Humfrey Hunter is a former journalist and public relations consultant who is now a publisher and literary agent. He lives outside London with his family. *The Storykiller* is his first novel.

The Storykiller

Humfrey Hunter

SILVERTAIL BOOKS • *London*

First published in Great Britain by Silvertail Books in 2016
www.silvertailbooks.com

1

ISBN 978-1-909269-37-8

To Charlotte

'The measure of a man's real character is what he would do if he knew he would never be found out.'
Thomas Babington Macaulay

Prologue

Jack didn't care he was late for work. Half an hour after the last of his colleagues had arrived, he stood alone outside the office building, slowly finishing his cigarette.

Neither did he care about his appearance. A crumpled grey suit a size too big, a creased white shirt, and a dark blue tie hanging a couple of inches below his open top button complemented the bags under his eyes and several days' stubble on his face. His black lace-up shoes were scuffed and unpolished; from his left hand dangled an orange plastic bag while his right cradled the cigarette from which he took deep, committed drags, smoke rising into his unwashed brown hair.

Though only in his early thirties, Jack looked worn out, too aged for his years. He was tall and thin, his skin was pale and his eyes were sunken, as though permanently recoiling from the sight of some horror witnessed long ago. He smoked quickly, but he was not hurrying.

His office stood on a dead end off a road leading east from Kensington into the centre of London. Jack watched a white van parked over the road on a yellow line, its driver shouting into his phone, window up. He saw the driver's face turn red as he shouted, turning mid-yell towards Jack. Momentarily, they stared at each other. There was anger in the driver's eyes and Jack quickly looked away, frightened of provoking a confrontation. He focused instead on the glowing orange tip of his cigarette, finishing it.

Ignoring the dozens of smoked-out filters on the floor around him, Jack walked to the public bin at the edge of the pavement. He bent down, stubbed out his cigarette on the ground and dropped it in with the rest of the rubbish. He sighed and turned to walk into the office.

He had taken one step forward when the woman appeared. She moved quickly and he felt the blows against his body almost before he registered her presence: one, two, three, four. His first thoughts were of surprise that he was being punched, in broad daylight, by a woman.

The woman stepped back, her chest heaving with quick, shallow breaths. She had a hood on and because Jack was much taller, he couldn't see her face; but he could see her hand, and registered the knife clasped in it. And then burning pain exploded in his stomach and chest. His legs seemed to disappear beneath him and he dropped onto his knees. The plastic bag fell out of his hand and he gave out a low moan as he toppled over onto his front, his arms lying limp next to him and the side of his face pressed against the pavement.

Barely able to breathe, Jack watched the woman start to run away. After a few yards she turned and looked back at him, as if to take photograph of the scene in her mind. As she did so, the hood fell away from her face and for an instant, her eyes met his.

The first people to get to Jack told the police he had a peaceful look on his face as he lost consciousness. He didn't scream or cry out. He didn't reach out for a comforting hand to hold and he didn't clasp his arms around his middle to try to stop the bleeding.

He lay still, with his eyes open and clear. One woman said he looked like he'd given up. A man defeated.

Three Years Later

3

Part One: Tuesday

1

I knew how much Tom Halliday had to lose when I saw the private hospital where he worked. A short hop from Notting Hill Gate tube station, the building was on a road which was so plush and smart it felt like I'd arrived on a film set. The hospital was four storeys tall and even from the outside you could tell the ceilings were high. The windows were large and tinted and with the dark brickwork it looked like the office equivalent of a stretch limo. The lobby was spacious, with a grey marble floor and a pair of blonde receptionists behind a giant mahogany desk. They sent me up to Halliday's office on the third floor with the kind of smile you don't get first thing in the morning from staff who feel underpaid.

I took the lift and found Halliday's office easily. This wasn't my first visit. I knocked three times and when he opened the door it was obvious what a mess he was in. His thick, salt and pepper hair was usually swept tidily back from his face but today it was ruffled and messy and his eyes were red and puffy.

'Thanks for coming,' he said, shutting the door behind me.

He'd asked me to come in and kill the story from the comfort of his office, I think partly so he didn't spend the day alone. I was happy with this arrangement, not least because travel time meant an extra hour each way on my bill.

Halliday looked at me and raised his eyebrows. His eyes were on the brink of watering. He was scared, and it occurred to me that this was a feeling he was not used to. Nor did it suit him. He was a vast chunk of ex-rugby player bulk padded out by twenty years of good living since he gave up the game. His size was part of what made his patients trust him so much. It also helped that he was known as one of the top knee and shoulder surgeons in the country. His love of motorbikes added a touch of cool danger to his image.

But he was in serious trouble. The hospital he'd worked at twenty years before was hell-bent on making him the scapegoat for their own cock-up. Later that day he was going to be handed to the media like a sacrificial lamb.

Halliday had three rooms to himself in the hospital. The reception room he'd ushered me in to was twice the size of my bedroom, but was still small. An empty desk implied his middle-aged secretary had the day off: wise decision, whoever made it. Halliday led me into his own office, a spacious room with cream carpet and a glass-top desk bigger than the mahogany beast in reception. I felt like I was in a City lawyer's lair.

I followed Halliday through another door into a meeting room oozing corporate reassurance. It was the kind of place you went for counselling, not to be interrogated. There was a round table and four chairs. It smelled of dry leather and old wood and money.

On the table was a big telephone of the type I'd seen in a million other offices. Next to the phone was a jug of iced water and two glasses.

'Are you okay?' I asked, filling both glasses.

'No,' Halliday said. 'I'm not bloody okay. I love my work. Every bit of it. I make a bit of money but I do NHS work for free one day a week. I don't have to do that. I give to charity. I don't deserve this.'

'You were just in the wrong place at the wrong time. But it's not over yet.'

I tried to sound reassuring but I knew Halliday wouldn't believe I could help him until it actually happened. Clients are always like that. I needed to do something to snap him out of his dark mood, even temporarily.

'I'll fix it,' I said, 'Now, how about making me a coffee before I save the day?'

Halliday's face was expressionless as he stood up and left the room.

I pulled the telephone towards me, switched it to loudspeaker and dialled a local number. It rang only once before she picked up.

'Jane Sharpe speaking.'

This was how people who wanted to appear busy and important answered the phone, quickly and in a tone which says you'd better not waste any of my time. Jane Sharpe was the PR director of the Fallon Park Hospital, the organisation trying to bury Halliday. Sharpe had only ever been a voice on the end of the phone to me, but I never imagined she'd be anything other than cold and serious in the flesh. I wasn't going to be angling for a face-to-face with her any time soon.

This conversation marked the end of the first part of my plan to save Halliday. Over the past week I'd spoken to Sharpe maybe a dozen times and on every call I'd made sure she knew I was ready to do the bidding of her and her hospital. I needed her to see me as a soft touch.

'So we're all set for today then?' I said.

Sharpe said, 'The press release is ready and as you and I agreed, the hospital won't proactively name Tom Halliday. But if a newspaper suggests his name to us we will confirm off the record that he's the surgeon involved. We think that's the fairest way to go for all concerned. Above all, the hospital doesn't want to lie to the press.'

'Fine,' I said. 'I understand what you have to do. Lying would be no good for anyone. And you'll send out the press release at—'

'Eleven o'clock. As we agreed.' She sounded smug. She had every right to be. I'd just given her my blessing to save her client by knifing mine.

I looked at my watch. Dead on 9.30 a.m. Ninety minutes to go.

'Let's see how it turns out,' I said, 'and maybe speak later, if and when the shit hits the fan. If you need anything in the mean time, you know where I am.'

'By the end of today you'll need me more than I'll need you.'

She hung up. She'd sneered those last few words, but maybe she thought she was being funny. Then again, maybe she really meant it when she spoke like that. Either way, that was the moment any guilt I might have felt at what I was about to do to Jane Sharpe vanished.

'What the hell have you done? They're going to ruin me!'

Halliday was standing in the doorway holding two white coffee mugs. He looked horrified. His eyes were almost popping out of their sockets and I could see veins of coffee running down the sides of the mugs and dripping onto the carpet.

I smiled at Halliday the way I imagined he did at his patients, calmly and gently. I wanted him to think I had everything under control. With my clients I work on the principle that if the energy I project is calm and relaxed, they'll be calm and relaxed. Same as when you train a dog. Unfortunately human beings aren't as obedient.

'Don't worry, it's all part of the plan,' I said. But Halliday looked a long way from convinced. I'd tried to sound light but Halliday's mask of doom was unmovable. He planted my coffee down next to me, lumbered over to the other side of the table and dropped into his chair.

'How's the motorbike?' I said, trying to improve Halliday's mood.

'It's not just a motorbike, Jack. It's a Ninja ZX-10R, the fastest bike in the world. Perfection on two wheels. And if you don't do your job I'll lose it. So please stop making polite conversation and get on with what I need you to do.'

Halliday slumped forwards. The words were said with polite desperation, not venom. That wasn't his style. He was a good man, Halliday, and I liked him, which was extremely rare for me. Generally I dislike people I meet until and unless they give me a reason to think better of them. Halliday had given me a reason. At our first meeting thirteen days ago I said his office made the NHS places I went to look like cesspits. Which they were. He'd frowned and told me I was being unfair. The NHS does its best, he'd said, and had far more important things to spend money on than smart chairs and fancy tables.

Halliday knew a part of the NHS was trying to destroy him and he was still sticking up for the organisation. That kind of loyalty made no sense to me. I told him that and he said the NHS was 'all about the patients', not bitter hospital bosses trying to save their own skins. As far as he was concerned, they weren't part of what mattered.

As I said, a good man.

Halliday lifted his head. He shot me the look of a man on Death Row who was desperately hoping for an eleventh-hour call from the Governor. 'So when are you going to start saving me?'

I flipped open my notebook and unfolded a printed sheet of names and phone numbers.

'Now,' I said.

This was the key moment, the hour when Halliday's fate would be decided. If I got it right, he'd be safe, his future secured. If not, his life would go down the toilet. I was nervous. I don't know if it was concern for Halliday or the fear that my ego wouldn't be able to handle failure but either way my guts were jumping and my head felt light. Whether I liked it or not, it was time to go to work.

My first call was to the Press Association, the highly-respected news agency which sent stories to every local, regional and national newspaper, magazine, TV channel and radio station in the country. Journalists rely on the Press Association. Their daily flow of unvarnished and unspun stories has been keeping the news media ticking over for years. As a result PA is one of very few trustworthy sources in a world of embellishers and downright liars. I knew if I could get them singing the song to my tune we'd be on the way to winning the fight for Halliday's career.

This was the first time I'd contacted a journalist since I had agreed to represent Halliday. Timing is everything in my business and if a story is going in tomorrow's papers there's no point talking to a journalist about it before today. Everything I do must fit in around the daily news cycle, which still exists now even though the internet dominates everything.

'Health Editor, please,' I said when someone on the news desk answered the phone. A click and it rang again.

'Hello, PA.' Becky Senior's northern voice was fast and harsh. She sounded busy. The best journalists always do. They either have a million things to do and never enough time to do them or are desperately trying to create that impression. If a reporter is stupid enough to sit around a newsroom looking anything other than rushed off their feet the chances are they'll be looking for another job pretty soon.

I knew Becky Senior by name and reputation but not personally, which didn't matter. Some people think stories are only ever killed because people like me have the right contacts and can call in favours but that's a myth. It's true that being best friends with an editor can help you get the right person on the phone, but if you really know what you're doing you can get the job done even if you're talking to strangers.

I put Halliday out of my mind. He was sitting across the table from me but I couldn't let that affect what I was going to say, no matter what he thought.

'My name is Jack Winter,' I said. 'I represent a surgeon called Tom Halliday and I have a story for you.'

I paused and let Senior's mind process the name she'd just heard. Halliday was famous in medical circles. His name would ensure she listened to me.

'Go on,' she said.

Now I had Becky Senior's ear. That meant Halliday's chances of survival had grown significantly. He didn't understand this. Yet.

'Tom is being set up by the NHS trust which runs Fallon Park Hospital. They want to make him a scapegoat for something he didn't do.'

Senior's silence meant she wanted to hear more, so I went on.

'At 11am you're going to get a press release from Fallon Park's public relations department. The release will say the hospital has had to write warning letters to just under a thousand former patients whose knees were operated on in the mid-nineties. Their problem is a piece of equipment which was used for five or six operations on different patients and then thrown away. It was washed and sterilised between uses to the accepted standards of the time but, as you know, those standards aren't the same as today's.'

I let this sink in. Halliday's face had worked its way through so many expressions that it now just looked contorted and strange. All I could read for certain was that the man was in pain.

'I'm still not sure why I should care,' Becky said. 'But go on.'

'The hospital has written to all the patients to tell them there is a risk a blood-borne infection has been passed on to them.'

'You mean like HIV, hepatitis, that kind of thing?'

'Exactly, and they need to be tested. The hospital is sending out a press release announcing this letter, basically trying to put the story out there before some terrified ex-patient goes to the papers and fillets them in public.'

Here was the moment where Becky would make her decision. For Halliday or against him. Every word of what I had just said mattered. Even the order in which I'd given her the information. I closed my eyes to help me concentrate.

'The risk to the patients must be tiny,' Becky said, her well-trained mind working quickly. 'Millions to one. But the headlines will be horrible – a thousand patients at risk of HIV because of unhygienic hospital equipment. Christ, that'll be bad news for someone. So why are you involved?'

'One surgeon performed all the operations and Fallon Park want to the world to think it was all his fault.'

'But if he did all the operations then it is all his fault.'

'It's not that simple,' I said. 'The hospital want to say he was a rogue employee and that means all these possible infections weren't their fault. But the truth is he did everything exactly as he was meant to. He followed the hospital's procedures to the letter and no one said anything at the time. They knew exactly what he was doing because they told him what to do and how to do it before he was allowed anywhere near a knee. And the surgeon is my client. I'm trying to stop his reputation from being trashed unfairly.'

'I get it,' Senior said. 'I see this all the time. The people who run NHS trusts can be very nasty when it comes to saving their own skins. Not the doctors, the administrators. They've gone for me a few times,' she let her voice drift. 'So what's the poor guy going to do? He has a lot to lose.'

I looked at Halliday. His eyes were watering, his face was red and he was breathing heavily.

'All he wants to do is put it on the record that he did nothing wrong, he is proud of his record and that Fallon Park are blaming him for things which are not his fault. They are trying to pin responsibility on him early so when the story reaches the public he's the villain, not them.'

I listened to dead air on the phone for several long seconds. The only thing I could hear was the drum beat of my heart.

'And this is the Tom Halliday who does all the footballers?'

'Yes, that's him.'

'Wow. If he gets the blame for this his career is over. I'm not surprised he's got you looking after him.'

'What Fallon Park are trying to do to him is outrageous.'

'Yes,' she said slowly, 'We'll see about that. I'll find out what the hospital has to say.'

'I have a statement from Halliday. I'll email it over now along with the press release.'

'Why were you so soft with her?' Halliday asked as soon I put the phone down. 'Couldn't you have pushed harder?'

'Wait and see,' I said. 'This game isn't simple; you can't force reporters to do what you want. Whichever way this goes it could be a big story and I can't ask her to not do her job properly. She'd lose all respect for me if I didn't play it straight. Sometimes you have to gently guide reporters towards where you want them to go. So gently they don't even notice.'

Halliday didn't seem convinced.

'How fucked am I?'

'Not even one percent.'

Over the next hour I made twelve more calls, all of which went exactly the same way as the first, which meant my plan had worked. Reporters are like customers to a used car salesman – they all work the same way. I used to be one so I could anticipate how they would react to the story and which parts would tickle their interest. I built Halliday's defence plan around that. And it had worked. This was the best possible start.

Halliday darted in and out of the meeting room every few minutes. Between calls I heard him on the phone talking to people about how their shoulders and knees were.

At 1105am the Press Association sent out Becky Senior's story and I couldn't have written it better myself. The first line said Fallon Park Hospital were trying to blame a surgeon for their own mistakes and after that it got worse and worse for them. Halliday's name was in the story but so was his defiant and strongly-worded statement. Written by me, of course.

'I can just about handle that,' Halliday said after reading the version on the BBC news website.

'Good,' I said, 'But we're not out of the woods yet. We'll have to wait until tomorrow morning when the papers come out to know for sure. But the signs are very positive.'

TV didn't seem interested in the story which meant it was boring and if a story is boring, journalists won't bother with it – the perfect outcome for us.

'We're finished for now,' I said. 'I'll call you later if anything major happens.'

'Thank you so much.'

We shook hands and I left.

I walked out of the hospital towards the tube. It was only then that I felt the weight of the morning lift off me. My job carries a lot of emotional pressure on days like this but having Halliday breathing down my neck all morning made it especially exhausting. I had no idea where my next client was going to come from so all I had to think about was whether to get a taxi straight home or stop somewhere for lunch.

And then my mobile buzzed. The name on the screen – Edward Valentine – made me forget about taxis or lunch. I'd been hoping for this call since I first spoke to Valentine a few weeks earlier, because if I could get him, he would be the biggest client I'd ever had.

During that first conversation it was Valentine's charm that surprised me more than anything else. In all my experience of dealing with powerful men, they were only friendly to people who sat even higher up the food chain. But that day Valentine showed me he was different. He had manners.

When he called, I was still dazed after my hours with Halliday, and there was no time to get my head together before I answered. But as soon as he started talking, Valentine's amiable tone made me feel better. Soothed, even.

'Winter, it's Valentine. Sorry to disturb you but I need your help.'

His voice told me a life story of comfort and security, expensive schools and nannies, country estates and long lunches. A long way from my own past.

'Don't mention it,' I said, disguising a cough. 'You know I'm available any time you need me. What can I do for you?'

'A friend of mine is in a spot of bother, Jack, and he needs the kind of assistance only you can provide. He's been a bit foolish and we need you to clear things up.'

I paused, my mind clearing.

'Who's your friend?' I asked.

'He's an MP, a good MP, the type this country can't afford to lose.'

'I always thought there were only two kinds of politician,' I said, 'Freeloaders and fanatics. I could happily lose all of them. What makes this one special?'

'He stands out from the rest, even to a cynic like you. He's the opposite of someone like me, who had every advantage money can buy. He dragged himself up with nothing but talent and ambition. He can inspire people, he can be a hero, and he's exactly what this country needs right now.'

Though I wanted to question Valentine's concept of heroism, preferring my heroes to have more than just talent and ambition, I kept quiet. Valentine had deep pockets and a big reputation so this was worth listening to.

'Sorry,' he said. 'I'm talking too much. I have a habit of getting a bit carried away when I care about something. What I really want to say is that he's a man worth saving because he'll make a difference. That's all. What do you think? His name is Adam Pryor.'

That was the moment where in a parallel life I said thanks but no thanks, told Valentine I had better things to do and wished his friend luck. Maybe even asked him to keep me posted on his progress. But I wasn't in a parallel life, and in this one I couldn't say, 'I'll do it' quick enough. I didn't even give it a moment's thought. And yes, I would regret that decision later on but believe me, when you spend every hour of your working day, and most of your night, putting out media fires for semi-literate sportsmen and D-list celebrities, the chance to work for one of the richest and best-connected men in London is not one you turn your nose up at. The fact was, I needed the money. I'd never wanted to be like that – taking a job simply because it paid well – but these days I had no choice.

I was glad the little girl with blue eyes in the photograph in my wallet wasn't there to see how desperate I'd become.

2

An hour later I found myself loping north from Clapham Junction towards Battersea High Street, on my way to find out exactly what kind of trouble Valentine's friend was in. I'd taken the train because I don't have a car – out of choice, rather than necessity – and steering my Vespa from my Earl's Court flat to south London after the morning I'd had was not a tempting prospect.

Sitting on the train I wondered what kind of man Adam Pryor would be. Some say politics these days is all about personalities. I disagree. It's more shallow than that. I say it's all about the surface – the look and the sound – and how those things are presented, which is my area of expertise. Americans like their presidents to sound like they're delivering the Ten Commandments and resemble retired athletes. We Brits prefer our politicians to appear more like a respectable head teacher. Gentle but firm, and gracefully intelligent without being belittling. I would find out soon enough which category Pryor fell into.

I came out of Clapham Junction station and made my way along Falcon Road. The area was typical of the suburbs immediately outside London's centre. Some roads had exotic names like Afghan and Khyber and Patience but it is almost a law of nature in London that the fancier the street name is, the shabbier the road. So I wasn't surprised to find that the house Valentine had sent me to was tucked away on plain old Trott

Street, where shiny black Range Rovers and Mercedes Benzes showed its residents' true calibre. Number thirty-nine was a two-storey semi-detached place at the end of the road, painted white and looking new, even though the Georgian design suggested at least a hundred years on the clock.

A couple of metres back from the pavement was a front porch that looked like something from the Chelsea Flower Show, with pots of blooms either side of the shiny black door. White shutters were closed discreetly over the windows. I prised open the iron gate – it made a kind of pleading squeak, as if I'd trodden on a depressed cat – and rapped the predictable lion's head knocker three times. Then I waited.

And waited some more. I checked my mobile and knocked again, louder this time. For a moment I worried I'd got the wrong address.

'Hold on,' a man called politely from inside. His voice, not deep and not high, but strong, carried through the wooden door unscathed. A few seconds later I heard the military clack of a strong, new latch and the door yawned open.

It was instantly clear to me that the man standing in the hallway would have been at home in the political worlds of both Britain and America – he met both countries' criteria. He had royal blue eyes that reminded you of the kind of English gentleman you only see in old paintings. Coal-black hair cut short at the back and sides and an Ivy League side-parting hinted at a man who had more pressing business to attend to than his hair but still liked to look sharp.

His suit was a lighter shade of black than mine – slate rather than coal – and a collegiate blue tie lay on top of his pristine white shirt. I liked the look. I always wear a white shirt, believing them to be unfailingly smart and having a row of identical ones in the wardrobe makes my mornings far less complicated than they need to be. But I don't do ties anymore, just an open-necked white shirt under a dark suit. I tell people it's an image thing – for my clients' sake I want to look sharp but not flamboyant or intimidating, the absent tie being the key. But the truth is that these days just the thought of having something tied round my neck makes me feel like I'm being strangled.

Adam Pryor, however, wore a tie well. On him it looked slick with his power suit and helped create the impression of a future world leader. I'd done my research so I knew about his background, a difficult childhood, born into poverty and a broken family. And I also knew who Pryor was today. The variety of politician who everyone liked, and I mean everyone: young, old, left, right, it didn't matter. Pryor was special. He said all the right things, about rewarding hard work, respecting people's rights to run their own lives, individuals taking responsibility for themselves, but also helping the unfortunate. And, of course, he had the right look, the right sound, the right everything. The blend was electoral magic. Political perfection.

But, as the old saying goes, if something looks too good to be true, then you can bet your last penny it's not true. And the fact Valentine had sent me to see Pryor proved that was right. If he really was political perfection, I wouldn't be here – the genuinely good guys never needed me.

Sure enough, Pryor's body language was that of an actor who'd fluffed the audition for his Hollywood meal ticket. He had sagging shoulders and a harassed expression on his face.

Which is how they all look. At first.

'Adam Pryor,' I said.

Pryor smiled weakly.

'Please,' he said. 'Do come in.'

He ushered me into the hallway. Polished wood flooring, Japanese vase beside a frosted-glass side table, a copy of *Vogue* casually slung on top. The air smelled of pinewood and lavender.

'Can I get you something? Tea? Coffee?'

'I'm fine,' I said. 'Where can we talk?'

'My study,' Pryor said. 'Pippa's at the courts. Big case.'

I nodded like I cared about the movements of his wife. Then I followed Pryor down the hallway. Before reaching the study we passed four open doors that opened into a dining room, a living room, a kitchen and a spare room filled with cardboard boxes. I was reminded of how deceptively large these terraced homes were. My Earls Court flat had none of these deceptive powers; slapped on the fourth floor of a humdrum mansion block, the place was so cramped, my ex liked to say, that you had to step outside the front door just to change your mind. But I liked my little flat – it was my home and everything I owned was in it.

Still, I doubted Pryor would have taken me seriously if he'd seen where I lived and compared it to his own house. But he hadn't and, like all my clients, never would.

'I take it you spoke to Edward,' he said, over his shoulder.

'He told me you had a problem.'

'Yes, and he told me you could fix it.'

'That depends.'

'On what?'

We reached the end of the hallway and a closed, four-panel oak door. Pryor rested his hand on the brass doorknob and angled his head at me, waiting for an answer.

'On what needs fixing.'

Pryor made a second attempt at a smile no more convincing than the first. He gingerly opened the door and motioned me into his study. I entered and paused just inside, taken by surprise. I'd

expected creaky old furniture and intimidating bookshelves, but
the study looked instead like a slab of corporate Britain had crash-
landed in the house, complete with ergonomic exec chair behind
a curved white desk, with a black laptop on top. The only features
which fit my expectations were the bookshelf to the right, filled
with serious-sounding political titles, and the bottle of Laphroaig
single-malt nestled between the volumes. The office was perfectly
ordered, almost surgically so, a slideshow of photographs on the
wall behind his desk providing the only personal touch. I cast my
eye over the snaps. They mostly appeared to be of Pryor at
university, decked out in his graduation gown and grinning at the
camera with his mates. He looked a little trimmer around the
waist and sported a little more hair on top, but not much. Time
had not been as kind to me.

Pryor gestured to the sofa. He perched himself on the corner
of his desk.

'You know who I am, I take it.'

'Minister for International Development, resident in the
department of the same name.'

Pryor inhaled and lowered his head.

'Christ,' he said. 'I'm in a real mess.'

His phone buzzed on his desk. Pryor managed to lift his head
– the effort seemed to require all his energy – and crane his neck
at the display. He looked back at me and let it ring off.

'Edward and I go back a long way, you know.' He traced his
fingers slowly along the edge of the desk. The phone stopped
buzzing. 'Tell me. Have you been doing this sort of thing for long?'

'The last three years, give or take.'

'And what did you do before?'

I noticed his left foot tapping on the carpet.

'Newspapers,' I said.

Pryor worked his face into a curious slant. 'Which one?'

'Does it matter? Whether or not I can help you is the important thing right now.'

I thought Pryor might press me on that point but the phone sparked up again. He tried to ignore it. The tapping had spread to his right leg. 'I'm screwed, aren't I? My whole bloody career in ruins. All because of one stupid little mistake.'

'What happened?'

'Edward didn't tell you?'

I shrugged. 'I didn't ask.'

I was being deliberately casual. An old trick of mine to help put the client at ease. But my laid-back attitude seemed to have the opposite effect. Pryor's lower lip trembled. He bit it and gave me his back.

'Oh God. Why is this happening to me?'

I left Pryor staring at the wall and counted to ten. Then I said, 'I could do with a glass of water.'

Pryor held his gaze level with the photographs for a moment longer then looked across the bow of his shoulder at me. 'Of course,' he said.

He paced over to the desk and took a bottle of unlabelled water standing next to the laptop. He poured some into a tumbler glass until it was three-quarters full – didn't spill a drop, I noticed, despite his anxiety – and handed the glass to me. I took a sip. It tasted like wine. He sat down, silent again.

'Do you remember Danielle Simons?' I said.

'Afraid not.'

'She was a ten year-old girl from Ealing who drowned on holiday.' I polished off the rest of my water and felt it settle in my guts like dew. 'This was about nine years ago. I was sent out to cover the story. My editor told me we absolutely needed an exclusive interview with this girl's parents. Shift more papers and all that. I asked around.'

I studied the empty tumbler. Drops of water slid down from the rim into the bottom of the glass.

'I was with another reporter and we managed to find out where the family lived. We got to the house. My colleague knocked on and off for an hour. Finally the door opened. It was the mum. She spat in my colleague's face and slammed the door shut. My colleague wiped the spit off and called out her name through the letterbox. Three hours later we had the interview.'

'Why are you telling me this?'

'Because you need to know what you're up against. The first rule of journalism is, ethics have no place in it. The second rule is, neither does privacy, especially not when everything you do is in the public interest. That's the pact politicians make. Step into public life as an MP and the public owns you. In the right hands newspapers are there to oil the wheels of democracy on behalf of their readers. And the third rule is a good reporter will never, ever give up on a story. The best reporters will do anything to get what they want. And believe me, the best are very, very good.'

Whatever you called them – journalists, journos, reporters, hacks, blunts or scribes – the men and women who chased stories for newspapers were lethal to men like Pryor and he knew it. I leaned forward in my seat, dead-eyeing him.

'I can help.' I said. 'But I need you to be completely honest. No secrets. If you hold back on me, if you tell me anything which isn't absolutely true, you're fucked. I guarantee it.'

Pryor clamped his eyes shut. Like a kid trying not to look at the bogeyman stepping out of his wardrobe. When he opened them again they were moist and red and strained.

He said, 'Her name was Kat.'

Pryor slumped into his executive chair and let his hands splay listlessly in front of him. His eyes gazed past my shoulder and bored holes into the wall. He said nothing and made no attempt to continue where he'd left off. I watched him and waited.

'Funny,' he finally said.

'What's that?'

'I thought your greatest hopes and worst nightmares were never supposed to come true.' He refocused his eyes and they met mine. 'Isn't that how the saying goes?'

'It's "greatest hopes and worst fears",' I said, folding my left leg across my right. 'And they're seldom realized. Jim McKay said it.'

'Never heard of the man.'

'He was a sports reporter at the Munich Olympic massacre.'

Pryor pulled a face. 'Oh, that bodes well.'

'You brought it up,' I said.

Pryor bolted upright and slapping his palms onto the desk. The hollow clap made me jump a little, which is not the sort of thing a man of my experience should be doing. There was a moment of embarrassed silence in which we both pretended I hadn't seen Pryor's little outburst. His body language had shifted so quickly it was like someone had flicked a switch inside his head.

'Have you any idea how much I stand to lose from all this? Have you? I'm second only to Scannell in the Department. One step away from being a Cabinet minister. I'm thirty-bloody-five and everyone keeps saying,' he threw his voice an octave higher, imitating a popular breakfast TV presenter, '*Adam Pryor is the rising star of Westminster*. Well, this could wreck everything. My marriage, too. I want children but that would be out of the question if this gets out. My whole life would be ruined.'

Silence settled around us, and I let the atmosphere drop down a notch or two. I brushed imaginary lint off my trousers to kill a few seconds. Then I said, 'In three years I've killed more than a hundred stories. And do you know how many times I've failed?'

Pryor blinked at me. 'No idea.'

'Take a guess.'

'Twenty?'

'None.'

Pryor blinked at me again. Now I detected something different in his eyes. They had grown narrow and curious. Like a cornered fox that's spotted a gap it can escape through. The fox has it easy, I reckon. He lives in constant fear of being torn to shreds by a pack of bloodhounds, but even this has its hidden blessings. His only concern, after all, is surviving from day to day. The things that worry me, like the prospect of waking up in thirty years' time alone and miserable and knowing I've wasted my life, don't stop a fox sleeping at night. Simply knowing he'll be alive for a new day means he's won. I got something of the same vibe from Pryor.

'You talk a good game,' Pryor said. 'But I could say that about quite a few people I know. I could also say those same people are untrustworthy. What makes you any different?'

I leaned forward and rested my hands on my thighs.

'Because I'm the best at what I do. I used to be a reporter and I know how to beat them at their own game. And trust me, right now, no matter what anyone else says, I'm the only person in the world who can help you. I'm your only option.'

'I'm curious,' he said. 'Why did you stop being a reporter?'

I paused, not sure how much to say. Clients didn't usually ask me that question. I decided to answer it, reasoning that if I shared something personal, that might help Pryor open up. But I would give him as little information as possible.

'I was involved in a story and someone died,' I said. 'I had a chance to save her and I missed it. The experience made me want to get out of the business.'

Pryor nodded. 'Sounds nasty,' he said.

'It was.'

He was warming to me. I'd Googled 'Adam Pryor' immediately after getting off the phone to Valentine, and the assorted articles I'd read described Pryor's background as, variously, underprivileged, poor or broken. He had grown up in Leicester, a place as alien to me as the dark side of the moon, and attended Corpus Christi College, Oxford, on a scholarship. He was, as Valentine said, a self-made man with an inspiring life story.

'Think of me as a lawyer,' I said. 'A bloody good lawyer who's getting you ready for trial. But good as I am, I can only get you off the hook if you've told me every last grain of truth.'

Pryor was intrigued by his cufflinks. 'You make it sound like I'm a guilty man.'

'Innocent men don't need me,' I said. 'I wouldn't be here if you were clean.'

Pryor sucked in a deep breath. Held it in for a few seconds before it leaked out of his nostrils. It stank of guilt.

'It happened last week. I'd been invited as the honorary guest speaker at the Oxford Union debate. They hold them regularly on Thursdays.'

He stiffened his neck. The veins protruded like tense rope. A fawning article I'd seen described Pryor as a self-confessed fitness fanatic. Adam Pryor, like every young politician of our age, felt the need to enthusiastically promote the cardiovascular benefits of discomfort.

'It's quite a big deal to be invited to speak to the Union. Tony Blair was an officer there. So was Gladstone. The Prime Minister spoke recently. And then they wanted me. As I say, it's a big deal.'

I resisted the urge to roll my eyes. I could imagine Pryor in front of the mirror, adjusting his tie and telling himself that here he was, the kid from an estate, getting ready to follow in the footsteps of the current leader of the country. I bet he'd even pictured the Union website one day gushingly announcing, 'Adam Pryor once graced our members with his presence…'

'Shouldn't you be writing this all down?' Pryor said, jolting me out of my stupor.

'I have a good memory.'

Which was true, though maybe less so after seven whisky sours. But it's also a house rule of mine never to take notes in front of clients. People tend to be intimidated by the sight of someone else recording their every word for posterity. They freeze up at the horror of being on some kind of stage and tend to measure their words more carefully. I didn't want that. I wanted the story uncut.

I said, 'Please go on.'

'Right. Yes. Well, after the speech I had a few drinks at the bar. Next thing I knew I was a bit drunk. I got chatting to this girl, a student. She can't have been older than twenty-one. One thing led to another, and…' He hesitated, perhaps hoping that the pause would fill in the blanks. One look at my curious expression told him otherwise so he stumbled on. 'And that was how *it* happened.'

It. Thank God for the invention of *it*, because without this single syllable the British respectable classes would be condemned to actually describe their nocturnal activities in painful detail. I nodded gravely at *it*. We both understood what he meant.

I said, 'Who knows about this? Your wife? Kat's friends? Has she told anyone?'

Pryor shook his head. 'No, I haven't told my wife and you're here so I never have to. And I very much doubt Kat would have told anyone. She said she's ashamed of herself for sleeping with a married man. But she still wants to do a story about it. Why? What's wrong with her?'

'Nothing,' I said. 'She's normal. This happens all the time. A secret is far too embarrassing for someone to tell their friends and family about but throw in a front page and a cheque and suddenly the world has to know.'

Pryor's expression was a mixture of confusion and anger.

'Tell me exactly how you met her,' I said.

Pryor said, 'The girl?'

No, the tooth fairy, I didn't say.

'Yes.'

Pryor scratched the back of his ear. 'She came over to me in the bar. She and her friend. A blonde girl. Afraid I can't remember her name but she was a knockout. She was the one who flirted with me at first.'

'And you didn't do anything with this first girl? The blonde?'

Pryor rubbed the knuckle joints on his left hand. 'Some gentlemen don't prefer blondes, Jack.'

It struck me as odd that Pryor would call me by my first name without asking if I preferred it that way. I always thought in a business situation people tended to check first. And this was business between us, regardless of how dirty we were about to get.

'Was Kat into you too?'

'No. Not at the beginning. She seemed, I don't know…'

The words seemed to die in his throat.

'Like what?'

'Like she thought she was better than me,' Pryor said.

He hadn't said it outright but Pryor had just revealed the real reason why he went for Kat instead of the blonde. Not because of hair colour or anything so trivial. Men like to claim that they prefer this girl's legs or that woman's face, but when you get down to the nitty-gritty details like those don't matter. No, Pryor had been attracted to Kat because she hadn't showed any interest in him at the start. I smiled inwardly. I'd discovered something about the real Adam Pryor. He liked the hunt.

'And then?'

Pryor rubbed his jaw. 'Pretty soon the blonde girl conceded defeat and wandered off. That's when Kat and I started talking. We hit it off quickly. She was into politics, she had the same interests. Even liked the same music as me, and let me tell you, a woman who knows her Miles Davis from her Thelonious Monk is a rare find.'

My stomach curled up in a cringing knot. Even as his life was in grave danger of toppling around him, Pryor still found it within him to make a smug joke about his night of fun with an Oxford student.

'What hotel where you staying at?'

'The Barker. It's where all the Union's guests are put up.'

'Did you take her back there?'

Pryor pursed his lips like he'd been sucking on a bag of lemons. 'You must be joking. Even I'm not that stupid. I still had enough of my marbles in the bag to know that was too risky.'

'So you went back to hers?'

'It seemed like a good idea at the time.'

Pryor shook his head at his own words. At that moment I felt sympathy for the man. How many of us decide to do something in the spur of the moment, only to regret it a few hours later? The difference between someone like Pryor and me is that if I slept with a student I could carry on my life like nothing had ever happened. I had no one to answer to. Pryor had voters and a wife to worry about, not to mention a gilded path to high office and a civic duty to resist from temptation. I knew which camp I preferred to be in.

'You don't know how it is at these events,' Pryor said. 'The girls are beautiful, clever and ambitious. And they're throwing themselves at you. It's not like I went looking for anything. I didn't need to.'

I listened to his excuse and said, 'Where did she live?'

'With her friend – the blonde one – in a house on Bullingdon Road, just up from the East Oxford Conservative Club.'

I nodded like I knew what that meant.

I said, 'Did anyone see you leave the Union?'

'I don't think so.'

'This is very important. Thinking so isn't good enough. I need to know yes or no.'

Pryor put a finger to his lip and considered my question for a moment. Then he dead-eyed me and said, 'Not a soul. I'm sure of it. The place had emptied by the time we left. Even the bar staff had called it a night.'

'What about the house? Was there anyone watching you arrive?'

'How much is Edward paying you, out of interest?' Pryor said, cantering his head at me.

'Enough,' I replied. 'Answer the question please.'

Pryor folded his arms. 'We walked back. Took us about fifteen minutes. Could have been longer. We were so lost in our conversation we didn't really keep track of the time.'

'And you slept in her bed.'

I'd meant it to come out as a question, but my lips betrayed me and instead it slipped out like a damning statement handed down by some pious judge to a celebrity on a drunk-driving charge. Pryor knotted his brow at me. I hurried on.

'What time did you leave the house?'

'Six-thirty, or thereabouts,' he said, without a hint of shame. I frowned. A man should always stick around for coffee. Another house rule of mine, you might say.

'Did you swap numbers?'

'She asked for mine,' Pryor said, digging his hands deeper into the crevices of his armpits. 'It was a mistake. I should have given her an old one. I felt guilty about leaving in a flash and, you know, but she only has my business number, not my personal one.' His voice was descending into a rambling, self-justifying monologue. Rather than point out the utter stupidity of Pryor giving her his business number – the phone provided by the House of Commons – I felt we needed to move on.

'Has she texted you? Called?'

'Yesterday. Last night. That was the only call. To say she was going to the press.'

'What about any other proof that she spent the night with you?' I said. 'I need you to really think hard about this, Adam. Did she take anything from you at all? A business card?'

'I don't have a business card,' Pryor said with a sneer. 'I'm an MP, not a salesman.'

'What about the blonde girl? Did she go home with you both?'

'No.' Pryor leaned back in his chair until the back plane was resting against the wall. I'd earlier noticed a curious dark smear on the wall at the spot where the chair now rested. I figured Pryor had done a lot of leaning in that chair recently. A lot of thinking.

'You said the blonde wandered off earlier in the night. Where to?'

'Don't know,' said Pryor. 'I saw her briefly later on chatting to some other chap. That was the last I saw of her.'

'And you didn't see her the next morning?'

'At the house? No.' He jerked his shoulders. 'Guess she had somewhere else to be.'

I watched Pryor silently while I soaked up everything he had told me. Silence is a wonderful thing. Use it correctly and people will feel compelled to fill it, often by revealing things about themselves they would normally never talk about. But not Pryor. He sat there with his hands wedged into his armpits.

He sighed and said, 'She's going to crush me. She says I didn't tell her I was married. She never damn well asked.' He snorted his disgust. 'She says she's going to go to the papers and tell them what I did. She says men like me deserve everything that happens to us.'

'Has she spoken to a paper yet?'

I asked again because of the importance of the question. Pryor's memory might have been jogged over the past few minutes.

'I don't think so,' he said. Then he saw my eyes narrow to arrow-slits, and he corrected himself. 'No, she definitely hasn't.'

'How can you be sure?'

'She told me she wants to do an interview and tell them the whole bloody story. She also told me,' he waved a hand dismissively, 'That I'm a disgusting pig and she hopes I burn in hell.'

Charming lady, I thought. I could see why this girl and Pryor made such a good match. My mind flashed up an image of them hurling insults and plates at each other right before they jumped into the sack.

'So what happens now?'

I stood up. Pryor locked his eyes on me and manners dictated that he rise out of his chair too. We stood there facing each other like a couple of men who had agreed a major business contract. Which is what we were, in a strange sort of way.

'I'm going to pay Kat a visit.'

3

I took a black cab from Battersea High Street, my right palm still warm from shaking Pryor's hand, and asked the driver to take me to Paddington station. He grunted. Modern cabbie-speak for, 'Certainly, guv.'

By the time the cab coughed me up on Praed Street next to Paddington, big drops of rain had speckled the windows. I unfolded myself from the back seat, handed a ten and a twenty to the driver and ducked into the station.

I purchased my return ticket, found an empty carriage, and watched as London slowly receded. The permanent buzz of traffic and thronging crowds was replaced by the reflective hum of the train engine. I closed my eyes. Everyone has a favourite place to think. Yours might be the gym or the walk on your way to work. Mine is undoubtedly a moving train. Whenever I'm stumped on how to save a difficult situation the first thing I'll do is head to King's Cross or Marylebone and buy a return ticket to somewhere a couple of hours away. Kidderminster and Peterborough are personal favourites. Once I arrive I'll turn around and immediately board the next train back to London. I'm not sure why, but something about the ticker-tape Middle England landscape swooshing by helps me concentrate.

And I had plenty to occupy me for the hour-long journey to Oxford. Partly I felt a twinge of sympathy for Adam Pryor. Most of my clients exist in a whirlwind of drugs and illicit affairs and the sad truth is that blocking stories for them is like being a

teenager who squeezes an unsightly spot; another one is bound
to crop up a few days later. But Pryor wasn't a serial offender. His
was a moment of weakness. Manna from heaven for newspapers,
disaster for the person caught up in the middle of it all. And now
he was facing ruin. I wondered how such a punishment could
possibly fit his crime.

I also wondered about his relationship with Edward Valentine.
Specifically, how it had started. The two men were hardly cut
from the same cloth. Valentine had a reputation as a brilliant
businessman and had been a multi-millionaire for almost as long
as I'd been breathing. I knew plenty of journalists who would have
shaken their heads in disbelief at the idea of working for the man
– their default reaction to anyone becoming rich and successful
is that they must be hiding a troop of skeletons somewhere. But,
even given my limited dealings with him, I didn't have that feeling
about Valentine. He struck me as a gentleman.

On the other side of the deal, Pryor was charismatic and had a
life story I could relate to, certainly one far closer to my own than
Valentine's. Clearly at some point in his political career their paths
had crossed, and it had benefited both men to stay in touch, one
as the big-hearted kingmaker, the other as the ambitious protégé.

I dug out my mobile. I had six missed calls and a voicemail, all
from the same number. I tapped the voicemail icon and pressed
the handset close to my ear.

'Dad, it's Emily. It's happened again. She's passed out. I'm going
to your place. Not sure how long I'll be there. Maybe I'll see you.
Bye.'

A familiar combination of sadness and frustration washed
through me. Emily was my daughter and she was now seventeen
years old, the age I was when she was born. I'd been the
stereotypical bad teenage father – I got scared and ran away – and

I'd been failing to make up for it ever since. Failing because I was unreliable. When I worked for a newspaper I was constantly being sent away from London on some story or other and the result was I missed countless days with her, often cancelling at the last minute which made her disappointment even worse. The golden rule of being a father to a daughter was to just be there for her and I broke it spectacularly.

As if having one problem parent wasn't bad enough, Emily's mother had become an alcoholic and these phone calls came every month or so now, when Emily would find her mother in a bad state and would want to get out of the house as quickly as she could. She had a step-father, a man called William Buckingham, who she was close to, but he couldn't shield her from moments like this. She had a key to my flat and would head straight there – it was only a couple of miles away from her home. Sometimes I was there but most of the time I wasn't. She slept on the sofa and looked after herself and for her it was a relief to only have one person to take care of for a few hours. I knew I hadn't been a good father to Emily and offering her a place to run to when she needed it was part of me trying to be better. I texted her back and hoped it wasn't too little too late. And then I took out my wallet and looked at the photo of her. I closed it before my focus on work got as broken as my heart.

The message from Emily reminded me of how important the Pryor gig was for me, and why I had pursued Valentine so hard in the first place. Three months ago I'd happened to catch Valentine on TV. He had been invited on to defend his decision to hire a notorious banker as the MD of one of his businesses. Despite starting amicably enough, I could see that Valentine wasn't putting on a good show. The interviewer threw a few pointed questions at him and when he tried and failed to bluff his way past them, she called him out bluntly. He ended up giving her a stare which said he thought the whole thing was beneath him and it wasn't this woman's place to question his decisions. He'd rather have been anywhere else in the world.

Big mistake.

The first rule of appearing on TV is to look like you're happy to be there, no matter what awkward circumstances are simmering away behind the scenes. But Valentine looked lost, like he did not have the first idea of how to play the game. At that moment I saw someone who needed my help. And who could pay me handsomely.

Valentine wasn't the only businessman in the world in that position. There were hundreds like him. But right now he was the only one who needed me. A few weeks ago I'd lost a client, a show business agent who wanted me to protect an actor client of his who'd slapped his wife in front of several witnesses. In a rare moment of conscience I'd said no, he deserves whatever comes to him and the agent said he'd never call me again. The weekly retainer they paid me stopped immediately and my bank account had been paying the price ever since.

After rolling into Oxford, I spent five minutes in the line for a non-existent taxi before deciding to walk to Kat's house on foot instead, which was probably for the best: I was thirty-four, ate badly and had an alcohol intake level that made my GP's eyebrows dance so I needed all the exercise I could get, plus I would have time to plan how I would approach Kat in light of what I'd found out from her Facebook and Twitter profiles. Like most students, she lived a very public life online.

Oxford in good weather is charming. So I'm told. On that Tuesday lunchtime the clouds were stacked across the sky and passers-by glanced warily upwards, wondering whether another ritual downpour was on the way. I made my way down Park End Street, which could have been any street in Britain with its Kwik-Fit and Domino's Pizza and bookmakers.

Park End became New Road. On my left was Nuffield College, a wide, grey stone building with brown-slated roof tiles and a tower with a wizard's hat spike on the top. The road morphed into a sort of trench dividing, on the right, humourless chain stores, charity shops and shabby independents, from the gothic facades of Magdalen, All Souls' and Queen's colleges on the left.

I left this English comedy farce behind and crossed the bridge at the Plain, which reminded me of an English summer in 1928 for some reason. I started down Iffley Road with its smug white and brown-washed Victorian townhouses. Google Maps directed me a couple of hundred metres along until I reached an intersection signposted by the Fir Tree pub on the corner. I took the left onto Bullingdon Road.

The homes lining Bullingdon were the poor twins of Iffley's town houses. Stumpier, uglier and fashioned from cheaper brick and mortar. The street was hunched and dark. Seen together from the corner of Iffley, the houses either side of the road resembled rotten teeth in an open jaw, poised to bite.

Midway up I found the house number Pryor had given me. The cars along parked along the road were all student hatchbacks, except for one: a black Range Rover parked across the road from my destination. It seemed oddly out of place, but then again there were spoiled students with rich parents in every university, so its presence could easily be explained.

There was no doorbell at the address. There was no knocker. There was a plant of some kind in a big blue pot. It looked dead. The top half of the door had a frosted-glass window pane. The lower half was panels of painted wood. The paint was peeling in places like an irritated scab. There were cigarette butts flattened on the ground and a black recycling box by the door. I rapped my knuckles on the window pane.

While I waited for signs of life I bent down and lifted up the recycling box lid. An old journalistic habit. Reporters don't root around people's trash anymore, but they do look for any clues about the person they're talking to. They're a bit like detectives, I suppose. One look inside the box told me that Kat and her friend read the *Guardian*, ate Special K – the strawberry variety – and drank a lot of gin.

Something stirred in the house. I heard the dull *thud-thud* of footsteps carting down the hallway. They were getting louder. I closed the recycling box lid and stood upright. A white-and-blue splodge was sweeping towards the window pane like an out-of-focus apparition. It stopped at the door and opened up halfway.

'Hello,' I said cheerfully to the blonde standing in the doorway. 'Is Kat home?'

My first thought when seeing this girl was, if Adam Pryor turned her down then either he has the strongest constitution in the world, or else he's crazy. She had the kind of face a man would punch a hole in the wall for. Strands of shoulder-length blonde hair were draped around her cheeks and shorter layers tickled the corners of a seductive smile. She wore slim dark-blue jeans that hugged her long legs, and a white linen blouse that slinked off at the collarbones and revealed a V of caramel flesh that left just enough to the imagination, and just enough not.

She smiled at me with her electric green eyes and said, 'So you're the man who's been parachuted in from London. How exciting.'

She must have seen the confusion etched across my face because she added, 'I'm a Valentine too. Edward is my step-father.

For my sins. He called me, woke me up, actually, and said you'd be coming to see us.'

My composure deserted me. I'd like to think it was just the shock of realising that she was Valentine's step-daughter. But her looks probably had something to do with it too.

'I've never met a story killer before,' she said. 'You must have lots of secrets.'

'One or two.'

The smile spread from her eyes to her lips and a crescent of it crawled up the expanse of her cheek. 'What's the biggest story you've stopped, then?'

I gave her the full-smile treatment back, eyes and mouth. 'If I told you, I'd have to kill you.'

She laughed. 'Are you playing with me, Mr...?'

'Winter,' I said.

'Do you have a first name?'

'Do you?'

'Only when I feel like it.'

She offered her hand. I took it. Her handshake was soft and light. Like shaking feathers.

'Zoe,' she said.

'Jack,' I said.

'Let's get one thing agreed now, Jack. You talk my housemate out of this ridiculous idea of hers and when you're done we'll do tequila shots and you can tell me all your secrets. Deal?'

Sense of humour and good looks. I liked her already.

'Afraid I need to talk to Kat first. Is she home?'

Zoe rolled her eyes. 'Of course she is. She hasn't stepped outside since it happened. I've tried talking to her but she's as stubborn as they come. Her dad's a barrister and her mum works for a charity or something, so what do you expect? Getting her drunk didn't work either. Are you going to come in, or do we have to do this whole thing on the doorstep?'

I entered. The hallway smelled of cigarettes. The place looked like it had been renovated not long ago but whoever organised the work forgot about the outside. Maybe that was deliberate. Maybe Zoe didn't want people to know a rich girl lived here. Once you were inside, the wealth was obvious. The furniture was all light wood and soft touches. I made a bet with myself that nothing in the house could be found in an Ikea catalogue. As I walked down the hallway with Zoe leading me the place felt like a fantasy world compared to my flat.

'How many people live here?' I asked.

'Just the two of us,' Zoe said.

A set of stairs tapered off to the right.

'And you're both in your second year?'

'No, just Kat. I'm doing a PhD in political science. You could call it a career break, if you were being kind. Truth is I'm twenty-five-years-old and still have no idea what I'm going to do with the rest of my life. I'm a proper twenty-first century girl.'

Zoe laughed and I smiled with her.

'This is a pretty big place for two people.'

'Yeah well,' Zoe said with a sigh, 'I'm not allowed to go slumming it. My step-father takes care of me.'

Of course he does. It had taken a few years for me to work it out but even I knew that was what fathers did. I shut down that train of thought before it got in the way of work.

We detoured into the living room on the right. Zoe wasn't lying about her father looking after her. There was a pair of expensive-looking leather sofas and a fifty-inch flat screen TV hooked up to the wall. Sitting on the sofa to the left was Kat.

She looked demure and younger than I expected. Her eyes were round and wide. They were circled red from tears or a lack of sleep. Or maybe both. Her skin was pale as uncooked chicken. She had tiny stipples on her cheeks and her lips were pink silk and sharp like cut glass. She wasn't the kind of girl who wore make-up. I felt my professional composure weaken as I realised she was only a couple of years older than Emily. Two years were nothing. The thought of Emily being in her situation made me feel sick. At that moment I knew Kat was far too young to understand what she was getting into. She needed my help too, probably more than Pryor did.

'I know who you are,' she said in a voice that wasn't so much cold as Arctic. 'Zoe's step-father has been calling me all morning. Trying to cover up for *him*.'

'Oh, for God's sake,' Zoe said, snatching the glass of wine from the coffee table and taking a gulp. There was no condensation on the glass, which meant it was warm and must have been poured a while ago. Zoe put down the glass, picked up a magazine and sat on the sofa arm.

I sat on the sofa opposite the two girls and composed myself. Hostility is something I'm used to in my line of work. Disarming it is tricky but I've had plenty of practice. I've learned that's always best to let the other person vent their steam before I make my moves.

'I'm not a slut.' Kat pursed her lips. 'If he had told me he was married I would never have slept with him. But the way he just said it the next morning, it was so off-hand.'

She hadn't looked at me since I entered the room. Her eyes were drawn to the floor and her hands were gripping the hem of her purple hoodie, The Hertford College crest emblazoned on the left breast.

'He didn't even say sorry.'

'No one is saying he's innocent,' I said softly. 'Personally I think you're completely right to feel the way you do. If I was in your shoes I'd feel the same.'

'I wouldn't,' said Zoe as she wet a finger and flicked through the pages of *Grazia*. 'You had a fling. Why are you making such a big deal about it? Move on. It's not like you're the first girl who ever fucked a married man.'

Kat's voice turned cold as she said, 'That doesn't make it right.'

I cleared my throat. 'Zoe, would you mind leaving us alone for a minute?'

Zoe rolled her tongue around her mouth. Both Kat and I were staring at her. Finally she said, 'Sure,' polished off her wine and marched out of the living room, slamming the door shut behind her.

Kat swung her eyes from the door to me. Her pupils were black and gleaming like little pools of oil.

I said, 'There's something you should know.'

'I don't care about him,' Kat said. Her voice was breaking like a crust of ice. 'He deserves everything he gets.'

'This isn't about him. It's about you.'

She looked away from me and stared at her dim reflection in the TV.

'It's too late anyway,' she said.

I felt something chill spider-crawl up my spine. I don't mind admitting I get a thrill at moments like this, when so much is at stake.

'What do you mean?'

Kat looked back at me. The weakness in her eyes had vanished. She looked defiant, her youthful courage was beating her naivety. She said, 'Because I've already agreed to do an interview. I'm meeting the journalist in a few hours.'

'Who's the interview with?'

'What difference does it make?' Kat said stiffly.

'I know a lot of newspaper people. Some are less bad than others. I might be able to give you a few hints.'

Kat went back to staring at the shiny blank expanse of the TV. 'She's from the *Sunday Legend*. Someone called me from *The Sun* but I'm not going to talk to a newspaper that degrades women.'

As she said this I couldn't help notice a folded copy of *The Sun* lying on the mantelpiece. But I didn't pursue the point. We all like to have principles. Whether we stick to them or not is beside the point.

'What was her name?'

'Rachel something-or-other.'

'I know who you're talking about. Rachel Kirk is her name, and she's good,' I said. 'But you need to understand that whether Kirk likes you or not, she can't protect you.'

Kat frowned at the TV. Said, 'I know how to look after myself.'

I respected Kat for the way she was standing up to me. She was clever and strong-willed and I could imagine a parent being proud of her. But like many people her age, she made the mistake of believing intelligence, passion and principles were more important than experience and battle scars. I had to convince her she was wrong.

'Maybe in your world you do,' I said. 'But you're in a very different place now. Tell me something, Kat. Have you ever Googled yourself?'

'I don't know,' she said in a bare whisper.

'Of course you have. We all have. What do you see under the search results? Let's see, there's your Facebook profile. Maybe you're mentioned in some obscure newsletter or the list of students at Hertford. But after tonight the first thing you will see on there will be the stories about sleeping with Pryor. And the thing people don't realise is those stories will be there forever. They will haunt you for the rest of your life.'

Kat looked vacant. It was impossible to tell whether she was listening to me.

'Do you really want that? To be remembered as someone who slept with someone more famous than them? Every time you apply for a job or date a new guy, this will be hanging around your neck. News doesn't die on the Internet, Kat. Even your children will know about it.'

'I don't care,' she said.

'Maybe not now,' I said. 'But you will.'

Kat turned away from me.

'He'll lose his job,' I said.

Her head turned far enough back around for me to see the pearly tip of a tear forming at the corner of her eye.

'Good,' she said. 'A man like that shouldn't be allowed to stay in politics.'

'But it's not only Adam who loses out.' I deliberately used Pryor's first name. It made him sound more human, more vulnerable. 'It's not even just you. Your family will suffer too.'

The tear broke free and glistened down her cheek. I edged forward on the sofa and softened my voice.

'Think about your mum,' I said. 'Breast cancer is a horrible thing to have. The last thing she needs right now is more stress.'

I'd checked out Kat's Facebook page and Twitter feed on my way to Oxford. It's amazing how much personal information people will post about themselves, free for absolute strangers to pore over. I knew a cop who said that many murders are solved not because of any forensic magic, but because your average criminal feels compelled to confess their crime and will either tell someone or do something which gives them away. The detective and I both rely on people wanting to share their traumas with the world so we can do our jobs.

'You need to think long and hard about your family,' I said. 'Do you want to bring them into this mess? I know what the reporters will do, Kat. They'll doorstep you day and night. They'll talk to your friends. Put your Facebook pictures in the papers. Follow you to lectures. And then what? You'll stop sleeping. Your grades will drop. Meanwhile your parents will have to keep their curtains closed and they won't be able to go outside because there'll be a pack of them outside their front door too. Your mum will be in tears. Your dad will blame you for this. He'll wonder why you didn't just let it go.'

'Stop it,' Kat said.

'Stop what?' My voice was gentle. Past experience taught me that the best way to act around someone like Kat was to empathize with her. I wanted to play the role of the friend who could help her out.

'You're trying to scare me, make me change my mind. But I won't.'

'If you're scared now, this is nothing compared to what a pack of journalists will do. They'll make your life a misery. All I'm doing is telling you the truth.'

And even though my motives weren't exactly pure I was telling her the truth. If she put herself out there as Pryor's fling she and her family would suffer forever. That was a fact. Newspaper journalists were ruthless, motivated and driven in ways she could never understand. They thought nothing of destroying people in the name of chasing a story. Like all the best reporters, I did things which would have disgusted people outside the business. Things that disgusted me now, to be honest. But I loved that world. It was the only place I'd ever felt at home.

Kat turned fully around to face me and leaned across the coffee table. Her cheeks had turned red and puffy and the skin between her upper lip and nose was gleaming with salty snot.

'What do you think my life has been like for the last week? It's been hell ever since that night. I keep thinking about that poor wife of his.' Her lips scrunched up. Her voice was scratchy. 'Every night he's sleeping next to her and kissing her. Telling her he loves her. He's a liar and I won't let him get away with it.'

Kat shivered. Then she rifled through the magazines on the coffee table and fished out a pack of unwrapped Mayfairs. Her hands were shaking as they unravelled the plastic and plucked the silver foil from the pack. She put a cigarette to her mouth, yellow lighter suspended in front of it.

'Do you mind?'

For a second I saw Emily sitting there in front of me, sparking up a cigarette as she fought to keep her nerves under control. If I was a religious man I would have prayed for Emily to never be in Kat's situation.

'I gave up a long time ago. But you go for it.'

I heard the crackle and fizz of burning tobacco as she lit up. The bittersweet smell of nicotine tickled my nostrils. I could taste its hot fuzziness in my mouth and for a brief moment I wanted a cigarette too. The craving passed, Kat went to replace the lighter and I reached out and held her hand.

I said, 'Just remember that you're the one in control, Kat. You have the power to stop this if you really want.'

She took a long pull on her Mayfair.

'I didn't ask for any of this.'

'No one ever does,' I said.

Kat sighed and blew out a stream of smoke that rose above us and ghosted into the whitewashed ceiling. 'So what am I supposed to do now? Just let him get away with it?'

'He's not getting away with anything. The man is sitting at home working himself into a blind panic. He can't sleep, can't eat. That's punishment enough, don't you think? And after this he's sure as hell not going to do anything like that again.'

At that moment I reckoned I'd sealed the deal. Kat was nodding and smoking and holding my hand and I was secretly congratulating myself on another story dead in the water and a few extra noughts on my bank balance. On the train journey back to London the champagne would be flowing and Emily would be waiting for me.

But they're funny creatures, human beings. The next moment Kat's demeanour changed like a weathervane spun around by a gust of wind. She sniffed, shook her head and snatched away her hand in a flurry, and suddenly the passengers on the 4.12 to Paddington were going to have to buy their own bubbly.

'No,' she said. 'My parents didn't bring me up that way. You don't know my mum and dad. They know right from wrong and so do I. They'll be proud of me. I'm going to do the interview,' she tipped ash into a glass tray, 'and there's nothing you can do or say that will stop me.'

At which point most people would have admitted defeat, made their excuses and left. But I'm not a normal person. I can be stubborn and argumentative to a fault and I'm also allergic to the word 'no'. If I hate anything in the world, it's that word. Which means hearing someone tell me 'no' makes my guts boil. More than that, it makes me want to get them to say yes. Especially when the person I'm trying to talk round is nearly the same age as my daughter and doesn't understand what she's getting into.

So I tried a new attack.

'This is a nice place,' I said, admiring the furniture. 'Must cost a lot in rent, what with only you and Zoe living here.'

'All the stuff is hers.' I noted that Kat didn't like referring to Zoe by name. There was some friction between them, I thought.

'And what about the rent?'

Kat took a final drag on the Mayfair.

'I pay my way,' she said.

'Yes, but is your way fifty percent of the rent?'

'I only use my bedroom so I pay thirty percent,' Kat said, stubbing out her cigarette in the ashtray like she was tapping out Morse code. 'The rest is hers. We agreed all this before we signed the tenancy contract. Not that Zoe would have a clue about any of that. Her father, sorry, step-father, takes care of it all. His name is on the contract and she doesn't even know how much this place costs per month. Every penny she spends goes on his credit card. Nothing's really hers. Anyway, what's your point?'

'Oh, nothing. Just that times must be hard with the rent, your tuition fees plus your mum's medical expenses and your dad not working so he can look after her.'

Kat froze. The last thin dregs of smoke drifted up from the crushed butt and cast a bridal veil across her features. She looked up at me, slowly. Her lips parted, slowly. I went in for the kill.

'I'm sure we could come to some arrangement,' I said. 'I think I'd be able to persuade Mr Valentine to make you an offer of ten thousand pounds, in cash, if you agree not to do this or any other interview.'

Perhaps you find the buying of silence repellent. Perhaps you think that truth is a commodity that has no market price, that it's a pure and immutable construct removed from the vulgar world of commerce. In which case you'd be wrong. In my world truth is bought and sold as often as oil stocks. Why should that be considered offensive? Ten thousand pounds would wipe out Kat's debts and let both her and Pryor go back to normality. In a world where African warlords slaughter their own people and fanatical terrorists blow themselves up on buses and airplanes, what's so bad about that? No one gets hurt. And it happens all the time, far more than you realise, or will ever know, thanks to people like me.

Except that the look on Kat's plain face told me she didn't see it that way. She shot me a look of such moral disgust I felt it stabbing my bowels like a kitchen knife. I think I might have even squirmed.

'Get out,' she said.

'Kat, listen, don't—'

'I said, get out of my house.'

Zoe's house, I wanted to say. But I didn't. I did what anyone else would have done five minutes before. I left. Kat sparked up another Mayfair as I walked to the door.

'Wanker,' she said to my back.

I found Zoe in the hallway, ending a phone call.

'Yes, okay,' she said, like a schoolgirl being told off. 'I'm sorry. I really am.'

The call ended abruptly and she gave me a forced smile as she put the phone on a shelf. Zoe hadn't struck me as the kind of person who could be made to talk like that to anyone, as if she was scared of whoever had been on the call with her. The ex-reporter in me was curious to know who that was. But it was none of my business and if I stepped out of line her step-father might hear about it and so I kept my questions to myself.

Zoe was halfway drunk but doing a good impression of sober and she made no attempt to hide the fact that she had her ear pressed to the living room door for the past twenty minutes. She raised her right arm so it was propped against the wall, blocking my exit. She cradled another glass of wine in her left.

'How did it go?'

'Not bad,' I lied. 'We're getting there.'

'Need to work some more of your charm?'

'She's a tough one to crack.'

Zoe sent another draught of wine down her neck. Her lipstick had left a blotchy-red imprint on the rim of the glass.

'Does that happen with every girl you try to charm nowadays? You find they're all tough nuts to crack.' She drew out the last word in a drunken slur. *Ca-rack.*

'Should you be drinking this early in the day?'

Zoe frowned at her glass. 'What's wrong with being merry at lunchtime?'

'Nothing, I guess,' I said. 'You must be hilarious by late afternoon.'

I moved up to her right arm. Zoe reluctantly lowered her arm and let me brush past. I stopped a few metres past her, removed a business card from my breast pocket, did a one-eighty and placed it in her hand.

'Tell Kat to call me when she changes her mind.'

I let myself out. It must have rained while I was talking to Kat because grey pellets now littered the pavement. The sky was so bleak that the streetlights were already on even though we were just shy of three o'clock. The black Range Rover was still parked opposite the house, looking sinister in the murky light. I wandered back down Bullingdon Road. By the time I reached Iffley I had increased to a fast stride. I had a new plan. If I couldn't stop Kat then I would have to kill the interview from the other end.

I needed to find Rachel Kirk.

4

I trudged away from the house and back towards the centre of Oxford. This job hadn't started well. I'd never seen anyone react to a cash offer in the way Kat did. Even the girls who made their livings chasing footballers preferred a cheque and anonymity to a smaller cheque and their faces in the papers. The brighter ones usually just asked for a bigger cheque rather than go ahead with the story and ruining their lives. But no matter how rude she'd been to me, Kat didn't deserve to have her life ruined over this. And that was certain to happen, I knew from experience. Kat might have been clever enough to study at Oxford but she didn't know how dirty the real world could get. I did. This was now possibly the strongest motivation I had to kill the story: to stop young, naive Kat from making a mistake which would haunt her and her family forever.

It was still only mid-afternoon on Tuesday and the *Legend* wouldn't go to print till Saturday evening but that wasn't my deadline. For me, as soon as Kat's interview went ahead the game would be lost. Rachel Kirk was my target now. The only trouble was, I didn't know where to find her. I didn't even know what she looked like. I'd seen her name in the paper and even killed a story she was working on but that was it. I wouldn't have known who she was if she slapped me round the face.

I read something once about how carrying out simple tasks helps the human brain work to its full potential. We usually only use ten per cent of our minds' thinking power but if that part is occupied doing something simple like walking or cycling, the other ninety per cent kick-starts and amazing things can happen. It's also how hypnotists reach the subconscious – they put the front ten percent to sleep and move in. So I started walking and let my brain get to work.

Bullingdon Road and Iffley Road were no more than background scenery as I strode back towards the centre of Oxford. How would I find Kirk? No one at the paper would tell me where she was, even my old mates. This was work. Even asking would be pointless. They'd laugh at me. I walked and thought some more.

I saw a Cafe Nero on New Road a few minutes later and at that moment I knew exactly how I'd find out where Rachel Kirk was. Some people sneer at clichés. I tend to believe them. If they weren't true, why would they be said so often by so many people? The one that popped into my head was *a chain is only as strong as its weakest link*.

I hurried into Cafe Nero and got a straight black coffee – I can't see the point of anything more complicated – found a table in a corner, sat down and pulled out my notepad and a pen. I pulled out my mobile and dialled the number for the *Legend*'s main switchboard.

'Travel agency, please,' I said.

The phone rang again and a woman answered.

'Hello,' I said, 'It's Nick Bull here from the *Legend*. I'm meeting Rachel Kirk in Oxford this afternoon and I wondered if you could tell me if there are any rooms left at her hotel for tonight?'

'Just a minute,' she said, 'I'll check for you.'

I heard computer keys being tapped quickly in the background.

'Yes,' she said, 'There are plenty of rooms left. Do you need me to book you one?'

'Not yet, thanks,' I said, 'I'm not sure if I'm staying the night. I'll call back later if it's confirmed.'

'OK. Do you need anything else?'

'Just the address, please,' I said, mock-embarrassed, 'I forgot to bring it with me.'

'No problem at all,' she said. 'The Barker is on Godstow Road'- she spelled it out for me-'and the postcode is OX2 8AL.'

I had no idea where Godstow Road was so I checked on my phone's map. Twelve minutes in a taxi or over an hour's walk. Not a difficult decision. I finished my coffee and waved down a taxi outside Cafe Nero. The driver wound down his window and smiled at me. So what people said about life in the provinces was true – people really were friendlier.

We arrived at the Barker: the place looked like an airport terminal. Smart and new, but still an airport terminal. I paid the taxi driver and realised another thing was true about life outside London – it's cheaper. I asked for a receipt and gave him a tip, something I never do at home.

Looking at the hotel Kirk had chosen, I thought it was funny how the younger, insecure reporters never go for the best hotels, even though the paper is paying. They don't want to rock the boat, don't want to attract negative attention for spending too much of the company's money. When I was a reporter I wouldn't have had a coffee in this place, let alone slept here. I'd have got myself a suite in the priciest hotel in the city and had a lovely time hammering their room service safe in the knowledge no one would call me on it. But I didn't work for a newspaper anymore.

I pushed through the glass door and the Barker's ground floor stretched out in front of me. To my left were the receptionists, two of them at a dark wood counter built into the shiny stone hotel wall.

The rest was smarter and more impressive than I expected from its exterior, classy even, with a white stone floor and then thick cream carpet under the chairs and tables. To my surprise I liked it. I also wondered why the hell they hadn't given the outside planning job to the same person who did the inside.

I headed straight for the more attractive receptionist and asked for a room for the night. I imagined where I'd stay if Edward Valentine wasn't paying my expenses. Wouldn't be here, that's for sure. We finished the booking and she handed over my room keys.

'Will there be anything else?' she said.

'Yes,' I said, thinking about the weakest link in the chain again. 'There is one more thing. I have a meeting this afternoon with another of your guests, Rachel Kirk. Has she reserved us a table?'

'Let me check,' she said with a smile. She typed on her keyboard and clicked her mouse a couple of times. A couple more clicks and she nodded and looked up.

'No,' she said, 'Not a table, a room. You're meeting in the Lavender Room at six o'clock. We'll have one bottle of red wine, one bottle of white wine and a bottle of still water waiting for you, as requested. The Lavender Room is down the corridor at the far end of the bar. You can't miss it.'

I gave the receptionist my best smile, turned and headed off on a recce.

Red and white wine – I was impressed. Rachel Kirk knew what she was doing. Nothing helps an interviewee talk more than a solid dose of alcohol.

I ambled over to the corner of the bar, looking around as I went, working out which seats could see what. There was only one door leading out of the bar area. I went through it and saw a short corridor which went straight ahead for about three metres and then turned left. I followed it and round the corner found two doors, a fire escape and the Lavender Room. There was one route in. Perfect.

The Lavender Room seemed like an architect's afterthought, someone thinking they were being clever by using a bit of spare space to create what hotels ambitiously call a 'meeting room'. I took a look inside. It was a small room, out of the way and discreet and at the same time, I guessed, too small to be used very often. There was a rectangular table with six chairs round it and a small black cabinet in the corner. Just enough space between the chairs and the white walls for it to not be a tight squeeze.

I went up to my room on the second floor, planning to kill a couple of hours watching TV news. It was too soon to call Valentine or Pryor because I had nothing good to tell them. My rule is you call a client when you have good news to share or when you desperately need something from them. Neither had happened yet.

Apart from room service and the TV, I didn't need anything else to keep me entertained. Twenty-four hour news channels are a dream come true. I'm a news junkie, I can't get enough. I don't care what format it comes in, paper, TV, radio, telepathy, doesn't matter, I have to have it. Addiction runs in my family. I suppose I'm lucky with my particular weakness. It's only killing me slowly.

At half past five it was time to go. I took the lift down to the ground floor and wandered casually into the bar. I took a paper from the selection laid out at the end, chose a table a couple of metres away from the door to the corridor which lead to the Lavender Room and sat down on the chair which faced it. My back was to reception. I ordered a whisky sour, opened the paper and got as comfortable as I could on the ridiculous seat.

At twenty to six a hotel worker pushed a trolley with three bottles on into the corridor. Three minutes later she came out with no bottles. At quarter to, I heard footsteps behind me. I didn't turn to look.

A woman wearing a dark blue skirt suit and light brown hair tied into a practical-looking pony tail came into view. From behind she looked unspectacular. Average height, normal body shape, medium heels. She had a large black handbag slung over her right shoulder and I could see the top of an A4 notebook sticking out. Doubtless there would be a small video camera in there too. Nowadays that was how newspapers operated – video and sound were as important as good old photos. She put her hand on the door and that was my moment.

'Rachel Kirk,' I said.

Kirk spun round.

'What?' she said.

She was clearly on edge. An older, more confident hack would have take this in their stride, the exterior calm and unconcerned while their brain calculated and schemed, like a swan gliding along the water's surface while its feet paddle frantically just below.

So this was Rachel Kirk. Her brown hair was pulled back from her face and she had bright blue eyes, slightly freckled skin, a little round nose and smallish but plump lips. She wore no make-up at all and seemed far better suited to being a doctor than a reporter, like her natural instincts were to care, not destroy. No matter, a few years at the *Legend* would harden her up.

'Who are you?' she said.

I stood up slowly, deliberately not smiling. 'Jack Winter,' I said, holding out my hand. 'And I'm here to tell you the girl you're about to interview is a liar.'

Recognition flashed across Kirk's face when she heard my name. Followed quickly by anger.

'How did you know?' she said.

'Kat is a liar,' I said, ignoring the question. 'There was no affair with Pryor. I repeat, there was no affair with Pryor. He did not cheat on his wife with her and he did not spend the night with her.' I paused, let those words echo round Kirk's mind. 'I suspect she's made the story up to get herself some attention and to bring down a politician from a party she doesn't like. Her entire family are a bunch of lefties. Pryor and his party represent everything they hate so she thinks she's going to make her parents proud by destroying him. And don't forget she's only nineteen. You need to be very, very careful on this one.'

I wanted to sow the seeds of doubt in Kirk's mind, make her nervous. I wanted her to start wondering if it would be wise for her to gamble her future at the *Legend* – her dream job – on this girl Kat, this *liar*.

Kirk might not have realised it but there was no true or false in my business. No difference between fact and fiction. The only measure I needed to bother with was deniability. If a story was deniable – and most of them were if you knew the game – then my rule was you denied it as far and as hard as you could and you never, ever showed weakness, right up to the day you saw that newspaper in court.

At the other end of the spectrum, when your client had no possible way out of the mess they were in, your best move was to apologise quickly and with Hollywood standard, Oscar-winning sincerity. But until Kat was on film telling the full sordid story, Pryor's dirty little secret was still perfectly deniable so I followed the first part of my rule.

I saw doubts appear on Kirk's face.

'Why should I believe a word you say?' she said. 'You're a nobody. I know your story. Everyone does. Why you left the paper, why you didn't even have the balls to come into the office to say goodbye to your old colleagues when you disappeared like a rat into a sewer. Everyone knows what you are. Everyone knows what you did. You're pathetic.'

I tried to visualise her words bouncing off me and disappearing into the distance. But I couldn't. Kirk had hit me where it hurt the most and she'd hit me hard. The best I could do was pretend not to have heard what she said.

'By all means listen to what she has to say,' I said, 'But remember what I've said to you here and now. This girl is a liar. She is making up this story. You'll see it for yourself if you focus on the details she comes out with. A good reporter always knows when they're being spun a line and you're a good hack so you'll know. Come and talk to me afterwards. I'll wait here.'

I sat down at my table and started reading my newspaper. I couldn't focus on the words on the page because the ones Kirk spoke were still swirling around my mind.

Out of the corner of my eye I saw Kirk stay still for a few seconds and then, without saying a word, turn and open the door. She slammed it behind her.

5.50pm. Kat was due in ten minutes.

I turned to check out what was happening in the rest of the bar. The guy who made my drink was fiddling about with the bottles in the fridge behind the bar. There were two overweight men in suits sitting at a table near the entrance, drinking bottled beer and talking quietly. The two women at reception were looking at their computer screens. There was no one else around. I sat and waited.

Six o'clock passed. I was reading the sports section now. When I was a kid I always read that bit before anything else but when I became a journalist that changed and now I still looked at news first. There was an interview with a young footballer, a kid born into poverty and who was as talented as any of the greats at that age but kept letting himself down by drinking or fighting or sleeping with indiscreet girls. I knew the type well. I'd represented enough. He was just a normal young man at his core, not bad or unintelligent, but full of physical health and hormones and now with a bank balance to make any young hothead's dreams come true.

But unlike most of us, his growing up would be done in public, with the world watching and waiting for him to make a mistake, which he was certain to do sooner or later because he was only human. I'd had enough of that kind of crap with clients over the past few years but if this job went pear-shaped maybe I'd give the player's agent a call. I'd have no choice. That's what my life had come to – chasing the football and celebrity gravy trains like all the other bloodsuckers.

Five more minutes went by. I'd read everything I wanted to in the paper and I sat and watched the door, letting my mind wander back to the days when I was in Kirk's position. Would I have been as easy to find as she was? Maybe. How would I have coped with a story killer on my tail? I would have changed my plans. But Kirk didn't know about me until minutes before her interview was supposed to start, so she didn't have time to change anything. My advantage over her was experience. I knew what she was going to do before she even knew I was around. How does a young journalist counter that? They can't.

At ten past six the door opened and Rachel Kirk appeared. She had her phone pressed to her ear and her eyes darted around. She hurried out and passed me with no acknowledgment. I didn't acknowledge her either. As she came back into earshot a minute later I heard the end of a message she was leaving. She was trying to sound friendly but couldn't hide the tension in her voice.

'…so give me a call, please,' she said. 'Hopefully you're just running a bit late. Hope to see you in a bit. Thanks. Bye.'

I heard her coming closer to my shoulder. She rushed past and back through the door. This time she didn't slam it.

I gave her ten more minutes and just before twenty-five past six I went to the Lavender room. I opened the door slowly and when it opened far enough for Kirk to be visible I saw hope on her face. But it was only for an instant. When she realised it was me at the door her expression changed. Her eyes dropped, her face slackened and her shoulders drooped. She looked beaten. I went to the cabinet and poured two glasses of red wine. I put one glass in front of Kirk, walked round the table and sat down.

'You don't know where she lives, do you?' I said, quietly. Kirk shook her head. If Kirk knew Kat's address, she'd have been there hours ago.

'And she's not answering her phone?'

Kirk shook her head again.

'What are you going to do?'

'I don't know,' Kirk said quietly. 'I haven't told the news desk yet.'

Right now, Rachel Kirk was experiencing the worst feeling in the world for a young journalist, when a story had gone badly wrong and you had to tell your bosses how and why. Every time that happened, it was the reporter's fault. No one else's. The facts, the reasons why it didn't work out, the freak lightning bolt of bad luck, none of it mattered. All anyone saw was a failed story with your name on. If Kirk was anything like me when I was her age, she was feeling physically sick.

'Can I give you some advice?' I said.

Kirk's head jerked up at me and her whole body seemed to spark into life. The defiance returned.

'What do I need advice from you for?'

I smiled my most reasonable smile.

'I've been where you are,' I said. 'I know how it works. I can help you.'

'Help me?' she said, now on the brink of tears. 'Are you joking? You ruined this story for me just like you ruined the Point Rail one. I haven't had anything since then, until this.'

Ah, the Point Rail story. I'm not surprised she bore a grudge. That was a simple one for me but a disaster for Kirk. The story started when an old woman who didn't speak English was put on a train by her daughter three hours from London. The daughter had paid for a steward from Point Rail to take her mother off the train when it got to London and escort her safely to the Point Rail office where her other child, a son, would be waiting.

Trouble was, that steward didn't show up. The old lady stayed on the train when it arrived in London and everyone else got off. She stayed on it when the lights went out half an hour later and she stayed on it when it was shunted onto some sidings near Watford a couple of hours after that. She wasn't found until 4am the next morning and ended up spending two weeks in hospital with hypothermia. It was a miracle the poor woman hadn't died. Her son was furious and phoned the *Legend* to tell his story.

Kirk took the call, got the story nailed down and was all set to see her name in lights when I got a call from the chairman of Point Rail. They were desperate. Could I help? Of course – for a fee.

I went in for a long meeting with some very stressed businessmen, came out and killed the story stone dead with one phone call. I simply let the editor know that if the story was printed Point Rail and all the companies its directors were associated with would no longer advertise with the paper.

Point Rail got the result they wanted and I got my cheque but all Kirk's good work was wasted. If it had happened to me when I was a reporter I'd have lost my mind. I'd have shouted and smashed things and seen off a couple of dozen whisky sours. I knew others who would have resigned on the spot. Journalists hate few things more than commercial realities crossing into their work. So I understood why Kirk didn't like me much. It was a compliment, in a way.

One more journalist hating me wasn't a great loss but friendly reporters could be very valuable so if I could do Kirk a favour now, when she was desperate, I would have her ear in future. I had lots of stories up my sleeve, I always did, and if I dropped one of those in her lap her week might not turn out to be the disaster it seemed to be now.

'It's nothing personal,' I said. 'You have your stories, I have my clients. We both do our jobs as best we can.'

Kirk looked like she wanted to smash one of the wine bottles over my head.

'There's a way out of this,' I said. 'We can turn this round for you.'

'No offence,' she said sarcastically, 'but you're not a reporter any more. Why the hell should I listen to you? I know all about you and your job.'

As she finished her sentence she obviously remembered something else she heard about me.

'Oh I get it,' she said knowingly, 'I'm the damsel in distress. Well, I'm not that stupid. I don't need to sleep with you to help my career.'

The look she gave me stung. She'd misunderstood me, but the damage was done. I smiled, stayed unflustered. This wasn't over yet. But trying to convince her that wasn't a proposition was a waste of time. I didn't need her to like me, just to listen.

'You know I used to be a hack?' I said.

'Yes.'

'Do you know what my biggest regret is?'

'No,' Kirk said, still not caring. 'But I'm sure you're going to tell me.'

'My biggest regret is leaving. Giving up. I had my reasons and at the time I thought they were good ones. But they look very different now that a few years have passed. I didn't listen to all the people who told me to hang in there, take it one day at a time. That it would get better. I wish I'd taken notice of what they said.'

Kirk gave a thin smile. There it was, a bit of sympathy.

'So what are you saying?' she said.

'I'm saying don't give up.'

'But I don't have a story,' Kirk said. 'I haven't had one for months. Whether or not I stay at the *Legend* won't be my choice soon.'

'I can help you,' I said.

'How?'

'You need a story for this weekend. I can give you one.'

She looked suspicious, but interested. Desperation makes people do funny things, especially reporters. I'd been there many times.

'What do you get in return?' she said. 'You're not coming up to my room.'

'I don't want anything,' I said. 'Just to help. People have done me favours in the past. I'm trying to do one for you now.'

Kirk ran her eyes over me, assessing her options.

'Think about it,' I said. 'Let's talk again when you've stopped chasing this nonsense about Adam Pryor.'

I stood up, reached into the inside pocket of my suit jacket, took out a business card and put it on the table.

'Could I have one of yours?' I said. Kirk took one out of her handbag and passed it to me. I took it, smiled and walked out slowly. I wanted Kirk to think I was leaving to give her time to stew on what I'd told her. I wanted her to think I had it all under control.

But the truth was I didn't. Not by a long chalk.

As soon as the door to the Lavender room clicked shut behind me I ran for the front door of the hotel and the taxi rank outside.

For the first time in years I felt that panicked tightening of the stomach I used to get when I knew reporters from other papers were beating me to a story, that same feeling Kirk had about calling her news desk with bad news.

Because I had no idea where Kat was, or who she was talking to. For all I knew she could have been making the biggest mistake of her life.

5

When a girl in Kat's position agrees to tell their story to a newspaper and then doesn't show up for their interview, ninety-nine times out of a hundred it means only one thing: another paper has waved a bigger cheque in her face and tempted her away. With the ink still drying on the new deal, that other paper will spirit the person away to another hotel, often abroad, and no reporter or story killer will get near them until every cough and spit is on record and in print.

And now Kat was AWOL, which meant this story was sliding away from me.

My options were disappearing fast. I could have called my contacts on all the different papers to ask if one of their reporters was talking to a student in Oxford about a fling she may or may not have had with an MP. But that would be like pointing a loaded gun at my foot and pulling the trigger just to see if it worked. The paper that was talking to her wouldn't tell me about it and the ones that weren't would instantly send reporters to Oxford on the hunt for the student who'd slept with a politician. Either way, my life would have got a whole lot more complicated.

That left me with one choice – head back to Bullingdon Road in case Kat was there. If she wasn't, all I could do was cross my fingers and hope for the best.

I got a cab outside the hotel and said I'd double the driver's fare if he got me there in five minutes, which he did. Cab drivers might be cheaper and more polite outside London, but there's one thing they all have in common: when there's extra money in it, they can all get there quicker.

The windows at Bullingdon Road were dark so I told the driver to wait for me while I rang the bell. There was no answer. I signalled to him to wait a little longer and took out my mobile. I had to speak to Valentine. My news for him wasn't all good, but I had to tell him what had happened. He was my paying client, after all. He had a right to know. I tapped the icon for his mobile and waited. He picked up on the second ring.

'The great Jack Winter,' he said, sounding like my call was worth celebrating. 'How goes it?'

'I have an update for you,' I said, trying to sound calm. I didn't bother with pleasantries. 'It's Kat. She was due to talk to a newspaper at 6pm but didn't show up, which is good news. But she's not at home so I don't know where she is. For all I know she could be talking to another paper. Zoe's not around either.'

There was a pause.

'OK,' he said, sounding obviously disappointed. 'Thanks for filling me in. Do you know what you're going to do next?'

'Of course,' I said. 'There are plenty of avenues for me to run up.' I didn't mention that I already knew most of them would be dead ends.

'Good. That's good to hear. Thanks Jack.'

Valentine's tone said that was the end of the call, unless I had something else to say, which I did.

'Wait,' I said, not wanting him to hang up. 'If you hear from Zoe please ask her to call me. I could really do with knowing if she's been in touch with Kat.'

'I will,' Valentine said and then, just when I thought the call was finished, he added an afterthought. 'And Jack, I feel I could be helping you a bit more. I haven't done a great deal to support you yet. Why don't I send you a car? Should save you a bit of time, having a driver.'

'There's really no need,' I said. 'I can get around perfectly well on my own.'

'I insist,' Valentine said. 'It'll make your life easier. When are you coming back from Oxford?'

'Some time tomorrow morning, I expect,' I said.

'OK,' Valentine said. 'My man will be in Oxford bright and early. He'll be at your disposal from then on. Chap named Naz. A good sort, very reliable. I'll send you his number. Call him when you want a lift somewhere. He'll go anywhere you want, night or day.'

'Thank you very much,' I said. There was no doubt that a personal driver would make my life less complicated.

I heard a quiet click and the call ended. Almost immediately my mobile buzzed as Naz's contact details arrived.

I got back into the taxi.

'Where to now sir,' the driver asked.

'Back to the hotel, please.'

He looked at me in the rear view mirror.

'Not there, was she?' he smiled lasciviously.

I didn't reply.

Back at the hotel, I went straight up to my room, took off my shoes and laid back on the bed. I hated to admit it but right now there was nothing I could do to help Pryor. If Kat was holed up in the Dubai Hilton with some hack funnelling champagne down her neck the whole show was out of my hands.

I had never failed to kill a story before. Not once. But this one wasn't like the rest.

I needed something to help me relax. I flicked on Sky news,

immediately muted the TV and ordered a good bottle of red wine from room service. As an afterthought I added a cheeseburger. I turned off the main light in the room and watched the images from the TV flickering on the ceiling. I wanted to find that serenity I get on train journeys, that sense of being away from the real world, away from my life. I wanted to turn this hotel room into a cocoon and come out with the idea that would change everything.

The red wine was a few minutes away so I tried a meditation trick my ex taught me because she thought I was too highly strung. I imagined white light going into my body through my eyes, filling up my head and then gradually working its way down to the tips of my fingers and my toes. On its way, this white light would take all the stress and tension out of me.

But amateur meditation didn't work for me. I couldn't get Valentine and Pryor out of my mind. This job might well have been my shot at the big time and right now more than anything else I needed to rest.

Room service came, and the bottle of wine was empty twenty minutes later. I didn't touch the cheeseburger.

***

There were three men in the call. Each was sat alone in smart, well-guarded offices with their doors shut and locked from the inside, one in London, one in Nairobi, and one in the Cayman Islands. The line they spoke over was untappable and unhackable and as clear as if they were sitting the same room.

'Gentlemen,' the man in London said. 'We are approaching the critical stage. But there is still a great deal for us to do. We must not relax. There must be no complacency.'

He paused. The silence told him no one else would speak until he told them to.

'The purpose of this call,' he said, 'is for each of you to update me on where you are with your respective areas of responsibility. So please do that.'

'We're on track and under control down here,' the man in Africa said. 'Our people are in place and ready. They just need to be told when to go.'

'Thank you,' London said.

'The same is true here,' one of the men in the Caymans said. 'The contracts are ready and we have finalised the structures of the investment vehicles.'

'Good,' the man in London said. 'Very good.'

Something in his voice didn't match his positive words and the two other men had already picked up on it. As a result the mood of the call remained low. They might have expected to discuss their excitement about the great wealth they would soon possess and maybe to enjoy some mutual back-slapping for their successes at performing what would be impossible tasks for anyone except a handful of people.

The man in London was pleased with the work the two men had done for him. But he, the leader, the architect of the whole scheme and the one who stood to make the most out of it, was responsible for the only part which was going so badly wrong it threatened to destroy all his hard work.

'I'll be in touch again soon,' the man in London said. 'Be ready.'

He disconnected the call without waiting for replies from the others and sat back in his chair. He was tantalisingly close to more money and power than he ever imagined was possible. So damned close. And now everything was in jeopardy because of a handful of idiots. Troublesome, irritating, stupid idiots.

Part Two: Wednesday

6

Rachel Kirk did not look pleased to see me when I knocked on the driver's door window of her car. Her motor was small and practical, not flashy. I smiled and waved and then watched as Kirk clocked me, sighed, closed her eyes and let her head slump forwards. She was parked across the road from Kat and Zoe's house and judging by the bags under her eyes and the empty coffee cup on the dashboard had already been there for a while.

Kirk turned the ignition key slightly and the window glided halfway down. Hardly a warm welcome.

'You found it, then,' I said in a positive voice.

It was seven o'clock the next morning and I'd come straight to Bullingdon Road. I wasn't expecting to find Kirk here just yet. I figured she'd get hold of the address eventually, but not this quickly. That was good work.

'I'm not completely useless,' she said, looking away from me.

'Anyone in?' I said.

Kirk looked at me.

'Why are you being so friendly?' Kirk said. 'You're not doorstepping her.'

Doorstepping is a regular feature of a reporter's life. Packs of reporters and photographers would spend days waiting outside the home of someone newsworthy, could be a celebrity, could be a train driver, depending on the story, waiting for them to come back in the hope of getting an interview or a picture. Waiting, waiting and then some more waiting. If you could handle the fact other reporters playing different angles were doing the interesting work and getting the glory, there were far worse ways to pass a day, especially when the weather was good.

But Rachel Kirk wouldn't agree. She was also wrong about why I was there – I was doorstepping Kat too, just for different reasons.

I stepped away from Kirk's car. Nothing positive could come out of our conversation.

A ring of the doorbell got no answer. I tried again in case they were on the typical student morning schedule but after five minutes where I could almost feel Kirk's eyes burning holes in my back. I knew what she was thinking. *Why is he ringing their bell? Why does he want to find Kat?* But I didn't have time to weave a web around that so I left. I had one more stop to make and after that it was back to London.

And then my phone rang. Tom Halliday was calling me. Normally I would have called him in an hour or two, having read or scanned every word of every paper looking for stories about him, which I hadn't done yet. But Halliday was clearly more anxious than most.

Even though I was ill-prepared, there was no sense hiding from him. I'd only have to call him back later. I sat up and rubbed my temples with the hand that wasn't holding my phone. I pressed the connect button and put it to my ear.

'Have you seen the papers,' Halliday said, not waiting for me to speak. His voice was lighter and quicker than last time we spoke. It didn't take a genius to work out why.

'Not yet.'

'There's nothing about me in any of them. Nothing at all. I can't tell you how grateful I am. You're a magician.'

'It's my job,' I said.

'I don't know how to thank you,' Halliday said.

'Just pay your invoice,' I said, 'that's all.'

There was silence. Not what I expected from a man as happy as Halliday.

'About that invoice,' he said, tentatively. 'How soon do you need the money?'

'My payment terms are fourteen days. You agreed to it right at the start. There's no small print on my contract. It's all there in big letters.'

'Yes, I know but…' Halliday's voice tapered off.

'But nothing. You agreed fourteen days.'

'Jack, I don't have the money.'

'Nice try,' I said. 'But I've seen your office. You're one of the country's top private surgeons, you're responsible for the knees of some of the best athletes in the world.' I quoted his own marketing literature back at him. 'Ten thousand pounds is nothing to you. You said so yourself.'

'Yes, but,' his voice tapered off again. This time I let silence get him talking. It didn't take long.

'I don't have as much as I used to,' he said, all the happiness now drained from his voice. 'They're going to take my home away from me, Jack. They want everything.'

A bad feeling was creeping over me. Another one to add to my impressive collection.

'What's happened?' I said.

'Gambling,' the word slunk out of his mouth, like it hoped no one would notice it.

I'd have slapped Halliday if he'd been standing in front of me.

'This isn't a joke, is it,' I said.

'No. I'm sorry. I joined a poker club, one of those smart places. I was winning and then I lost and then'-

'Save it for Gamblers Anonymous,' I said. 'I'm not interested. I want my money. My work isn't a hobby.'

'Jack, you don't understand. I don't have the money. I owe so much I might have to sell my house. My motorbikes are next to go. In fact, do you want a motorbike to cover your invoice? You could upgrade from your Vespa. You'd love it.'

'No I wouldn't love it,' I said. 'What I'd love is my money.'

The truth was motorbikes terrified me. My Vespa topped out at 32mph going downhill into the Hyde Park Corner underpass and that was quite enough speed for me. I wanted the cash. That was the only reason why I killed stories. It wasn't for fun.

I was about to explain this to Halliday in the bluntest terms I could think of when I coughed a horrible, raking wheeze, the kind of noise you hear from lung cancer victims on anti-smoking adverts. And then another one.

'Sorry,' I said, when my throat started behaving again. I wished I hadn't picked up the phone.

I usually enjoyed these conversations, the praise and the happiness in the voice of the client were good for my ego, and it should have been especially true with Halliday because I liked him. But not today.

'Are you okay?' he said.

'I'm fine.'

'You sound like shit,' he said. 'And that's a medical professional talking.'

'I'm fine. I had a big night last night. Out with some mates. You know how it is.'

I didn't want him to know I spent the night alone with a bottle of wine and a hotel mini bar.

'Ah, I see. Good lad,' Halliday said, relieved. He paused and sounded serious when he spoke again. 'I don't think you understand what you've done for me. My work is my life. I'm so sorry about the money. I'll make it up to you, I promise. If it wasn't for you I'd have lost the only thing I have left and I am deeply in your debt. If you ever need anything, just let me know. I mean absolutely anything.'

'I need ten grand.'

'Jack, please. This is hard for me.' Halliday sounded hurt.

'Piss off,' I said, and ended the call.

Adam Pryor and the money he would bring in were even more important now.

As I reached Hertford College I began to understand why Pryor found Oxford intoxicating and dangerous. It wasn't simply the attractive young women throwing themselves at him. It was the history, the atmosphere, the architecture. All of those things with the man's ego thrown in would blend to form a potent cocktail. If I were Pryor I'd have slipped up too, just like I was slipping up now.

The Pryor story was turning out to be about control more than anything else. Sometimes my job was proactive, getting out there and getting the first hit in for a client, and sometimes it was reactive, responding carefully to something someone else said or did. But I'd never had one like this before, a story which was a mix of both and which had kicked off with this kind of intensity so early in the week.

The knot in my gut which had been there since I woke up was slowly tightening as I walked away from Kat's college. She wasn't there. I wasn't expecting anything else.

I had to go back to London. Right now there was nothing I could do in Oxford for Adam Pryor's glittering political career and, of course, Emily was in my flat. Some time with my daughter would be very welcome. I started to walk towards the railway station but stopped when I remembered Valentine's offer of a driver. A warm, comfortable car was much more tempting than a crowded morning train and much quicker, too. I pulled out my mobile and called the number Valentine sent me. My call was picked up on the second ring.

'Is that Naz?' I said.

'Yes,' he said. 'And that's Jack Winter. Where are you and where would you like to go?'

I told him where I was and my destination.

'I'll be there in five minutes,' Naz said.

His voice was confident and businesslike. He sounded more like a soldier than a chauffeur.

As I waited for Naz I made one call, to Pryor. He didn't answer. I left a message.

'Adam,' I said. 'Don't forget what I told you about truth. You have to tell me everything. If you hold anything back, I can't help you. I need to know everything.'

A shiny, new black Range Rover with tinted windows glided to a halt in front me. The passenger door opened and a man looked at me from the driver's seat.

'Jack,' Naz said. 'Get in.'

He said it in the way a man does when he is used to being obeyed. I sat down and he stuck his hand out for me to shake.

'Good to meet you,' he said as we shook hands. His grip was surprisingly strong. I smiled and nodded back.

Naz looked to be about the same height as me and wore a green, round-necked wool jumper with a blue shirt underneath, blue jeans and shiny brown brogues on his feet. He was in his mid-forties, had short, ginger hair and was cleanly shaved, with bright blue, alert eyes which he turned back to the road as soon as I closed my door.

Because I'm the nosy type, I looked into the back seat. There was a green Barbour coat rolled up tidily on the seat behind Naz and the seat was so spacious I could have got a good night's sleep on it.

Every time I sat in one of these monstrous cars I understood why the people who could afford to bought them. You sat above everyone else on the road and behind metal walls which insulated and protected you from the messy realities outside. In principle I didn't like that approach to life but I knew if I had the means I'd most likely be driving one of these myself too. They make you feel strong, safe and dominant.

Naz's driving had a similar effect. He was efficient, smooth and precise, even in city traffic. His hands never crossed and he constantly checked his mirrors. He was obviously highly trained and I was sure from that and the way he was dressed – an off-duty soldier's version of casual – that his training happened in the military.

I noticed something else about Naz. I've known two types of soldiers: ones who take lives and are haunted by their actions, who cry and drink and lash out, and others who kill in the line of duty and don't give the consequences a second thought. These men are professional killers. Inflicting death is their job and they get on with it with no fuss and no regrets, like machines. They are the best and the SAS is full of them. I was confident that Naz was one of these professionals and, as they all did, he scared me. Many of them ended up working as bodyguards for rich men like Edward Valentine when they left the Army and wanted a payday. So I had a good idea that Naz was more than just a driver.

'How's the job going?' Naz asked, a few minutes into our journey. He sounded like he was simply making polite conversation and didn't really care about what was going on. I wasn't sure if he was off duty or on.

'It's challenging but I'm making progress,' I said.

'Nothing worth working hard for comes easily,' Naz said.

'Very true,' I said.

I stopped there. I wasn't sure if Naz was aware of what I was doing in Oxford and I knew better than to tell a stranger too much about something so sensitive. Also, an hour of peace and quiet would make for useful thinking time. And I had plenty of that to do.

Naz and I didn't speak again until we arrived at my home. We shook hands as I got out of the car.

'Thanks for the lift,' I said.

'Any time,' Naz said. 'Call me if you need the car again. Or any other kind of help. I'm always around.'

The door closed and the Range Rover pulled away. It disappeared smoothly and powerfully into the traffic. I wasn't sure whether to feel frightened or protected.

I was about to pull out my keys when my phone rang. I answered it and the voice at the other end was cockney and hoarse and sounded like someone doing an impression of a dirty old man.

'Winter, you bastard,' he said, 'you never ring, you never write.'

It was Nick Bull, an old newspaper friend – the man whose name I borrowed to find out where Rachel Kirk was in Oxford. We used to work for the same paper and drink similarly inadvisable amounts to ease our consciences. Bull was a good guy, an old school reporter with fifteen years' more experience than I had. But not always the most charming man in the world.

'I hear you spoke to the delightful Miss Kirk,' he said. 'But you didn't have time for me. We have a name for you people.'

'Let me guess. Younger, better looking and richer than you?'

'Remember who you're talking to, boy.'

'I've been trying to forget you for years now.'

'Very funny. Smooth bastard. Anyway, this isn't a social call.'

'What is it then, sexual harassment?'

'Behave,' Bull said. 'I need to talk to you about a story. I think you and your new high-powered contacts might be able to help me with a little something.'

Every time I got a call from an old newspaper friend asking for a favour all the old excitement and energy would flicker back into life. I already wanted to know everything about the story, the five points you're trained to look for: who, what, where, why and how. But I couldn't tell Bull that now.

'Why should I help you?' I said.

'Because now you're in public relations you need all the good karma you can get. Meet me at seven at the Pit.'

Emily was finishing packing up her bag when I opened the door. I was too late, as usual.

'Hey,' she said with half a smile. She was pleased to see me but disappointed I hadn't come sooner – the same old story and the reason I only ever got half a smile from her.

I looked at my daughter and couldn't help comparing her with Kat. They were very different physically; Emily was slightly taller, not so petite, had lighter hair and her mother's blue eyes. But they could have passed for the same age. In fact Emily could have been older. The realisation terrified me.

'Are you okay?' I said.

'I'm fine. I'm used to her being drunk. She always says sorry and I know she's ill so I can't stay angry with her.'

She sounded tired, worn down. And I couldn't do anything to help.

'Did you find everything you needed?' I said, hopefully.

Emily smiled and shook her head. 'Of course I didn't. I went shopping for what I needed. I used your card and I left some stuff in the fridge for you. It looked a bit empty.'

'Thanks,' I said. Emily had my credit card for emergencies. Another small gesture I'd made.

'Where are you going now?' I said. 'Do you want to stick around for a while? We could go out and eat somewhere.'

I would have cancelled my drink with Bull in a flash for Emily. But she shook her head.

'I have to go home. William's back and Mum is feeling better today. I should be there. It's important to support her when she's feeling bad about herself. Makes it less likely she'll go on another bender. That's the idea, anyway.'

'Ok,' I said. 'I understand. You should be there.'

There was a moment of awkward silence. Emily broke it.

'I'd better go. Thank you for having me.

'Any time. I'm sorry I wasn't here.'

Her expression softened. 'It doesn't matter. Sometimes you can help me without even being here.'

She hugged me more tightly than I expected and left.

After the door closed I checked my fridge. In it were fruit, vegetables, a packet of fresh salmon, a carton of orange juice, and a pint of organic milk. My daughter was trying to make sure I ate properly. Part of me was touched. Another part was embarrassed.

Down Adam and Eve Court, a narrow paved road which runs off Oxford Street between two well-known clothes shops, that's where you'll find the Pit, real name The Miner's Hat. The Pit is more apt. It's a dark, dingy, cramped place with a small bar, uncomfortable chairs, dark floors and dirty walls which are still marked with tar stains, five years after smoking in pubs was banned. Bull and I go there for privacy. Very few people know about the Pit and even those that do tend to avoid it.

Bull and I had been coming here for years and still knew nothing about the background to the place. There were always new staff in, always foreign, and no one there knew anything about us either. We found the Pit by accident on a long night out a long time ago. We'd had enough of paying £10 for a whisky sour in the smart bars and found the Pit when Bull went down what he thought was just a dark alley for a toilet break. We had been coming here ever since.

Bull and I were standing at one end of the bar, in a corner, away from the handful of other drinkers and the two staff. Bull was short and stocky and he could put away more than men twice his size. He had a full head of brown hair flecked with grey and somehow managed to still look healthy, despite his lifestyle and his temper, which I used to enjoy pointing out was even shorter than him.

'There's no way round it,' Bull said, frowning. 'You've ruined that girl's life.'

'It's a cruel world,' I said. 'If she's going to play with the grown-ups she shouldn't expect to be treated like a kid.'

Bull laughed. 'You really are a tosser. What a thing to say.' He shook his head. 'I'm not joking, you know. Kirk's career is going down the toilet and you're the bastard pulling the chain. The poor girl has had two great stories in the palm of her hand, two brilliant opportunities to show what she can do and you've ruined both of them. Now she's getting a reputation for being unlucky and you know what that means.'

I did know. There is nothing worse than an unlucky hack. You can be stupid, late, ugly, rude, drunk, high, even violent, it doesn't matter, as long as you get the stories. But if you're unlucky, you could be the lovechild of Audrey Hepburn and Warren Beatty with the brain of Einstein and the charm of JFK and you'd still be finished because your editors won't trust you with on any of their stories.

'You remember what being a young reporter was like, don't you?' Bull said.

Of course I remembered. Back then I was boiling over with ambition and enthusiasm. Nothing mattered more than proving myself and that meant getting stories. Friendships, relationships, family, my health, they all took a back seat. The job came first.

We were all the same – it becomes your life. In those first couple of years success tastes so sweet it brings tears to your eyes. You are living out your dreams. The flipside of the glory is that setbacks, even small ones, make you feel like your world is falling apart. I'd be lying if I said I didn't feel sorry for Kirk.

'What choice do I have?' I said. 'I'm just doing my job.'

Bull looked down at his empty glass.

He waved at the barman. 'Another round please, two each again. Ta.'

Four more whisky sours. They were Bull's drink of choice and had been for decades. I'd never had one before we met but after a few nights out with him I was addicted to them. Beer didn't really cut it next to whisky, lemon juice and sugar, preferably straight up. I didn't mind if the whisky was cheap. They all tasted the same to me.

Tonight we'd had half a dozen already and Bull was drinking faster than me, as always. I could go drink for drink with most people but with Bull I struggled. He was a veteran boozer, his career fuelled by alcohol, whether it was bonding with his colleagues and bosses or getting contacts so drunk they spilled their guts to him. In the cold light of the next morning Bull would replay the conversation in his mind and pick through their indiscretions until he found a golden nugget which would make the front page. Very few reporters did that anymore because expenses weren't what they used to be. But Bull was old-school. He treated every drink like it was the last before kicking-out time.

'I can't believe you're spending your life doing that shit,' he said. 'After everything you did at the paper, everything we did together, how can you do it? How can you live down there with the scum?'

'It pays the bills,' I said.

Bull downed another sour and looked at me. The pub was hot and muggy and that combined with the whisky was making my head light. I was relaxing but Bull looked like he had something serious on his mind.

'You could still come back,' Bull said. 'You know the Princess, she's loyal.'

The Princess, Jennifer Shaw as she was known to most people, was the editor of the daily paper where Bull and I worked together until I left newspapers. Shaw was a brilliant editor, demanding and tough but also supportive, like a kind but scary headmistress. Her staff would have run over hot coals for her, me included. A couple of years after I left, she moved to the *Sunday Legend* and Bull was the first person she hired. He was also the only person who called her Princess to her face.

But I didn't work for her now. I wasn't a journalist any more but at moments like this I wished I still was. Whisky and regrets. Not a good mix.

'What do you want?' I said. 'Why did you call me?' I'd stopped enjoying our reunion.

'I'm serious about you coming back,' he said.

'I can't,' I said, feeling myself tense up. 'Not after what happened.'

'Relax,' Bull said, putting his hand on my shoulder. 'No one blames you.'

I flinched at Bull's touch. He'd picked the wrong subject.

'Easy for you to say,' I said, turning to look at him. 'But you don't know what it was like for me. Even if I didn't think I was to blame, everyone knows what happened. Everyone. At the *Legend* and every other paper. And will never, ever forget. You know that. I'll never be able to move on.'

Bull looked at me and spoke quietly.

'Coming back and starting again is the only way you'll ever be able to move on.'

I'd had enough. A combination of alcohol and exhaustion meant my patience had run out.

'For the last time,' I said, 'What do you want?'

I was surprised at how abrupt I sounded. Bull puffed out his cheeks. He was surprised too.

'OK,' he said. 'All business, then. Fine by me.'

He reached into his pocket and pulled out a sheet of paper. He unfolded it and put it in front of me. There was a mobile number written in blue ink.

'This number,' he said. 'I need to know who pays the bill, who's been calling it and who it's been calling. Standard stuff. Past two weeks should do.'

'No problem,' I said. 'Usual terms?'

'If you can get the details to me by Friday morning it's two grand, cash.'

I folded the piece of paper and put it in the inside left pocket of my suit jacket.

'Where did the number come from?' I couldn't help myself. The old instincts were still there.

Bull shot a look at me that said he still knew who I was. His eyes were clear and focused. How he could be like that after what we'd drunk was a mystery.

'I was out for lunch with a contact today, somewhere posh, one of those prehistoric gentlemen's clubs where they don't let ladies in. You should have seen the Princess's face when I told her. Anyway, I overheard a conversation at the next table.'

I wasn't surprised. Bull could have been out for lunch with the Prince of Wales and Marilyn Monroe and he'd have still been ear wigging the next table if he thought there might have been a story in it.

'Bunch of well-dressed sorts,' Bull said, 'They were talking about how much they were going to make from some deal and I was listening in because my pal had gone to the little boys' room and then heard the words Mozambique and mobile phones. I was thinking, what the fuck is that all about? What a strange combination. And then one of them said the magic word.'

'Which magic word?' I said, 'You have a million.'

Bull polished off another whisky. He looked excited, alive.

'Offshore,' he said, with a twinkle in his eye, 'This season's favourite.'

Bull detested the idea of money being taken out of the country and exposing rich people dodging taxes was one of the great joys of his life. This phone number was how it could have started – one bit of information appears, you see what it leads to and then see where that one takes you and so on until you've assembled enough of the jigsaw to make a story.

'When they left I had a crafty butcher's at their bill,' he said. 'Four grand. On lunch. Fuck me. And the tip was only forty quid. But that wasn't the interesting part. One of those clowns left a business card on the table and yours truly grabbed it. There was nothing on the card except a phone number. And that's the number in your pocket.'

'Have you called it yet?'

'Don't be daft. I'll call it when your man's done the business.'

My man was Karl Wake. He worked for one of the big mobile phone networks and had been providing me with inside information for years; numbers, messages, call records, texts and so on were worth serious money to reporters, especially if everything could be done secretly which, make no mistake, it could be. This was all highly illegal, of course, and because trust was important, I was still the only person he'd deal with, even though I wasn't a journalist any more. No one else even knew his name.

'So this is a fishing expedition?' I said.

Bull grinned at me. 'How do you think Watergate started? Greatest fishing expedition of all time.'

'You always say that,' I said. 'Give me a minute.'

I dug out my mobile and texted Wake the number. I gave him the terms, a grand – the second one was mine – in cash if he got me the details by Friday morning. He replied almost immediately. 'No problem,' the message read.

The room around me was beginning to wobble. Those whisky sours were starting to kick in now. I was approaching the point of no return. A couple more and I'd be kicking my door down at 4am with no idea of where I'd been. If I was lucky.

'Another?' Bull said. I needed a trapdoor but I'd never been able to say no to another drink from him.

And then my phone sparked up, just in time. Bull nodded to say he understood I had to take it and then turned and ordered another four drinks.

Pryor's name flashed up and I made my way out into the sticky night. I heard shouts and laughs from groups of drunks a few

yards away as they ambled along Oxford Street past the end of
Adam and Eve Court. There were sirens blaring further away –
typical late night London noises. I tapped the answer button and
pressed my mobile tight to my ear so I could hear what he was
saying.

'We need to talk.' No time for pleasantries. He sounded
anxious.

'Right now?'

'Yes, it's urgent. Come to my house.'

I took a deep breath and tried to clear my head. I had left merry
behind and was well on my way to being smashed. The last thing
I wanted was to be dealing with the unfortunate consequences of
Pryor's loose interpretation of marriage vows. But work was work,
no matter how pissed I was.

'I'm on my way,' I said.

Just as Bull understood I had to take Pryor's call, he understood
the summons meant our evening was over. I left the Pit and hailed
a black cab on Oxford Street. I spent the journey wondering why
Pryor needed to talk to me and trying to sober up, which isn't
easy in a moving London taxi. After twenty minutes it spat me
out a hundred metres down the road from Pryor's house. I
thought the walk might do me good, help clear my head. I could
just about move in a straight line, but it was close. At times like
this I wished I was teetotal. It's good to dream, I suppose.

7

I reached number thirty-nine sooner than I'd have liked. The lion's head knocker on Pryor's front door echoed like a giant bell into the quiet of the night and seemed to shake the blood in my head. I was rubbing my temples wishing I was at home with a pint of water and a kebab when the door opened.

One look at Pryor told me I wasn't the only one who'd spent the evening inside a bottle. He looked like I felt, tired and messed up and far worse than the day before. His eyes were puffy and red and his skin looked grey, like his insides were slowly drying up and dying. The top two buttons of his shirt were undone and his sleeves were rolled up untidily, his right one halfway up his forearm and his left up to his elbow. He turned away from the door and set off quickly towards his study door. I shut the door behind me. He didn't look back and neither of us spoke.

He opened the oak door to his study and motioned for me to go in past him. He turned to close it but stopped when a female voice came from one of the rooms we'd passed along the hall.

'Aren't you going to introduce me?' Pippa was slurring her words slightly, like she'd had one too many at a cocktail party and was trying to making herself heard.

I turned back into the hall and saw her. She was tall and classically good looking, the aloof, superior type, with dark red hair cut into a very precise bob. She wore black trousers and a white blouse. She came towards me with a glass of white wine in her left hand and a wobble in her step, and as she got closer I saw she was looking me straight in the eyes.

I looked her up and down. Her body seemed hard and bony, with no curves. Her presence screamed entitlement and ego and nothing sensuous or fun.

'I'm Pippa,' she said, holding out her hand for me to shake. It was cold and limp. I smiled politely but didn't say anything for fear of breathing whisky fumes on her. She took her hand away and put it on my left bicep. My arms aren't what they were a few years ago but she seemed to like what she felt because she smiled and raised her eyebrows.

'I know who you are,' she said, looking me in the eyes again. 'You're the man who's come to save the day.'

Her hand was still on my arm and from the look in her eyes and the slow, husky way Pippa was talking I half-expected her to suggest we adjourn to her bedroom. I turned to Pryor for some kind of guidance but all he did was stare at the floor.

Pippa let go of my arm. 'Make sure he takes care of this,' she said to Pryor, not looking at me anymore. 'And make sure he does it quickly.'

In my line of work clients were rude as a matter of course and in all kinds of offensive and imaginative ways but that was the first time I'd been spoken to like a servant. I'd been called scum, a traitor, a whore, a fluffer and even a Nazi. Somehow this was worse.

Pippa turned and tried to strut back to the room she'd come from but she was wobbling too much to carry it off. Pryor sighed and shut the study door. He trudged round to his chair with his head still tipped forward. I didn't blame him. I wouldn't speak to someone else's cleaner the way his wife just spoke to us.

Pryor sat down behind his desk. I took the chair in front of it without being asked. The bottle of whisky I'd noticed last time was now on his desk and about a third was gone. There was a half-full tumbler next to Pryor.

'First things first,' he said in weary voice, 'Whisky? It's good stuff, £300 a bottle.'

I nodded. He carefully picked up another glass from the shelf next to him, turned and poured me a glass with slightly less in it than the one he'd already been drinking out of.

He pushed the glass over to me and raised his.

'Cheers,' he said. 'To the future. Whatever it brings.'

He drank a sip and then looked admiringly into his glass. I picked up the tumbler and it was heavy and obviously expensive. I tasted the whisky and thought it was okay. Nothing more. But I kept my thoughts to myself and nodded to indicate my appreciation. And then I took another sip. Free whisky is still free whisky.

Pryor breathed in and out slowly and deeply. He tipped his head back, stretching his neck, and brought it forward. All these movements seemed deliberate yet slightly clumsy. He was used to people listening to him, I realised, and basked in the attention. It was just his usual moves didn't look quite so smooth when he was half-smashed. I hated this self-absorbed posturing. He was behaving like a drama student, not a politician. I wanted to slap him.

'I'm sorry about Pippa,' he said. 'She loves all this,' he waved his hand around the room, 'and she's very ambitious for me. That makes her a bit, well,' his voice faltered, 'difficult. She wants to wait until we're what she calls *financially secure*'- he layered the words with sarcasm —'before we have children. Whatever the hell that means. I think there's never a right time to start a family so why not get on with it but Pippa won't have any of it. What can I do? Nothing. I can't force her.'

Pryor looked at me with real sadness in his eyes. The man wanted to be a father – he wasn't a machine after all. I felt a shot of sympathy for him. My father issues were different to Pryor's – mine were to do with being too young and stupid to understand what really mattered for too long after Emily was born, while his were domestic – but I felt like I'd discovered some common ground between us.

Not that this made Pryor and me blood brothers, but I looked at him slightly differently now. Maybe I despised him a little less. Whatever, I'd now seen and heard enough to be confident I could guess the lie of the land in Pryor's relationship with his wife. Pippa wanted to be the Prime Minister's wife and God help Pryor if he fucked it up for her. I could see exactly why he couldn't resist a night with a friendly young university student.

And I didn't need to ask what he'd told his wife about the affair allegation. I knew enough about men staring down the barrel of ruin to know he'd have sworn blind there was no truth whatsoever in the rumours, that it was all lies and he would never, ever lay a finger on another woman and I was only here as a safety precaution. Pippa was his one and only. I'd used some of those lines myself, once upon a time.

'I've seen far worse,' I lied. 'What do you need to tell me?'

'It's complicated,' he said.

'It always is,' I said.

He touched his fingertips together in front of him and seemed to check all ten were present and correct before starting to talk. I was getting bored, even with a glass of whisky in my hand.

'A few years ago I was in a car crash,' he said, slowly and precisely. 'A woman died.'

'How many years ago?' I said.

'Ten.'

'Who was driving?'

'Not me,' Pryor shook his head.

'Then what's the problem?' I said. 'If you weren't driving it's not your fault, end of story. And we can sue the balls off anyone who says otherwise. You don't need to worry.'

Pryor breathed slowly and deeply again.

'There's no way anyone can ever find out about this but I want you to know about it,' he said, emphasising *you* and looking at me like he wanted me to feel how special he thought I was. The old politician's trick.

'You said no secrets, right?' Pryor said.

I nodded. 'Go on.'

'There were three of us in the car. Me, my sister Imogen and Harry Slew, a friend I grew up with. He lived near us. Harry was driving that night. We hit another car and a woman died. It was horrible.'

Pryor closed his eyes. Crash scenes were replaying in his mind. I couldn't let him dwell on them, not with all that whisky and self-pity brewing up inside him. I'd have been there all night.

'And?' I said. 'What happened next?' I wanted facts, not feelings.

Pryor's eyes blinked open as he snapped out of his stupor. Maybe a backhander wouldn't be necessary after all.

'We'd all been drinking and Harry was charged with causing death by dangerous driving,' he said, still in that annoying, precise way of his. 'And in the weeks leading up to the trial things got really nasty. The poor guy had some kind of breakdown and started making all kinds of threats to me. He said he would tell the world my darkest secrets if I didn't get him off.'

Here we go, I thought. Here it comes. No one is ever as clean as Pryor seemed. He shrank a bit in his chair.

'You have to remember this was ten years ago,' he said, opening his hands to give extra sincerity to his words, 'And back then I was only on the verge of becoming an MP. I was ridiculously young for it and getting lots of attention. Anyway, Harry saw me as his way out. He thought I had influence and he knew things about me from university which could have ruined everything.'

Pryor paused. More goddamned drama.

'What things?' I said.

'Nothing too bad,' he said, looking down at his whisky. 'Just the usual experimenting with drugs, that kind of thing. What most people do when they're young. But things which would have made terrible headlines. You know what I mean.'

'Of course.'

Pryor was right. It was different now but even ten years ago times were different and a story about teenage drug use would have finished a young politician.

'So he blackmailed you?' I said.

'He tried to.'

'What do you mean he tried to?'

'This is where it gets complicated,' Pryor said, looking towards the window and taking long breaths.

He turned back to me and then spoke again. 'I've known Edward for a long time.'

'Edward?' I said.

'Yes, Edward Valentine,' Pryor frowned. 'I've known him since I was a student, long before I started out in politics properly. He's always looked out for me, mentoring me, if you like. He introduced me to people, gave me advice, help, whenever I needed it. So when Harry started making all these threats, I was out of my depth. I went to Edward and he said he'd sort it out. And he did.'

'What do you mean? How did he sort it out?'

I still couldn't see what was so urgent about all this.

'Edward got Harry the best defence lawyer money could buy.'

'And?'

'Harry was acquitted.'

'So what? Adam, I'm beginning to think you're wasting my time.'

Pryor couldn't look me in the eye.

'I lied,' Pryor said.

'To who?' I said, my drunken mind now all but lost in the details of the story.

'I lied in court,' Pryor said. 'To help Harry's case, I lied. I swore on the bible that he was sober and that the accident wasn't his fault. You wanted it, so there it is. That's my darkest secret.'

Pryor took a quick gulp of whisky and put his glass back down hard on his desk. I loosened the grip around the glass in my right hand and rolled it gently backwards and forwards between my thumb and fingers. I was trying to buy some time, to think clearly. Lying to help a friend didn't sound like the greatest sin in the history of mankind. But this was deceptively serious. Pryor didn't just lie to help a friend. He lied in court to change the outcome of a trial. That meant he was guilty of perjury and our legal system really doesn't like people interfering with justice. If it ever got out, this secret would kill Pryor's political career instantly and soon after that he would be in jail. There would be no way back for him, ever.

'Tell me what happened,' I said. 'Who asked you to lie?'

Pryor leant forward again, dipping his head and hiding his eyes from me as he gave his confession.

'The lawyer Edward hired,' he said. 'He put together a statement for me and said if I wanted Harry to get off I should sign it and be prepared to stand up in court and repeat every word. So I did. And Harry got away with it. I made a good witness.'

Of course you did, I thought. Good politicians have to be effective liars.

'That's perjury, isn't it?' Pryor said. 'What I did. I could go to prison for that.'

'There's no "could" about it,' I said. 'You probably perverted the course of justice as well. And if the CPS were feeling creative they might throw in a charge or two for you being an accessory to whatever Harry did. It wouldn't be pretty for you.'

Pryor's immaculately shaped dark eyebrows twitched upwards once and then almost immediately his gaze moved to his hands.

'I didn't want him to go to prison,' Pryor said, sounding like he was pleading with me. 'That's all. You must understand that. Harry was my best friend. He was crazy sometimes and caused me all kinds of problems but if I could do something to stop him from going to jail I had to do it.'

'Tell me something,' I said. 'Where's Harry now? He's the one you need to worry about.'

'I don't know,' Pryor said. 'That was the other part of the deal. After the case finished Edward gave him some money to disappear, to start a new life somewhere else.'

'And he went?'

Pryor nodded. 'He went abroad. I don't know where.'

'Just like that? He dropped his entire life and disappeared? Didn't anyone kick up a fuss?'

Pryor looked at me with raised eyebrows and said, 'Harry didn't have much of a life to drop.'

I shot him a confused look. Pryor let out a long, slow breath and when he spoke he sounded like he had taken a huge weight off his back. I knew without having to ask that he'd never told anyone this before.

'Jack,' he said, with sadness in his eyes. 'You don't know what it was like where we grew up. Some council estates are okay but ours was horrible. It was as poor as you can get and that was before heroin arrived. After that it was chaos. There were drug dealers killing each over territory and you never saw the police. The turnover of tenants was fast. Someone would be around one week and then gone the next, usually an addict dead after an overdose. Flats were empty then filled then empty then filled again and again. And no one took much notice of anyone else because they were all too busy trying to keep their own lives in some kind of order. I thought I was helping Harry to start a new life away from all that.'

Pryor's eyes left me and looked instead at a spot somewhere in the distance behind me.

'It wasn't like this neighbourhood,' he said, 'with everyone wanting to know everyone else, bringing round bottles of wine and cakes to welcome the new neighbours. Dinner parties and all that. Where I grew up, all we did was try to survive. And that's individuals, not even families. I know what broken Britain really looks like.'

And there he was, making a political speech again, complete with a headline-friendly sound bite. He even paused for dramatic effect. He sounded sincere, but I could have done without the grandstanding. It made me think less of him, which perhaps wasn't fair given the life he'd lived. But his rhetoric had power because I found myself thinking through the journey he'd been on, from that grotty estate to here. He had achieved something amazing, something really special, much more than I ever had. It didn't seem right that so much should be lost because of that one night of passion with Kat or the lies he told in court to protect a friend, because that's what he was doing – protecting a friend. There are far worse things a man could do. I nodded for Pryor to continue.

'Harry lived on his own,' Pryor said. 'His father vanished years ago and his mother didn't care about him. He didn't have any brothers or sisters either and no girlfriend. When he went away, no one cared enough to look for him.'

'This isn't what I was expecting to hear when I came here,' I said. 'I understand why you stuck up for Harry but Edward Valentine is a reputable, wealthy man, a public figure. Why would he be involved in something like this? He must have known what was going on with the lawyer and your dodgy statement. So why did he help you? Why would he want to be part of that?'

'Don't forget that back when the car crash happened Edward wasn't the mighty figure he is today,' Pryor said. 'He was crawling up the greasy pole, not sitting at the top looking down at everyone else. He wanted to do people favours and he helped me because he liked me. I know he still does. But at the same time people don't do that kind of favour for nothing.'

'What does that mean?' I said.

'I was a kind of investment for Edward,' Pryor said. 'He knew I was a hot political talent and he might have thought I'd be useful in the future. With our history, the higher I go, the better it is for Edward.'

And that, I now saw, was why Valentine called me – Pryor needed to be protected because he mattered to Valentine in the way a business investment matters. In the same way Pryor needed Valentine's help after the crash. Two men working together, helping each other but really only looking out for themselves.

'He told me you were friends,' I said.

Pryor smiled, pleased to hear this. 'I suppose we are,' he said. 'Friends. But there's more to it than that. There always is.'

I knew enough about the world to realise the people who made it to the top of the power tree didn't do it by playing by the rules but compared to the skeletons in some people's closets, Pryor's sins were tiny. Next to what he might do for the country, the things he'd done wrong ten years ago looked very small.

At that moment I was glad I'd taken Pryor on as a client. For the first time since I left newspapers I had a cause to fight for. I was motivated by more than money.

'What do we do next?' Pryor said.

'Nothing,' I said. 'You were right to tell me about the crash but it must stop there. You don't talk about what happened to anyone, ever again. If anyone ever hears about this, I'll protect you. Despite what people think, it is possible to bury secrets, especially when they involve what did or didn't happen on a dark night ten years ago when someone else was driving a car and especially when you've got someone like me around. You're in safe hands.'

'Thanks Jack.' He said.

'I need to go,' I said.

'Of course,' Pryor said. 'It's late. I understand. Can we speak tomorrow? We're going to need to talk again.'

'Yes,' I said. 'I'll call you.'

We stood up and shook hands but Pryor didn't let mine go.

'I'm glad I can trust you, Jack,' he said, hardening his grip. 'Good things happen to people I can trust.'

***

The man smiled to himself as he walked out of Oval Tube station, pleased his difficult day was nearly over. His plans for the next few hours were simple: a drink, a bite to eat, a long bath and then bed.

He turned right and walked past the orange-jacketed man giving out copies of the Evening Standard, taking a paper on his way to read later in the bath. After five minutes' walking, two right turns and a left, the man was outside his blue front door.

He opened the door and walked in. He closed it behind him, put down his briefcase, took off his dark overcoat and hung it up on one of the hooks behind the door. He switched on the hall light and warmed his hands on the radiator by the coats. It was cold outside – spring felt late this year – and the sudden heat on his hands made the rest of his body shiver.

He picked up his briefcase and a small pile of post from the floor behind the door and walked upstairs to his study at the top of the house. On the way he passed the two bedrooms on the first floor, the one he shared with his wife when they were in London and the spare room which his son and daughter fought over when they were both in town. The noise of their last argument over sleeping arrangements replayed in his head. He smiled at the memory. Of all the good things in his life, those two confident, boisterous young people were the best.

He continued up to the second floor where there were two more rooms: their second spare room, the one his children battled to avoid because of its size, and then the study. This was his room. Walls lined with books and a black leather chair behind a solid-looking wooden desk.

The man put the letters and his briefcase on the desk. He undid his top button, loosened his tie and sat down. Letters first, then a drink, he decided, knowing if he didn't get the chore out of the way before he began relaxing then the envelopes would be left unopened until who knew when.

He turned on his desk lamp and picked up the mail. There was an offer from a credit card company, another from a satellite TV provider – both quickly binned – and a handwritten card, a thank you from a friend for a dinner party he and his wife gave the previous week.

The last letter lay face up on the desk. There was no name on the envelope. Odd that such a thing was delivered with the post, he thought, and then he opened it.

Inside was a single photograph. He took it out and placed it in the middle of his desk so it was spotlighted by the lamp next to him like an exhibit in an art gallery. The photograph was small, the size of a holiday snap, but clear enough for him to know exactly what he was looking at.

He lifted his elbows up onto the desk and rested his forehead in the palms of his hands. He wanted to throw up. His head was light and his legs felt empty and useless. His lungs tightened and he tried to control his breathing. In and out, slowly and deeply, he told himself. In and out, slowly and deeply.

The man sat still for a moment and then stood up and walked to the small table on the other side of the room. He picked up his favourite brandy, unscrewed the top and drank two large mouthfuls straight from the bottle. He looked at the label and remembered his son giving it to him last Christmas. He put down the brandy bottle, walked out of the room and down the stairs.

A couple of minutes later he came back upstairs holding a length of thin blue rope. He knelt down on the floor outside his study with the brandy next to him. He looped the rope twice around two banisters and tied it tightly. He took the other end, turned it back and tied it loosely around itself with a solid knot. He opened up the loop and put it over his head. He took another swig of brandy, larger this time.

The man was tall and fit and stepped easily over the banister. Once he was on the other side he lowered himself until he was hanging by his hands from the lower part of the wooden columns while his legs dangled beneath him. Below him was a drop down two staircases.

With only the tiniest hesitation he closed his eyes and let go of the banister.

He fell several feet but not far enough to break his neck and finish it immediately. He knew this could happen and after he stopped with a jerk the man hung in mid-air waiting to suffocate, knowing these would be the most agonising minutes of his life. But the carotid arteries on either side of his neck had been compressed by the rope and virtually the entire supply of oxygen-rich blood pumping from his heart to his brain was cut off instantly. And so after only thirty seconds the man lost consciousness, though he barely felt out of breath.

Slightly less than two minutes later, when his brain was damaged beyond repair and the rest of his body ran out of oxygen, the man shuddered once and died.

Part Three: Thursday

105

8

'Good morning,' I said, trying not to sound too hung over. 'Please could I speak to Robert Castledown?'

'Robert?' an elderly woman said. 'Robert Castledown?'

'Yes,' I said slowly, 'Robert Castledown.'

He was Kat's father. It was a long shot but for now it was all I had. I needed to find her.

'The Castledowns don't live here,' the woman said. 'They live next door. Number 30. This is 28.'

'Oh,' I said, 'I'm so sorry. I thought this was their number. I must have dialled the number wrong.'

I reeled off six digits.

'No, that's my number,' the lady said. 'Wait a minute. I'll find you theirs.'

I heard a drawer open.

'Yes, here it is.'

'Thank you so much,' I said, after she read out the number. 'I really do appreciate it.'

'You're welcome,' she said.

It had taken me only a few minutes to get hold of Kat's parents' home number – doing exactly what I'd have done as a journalist. I had several lucky breaks along the way: her distinctive surname, which always helped, and the fact she had put her home town, Ipswich, on her Facebook profile, narrowed down my search to the Castledowns of Ipswich. A check of Companies House's online database showed up a Robert Castledown resident in Ipswich, complete with his home address.

Directory Inquiries said the address's number was ex-directory but that wasn't a problem. Their neighbours' numbers were available so I just rang round them being as charming as possible until one decided to help me. The old lady was the second I tried.

My third call would be to what I was almost certain was the Castledown family home. I had to tread carefully. As far as I knew they had no idea of the situation their daughter was in. I rang immediately and a serious-sounding man with a deep voice answered on the third ring.

'Hello,' he said.

'Hi,' I said, trying to sound young and chirpy. 'Is Kat there, please? It's Johnny.'

'I'm afraid not,' he said. 'She's in Oxford. And probably in the library by now.'

'I'm sorry,' I said, 'I must have called the wrong number. Hang on'- I pretended to look at my mobile screen –'yes, I did. I meant to call her mobile. I'll try her now. Sorry to bother you.'

'No problem.'

Kat's father hung up.

I sat back on my sofa and wondered what the hell I was going to do next.

I was in bad shape. I'd woken up lying on my front on top of my duvet, fully clothed. I even had my shoes still on my feet. There was a whisky bottle on the bedside table, empty, no glass, in front of the picture of Emily. I couldn't remember putting it there.

But I did remember that I had to find Kat. I got up immediately and set about finding Kat's parents. That was a quarter of an hour ago now and the full extent of my hangover was becoming painfully clear.

My tongue was spongy and dry and tasted disgusting and my head and insides felt like they were rotting. My feet were swollen and my legs felt hollow. My clothes were damp and clung to my skin. There was a film of grime on my face and my eyes were sticky.

I'd found out plenty of times before that a whisky hangover felt like you'd been poisoned. But I never learned my lesson.

The dark brown curtains in my bedroom were half open, or half shut, depending on how you looked at it. They were always like that – I wasn't big on general housekeeping – and not for the first time I was grateful that the window was small and faced another building, letting in virtually no natural light. At that moment, direct sunshine might have killed me.

I lay back on my bed. My head ached and my stomach was growling. I knew I needed to eat something or else I'd be at half pace all day but my guts were telling me to leave them the hell alone, especially when I thought of all the healthy produce in my fridge courtesy of Emily. I looked at the empty whisky bottle again, with the photo frame behind it and felt a pang of shame. Or maybe it was fear. Either way, I knew I couldn't keep doing this to myself.

I'd known a few alcoholic ex-journalists who ended up dying in pools of hard liquor and I didn't want that to be my fate. I was too young to make waking up next to an empty whisky bottle a regular event in my life.

But this was already happening more often than was healthy. I needed to make changes, I knew that. But what could I change? I need something to make me want to live a better life. Maybe I should move on from this job, I thought. Maybe I should cut my links with Edward Valentine and all my other clients and go and find something better to do. I'd even let Halliday off his ten grand. By the sound of things he needed it more than I did.

What I really wanted, deep down, to do was go back to newspapers and for things to be how they used to be. But there was no way that could ever happen, despite what Bull said about there being a place for me at his paper whenever I wanted it.

Maybe I'd just think about it another time, because right now my mind was stuck in neutral. And I needed the money.

I looked at my mobile's clock. It said 9.13am.

I wandered slowly out of my bedroom and into what estate agents call an 'open plan living space'. What they mean is a kitchen and sitting room combined because there wasn't enough space to have them separate. I filled the kettle and switched it on, then checked the cupboard for teabags. None. Coffee? None of that either. I made do with the orange juice Emily left me. The stuff wouldn't make me feel any better but she would be happy I was drinking it. I sagged down on the sofa feeling like a deflated balloon and flicked on the TV, straight to Sky News as usual.

The channel's logo screen appeared then disappeared, to be replaced by a serious looking woman sitting behind a desk. She had glossy dark hair and wore a bright red suit jacket. I knew her by name and reputation, one of those highly intelligent and beautiful women who managed to be intimidating and sexy at exactly the same time.

'Welcome back,' she said. 'Before we move onto our next interview, we have some breaking news for you.'

The words 'BREAKING NEWS' appeared on the screen behind her with a fizzing noise. Very dramatic. She looked at the piece of paper, holding it up just high enough for viewers to be able to see it in order to give the impression it had just that second been put in her hand. She was a smooth performer.

'Cabinet minister Andrew Scannell, Secretary of State for International Development, has been found dead at his London home. We have no further details at the moment but will bring you more when we can.'

A Cabinet Minister has died, I thought, that's one hell of a story. I'd have loved to be a reporter covering something like that, digging into the story behind the headline. I was beginning to feel nostalgic for the adrenalin I used to feel at moments like that.

And then my mind slipped up a couple of gears for the first time that morning. A surge of energy went through my body and my hangover vanished.

Andrew Scannell was Adam Pryor's boss.

This was huge for Pryor and I needed to know more, quickly. James Warrington, Sky News's political editor, was immediately on hand to help.

'James,' said the anchor. 'What more can you tell us?'

'The details are vague at the moment,' Warrington said. 'But what I can tell you is the police aren't looking for anyone else in connection with the death.'

That statement – the *police aren't looking for anyone else in connection with the death* – meant it was suicide. Journalists couldn't say so for certain until an inquest into the death had been held but for Warrington to come out and say something like that – everything except for suicide – live on TV meant he'd been given a completely reliable briefing that Scannell had taken his own life.

With Warrington in full flow, the screen above the 'Breaking News' cut to a shot of some policemen standing outside a small terraced house with a yellow plastic ribbon across the entrance. Scannell's home. The contrast with Pryor's place shocked me. Scannell's house was neat but smaller than Pryor's and, what struck me most of all, far less flashy, even though he was Pryor's boss. Which of them was the more normal MP?

'Right now, though,' Warrington said, in response to a question I didn't hear, 'The only thing we can say for certain is that this is a tragic blow for a Government already in crisis. All immediate concerns will be for Andrew Scannell's family, of course, and our thoughts and condolences are with them.'

He paused to ensure his words were noted.

'Tell us about Andrew Scannell,' the anchor said.

'Andrew Scannell was an extremely popular MP,' Warrington said, looking genuinely sad as he spoke.

'He was one of that rare breed who has support among all parties. I knew him well and I liked and respected him very much. Andrew Scannell was his own man, principled and knowledgeable, driven by the urge to do some good for the world as much as by his own ambition and he will be sorely missed.'

Warrington was interrupted by the anchor, who seemed to be telling him off for spending too much time eulogising Scannell.

'James, at some stage the Government is going to have to get back down to business and Andrew Scannell will need to be replaced. Who is in line for that Cabinet seat?'

Warrington prickled slightly but remained professional. 'The obvious choice is Scannell's deputy, Adam Pryor. Pryor is young but highly regarded. He's a great talent and many see him as a future leader of both the party and the country. He is known to be extremely ambitious and this could be a great opportunity for him.'

'But will the Prime Minister want to promote one of his future rivals at such a difficult time? He's under a lot of pressure at the moment and now might not be the time to give a young hotshot his big break.'

Like the anchor, I didn't really care about Scannell either. Pryor's promotion prospects were all that mattered to me.

'It's far too early to make a call either way on that,' Warrington said, 'But my instinct is he will. If Pryor was passed over for this then the support he already has in the party would be entrenched even further and he and his backers would also be firmly set against the Prime Minster. I think the Prime Minister will want this young man on his team, backing him up rather than undermining him.'

'Can you tell us more about Adam Pryor?' she said.

'He's the coming man,' Warrington said. 'He is intelligent, charming, adored by the party and an inspirational figure to those outside it. Adam Pryor was born into a poor, fatherless family on a deprived council estate and yet managed to become the man he is today, thirty-five years old and thought of by many, me included, as a future Prime Minister.'

Those words gave me goose bumps. I was working to save the career of a future Prime Minister. What a client Pryor might turn out to be. Valentine never asked what my hourly rate was. It just doubled.

And Warrington still wasn't finished praising Pryor.

'Anyone who saw his reaction to the riots in London last year could not fail to have been impressed. He was on the streets at Clapham Junction near his home appealing to looters and thugs to stop destroying their own communities, rallying supporters and occasionally getting physically involved himself. His popularity is immense, across all ages. He is the outstanding politician of his generation. In fact, I would go further than that. I've been covering politics for almost thirty years now and he is the most impressive young MP I have ever seen. And that includes Blair, Cameron, Aitken, Brown. All of them. Pryor is special.'

'But will he want the job?' The anchor said. 'It's a big step up to the cabinet. Will he feel ready for that kind of challenge?'

Warrington looked at her with something very close to contempt in his eyes. He paused before he spoke. 'Of course he would. Filling Scannell's seat at the cabinet table would be a huge promotion for Pryor. He would be a cabinet minister while still in his mid-thirties. That is a great achievement and it would give him a wonderful opportunity to make himself known to the wider public and position himself as the next leader. In short, it's his shot at the big time.'

His shot at the big time.

The anchor cut away from Warrington and started talking about share prices again.

Halliday's unpaid bill didn't matter anymore. Nothing else was important now, except for Pryor. I had to save his career to make mine. With Scannell out of the way and his status about to be elevated a level, he was going to need me more than ever.

I turned the volume down on the TV and began to think.

Strategies, plans and ideas turned over and over in my mind, crystallising into one clear form and then metamorphosing into something else and after that something else again. I was getting nowhere.

First things first, I told myself. Don't think too far ahead. Deal with the next issue in the queue and look at the rest later.

I closed my eyes and waited for inspiration.

My phone buzzed on the table and my eyes snapped open. I didn't know how long they'd been shut for. The text was from Wake, saying he had the numbers I'd asked him for and would meet me in the usual place in an hour, where the exchange would take place.

The news about Scannell's death would have huge implications but I didn't have time to think about them right now. I had an obligation to Bull to fulfil.

He and Karl Wake had never met. And if they and I had anything to do with it, they never would. They had never even asked each other's names and that arrangement worked fine for all of us. Both got what they wanted, and so did I, the conduit for information and money and happy keeper of half the latter.

Before that, though, I had to get cash from Bull. Only then could I go to Wake, swap the cash for the numbers and then deliver the numbers back to Bull. Not very high-tech, I know, but our system was carefully thought out and while it might only have been one step behind even pigeon post on the evolutionary ladder, it kept us all protected.

I texted Bull and told him to meet me in the usual place in half an hour. And to bring the money with him. I showered, put on a clean shirt and suit and jumped in the first available cab I saw outside the flat.

Fifteen minutes later I stopped the taxi outside the Hand and Flower pub on Hammersmith Road and started walking east. Bull's office was about a mile further into town. I never went too close in case a familiar face saw me with someone who shouldn't be speaking to me, like Bull.

It was a plush area, full of rich people and tourists. The shops weren't vast or designer – nothing like Knightsbridge or Kings Road – but for some reason the area attracted money. It felt wealthy but not showy, the kind of place old money lived, where you saw battered old Land Rovers parked outside terraced houses worth millions, passed down from generation to generation along with hundreds of acres and a manor house somewhere in the countryside.

I passed a few shops, an Iranian restaurant I had fond memories of, and then stepped into the Starbucks by Waterstones. It was far enough from the *Legend* to be private but also close enough for Bull to get there at short notice.

I queued up, ordered two black coffees and two cheese and Marmite paninis. I still hadn't eaten and that snack was the closest thing to a hangover cure on Starbucks' menu. I got the drinks and sat down at a table at the back, away from passing eyes.

I looked around. The place was empty except for a pair of Japanese girls talking quietly but intensely at a table in the corner. Perfect. A server came over with the sandwiches and I immediately picked one up and took a bite. The melted cheese and Marmite was just the right side of boiling hot to be eatable.

'One of those had better be for me,' Bull said from above me.

'No way,' I said through a mouthful. 'This is my breakfast and lunch.'

'Unlucky, kid,' Bull said, and then picked up the second sandwich and took a huge bite.

'You bastard,' I said. 'I wanted that.'

'This should make up for it,' Bull said, and reached into the inside left pocket of his suit jacket. He pulled out a white envelope and handed it to me. I took it and quickly tucked it in the inside right pocket of my suit jacket.

'Shouldn't be more than twenty minutes,' I said.

Bull nodded and after taking a long gulp of coffee I walked out of Starbucks and turned right, in the direction he came from. I didn't need to open the envelope to check what was in there. It would be two thousand pounds in used fifties, taken from the *Legend*'s petty cash store, signed for by Bull as being necessary for something he was working on and split into two equal bundles.

That was how newspapers use to work for all trusted reporters.

If you needed cash, you got it, with a minimum of questions asked. The security system was simple. Those who took the cash and brought stories in were trusted and given it again the next time they asked. Those who took the cash and didn't bring anything back weren't trusted and didn't get another chance. It was survival of the best and, of course, the luckiest.

Now only a few papers did that for very few reporters, but it wasn't about trust any more. Now it was all about the cash, or the lack of it. A combination of the internet, twenty-four hour news channels, newspaper price wars and relentless cost-cutting had newspapers on their knees. A couple of big ones were only one more squeeze away from death. Newspapers were run on tiny budgets compared to the old times, the final years of which I just caught, and the coffers were shrinking all the time. That's a sad story if you love newspapers like I do.

Bull, though, was an old school reporter with an old school editor. If he needed cash in a hurry, he got it, whether it was paying someone for documents, a favour, a number, a name, whatever. He was high enough up the food chain to be able to waste a few thousand without damaging his reputation. His bosses knew Bull would bring in the goods eventually, a story big enough to get the *Legend*'s name on all the TV channels and all over the other papers.

My old instincts were still there and I wanted to know what he was working on this time. But I couldn't ask. It would be humiliating, especially after our conversation last night.

I took out half the money and put it in my trouser pocket. I crossed the road from Starbucks and went straight into the bookshop opposite.

I walked down the stairs and went straight to the till in the basement floor. Behind the counter was a tall, heavy woman with fuzzy brown hair and a nose ring. Next to her was a short, skinny, pale man in his late twenties. He looked like a skateboarder who hadn't eaten for a month. His long hair was pushed behind his ears and by my reckoning he had added two more earrings since the last time I saw him.

'Excuse me,' I said to Karl Wake. 'I'm looking for a book about chess. I'm a beginner and I'd like to learn more about the game.'

'This way sir,' Wake said, ushering me away from his colleague. We stopped by the games and pastimes shelf and I looked at Wake. He shook his head. Not yet, he meant. Someone was watching us. We had to make small talk instead.

'You know I'd destroy you at chess,' he said.

'Not a chance,' I said.

'Maybe. I guess posh people like you learn the game at school.'

I laughed. 'I'm not posh.'

'Where do you live?' Wake said.

'West London,' I said, being inexact by instinct, even though I trusted Wake.

'You would live in the west, wouldn't you,' he said, gazing at the shelves.

'Why?'

'You're posh. Posh people always live in the west of cities.'

'What?' I said. 'Where did you get that from?'

'It's a fact. You should read more. In the northern hemisphere the west of a city is always posher than the east because the wind blows west to east. The gulf stream. It comes off the Atlantic and sweeps across the continent. And so when the Industrial Revolution happened, all the rich people wanted to live upwind of the stinking factories, which meant going west, against the wind, and that meant the poor people could only afford to live in the east, where they got covered in fumes all day long. Hence the difference between east and west London.'

Wake glanced over my shoulder.

'Now,' he said, and I handed over the envelope with the cash in. He looked inside and seemed satisfied because he reached into his back pocket and took out a crumpled sheet of A4 paper folded into quarters. He turned and walked back towards the counter. I followed a few seconds later.

'Sorry we didn't have the book you wanted,' he said, for the benefit of his colleague.

'No worries,' I said. 'Chess is too complicated for me anyway.'

When I got outside the shop I unfolded the piece of paper and saw two columns of phone numbers written in blue biro. At the top were two headings, INCOMING and OUTGOING, and there were about twenty numbers below each.

This was the most important part of our system. In order for Wake's scam to never be found out, he could leave no trail. We had worked through everything very carefully at our first meeting.

Wake had two jobs, in the book shop and at the mobile phone network. He was trying to save up as much money as he possibly could. I never asked why. As part of his job at the network, Wake had access to a lot of information and that information was what Bull wanted.

Wake could look at it as much as he wanted without arousing suspicion but if he printed anything out, ever, even one sheet, there would be concrete evidence against him which, if it was found, would land him in jail. So instead of printing lists of numbers, he wrote them down by hand on a piece of paper and then handed me the paper. There was no electronic trail, no paper trail, nothing. Wake even made sure whatever was under the piece of paper he wrote on was a hard surface and wouldn't have his writing indented on it.

The system was as close to perfect as it was possible to get. The money was untraceable – used notes and not signed out for me specifically – and Bull copied down the information on the pieces of paper I gave him and then burnt the originals. Every time. Bull would never tell anyone where his information came from and neither would I. Through his job Wake was able to wipe any records of our mobile phone contact and there was no trail of emails to follow either. In the days since phone hackers started being arrested we had to take extra precautions.

The job at the bookshop made it extra convenient. Bull had no idea what went on. He never saw me go into the bookshop. I think he assumed either I had the numbers with me when I arrived and walked out and back in to make the whole thing seem more dramatic or it really was dramatic and some shady character would appear from nowhere outside the cafe and hand me a package. The truth, as ever, was somewhere in the middle.

I walked back into Starbucks and sat down. Bull smiled. I gave him the piece of paper.

'Thank you,' he said. 'Now, get comfortable because we need to talk.'

Bull saw the hesitation in my face. He knew I wasn't keen to hang around, not there and not with him.

'I mean we really need to talk,' he said. This time all the fun went out of his face.

'What about?' I said.

Bull moved closer to me.

'Edward Valentine,' he said quietly. 'There is something very wrong about what he does and you need to get away from him.'

9

'I'm saying this to you now because we were friends once,' Bull said, 'and believe it or not there are people out there who care about you.'

Bull paused, and when he spoke again his voice was iron.

'You must stop working for Edward Valentine. You must stop people associating you with him and you must break every link you have with him as soon as you possibly can. I don't know how much he's paid you but whatever it is, you must stop accepting money from him, for your own sake.'

I had never seen Bull like this before. He had been angry with me plenty of times, to the point of violence occasionally. But never anything like this.

I believed he was genuinely trying to do me a favour, or at least he thought he was. But what could he know that I didn't? There was a good reason why I couldn't turn my back on the biggest client I'd ever landed just because some hack – barely even a friend of mine any more – didn't like him.

'I'm not rich,' I said. 'And Valentine is going to pay me a lot. Right now I don't have any other options.'

'You do have options,' Bull said. 'You could come back to the *Legend*. You know you want to. It's where you belong.'

'No,' I said. 'I can't even walk past the office. How could I work there again? It's history.'

'Oh stop being so melodramatic,' he said. 'That woman's not going to stab you again, is she? Not from where she is. You were unlucky, that's all. It could have happened to anyone. What happened was not your fault. And I'll tell you something else about options. If you stay with Valentine you will have no options. None at all.'

Bull pointed his finger at me. He looked like he was about to explode.

'And,' he said, trying hard to keep his voice down, 'When it all goes wrong for you with him, which I promise you it will, I won't be able to help you. The *Legend* won't take you back. No paper will touch you. No one will hire you to kill stories either. You'll be finished. You need to move quickly Jack. I mean it. Today. Get back where you belong or your life as you know it is over.'

Bull wouldn't be like this if it wasn't serious, I realised. The coffee and sandwich churned in my stomach. What if Bull was right and I really didn't know what I was getting into with Pryor and Valentine? More than anything, for my sake and Pryor's, I needed to know what Bull knew.

'Fine,' I said, 'I'll walk away from Valentine.'

Bull relaxed in his seat.

'But,' I added, 'Only if you tell me what you know. I can't just leave because you say so. I need to know what you know about him which is so terrible. I did my due diligence on the guy. He has no criminal record. He's not been linked to anything dodgy before. I know he's rich and powerful and I know you hate people like that so I can't just go on your word.'

'Answer me this, then,' Bull said. 'If he is such a straight shooter, why does he need so many bodyguards? They're with him all the time. Tell me why.'

Bull was right about Valentine's personal security. In every photo I'd seen of him, there were a couple of mean-looking men in dark suits lurking in the background. But what did that mean?

They might be just another way of showing off, an accessory rich people have, along with their watches and cars worth more than my flat.

'That means nothing,' I said. 'You're speculating. Bodyguards are accessories these days. Every rich person has to have a couple. They're status symbols, not proof people want to kill him. I need facts. Real information. Not guesses. There's too much at stake. Give me that and I'll leave him alone.'

Bull looked away from me, thinking. His mouth tensed.

'I can't,' he said. 'Not here and not now.'

'So when and where?' I said.

'Tonight, seven o'clock,' he said. 'Come to my house. Maggie and the kids are over with her mum so we can talk properly. I've got some beers in, we can order a curry. It'll be like the old days.'

I smiled. Good memories ran through my mind. The idea of being on the same team as Bull again felt good.

'OK, I'll see you tonight,' I said. 'But before that, I have two questions. First, where is Kat?'

Even if I was going to follow Bull's advice and stop working for Valentine, Pryor was still my client and my future and Bull was always a good source of information.

Bull looked confused. 'Who?'

'Don't mess me around,' I said. 'Kat, the girl who Rachel Kirk was supposed to meet at the hotel in Oxford.'

Bull shook his head. 'I have no idea. No one does. Rachel hasn't shown her face in the office and the whispers I hear are that her luck has really run out this time.'

That was what I expected to hear. I knew Bull well enough to be able to tell if he was lying and he wasn't.

'OK,' I said. 'Second question, what do you know about Andrew Scannell?'

'Not much, other than it's a great story,' Bull said. 'Politican tops himself. That'll keep us in words for the next week or three. The cops are saying nothing at all. Completely zipped up. And that can only mean one thing. There are dirty secrets waiting to be dug up.'

'So it was suicide, then?' I said.

'Yep, he hung himself. But that's all we know.'

Bull's eyes were dancing. A reporter to his bones, right now he was in his element, hungry for more information, desperate to dig further into the story, to find out what dark secrets were being hidden from public view. I was like that once and he caught the end of a wistful look in my eyes as I thought about who I would have called, how I'd have contacted Scannell's friends, family, neighbours, university buddies, anyone who might know anything about Scannell's life.

Bull smiled at me. 'Time was,' he said, 'you'd have been digging around yourself right now. You'd have got it all, wouldn't you? Photos, interviews, old flings. I know you would have. You learned from the best.'

'I didn't realise I'd ever met the best.'

'Very funny. You miss it, don't you? Go on, tell the truth.'

I was in the process of deciding whether to be honest with him or tell him there was nothing about working with him anyone in their right mind could miss when his phone rang. He looked at the screen.

'I have to take this,' Bull said.

'No worries. See you tonight.' He stood up and left.

When I was a young reporter, only a couple of years into my first job, I was covering a murder story in a village out in Kent. A woman had shot her husband and his mistress, a straightforward crime of passion. She'd been arrested at the scene, the gun in her hand, no attempt to escape and no denial. She was charged with murder the next day and thanks to Britain's contempt of court laws – the ones which say no newspaper can publish anything which could prejudice someone's right to a fair trial – just about the only publishable revelation was what this woman looked like. So the story became a race for the first picture of her.

And I won the race. I talked to a couple of dozen people in the village and eventually spoke to a farmer who either liked me or saw an opportunity to earn himself a bit of extra money. He said he had a photo of the woman and would give it to me, for £500 in cash. I called my news editor and he said yes, go for it and claim the money back on expenses later. I got the cash out on two credit cards and swapped it for the photo. The farmer, a big, bluff, jolly man who was sharper than he looked, peeled off five twenty pound notes and gave them back to me.

'What are they for?' I said, shocked.

'Call it luck money, Jack,' he said. 'I was lucky so I'm giving you some back. You have to be good to Lady Luck. Show her some gratitude. You can't take her for granted.'

Luck money. I knew what that farmer meant. But as I walked away from Starbucks I realised I would need a lot more luck money than the thousand in my pocket if I was ever going to do something better with my life.

And then my phone vibrated in my pocket.

I fished it out and saw an unfamiliar number on the screen. Instinctively, I answered. I didn't usually answer numbers I don't know, especially withheld ones, but when it's a mobile I make an exception because I'm curious to know who, which individual person, has my number. New clients, sometimes.

'Is that Jack Winter,' a female voice said. 'I'm looking for Jack Winter. Is that you, Jack?'

She sounded panicked and was rushing her words. She also sounded familiar. It was Zoe, but different. Very different. All that cool, sexy aloofness she'd shown when we met at her house in Oxford had vanished. She sounded frantic, desperate.

'Yes,' I said, 'It's Jack here.'

'Please come to Oxford,' she said. 'I need to see you. I don't know where Kat is and I'm scared.'

My first thought was, what could she possibly be scared of? Whatever it was, it was real enough for her to sound genuinely desperate. I found myself not feeling quite so light and serene any more.

'What's happened?' I said.

When Zoe spoke I could hear she was crying.

'Someone's taken her,' she said. 'I think it was my step-father.'

My mind scrambled.

'Why?' I said.

'Not on the phone,' Zoe said. 'Please come.'

'I'll be there as soon as I can,' I said, and ended the call.

I was sure that Zoe couldn't be right, that Kat hadn't been taken by Valentine, but if she was then Zoe wasn't the only one who was in trouble. I was too, because it meant I was working for a kidnapper.

The quickest way to Oxford was by car with Naz driving. But Naz worked for Valentine and if Zoe was right and he started asking me questions about why I was going there I'd be in trouble. Naz didn't seem like a man it would be wise to lie to. So I took the train and used the time to order my thoughts.

I had to get Pryor out of trouble, talk to Zoe, and then there was Kat. The more I thought about it, the less I believed she'd been taken by Valentine. The idea of him doing something like that seemed so unlikely, for the simple reason that he hired me. If he wanted to shut her up, why didn't he just kidnap her to start with? I wasn't necessary. But I still needed to find Kat and talk to her, for Pryor's sake. Zoe sounded distraught, but she was my only lead on Kat right now and so I had to go to Oxford. As Kat's flatmate and Valentine's daughter, Zoe was too important to ignore. When I found Kat, I'd then have to stop her from making the biggest mistake of her life.

I had plenty of time to see Zoe, calm her down and be at Bull's house for 7pm, and until then I would focus on gathering information which would help Pryor. I couldn't see how anything Zoe was going to tell me could harm him. But now Pryor's boss was dead the game was even more serious. I decided to call him. Time on the phone to clients when you aren't giving them bad news is never wasted. It makes them feel like they need me.

I took out my mobile and made the call. Apart from anything else, we needed to talk when we were both sober. Pryor answered instantly.

'Jack,' he said, 'It's been a hell of a day. Everything's happening and I need to know you've got Kat under control.'

I found this often happened with busy clients. I would call them and they would answer the phone and immediately start talking as if they had called me. I imagined they had a 'to do' list and hadn't got down to calling me yet. Either that or they were too scared to. I tended to bring bad news.

'Everything's fine,' I said, 'The *Legend* still has nothing.'

'Good, that's very good. There's a lot at stake, you know, now Andrew's not with us anymore.'

Pryor didn't sound upset at all, not about what he'd said to me the previous evening or about Scannell's death. Just because they had worked in the same department, that didn't mean they were friends, so maybe he really didn't care. I knew enough about politicians to know they were a devious, competitive bunch of backstabbers, most of whom had had their consciences amputated at birth. Perhaps I'd been naive but I didn't think Pryor was like that, so I was shocked by his complete lack of sadness at the death of his colleague. Just like the first time we met, he reminded me of a cornered fox, his mind working out angles and plans and routes, all directed towards achieving the best possible outcome for himself above everything and everyone else.

'How are you doing?' I said, trying to find Pryor's human side. 'I was sorry to hear of his death, by the way. I hope you're coping.'

Pryor immediately switched into politician-live-on-TV mode. 'It's very sad,' he said. 'Andrew was a good man and a great politician. He taught me a lot about being an MP and why what we do is so important. I looked up to him and I'll miss him.'

There he was again, speaking in perfect soundbites, the real man hidden away. I could picture the frown he would have had on as he spoke. That little performance would have worked perfectly on TV. He was good, and he kept on proving it. I decided to be more blunt, to remind him we weren't talking live on Sky News.

'Are you going to get his job?'

There was silence. Pryor was thinking about what to say to me. Did he trust me? I thought I might be about to find out.

'I can't talk about this,' he said quietly, 'Not to anyone.'

I knew from the tone of his voice that talking about this to someone was exactly what he wanted. He wanted to boast, to preen, to fluff up his feathers and impress someone. Probably, anyone would do. I could be that person, or at least pretend I was.

'It's a little late for us to have secrets, don't you think?' I said. 'I already know more about you than I want to. And I need to know for professional reasons anyway. If you're about to be promoted in a blaze of publicity then the papers will be going through your past with a fine tooth comb. You can't afford to have secrets from me.'

'OK,' he said, accepting the situation very quickly. 'I'll tell you. I've had the nod.'

'The nod?' I said.

'Come on Jack, keep up. I mean I've had the nod from the PM that the job is mine. I assume you know who the PM is?'

'Congratulations,' I said, ignoring the jibe. I knew exactly what he meant but I wanted him to say the exact words, not just hint at them. 'When will it be announced?'

'Oh, not for a few days. They want to let the dust settle, show respect, that kind of thing. But I'm already being briefed. The civil servants are all over me. It's only one notch up into the cabinet from where I am now but it's a huge step forward. Quite a change, I can tell you. But I'm on top of things. These are exciting days.'

From Pryor's tone you would think his promotion was purely due to his own merit and nothing to do with the untimely and tragic death of his boss. I was finding it hard to work out exactly what I thought of him. Sometimes I liked and respected him for his good heart and what he'd achieved while at other moments I thought his cold-eyed ambition was disgusting. This was one of those other moments.

'I have big plans, Jack, big plans,' he said, now going full throttle on the boasting. 'And I tell you what, do you fancy being my press secretary? I'll need someone to look after me full-time now and I can't stand the chap Scannell had. A ghastly little man called William Buckingham. He'll have to go.'

I couldn't tell if Pryor was serious about the job offer or was blustering. If he was serious, if the offer was genuine, then I would be very tempted by it. Valentine's words about him in our very first conversation stuck with me. How special he was, his background and abilities, were more important than his flashes of arrogance or ambition. Working for a future Prime Minister was a great opportunity.

But there was a problem. William Buckingham was Emily's stepfather. The man her mother met on her first day at university, when Emily was two months old and I was a stupid, scared teenager who ran away from responsibilities I should have been grateful for.

William Buckingham now worked for the Civil Service, one of the unelected men of power who work away behind the scenes, advising cabinet ministers like Andrew Scannell and, maybe, Adam Pryor. Buckingham was a high-flyer too. How would Emily react?

First I would have to decide if I could work for Pryor? Could I be with him every day? The way he spoke was something I disliked intensely. I bet they didn't use words like 'chap' and 'ghastly' on the estate Pryor came from in Leicester. It was as if he was assuming a new personality now he was a level further up the power ladder, one which sounded more what the newspapers call clubbable, shorthand for an upper-class vocabulary and accent. Maybe that was how it worked in politics. They went into that world all looking and sounding different but after a few years they were clones, like a long line of sausages popping out of a factory. Not for long would Pryor be the man of the people who'd shone in the riots.

But taking the job would mean I gave William Buckingham's career a shot in the knees. Did I want to do that? Sometimes yes and sometimes no, and which answer I chose was usually dependent on how much I'd drunk. Of course, Pryor knew nothing about my link to Buckingham.

'I might well be interested,' I said. 'I'd have to look at my commitments to other clients but it's definitely something we should discuss. Thank you.'

'Excellent,' Pryor said. 'I'm going all the way, you know. All the way to the top. Unless Kat spoils it. What's going on with her?'

'Not much,' I said. 'No one has seen her since Tuesday.'

'Is she talking to the press?'

'No, I don't believe she is.'

Not to my knowledge, would be a politician's answer, a defensive line which was neither the truth nor a lie. But I wanted to sound confident.

'Then what have we got to worry about?' Pryor said.

'Right now, probably nothing,' I said.

'Good. I'll call Edward and give him the good news.'

'OK, I said.' 'Of course, let me know if you hear from her and—'

Pryor interrupted me. 'Jack, you're being paid to sort this out for me so get on with sorting it out. Your job is to make damn sure that girl doesn't breathe a word about what happened. I suggest you do that.'

I counted to five and then replied, clearly and slowly and in the calmest voice I could produce.

'Will do,' I said.

The fact was, Pryor would need me even if Kat kept quiet. I was sure Bull was gunning for Valentine and I had no idea what dodgy connections might exist between them. But even if there were none, Pryor was about to jump into the crosshairs of every journalist in town purely because of his new job.

Whenever someone new appeared at top of any profession in the public eye, but particularly politics, an army of reporters goes to work raking over that person's past, racing to find some terrible secret to destroy them with. Illicit love affairs or some kind of dodgy financial arrangement or a hidden criminal conviction were pay dirt. Countless politicians' careers had been cut short that way, buried secrets dug up and thrown like grenades from the pages of newspapers.

It sounds nasty – it *is* nasty – but it's also what you get when you have free speech in a democracy. The media is allowed to tell the truth. Journalists do messy, horrible work, break the law sometimes and are punished for it, but the ultimate reward of their work is the defence of something important. And to politicians they're especially dangerous, which Pryor was finding out.

'I'm serious about the job,' Pryor said, as if he was a mind reader.

'So am I,' I said.

And then something occurred to me, a small thought at the back of my mind.

'Do you mind if I ask you a question?' I said.

'Of course not,' Pryor said. 'We have no secrets now. I could ask you questions if I wanted to.'

'Has Edward Valentine ever asked you for a favour?'

When he replied, Pryor's voice was icy. 'Edward has never asked me for anything.'

His contempt for the question and absolutely certain answer made me wonder about the balance of power in their relationship. Valentine had seemed to be the senior partner, but now I wasn't so sure. Pryor's confidence had made me question that assumption. I knew that in any power structure the man who thinks he's in charge isn't always right. So if either Valentine or Pryor thought they were the other's boss, either could be wrong. They were complicated men and I was in the middle of a messy situation.

'Good,' I said. 'I didn't think he would have.'

Yet, I thought, but didn't say.

10

My planned rendezvous with Bull meant my time in Oxford was going to be limited. I would go straight to Zoe's house and get there by 3pm. I would be able to stay for two hours at the very most so I could get the train back to London in time. I wasn't planning to cut corners – Pryor and Kat had started to matter too much to me for that to be an option – but I couldn't see why I would need to spend more than two hours calming Zoe down and getting an explanation from her. I thought that was all I would have to do, because no matter what angle I looked at Kat's disappearance, I couldn't believe Valentine would have kidnapped her. Why would Valentine, with all his power and money, do something like that? Valentine was powerful, but he didn't strike me as the sort of person who arranged kidnappings. He was a businessman, not a gangster. Why would have hired me in the first place if he wanted to snatch Kat off the streets? I had no answer.

Even so, I didn't have time to waste so as soon as the train arrived in Oxford I made straight for the taxi rank, pushing a couple of people out of the way as I hurried along, and told a cabbie to take me to Bullingdon Road as quickly as he could.

I knocked on the scruffy door and waited. The door opened slowly and Zoe appeared. She had bags under her eyes and red rings around them. Her blonde hair was pulled back into a pony tail and she had no makeup on. She wore a long, baggy black roll-necked jumper which hung down further than most miniskirts and instead of clingy jeans she had on baggy tracksuit trousers. The contrast between now and the first time I'd met her was completed by her footwear. Two days earlier she'd been wearing slinky heels which made her hips swing when she walked but today she had only socks on her feet. She was still a knockout.

And that was before she threw her arms around me.

'Jack,' she said, her face tight against my chest, 'I'm so glad you came.'

I couldn't very well stand there and not hug her back so I gently put my arms around her shoulders. Somehow my right hand ended up on the back of her head and without making any conscious decision I started stroking her hair. Unprofessional, I know, but no healthy, red-blooded man could have done anything else.

We stood in that clinch for nearly a minute. Eventually Zoe slowly moved away from me and led the way into her sitting room.

There was already a glass of white wine waiting for me on the coffee table in Zoe's sitting room. There was a half full bottle next to it. I wondered if it was the first one Zoe had opened today.

The room was in chaos compared to the last time I visited. There were several empty wine bottles on the floor by one of the leather sofas, the cushions were scattered around randomly, not perfectly arranged like before. There was a cigarette packet next to a full ashtray and a plate with half a piece of toast on it. The curtains were closed, keeping out the daylight, and the room smelled like it needed airing.

Zoe sat down at the end of one of her sofas with her back to the arm and her legs across the cushions and gestured for me to sit on the same one, close to her. I ignored her and went over to the window. I opened the curtains wide and pulled up the sash window as far as it would go. The six-inch gap at the bottom let in some very welcome clean air.

I turned back to Zoe. Her eyes were slits as she got used to the sunlight. I wondered when she last went outside.

'Sit down,' she said, pointing at the space next to her, 'Please.'

If I had more time to spare I'd have sat further away but I couldn't afford to play games and wait for her to open up to me. I needed her to tell me why she thought Kat had been kidnapped so I could see if there was anything in it, and then get on my way back to London. I sat down and Zoe immediately wedged her toes under my thigh. I looked at her and she gave me a shy smile.

'My feet are cold,' she said.

I smiled back. I was uncomfortable but if the intimacy made Zoe relax I would go with it in the hope she would start talking more quickly. That was my professional reason, anyway. Zoe reached out her left hand and passed me a glass of wine. Then she picked up hers and raised it to me.

'Cheers,' she said.

'Cheers,' I said back, and leant forward to clink our glasses together. She frowned and pulled away.

'No, Jack,' she said, 'We don't touch glasses. It's not the done thing.'

I thought only characters in Jane Austen books said things like that. I smiled. It would take more than that to embarrass me. Zoe took a long gulp of wine, closed her eyes and I saw her body relax. If this was what she did every time life threw something difficult at her Zoe would have serious drink problems in future. I knew the signs well enough. I saw them every time I looked in the mirror.

I felt an urge to tell her that, to warn her that if she doesn't watch it alcohol will cost her everything she cares about, including her looks.

I decided to hurry things along.

'I don't have much time,' I said. 'So, let's talk. Where are we?'

Zoe looked into her glass and swirled it around, watching the liquid circling. It was a beautifully executed dramatic pause. In fact, Zoe could have taught even Pryor a thing or two about theatrical presentation. Eventually she turned to me and spoke.

'OK,' she said, breathing out heavily, as if to say she was ready. 'What do you need to know?'

'What do *I* need to know?' I said. 'You were the one who summoned me here. I assumed you'd have a list of things you were ready to tell me.'

'Sorry,' she said. 'I've had a terrible day.'

'Fine,' I said. 'I'll ask the questions. What do you think has happened to Kat? And why do you think it?'

Zoe looked at me and I saw her bottom lip tremble. She put her glass down hard on the table and it nearly toppled over. The wine sloshed around and a bit slopped out onto the table before the glass righted itself. Obviously not a cheap drinking vessel.

'Oh God,' she said, and put her face in her hands. The tears flowed immediately.

Watching Zoe crying, I thought to myself, she knows something terrible. Was Kat in serious danger? Looking at Zoe, I thought for the first time that she might be. I felt a lump coming up my throat. I fought it down. How had I let this situation get so out of control? Wherever Kat was, whatever trouble she was in, it was all my fault. If I'd managed to talk her into keeping quiet none of this would be happening.

'Talk to me,' I said. 'We need to move quickly. Tell me what happened.'

I tried to sound like I knew exactly what to do next.

'This morning,' Zoe said through her tears. 'The doorbell rang. I was upstairs so Kat answered it. I heard her talking to someone, a man, but I couldn't make out what they were saying. Then I heard her shout "no", like she was scared. Really scared. As I ran downstairs

I heard a car driving away. The front door was open and she'd gone. Disappeared. I've tried to call her a hundred times since but her phone has been switched off. Oh God, Jack, what have I done?'

'It's not your fault,' I said, for my own benefit as much as Zoe's. 'You haven't done anything wrong. We can't even be sure Kat's in danger.'

That was my polite way of saying Zoe's account of Kat's supposed kidnap had holes in it. I imagined what the police would say if we called them and said she'd been taken against her will on the basis of what Zoe had heard. Their questions would lead nowhere. What did Zoe see? Nothing. What did she hear? Possibly some raised voices, possibly not. Did she see the car? No. Did she see anyone taking Kat against her will? No. There was literally nothing for them to go on. No evidence of an abduction, nothing at all. Except for the fact a student had not been at home for a few daylight hours, which would be even less interesting to a policeman than a cat stuck up a tree.

But I wasn't just looking at cold facts. From the way she was behaving, it was clear that Zoe was convinced something bad was happening. I had to handle her carefully. There was one more question I needed to ask.

'You must tell me why you think your father is involved,' I said. 'That'll help us work out what to do. Tell me everything, please.'

She shot a vicious look at me. 'He's not my father,' she said, eyes narrowing like an angry cat. 'He's only my step-father. There's a huge difference.'

'Sorry,' I said. 'A slip of the tongue, that's all. I know he's only your step-father.'

Zoe's eyes told me I was forgiven. And then she started talking.

Her voice thick with tears, she said, 'There's so much,' and then stopped again, almost choking.

I waited a few seconds, wanting her to calm down, and said, 'So much what? I don't understand.'

Zoe looked over my shoulder at nothing. Her eyes were staring into space, unfocused but not empty.

'It should have been me,' she said.

It should have been her? What did that mean?

'You'll have to give me a bit more than that,' I said. 'I have no idea what you're talking about.'

'That night,' Zoe said, 'With Adam Pryor. He wasn't supposed to want Kat.'

'I know he wasn't,' I said. 'He's a married man. And an MP.'

'No,' she said, her voice insistent now. 'It should have been me who slept with him. That was the plan.'

I suddenly had the feeling I was being shown the world from a different angle, a viewpoint I'd never had before, seeing round corners and into shadows I didn't know existed.

'The plan?' I said. 'What, as in you both went for the same guy and she got him?'

Zoe's body went rigid.

'No,' she said, 'It wasn't a plan with her. It was a plan with my step-father.'

The composure which Zoe briefly showed vanished as she leant into me and put her arms around my chest again.

'Hold me, Jack, please.'

Her body was convulsing as she wept. She was snatching shallow breaths and for a second I worried she might have been having an asthma attack, maybe a panic-related one, assuming they were possible. I stroked her back firmly and tried to soothe her. There was nothing else I could do.

While I waited for her to calm down so I could ask more questions, I tried to order my thoughts.

A plan with her step-father.

What on earth did that mean? Why would her step-father want her to sleep with Pryor? Did he want Pryor to cheat on his wife? Did he want to break them up? If he truly had Pryor's best interests at heart I could see the sense behind that. I had met Pippa after all. But why use his own step-daughter as the bait? That was appalling. In all my years poking around in people's dark secrets, I'd never heard anything like this.

'A plan?' I said. 'You and your step-father had a plan for you to sleep with Pryor? Are you serious?'

Zoe nodded. The flow of tears had stopped now. I hoped she had run out. I needed some answers. This was as bizarre as any story I'd ever killed or written.

'What happened?'

I saw another look on Zoe's face, one I hadn't seen before. This wasn't sadness or grief. It was shame.

'Daddy was desperate for me to sleep with him.'

I've heard many people say many strange things in my time but those words would have taken the gold medal by half a lap. They made my mouth hang open.

Zoe clasped her hands together in front of her as if she was at prayer, closed her eyes and said, 'I was supposed to film it.'

Zoe collapsed into me and sobbed. Again, I held her and stroked her head for what must have been nearly ten minutes. When she stopped, I spoke.

'Tell me that again,' I said. I knew what I'd heard but I needed it to be repeated.

'I had a camera in my bag,' Zoe said, still with the side of her face pressed against my chest. 'I was supposed to have it pointing at the bed while we…while we…'

'I know,' I said, as her voice faded away. And without thinking

I kissed the top of her head. My body tightened as I realised what I'd done. Zoe responded by moving her hips closer to mine on the sofa, so she could lean against me more comfortably. When she stopped moving her left arm dropped so it was lying across my lap.

I tried to focus on the story Zoe was revealing to me. Valentine wanted her to film herself in bed with Pryor and there were two possible reasons why Valentine could want that kind of video. The first made him a sexual deviant. The second made me think of why I'd used hidden cameras when I was a reporter: to get evidence of someone doing something they didn't want anyone to know about, like being unfaithful.

I could think of no other reason why Valentine wanted that tape. He wanted proof that Pryor had done something wrong. But Valentine's ultimate motive had to be different to mine when I was a hack. Valentine couldn't possibly want to publicly shame Pryor. His golden boy would be destroyed. And not only would Pryor be destroyed, but Zoe would be too.

Either way, that left only one possibility.

Blackmail.

Zoe spoke again. This time her voice was clearer.

'I was supposed to give the bag to a man who works for daddy,' she said. 'He was going to come to the hotel the next morning and take it away with him.'

'But you had nothing to give him,' I said. 'Because Pryor came back here with Kat instead.'

I tried to think of something to say to lighten the atmosphere. Before I could, Zoe spoke.

'There's a first time for everything, I suppose,' she said.

'What do you mean?'

I expected Zoe to say Pryor was the first guy to choose Kat over her, that the university rugby team captain and whoever else Zoe had gone after had always, always gone for her over any other girl. But she didn't say that.

'That night was the first time the plan didn't work,' Zoe said and Bull's words of warning about me being mixed up in something far bigger than I could imagine began playing on repeat in my head.

Before I could say anything else, Zoe pulled away from me and sat up straight.

'Let's get out of here,' she said. 'I need some air.'

I needed some too. Zoe's theory about her father taking Kat didn't sound so far-fetched any more. If Zoe was telling the truth – and I'd seen enough liars in my time to think she was – then Valentine was capable of much worse than I thought. I thought of Kat and the danger she might be in and the world began to feel very dark.

We left the house and walked in silence to the end of Bullingdon Road and turned right on Iffley Road. We passed the athletics track where Roger Bannister ran the first four-minute mile. If this was a social visit I might have mentioned that. But it wasn't.

'Where are we going?' I said.

Zoe smiled weakly. 'It's a bit early for that kind of conversation,' she said. 'We've only just met.'

I appreciated the attempt at humour but I wasn't in the mood to laugh. Zoe had put on a dark coat and a pair of trainers. She walked on my left, away from the road. The afternoon air was cool and there were light grey clouds in the sky. It didn't look like a storm was on the way but I half-expected thunder to rumble overhead any second anyway. It was that kind of day.

Zoe was looking at the ground in front of her as she walked.

Without thinking, I reached out my left hand and stroked her back. She reached out for my arm and I thought she was about to push me away but instead she took it and held on as we walked, both her hands around my forearm. I put my hand in my trouser pocket to anchor it.

This was how couples walked. Not something I'd experienced for a while.

I looked at my watch. It was half past four already. That meant I had to leave in half an hour if I was going to make my meeting with Bull. That didn't seem likely.

'I don't understand why your step-father would make you do this,' I said. 'So if you can tell me anything which might help explain what's going on, I'd really appreciate it. I have no idea what he's up to.'

'I'll need a drink in my hand first,' Zoe said, stopping. She checked for a gap in the traffic and then set out quickly across the road, pulling me behind her. She turned down a short street of terraced houses. At the end, about fifty metres away, was a small, traditional looking pub.

We didn't speak until we were inside. The bar stuck out into the middle of the room in a u-shape. The pub wasn't modern or smart but felt comfortable and cosy, with dark wood walls and painting of peaceful country scenes on the walls.

'Large glass of dry white, please,' Zoe said. 'But not the house stuff. It's disgusting. Get me Chablis.'

She walked off to a booth in the far left corner. I bought two large glasses and took them over. I sat down on the brown leather bench opposite hers. The booth could have sat four people if they didn't mind being crammed together. For two it was fine and the table was narrow so when Zoe and I sat normally our faces were about eighteen inches apart. Zoe took a large gulp of wine and closed her eyes. There was a light above us and it shone down on her face. She looked stunning, beautiful and vulnerable and powerful all at the same time.

Her eyes opened and she caught me staring. I flushed and looked away.

'So,' Zoe said, 'Let's talk about my step-father.' There was sarcasm in her voice, like she was mocking therapists who insist on blaming their patients' parents for everything that goes wrong in their lives. I could see her boiling up again. She'd been calm while we were out walking but now she was sitting down with a drink in her hand Zoe was back on that emotional tightrope.

'I suppose I should tell you what I've been doing for him,' Zoe said, and swallowed another mouthful of wine. I did the same. I know from my own experience that if someone is drinking hard and their companion isn't, then the drinker's mood can sour easily. And when the companion wants the drinker to start talking, that's no good. I've been on both sides of that deal.

'You don't have to tell me anything,' I said, knowing that to push her too hard would make her clam up. 'But remember all I'm trying to do is make sure Kat is okay and keep Adam Pryor's career on track.'

'Isn't my step-father paying you?' she said. 'That's one of his tricks, you know, controlling people with his money.'

I looked at Zoe's expensive handbag, her expensive haircut. Thought of her expensive flat which Valentine paid for. The picture was still incomplete but gaps were gradually being filled in.

'He was paying me,' I said. 'But I'm not sure that arrangement is going to last forever. I'm not sure whose side I'm on now.'

'So where are your wages coming from?'

'Right now, there aren't any wages. No one is paying me.'

'Then why are you here?'

'I was originally employed to work on behalf of Adam Pryor and I'm still doing that. He doesn't deserve to lose everything over this.'

'What will you get out of it? Don't tell me you believe in karma.'

'Pryor might not have the money to pay me as much as your father did but in the long term I'll be looked after. He'll owe me a favour. That's part of what I get out of this.'

'Only part?' Zoe said, and raised her eyebrows.

I knew my honesty was a good idea. She was too cynical and far too clever for me to be able to pull the wool over her eyes.

And I had one card left.

'But Kat is the main reason,' I said. 'I can't walk away from this until I know she's safe. If I'd convinced her not to tell her story, she'd be fine. Kat's why I'm still here.'

Zoe held her wine glass by its stalk and turned it in small circles. The liquid began to rock and then spin in time with her movements. Then she stopped, set it back down and watched the wine settle. When the surface was flat she looked at me and I saw tears in her eyes.

'I don't know where Kat is,' she said. 'But I know my step-father is an evil bastard.'

Tears swelled in the corners of her eyes. I leant towards her and fought the urge to grab her hand and tell her everything would be okay. I tried to be professional.

'Then help me find her,' I said. 'And help me stop whatever it is he is doing.'

Zoe tipped her head forward so I couldn't see her face. I didn't move or say anything. I know how easy it is to ruin moments like this, when someone is about to tell you something big. Push too hard and they shut up forever. I stayed still and waited.

This time it didn't take long. Barely a minute later Zoe raised her head and looked me straight in the eyes with a combination of defiance, shame and detachment.

'I will help you,' she said. 'But we can't call the police. You must promise me that.'

I nodded, not really meaning it.

'Adam Pryor was my seventh MP,' she said. 'The plan worked with the first six.'

I nodded for Zoe to continue. I made sure I didn't look shocked or judgemental as she spoke. She wanted to talk so I just listened and collected facts.

'I met them all at the debates,' she said. 'They're organised by the Union. I help them get political speakers every now and then. Whenever my step-father suggests it. I'm not on any committees or anything like that but if he suggested someone they were always welcome. The committee all know who he is and his name gets me invited to everything. Some of them, the ones who want to be politicians, treat me like royalty. My life is all about Edward Valentine.'

Zoe almost spat out her step-father's name.

I knew from Pryor how the next stage worked. There was the debate, where the MP spoke, usually well, followed by a lovely dinner, lots of wine and then drinks in a bar afterwards. A grand occasion, followed by the mix of attractive, ambitious and intelligent young women all dressed up and keen to make friends with powerful men with big egos who were away from home for the night. It wasn't difficult to guess what happened next.

I imagined Zoe getting one of those men in her sights. I doubted any man in the world would be able to resist.

Zoe seemed to know what I was thinking.

'My part was easy,' she said. 'You know what men are like.'

I nodded. I knew all too well.

'Some of them thought being with me could become a way of influencing my step-father. Men can be so stupid, even the clever ones.'

Zoe finished her wine and I did the same.

'Another one?' I said. She nodded and I went to the bar.

The pub was virtually empty so I didn't have to queue for service. I ordered a double whisky with our two glasses of wine. Old habits die hard. As I stood waiting for our drinks I let the information she had just given me sink in. Zoe was one hell of an asset for her step-father. And what an ice-cold piece of work he must be to use his own stepdaughter like that. His own family – not flesh and blood but definitely family – sent out to have sex with politicians on film.

I didn't want to think about how he persuaded Zoe to go along with his plans. That wasn't relevant to the job I had to do.

The drinks arrived and while I was waiting for my change I downed the whisky. I felt the familiar fire move from my throat to my stomach, where it settled, warm and comforting. Nothing else could do that to me.

When I got back to the table Zoe wasn't looking at me. I put her glass down and sat down with mine. She seemed unsure of what to tell me next. It was time for me to take control of the conversation. I had a gulp of wine and then spoke.

'Zoe,' I said, deliberately using her name for the first time. 'Can I ask you some questions?'

She nodded.

I started with one I already knew the answer to.

'Do you know why your step-father wanted you to do all this?'

'Isn't it obvious?' she said. 'He wanted to have something on them. Something he could use to threaten them with.'

'So blackmail?'

'You're quick, aren't you.'

I ignored the barb.

'Who were the MPs?' I said.

Zoe listed six names. I recognised two. One, Michael Hicks, I knew was in the Foreign Office, not the Secretary of State but one of his ministers. The other name I recognised, William Cleave, was a leading member of the Opposition. So Valentine had feet in both camps. The other four I didn't know but committed to memory.

'Was there anyone else? Anyone other than those six MPs?'

'No,' Zoe shook her head slowly.

'Why those six?' I said.

Zoe shook her head. 'Just because my father's in politics doesn't mean I know anything. I don't know much about what my father does, except that he likes to control people.'

'When did they happen?'

'All in the past year.'

'Did your father want you to ask any specific questions?' I said. 'As in, did he want you to get information out of them?'

'No,' Zoe said. 'He just wanted me to fuck them on film. I'm not a spy. I'm his whore.'

She looked away.

I wanted to know how Valentine persuaded Zoe to take part in his scheme but I didn't know how to ask.

I drank the rest of my glass of wine in two mouthfuls and tried to look at the bigger picture. But all I could think was that if I was still a reporter this story would have made my career. Young reporters are told the biggest story anyone can ever get is one which brings down a government. This might not have been the British Watergate or a present-day Profumo affair but it wasn't far off. It was easily the biggest story I'd ever been involved in, including all my years in newspapers.

I could have written the headlines there and then but that wasn't how I used my secrets any more. I had to come up with a different plan to help Pryor, Kat and Zoe. But the wine and whisky had made my head foggy and I wasn't thinking clearly.

'Why did you do it?' I said, my hack's mouth springing into action before the polite side of my brain could apply the brakes.

'Sorry,' I said. 'You don't have to answer that.'

'No, it's fine,' Zoe said, wearily. 'I'd have to tell you sooner or later.'

More wine, and then she spoke. 'It's my mother,' Zoe said. 'She's ill. Depression, anxiety, that kind of thing. She's been like that all my life, in and out of different places. Tried to kill herself three times. He pays for her treatment and he'll cut off the money if I don't do what he says. Same for my money, so Mum and I would be left with nothing. But she loves him too, for whatever that's worth. More than anything in the world. He rescued her, after all. Rescued us, actually.'

Zoe went quiet.

'What do you mean rescued you?' I said.

'Mum is from a very old, wealthy family,' Zoe said. 'With estates and titles. But when she had me, they cut her off. She was young and not married to my real father and they were ashamed of her. After my real father left, Mum was desperate and then Edward came along and saved the day. The marriage was convenient for him too, I think. Mum still had lots of contacts, even if she was cut off from the family and a wife from the right background made him look like part of the establishment.'

'How old were you when they met?' I asked.

'Two,' Zoe said. 'He's been around as long as I can remember. He calls me his daughter. Won't use the "step" word. So, you see, I'm stuck. I have to do what he says. I don't have any brothers or sisters. I'm all she's got. And that's why I can never, ever go to the police about him. Mum and I would be destroyed. Do you understand?'

Zoe looked at me, wanting reassurance. I reached over the table and held her hand. 'I understand,' I said. 'I'll do whatever you want. If that means not calling the police then fine. I won't do it. But what about Kat?'

'We have to find a different way,' Zoe said.

If I knew a call to the police would save Kat's life, I'd make it instantly. But until that moment, which might never come anyway, I had nothing to lose by doing what Zoe wanted, so I nodded.

'Thank you,' Zoe said. 'Now please take me home. I want to get out of here.'

Outside the pub the grey sky was a few shades darker than when we arrived. We walked back to Zoe's house without speaking. This time there was no contact between us. Zoe walked with her arms wrapped around her, as if she was trying to keep warm.

Zoe opened her front door and walked in. She didn't close it behind her so I followed her in and shut it for her. She stood at the bottom of the staircase and took off her dark coat. She hung it on the banister and stood still with her hands on the coat. There was a mirror on the wall to my right and in the reflection I could see the side of her face. Her eyes were open and she looked like she was thinking about something.

After a few seconds she turned and started walking towards me. Her eyes were still pointed at the floor. It was only a couple of metres but she took her time, drawing out the moment. And then she was in front of me.

She started playing with the middle button on my suit jacket. I looked down and watched her fingers moving over it, turning one way and then the next.

Her fingers stopped moving and she grabbed a handful of the jacket, with the button in the middle of her fist. Her hand stayed still and I stopped looking at it. I looked at her face instead.

Her eyes were already aimed at mine.

I kissed her immediately. I couldn't wait any longer.

Nothing else mattered. Not Kat, not Pryor and not Edward Valentine.

11

'Don't worry,' Zoe said. 'I didn't film us.'

'Shame. I'd have liked to see it again.'

'Well maybe in a while we can have a repeat performance,' she said. 'But that depends on how long it takes an old man like you to recover.'

Zoe had a point. I would need some rest after what we'd just done.

I was lying on my back in the middle of Zoe's huge white bed, relaxed, calm and warm under the covers. Zoe was lying on her side on my left, facing me. She was holding my left hand with her right and rested her left one on my shoulder. Those touches, which she instigated, were yet another surprise on a day full of them. But what surprised me even more was that I didn't mind. In fact, I liked what Zoe was doing. I was normally the guy who gets out of there as soon as is polite. Sometimes even sooner.

But this time that wasn't how I felt. I wanted to relax and stay close to Zoe, not get home and be on my own as soon as possible.

Her bedroom was at the front of the house and was as big as my flat. And it was a perfectly presented room. Everything was white, the wardrobe, the dressing table, a large chest of drawers, the sheepskin rug on the white floorboards, the silk cushions on the bed which were now on the floor. Our clothes had got lost on the way up so there was nothing but white. There were no family photos, in fact no photos of people at all, only one of a dog. The room belonged on the pages of some high-class interior design magazine and would, I'm sure, have given a psychologist plenty to think about.

'So, Jack Winter,' Zoe said. 'I want to know about you.'

'Ask me a question,' I said. 'I'll tell you anything you want to know.' And I meant it.

'How did you become a story killer?' She said it breathlessly, as if I was Batman, but with gentle sarcasm.

'I was a journalist originally,' I said. 'A newspaper reporter, I mean. And then I went over to the other side. Instead of writing news stories, I stop them.'

'Do you like your job?'

I hesitated. 'Sometimes,' I said. 'Like now.'

'Interesting. But you're not working now Mr Winter. Did you like being a journalist?'

'I loved it,' I said. 'Best job I've ever done.'

'So why the change? Why did you leave your newspaper? Why leave a job you love for one you only like when you're in bed with me? What made you change?'

Zoe was joking but she had a serious point and she'd asked the question I had never answered. Other people had found out what happened but I had never actually told anyone everything. Not once.

But there was something about Zoe and this moment which made me want to tell my story. Maybe it was because of what I'd found out about Zoe a few hours earlier, even if I didn't fully understand it. All I knew was at that moment, in Zoe's bed, I wanted to tell her.

'Does the name Daisy Gill mean anything to you?' I said.

'Of course,' Zoe said. 'The little girl who was killed by her teacher. What was it? Four years ago?'

'More like three but you're right on everything else. I was a reporter back then and I was sent to cover the story. Clive Birch was one of the first people I met.'

'The teacher?'

'Yes, the teacher. He lived close to the school and was out there from day one, getting involved with searches, giving the police information, basically doing anything he could.'

I paused. This was the start of the part I was ashamed of.

'Birch and I got on well. We talked, he gave me stories and he helped me out once or twice, letting me use his house to charge my phone and computer, to watch news bulletins on his television so I could keep track of the competition, that sort of thing. I spent hours in his house and I didn't suspect him, not once. The thought didn't even cross my mind. All I wanted from him was a promise that he wouldn't let any reporters from other papers have his photos of Daisy from their school trips or hear his stories about her before I did. I wanted him to be my source and mine alone. And he was. I cleaned up. Everyone else was using my stuff the day after we printed it. I won, day after day. I was going to get awards, everyone said so.'

'You couldn't have known,' Zoe said, already seeing where I was going. 'You were just doing your job.'

'Maybe,' I said. 'But when the story and investigation started to go cold ten days in and the media began moving on, I still didn't suspect Birch. We parted as friends, promising to keep in touch, to meet again. I liked him. I even sent him a case of wine as a thank you.'

Zoe took her left hand off my shoulder and put it round my chest, moving herself closer to me so our bodies were touching. I continued, looking up at the white ceiling.

'Five days later Birch walked into the local police station with a lock of Daisy's hair in his hand and told them where she was. They found her body in his cellar. She'd been dead for two days.'

'That's not your fault,' Zoe said. 'None of that is your fault.'

'Really?' I said. 'Are you sure about that? When Birch walked into that police station, Daisy had been dead for two days. That means every second I spent in Birch's house, Daisy was alive. She was lying somewhere, terrified and alone and probably in all kinds of pain and crying for her mother and father while I was busy patting myself on the back for yet another front page exclusive.'

'You couldn't have done anything,' Zoe said. 'You can't blame yourself.'

Zoe was wrong. I could and I did.

'I was the only person who could have saved her,' I said. 'And I didn't do it. I was too busy toasting my own brilliance. That's why I left newspapers. After I found out Birch had been arrested I knew I couldn't do it anymore. I tried for a while but it didn't work. I was reminded of it every day and I couldn't handle the guilt. I couldn't even go into the office. The shame was too much.'

'But you weren't guilty of anything.'

'I think I was,' I said. 'And I wasn't the only one. Can you feel those?'

I moved Zoe's right hand over the four small scars on the left side my stomach and then the larger long one which ran down the middle.

'Yes, I feel them,' she said.

'The small ones are where the knife went in and the big one is where the doctors opened me up so they could sew my guts back together.'

'You were stabbed? By who?'

'Sharon Gill. Daisy's mother. In her eyes I killed her daughter.'

'But that's ridiculous. The teacher killed her.'

'It's not ridiculous,' I said. 'I could have saved her. If I hadn't been so obsessed with keeping Birch all to myself and had stopped to think about more than just my by-lines I might have. If I was Sharon Gill I'd have done the same. Except I wouldn't have missed my heart.'

And it was true. Whenever I thought of Daisy Gill I thought of Emily and how I would feel if someone failed her the way I failed Daisy. Those thoughts didn't make me feel good about myself.

Zoe didn't say anything. She turned my face towards her with her left hand and kissed me, softly at first and then with urgency.

The second time, there was more than just desire between us.

By the time I opened my eyes, the sun had gone down. A combination of moon and street lighting shone weakly through the window, leaving most of the room covered in shadows. Zoe's bed was warm and comfortable and I had no idea what the time was. Part of me wanted to lie close to Zoe and sleep as deeply as she seemed to be, but the part which was now sobering up knew I had some serious thinking and planning to do and it was that part which got its way.

I got out of bed as quietly as I could and crept across the room towards the door. The floorboards were cold under my feet. I opened the door and shut it behind me. The only sound I made was the click of the handle as it closed.

I found my underwear at the top of the stairs and put them on. My trousers had been dropped half way down. I picked them up on the way and I put those on too. All Zoe's clothes were in one pile in the hall. I wouldn't forget those coming off for a while, that was for sure.

I went into the kitchen at the back of the house and turned on the light. Like the rest of the place, it was immaculately designed, with bare wooden floors and work surfaces and cream cupboards.

The room was homely and comfortable, like a country kitchen. An expensive country kitchen.

There was a cupboard with glass doors above one of the surfaces and I took out a large glass. The tumbler felt heavy in my hand – even the drinking vessels were classy. I filled it with water from the tap, drank half immediately, refilled it and then walked back through to the living room.

I sat down on the leather sofa and put the glass on the coffee table. My suit jacket was next to me – it was the one garment not just thrown aside. I pulled my mobile out of breast pocket and checked the time. Half past ten. I'd been asleep for a few hours. I figured I'd earned the rest.

The missed calls and text messages I had from Bull implied he didn't agree.

Where the fuck are you?

Why aren't you here?

Answer your phone fucker

And then anger turned into concern.

Call me, Jack. We need to talk. Seriously. I don't care how late it is. Just call

I was angry that I'd missed my meeting with Bull, and so was he. But my night with Zoe was worth his wrath. I could wait another day or two to hear what he had to say.

Kat was missing and I had to do something about it. I had to find her. But how? Calling the police was out of the question. Edward Valentine's part in it, if he had one, was the big unknown. I needed a plan.

Twenty minutes later I went back upstairs and crept into Zoe's bedroom. I switched on the lamp next to the side of the bed where she was sleeping and sat gently on the edge of the mattress. She was lying on her side, facing the lamp and asleep she was even more beautiful. Her face was relaxed and serene. Carefree. I realised what a huge amount a person like her must carry with her every day, no matter how perfect her life looked from the outside.

I hoped what I was about to do would make everything better for her.

I put my hand on her shoulder and moved it gently backwards and forwards. Her skin was soft and warm.

Zoe opened her eyes but the light made them immediately close sharply. She pulled the duvet over her head and moaned quietly. Then the duvet lifted. 'Come here,' Zoe said as she wrapped an arm around me and tried to pull me under the covers with her. I let myself get drawn in slightly but I didn't relax.

'We need to talk,' I said. Zoe moaned again. She was drowsy and wanted to go back to sleep. But this wasn't the time for sleeping.

'I'm serious,' I said. 'Now.'

'Mornings are for talking,' Zara said. 'Nights like this are for sex and sleeping. Don't spoil it.'

'Listen to me,' I said. 'We need to talk about your step-father.'

Zoe's sleepy smile disappeared. 'I hate him,' she said. 'What else is there to say?'

'This isn't about saying anything,' I said. 'It's about doing something.'

'I'll do anything you want me to, Mr Storykiller,' Zoe said, 'you're going to save me.' She pulled my head close to her and closed her eyes. Her face had softened again.

I spoke for nearly two minutes. When I'd finished, Zoe nodded once and got out of bed.

Ten minutes later we were on our way to London courtesy of the account Zoe's father had set up for her with a local taxi company. Our car was a huge silver Mercedes with black leather seats and a suited driver. The irony of who was footing the bill for our luxurious journey was not lost on me.

Zoe and I were sitting together in the back on a car seat that made my sofa look like a bus stop bench. I had my arm round Zoe. She hadn't said a word since she ordered the car. As soon as we got in, after she'd given the driver the small bag she had packed in a couple of minutes after getting out of bed, she had moved across and sat close to me. The driver didn't say anything about the legal requirement for us both to be wearing seatbelts. I guess he was paid enough not to make a fuss about things like that.

The car took about an hour to get to my flat in Earls Court, just under sixty miles away.

In an ideal world I wouldn't have taken Zoe there. I didn't let many people see it. But there were things in there I would need tomorrow and that meant I had no other option. It was too late to park her in a hotel and come back there alone. Too late and too inconvenient. And I wanted her with me.

Zoe didn't comment on the poverty of her surroundings as we walked up the stairs to my front door. I showed her in, switched on the light and pointed out the bathroom and bedroom. She spent a couple of minutes in the bathroom with the door shut and when she came out she was naked. She stopped in front of me and gave me a kiss which lingered long enough to make me wish I was ten years younger and a whole lot fitter. She pulled away and smiled, fully aware of the effect she had.

'Good night,' she said, and walked into my bedroom. When the door shut behind her I checked the time. Half past midnight. Too late to call Bull.

What couldn't wait was checking I had what I would need for tomorrow. I walked the couple of metres to my desk and I pulled out a box file from under it. Months had passed since I last needed what was inside. I put it on my coffee table, sat on the sofa and opened the lid. Everything was exactly as I remembered.

I closed the box and took stock of where I was. It was the end of the strangest day of my life. The Pryor situation had advanced because I now knew Edward Valentine had tried to set him up but I didn't know why.

Kat was still missing.

And then there was Zoe.

I leant back into the sofa, closed my eyes and tried to do some logical planning.

But I couldn't focus. My mind was fizzing with bitter anger at Edward Valentine. For what he was doing to Adam Pryor and for what he might have done with Kat.

And, most of all, I was angry with him for what he'd put Zoe through. That anger was pure and dark and more than anything else that had happened it meant I wanted to take him down. Every trick I'd ever learned, every ruse, every ploy, I would use them all against him. I didn't care if I never killed another story again. Destroying Edward Valentine was all that mattered.

And I knew if I could do that, Pryor's career would be okay and maybe so would Kat. I also knew maybe was the best I could do for her. And Zoe? I'd find some way to make sure she was fine.

I closed my eyes and imagined a happy ending to this mess.

***

The girl lay in the boot of the car with her hands and feet bound together behind her, tape covering her mouth, a black bag over her head and feeling the kind of fear she thought only existed in movies; a cold, paralysing terror which seemed to be tightening around her lungs like a fist.

Her shoulders and knees ached desperately after hours forced into this unnatural position, her wrists were burning and her hands were numb. And with her body stuck in this terrible shape it was becoming worse with each passing second.

She hadn't cried for a long time now. Exactly how long she didn't know – could be an hour, could be three. She'd wet herself, too. Her jeans were cold against her legs and the skin underneath was beginning to feel tender and sore.

But the worst was her stomach. It wasn't injured. It was where the fear had gathered. It was electric and angry and seemed to be forcing unbearable pressure into her guts and out of them at the same time. She felt like she was being tortured. Or caged like an animal awaiting slaughter in a dark and cramped abattoir.

She felt less than human, like she didn't matter anymore.

The opening of the car boot brought relief and then, very quickly, panic as she was lifted out in silence by strong hands. She was no longer trapped in that tiny space but she did not know where she was or what they were going to do with her. Behind the tape, she screamed. Tears reappeared quickly. Until this moment she thought she had none left.

She was dropped onto the ground. It felt cold and damp against her cheek and smelt like dirt. Where was she?

When they grabbed her a few hours earlier, she hadn't even seen them coming. The shift from moving steadily along a pavement to lying in the back of a car with a bag over her head was almost instant. She didn't see their faces, didn't see their vehicle, not even their shoes. She had no image of her kidnappers.

But what she did have was an idea of who they were working for. Unless this was some moron's idea of a joke, there was really only one possibility.

Part Four: Friday

12

My phone woke me up, again. It was on the coffee table when it rang and I was lying on my sofa, still fully clothed. I hadn't made it to my bed. Even for me that was unusual. This week really was running out of control.

I couldn't remember when I'd done it but some time during the night I'd laid down on my side with my legs curled up. My head had been pressed up against the end of the sofa and my neck and back were painfully stiff. When I sat up the clicks and crunches in my body made me wince. And then there was my head, clogged with yet another hangover.

As my hand moved towards my mobile I remembered Zoe was in my bedroom. I'd blown my chance to spend the night with her for the first time and I was not happy about it. I hoped when this was all over there would be plenty more chances for us but that was a long way from being certain.

And then I saw the name flashing up on my mobile screen: Adam Pryor. The thought of ignoring him flitted into my mind. But I dismissed it. Today wasn't a day for hiding.

'Jack,' he said, before I had the chance to speak. 'We need to talk.'

'OK,' I said, my throat was dry and my voice hoarse. 'I'll come and see you later. When's good?'

'Later isn't good,' he said.

'I can do sooner than that. How about at your house in an hour?' I said.

'No,' Pryor said. 'It has to be now.'

'Now?' I said. 'But I'm at home. It'll take me a while to get to you.'

'No it won't. I'm outside.'

'You're outside where?'

'Outside your house,' he said. 'I'm downstairs in the car waiting for you. Something very troubling has happened and I need your help so you'd better pull yourself together fast. I'll give you ten minutes to get ready. Hurry up and get down here.'

He ended the call before I'd had the chance to reply. His tone was commanding and clear. He would not stand for me taking any longer than ten minutes. I was still half asleep and not in the mood to argue anyway. I was also incapable of even guessing what he was going to tell me. All I knew was that for Pryor to have turned up outside my door this early it must be serious.

I slowly stood up. My knees creaked and my shoulders hurt. I stretched my arms above my head and then out to the side. Maybe Zoe was right. Maybe I was an old man. But there was still fight left in me.

I dropped what I was wearing, my shirt, trousers, boxers and socks, where I stood and went straight to the bathroom. I called it that even though there was no bath. Just a shower cubicle, a sink and a toilet. According to the estate agent that was one of the reasons why the place was so cheap. But it was fine by me. I wasn't the type of man who enjoyed a long soak with a glass of wine and a book.

I liked my shower. On a lazy day I had it hot and stayed in there until the steam was so thick I couldn't see the door. But this wasn't one of those mornings. I washed under hot water and then slammed the dial onto its coldest setting for thirty seconds to wake myself up.

As always, the experience was hideous. Anyone who did that regularly or for pleasure was insane in my book. But when I urgently needed a bolt of instant energy fired into my body, there was nothing better.

I dried myself in the bathroom and then went to my bedroom with the towel wrapped round my waist. I opened the door quickly but didn't turn the light on. I knew where everything was and didn't want to wake Zoe up too abruptly.

But she woke up anyway.

'Hey,' she said sleepily.

I flicked on the lamp by the side of the bed and she blinked as the light met her eyes. Bull once said to me he knew he was in love with his wife when he saw her first thing in the morning after a big night and thought she looked even more gorgeous in those moments than she did when she was all dolled up and ready to go out the previous evening. Zoe had a similar effect on me and it was frightening.

'I have to go out,' I said, opening the wardrobe. 'But I won't be long. A couple of hours at the most. You can go back to sleep.'

'Sure you haven't got time to come in here with me first?'

Zoe lifted the duvet and showed herself to me.

'I'd love to but this old man has work to do,' I said. 'When I get back I'm all yours.'

'I'll hold you to that,' Zoe said and wrapped herself up in the duvet.

I dressed quickly in a white shirt and my best suit, dark grey and single breasted, and most expensive shoes. I guess you could say I wanted today to go well.

I turned and saw Zoe watching me.

'Very nice,' she said. 'I look forward to crumpling you later.'

It didn't take me long to find Pryor and his car. There was a huge black BMW double-parked on the road just outside the door to my block. The back windows were blacked out and I could see the outline of a man in a suit in the front seat. He was not a big man, but then the best bodyguards never are. And Government-trained ones are the best.

At gatherings of the powerful it's the quickest way to separate the wheat from the chaff. Look at the muscle. If you see a man accompanied by a handful of wiry, slightly underfed normal-sized males, he's a big dog. The guys with the twenty-stone lumps around them are the ones the assassins either don't care about or know they can get whenever they want. The weasel bodyguard would have time to kill you a thousand times before the weightlifter even touched you.

Pryor's man was out of the car before the front door shut behind me. He moved smoothly round to the door behind the passenger seat and opened it for me with the self-assured courtesy of a man who knew he could handle himself. I can always pick them. It's the opposite of what I see in the mirror every morning.

'Thank you,' I said.

The weasel said nothing. Just gave me a knowing smile and held the door open. The calm, confident way he went about his work reminded me of Naz.

After the driver shut the door behind me – just a smooth click – I turned to Pryor. He had his right elbow resting on the door. His hand was balled into a fist and it was pressed hard against his closed mouth, like he was about to take a bite out of his thumb.

He was dressed immaculately, as always, in a black suit, light blue shirt and dark blue tie and had already shaved, unlike me, but the skin on his cheek was red and angry. I knew from my own bad days how men carry the physical symptoms of stress on the skin of their faces. Pryor had several: dry, flaky patches around his nose, the shaving rash and dark rings under his eyes. He looked like a man battling demons and losing.

'Adam,' I said. 'What's going on?'

Pryor paused, looking out at the people outside the car, the early commuters rushing along Earls Court Road towards the Tube station.

'Not here,' he said. 'We can't talk here. Wait until we're at Portcullis House.'

Pryor's paranoia seemed over the top. But maybe he had good reason to think someone would be listening. Maybe his bodyguard wasn't trustworthy. Then again, maybe this week of intense stress had got to Pryor and he was cracking up. I'd seen it happen before. I decided not to do anything which might inflame him even slightly so I kept quiet. I had nothing important to say anyway.

At this time of the morning London's roads were relatively quiet so the journey didn't take too long. We turned west onto Old Brompton Road, passing lots of upmarket furniture shops and then turning left onto Onslow Gardens as we moved through Kensington. We turned right onto Cromwell Road and headed west towards the centre of town. The car zipped passed the Natural History Museum. The sight of it seemed to snap Pryor out of his stupor.

'No one would build that these days, you know,' He said. 'No one would have the balls. Everything is far too politically correct now. No one sees the value in national pride any more. No one wants to celebrate the past and use it to galvanise the present and future. Look at it, Jack. I mean it, look. Really look. They built that in the 1870s. What the hell has our generation achieved that can bear comparison with that?'

I turned away from him and glanced at the museum. I had to admit, it was a spectacular structure.

'That, Jack, is what this country should be aspiring to,' he said, like he was practicing a speech. 'That is a majestic tribute to history and learning. This country should be proud of its past.'

And then Pryor went quiet again, turning back towards the window next to him and away from me.

A couple of minutes later we came to Hyde Park Corner. The road split into two, with the right and middle lanes sloping downwards into the underpass. We took the left hand lane and stayed above ground.

'You know what that makes me think of?' Pryor said, pointing towards the tunnel.

'No,' I said. 'I have no idea.'

'Princess Diana,' he said. 'I know it's morbid but every time I see that tunnel I think of the crash which killed her.'

'Her crash was in Paris,' I said, more dismissively than I'd intended.

Pryor narrowed his eyes at me and went quiet again. I didn't mind. He was obviously in a strange mood and I didn't want to hear more of his thoughts. I wanted to get down to business, not be his therapist.

Outside the car, London's streets were dry and uninspiring. Until, that is, the Houses of Parliament came into view.

I knew British politics had been carried out here since before the sixteenth century, when it was the king's palace and the place where he would meet the lords of the land to decide how things would be run. This little plot of land on the north side of the Thames had been the centre of power ever since. I found the history of the place awesome.

Portcullis House was the modern building opposite the House

of Commons. It was about ten years old and was built as an extension to the old buildings across the road which were full to capacity. I knew what it looked like – a big, brown building with rows of black chimneys on the roof – but had never been inside. It was the latest incarnation of the progress of our great political system.

The driver dropped us outside Portcullis House, across the road from the Houses of Parliament and with the river just beyond, and showed no emotion as we left his protection. Pryor led the way into the building. The entrance was relatively small, a front of one storey wall-to-ceiling windows with two revolving doors in the middle. I could see light and space through the glass.

We went through the left hand doors and immediately inside joined a short queue for a luggage scanning machine. I emptied my pockets into one of the boxes. All I had was my wallet, phone and keys.

Before I could join him on the other side of the security barriers I had to have my photograph taken. I looked into the lens, as instructed by a fifty-something man in uniform who looked like a nice old uncle rather than a highly-trained protection specialist, went through the scanner without arousing its interest, received my pass and picked up my things.

Pryor used his pass to get through the next layer of security, another revolving door, and then turned, pressed a button and gestured for me to follow him in.

The hall of Portcullis House was spectacular. It ran all the way up to the clear roof and looked like an upside down glass-bottomed ship. Natural light flooded in. The floors were beige marble and the walls were light wood. There was even a water feature down the middle. All around it were chairs and tables where a small scattering of people sat going about their early morning business. The space was about the length of half a football pitch and was immaculately clean.

On the left, where we stood, were a series of wooden doors leading, I assumed, to the literal corridors of power. On the other side was a glass wall with a cafe behind it. There weren't more than about thirty people in sight in the whole place and I could easily imagine it getting much busier.

Pryor set off towards the far left corner of the room. He stopped by a coffee bar built into the wall. There was a sign above it saying 'The Despatch Box'. A nice touch.

'I'll get the coffees,' he said. 'You find us somewhere to sit.'

I was about to nod my agreement when he spoke again.

'Over there,' he said, pointing at the tables on the other side of the hall, where there was no one else within twenty yards. 'We'll sit on one of those tables. Where it's quiet.'

I went and sat down while he got the drinks. I pulled out my phone to kill the time. I was thinking about whether to text Zoe when Pryor reappeared with two coffees in takeaway cups and lids.

Pryor put the coffees on the table and sat down without saying a word. He looked around slowly, and when he was satisfied no one was within earshot, picked up his coffee, drank a sip and lent forward.

'You haven't found Kat yet, have you.' Pryor said. It wasn't a question, so I answered quickly.

'No.' I said. 'She didn't come home yesterday.'

'Do you think you will? Find her, I mean.'

'I don't know. I hope so. But the truth is I don't know.'

'I expect she's hiding somewhere planning her big newspaper story.'

'Maybe,' I said. 'It's possible.'

Pryor took another mouthful of coffee, leant towards me, and then spoke quietly.

'There's something else we need to talk about. Do you remember asking me if Edward had ever requested any favours from me?' he said.

I nodded.

'Well,' Pryor said. 'Now he has.'

He looked around again, more quickly this time, and I noticed how bloodshot his eyes had become since I first met him only a couple of days ago. He drank some more coffee.

When he spoke again Pryor lowered his voice even further. He was getting more and more agitated by the second, as if he was fighting hard to stop himself from panicking. He looked genuinely scared.

'He wants something from me,' Pryor said. 'And he's threatening to make my life very difficult if I don't give it to him.'

I said nothing. Pryor waited for a reaction. The revelation he had just dropped, he was entitled to one. But I didn't give him a reaction. I didn't give him anything at all. I simply sat there, looking at him and not really looking at him at the same time.

I knew he was going to be blackmailed but I couldn't tell Pryor that. Not yet, anyway. Until I did, I would try to pick as much information out of him as I possibly could.

'That doesn't make any sense,' I said.

Pryor managed to make his face look confused, offended and defiant all at the same time. I could see that mask working on the Commons benches. I could see it working at rallies and speeches and wherever the hell else it is that politicians go to on their vote-grabbing tours these days.

'What do you mean?' said Pryor.

I tipped sugar into my coffee. Lots of it. Three sachets of the white stuff. Not the suspicious brown grains or the imposter sweetener. I needed a real sugar fix. I stirred and explained.

'Blackmail is one guy threatening another guy with a secret he doesn't want the whole world to know about,' I said.

'I bloody well know what blackmail is,' Pryor snapped.

'But the other thing about blackmail is, it only works one way,' I said.

'I don't follow.'

'Blackmail is like your heart rate on a first date. It goes up, not down. You don't have rich and powerful people blackmailing people less rich and powerful than them,' I said.

Pryor frowned at my implication that he was less rich and powerful than Valentine. Harsh, but true. He cleared his throat.

'So what you're saying is—'

'I don't understand why Valentine would blackmail you. He has everything to lose and little to gain. You're not even in the Cabinet yet. What can he squeeze out of you? What can you do for him that he can't do for himself?'

Pryor drank coffee. Frowned, like he didn't like the taste of it. Drank some more, like he had started it so he had to finish it.

'You're forgetting that I'm about to become Secretary of State for International Development. I wouldn't say this on record, of course, but it's a funny old position. The Department is less than twenty years old. It doesn't have the glamour of Defence, and it doesn't have the grand sense of purpose of Education or Health. But it is a position that has a lot of influence. We're not a global military power these days. Not standing alone, anyway. We rely on soft power. International Development is a key part of that. We look like a charity but we also get involved with the dirty work. So I'm about to take a relatively minor Cabinet role, but one with a lot of sway.'

I nodded. Pryor paused a beat. Like he was an actor waiting

for me to remember my lines. I didn't remember my lines. He smiled wanly and hurried on.

'My point is, in a matter of days I will have the keys to something Valentine wants. Something that he needs my help to get.'

I nodded again.

'So what are we talking here? Money?'

Pryor shook his head.

'What do you know about the Government Investment Corporation?'

'About as much as I know about rocket science,' I said. Pryor threw up that weak smile again.

'The GIC was founded after the Second World War, as the investment arm of the British government,' Pryor said. 'What they call in business circles a Development Finance Institution. Their funds are used to invest in infrastructure and stimulate the private sector and enterprise in the world's poorest countries.'

'A cynic might say it sounds like a cheap way of buying influence,' I said.

'And an optimist might argue that it's better than foreign aid and sacks of rice because the only long-term solution to poverty is sustainable business, employment and taxes,' Pryor said, his voice suddenly hard and cold, like the blade of a knife. He gave me the full-blown forced smile now. I wondered if he really believed in the kind of PR spin he'd just fed me. Probably he did. Probably he'd been spoon-fed the same old lines since he'd first stepped into politics. In my experience, tell somebody something enough times, and they'll start to believe it.

'It's not exactly Bono and Live Aid, I know,' Pryor raised his hands in mock surrender, as if he was anticipating a howl of protest from me. But I sat there and listened and sipped at my coffee, and he went on.

'The GIC used to be a noble organisation. Did a lot of good work, you know. It started out in Kenya, Zambia, Malawi. Places like that. This is back in the Fifties. It was agricultural investment. Buying up land to grow tea, that sort of thing. Anyway, by the mid-Eighties the GIC branched out into other areas. Oil. Cement. Local equity schemes. Then in the late Nineties they launched the first pan-African mobile phone network.'

Pryor paused a beat, like I should care about this information too. I didn't, but I nodded again, like I was really soaking this all up. In the back of my mind I was thinking that this was Pryor's way of making small talk. Banging on about nothing, to avoid telling me something. People do that a lot, when they have something they need to get off their chest.

'It sounds like a lot of fingers and a lot of pies,' I said.

Pryor nodded enthusiastically. He was warming to the subject. 'The reach is huge. But the fund has become something of a problem lately.'

'How so?' I said.

'I said the GIC used to be a noble organization. The reality today is very different. It's become a political embarrassment. At least, that's the sentiment in Whitehall.'

'Embarrassing how?' I asked.

'It used to be about helping developing countries. But recently the GIC has started to behave more like something from the shadiest corners of Wall Street. It's been aggressively pumping equity into some pretty corrupt regimes. Places like Equatorial Guinea, where backhanders to presidents get you a slice of serious deals. I'm surprised you haven't seen the articles about it.'

I shrugged. 'I don't really bother with world news.'

'Yes, well. Stories of a government-sponsored investment fund propping up septuagenarian dictators isn't good PR.'

Pryor finished his coffee and cold-stared at the cup in his hand for a long moment. Like he'd just spotted a cockroach at the bottom.

'Some of the investments haven't been too shrewd either,' he said, leaning forward and replacing the cup on the table. 'Lost quite a bit of money last year. Again, it makes the government look bad. So they're looking to sell it off.'

'They can do that?'

Pryor smiled at me. I felt like the kid at the back of the class who figures out the maths problem about a year after everyone else.

'This is the government,' said Pryor. 'They can do whatever they want.'

I shrugged again. I was growing restless. The coffee had put me on edge, and my left foot was tapping away under the table, like all the energy in my body was fizzing out of my toes.

I said, 'Big deal. The government sells off a liability and stashes the money in its back pocket. Nobody loses. What the hell has this got to do with Valentine?'

Pryor folded his hands across his lap. Tightened his face and did a little twist of his neck. Like he was preparing to make some grand statement.

'Edward,' he said, 'wants to buy GIC.'

He looked at me for longer than a little while. I felt like I had to say something. I said, 'So?'

Pryor blinked.

'He's willing to offer a hundred million.'

Pryor kept looking at me funny. I blanked a look back at him. Then I recognized the look in his face. The same look I'd seen the first morning at his house. Fear.

He said, 'The problem is, GIC is worth two hundred times that.'

13

The thing about money is, once you get past a certain number, it kind of loses its meaning. A million sounds like a big number to me. But I've known for a long while that a million sounds like a lot less to the footballers whose affairs I cover up every now and then. To them, it sounds like a couple of months' wages, an extension to their country pad, or the amount a celeb magazine will pay to have the exclusive rights to their wedding to some B-list singer. It doesn't sound like much to them. But I bet a hundred million sounds like a lot to a footballer. A hundred million sounds like a lot to anybody. I bet even Russian oligarchs would hesitate to sign a cheque for a hundred million without asking what it was for.

So to me, the difference between a hundred million and a number two hundred times as big was not really any difference at all. They were both vast sums of money.

Pryor adjusted the cuffs on his shirt and waited for me to fire another question at him. I spent three or four seconds working out two hundred times a hundred million, and another three seconds thinking that twenty billion was more money than I could even imagine. What did it look like? Could you fit twenty billion in a hotel room? I didn't know. I somehow doubted it. Then I spoke up.

'If it's worth so much more, why is Valentine making such a small offer? He must know they'll reject it out of hand?'

'They won't,' Pryor countered. He sat back and took a deep

breath, like a man about to do a bungee jump on an elastic cord he didn't completely trust. Finally he was getting to the important part. 'You see, nobody else knows the GIC is worth that much.'

I frowned. 'How can they not know?'

Pryor glanced across his shoulders. As if he was worried someone was snooping in. Then he leaned in close to me.

'The whole point of the GIC is that it holds shares in a dizzying portfolio of companies in a lot of countries. And the companies the GIC has a stake in then have stakes in their own local enterprises. And they have stakes in other businesses, and so on and so on. Keeping track of who owns what in which business is like trying to keep track of a single drop of water in a bath. Not many people know what interests GIC has. Apart from Valentine. That's why he knows the valuation of the company is so low. Because it has secret shares in potentially lucrative investments.'

'How do you know about it?' I said.

Pryor looked at me like I was a stupid child. 'Edward told me,' He said. 'Just before he started with the blackmail.'

I nodded. Sipped at my coffee. Then wished I hadn't. It had gone tepid. I drank it anyway. I needed the caffeine fix more with every word popping out of Pryor's mouth.

'You remember me telling you about the mobile phone network?' He said.

'The one that spanned Africa. How could I forget.'

Pryor ignored my sarcasm. 'That's the one. Well, that was one of GIC's big success stories. They made a vast pile of cash from that enterprise. I'm talking mountains of the stuff. That's what Valentine has his eyes on.'

'A phone network that already exists? In Africa?'

Pryor slow burned at me.

'Ten years ago, your scepticism would be understandable,' he said. 'But times have changed, Jack. People are talking about China this and India that in the news, sure. But the real emerging markets are in Africa. It's the last great untapped economy of the world.'

My mobile buzzed like mad in my jacket pocket. I felt it thudding against my chest. I felt my heart beating almost as fast. I ignored the call. I had to. This conversation was too important to interrupt.

A dark-haired waitress came over and scooped up our coffee cups. She was pretty but looked tired and depressed. Skin pale as bleach. Her name tag said her name was Monika. Eastern European. I wondered briefly how many MPs had tried to sleep with her. More than one, I was willing to bet. Call it the cynic in me. Pryor eased back into his chair. He was talking at me as much with his hand as his mouth now. Making exaggerated waves and gestures. I guessed I was supposed to be impressed.

'You have to look at it this way,' he said. 'There are a billion people in Africa. Today, most of them don't have the Internet. But things move quickly over there. Most countries on the continent aren't saddled with tired old infrastructure. Unlike Britain, say. If they want to lay down new fibre-optic broadband that stretches from Dakar to Djibouti, they don't have to dig up the old one first. They just go ahead and install it. What takes ten years here, they can do in one year in Africa. Today much of the continent isn't connected. Tomorrow, they'll be using wifi and Facebook. Africa is the future, Jack, I'm telling you. And the company GIC has a stake in is going to be a big part of that future.'

'What's the company called?'

'AMob,' Pryor said. The name meant nothing to me. 'Stands for Africa Mobile, as you might guess.'

I kept wearing my sceptical face. I felt like I was being sold some dodgy timeshare by a holiday rep, waiting for him to get to the important bit – the actual price, the bare numbers. I looked around. Old men in suits blathered away to younger men in suits, in between shooting frowns and glares at their phones.

'So there's money in mobiles. But there can't be that much. Not twenty billion pounds of money.'

'That's where you're wrong, Jack. Telecommunications is big business in Africa. People use it for all kinds of things. Mobile banking, for example. The mentality is different there. It's safer and easier to bank on your mobile than visit your local branch. Something like a quarter of Kenya's GDP passes through the M-Pesa mobile network. You've got companies focusing on mobile in Africa, posting revenue of eight and nine billion pounds.'

I sat up now. Took notice.

'The point is,' Pryor was saying as I tuned back into the conversation, 'African mobile is a goldmine, and Valentine knows it.'

'Sure,' I said. 'But he's not the only person who knows this, by the sound of it. Those other companies have figured it out pretty good too.'

'They're only part of the equation,' said Pryor. 'Health. E-commerce. Banking, what have you. All of this is very nice. But the real king will be the person who can roll out a superfast service across Africa, on a single network. One that can handle the enormous volumes of traffic that are going to be generated over the next decade. Whoever owns that network will be rich on a scale most people can't even imagine.'

I nodded. Joined the dots in my head. A picture was beginning to emerge. There were parts of it I understood, and parts I did not. I needed answers, and I needed them today.

'You're talking about a superfast version of that pan-African mobile company you mentioned,' I said.

Pryor's head bobbed up and down.

'And that's exactly what AMob is. Except it's way more advanced. The technology can be set up easily enough. If it works then it'll rake in more money than—'

Pryor stopped abruptly. He flicked his eyes up from the table and held them at a point past my shoulder. I glanced behind me. A guy in his fifties was strolling past and trying very hard not to look in our direction. Then he nodded briefly at Pryor. Pryor returned the nod. He waited for the man to pass out of earshot. Then he continued.

'Let's just put it this way. Whoever ultimately owns AMob is sitting on billions in shares. Billions and billions. Now here's the thing. Edward knows about the mobile contract. Don't ask me how. He hears stuff on the grapevine before it's even left someone's mouth.'

'But no one else knows?'

Pryor made a pained face at me.

'AMob is owned by Redstone Limited. It's an offshore shell company, effectively created to conceal the identities of the investors in AMob. GIC is the majority investor, it's simply that no one knows about it because the trail has been so well hidden.'

'So Valentine will buy up the GIC and then reveal the shares and the real value of the company?'

'Correct,' said Pryor. 'Soon as the news about the stake in AMob goes public, the value of the GIC shares will go through the roof. Valentine, as the owner of the newly-privatized GIC, will be sitting on more than twenty billion pounds. Could be even more, if the stock market is in a good mood.'

The air in the café was warm and stale. I loosened my collar a little. Was glad I wasn't wearing a tie. I looked at Pryor and wondered how he managed to wear his without breaking into a sweat.

'So tell me,' I said. 'What's your role in all this?'

Pryor looked quizzically at me. 'GIC is a government enterprise, Jack,' Pryor said slowly, as if I was having trouble grasping the concept. 'That means no sale can be pushed through without the approval and support of the relevant minister.' He coughed. 'In this case, the Secretary of State for International Development.'

'Meaning, you.'

'Meaning me, yes.' Pryor smiled at his shoes. He was trying to hide it, but I saw that smile all right. It told me he was pleased with himself. No matter that the man who'd been in the seat a couple of days ago had died. All that mattered in Pryor's head was that he was now the one with the impressive job title.

I waved to Monika. She started walking over. I needed more coffee. I said to Pryor, 'So Valentine wants you to rubber-stamp the sale of GIC to his company, right?'

'Correct,' Pryor said. 'That's what this is all about.'

'But I thought you said selling off GIC was a good thing. What about all that stuff you told me about bad publicity and being a liability?'

'All that is true.' Pryor yawed his head this way and that, like he was trying to relieve some chronic knot of tension in the back of his neck. 'But you're forgetting something. If I allow Edward to buy GIC, I'll be shredded by your mates in the media once GIC reveals the stake in AMob. I'll look like a complete idiot. Christ, I can see the headlines now,' Pryor slumping back in his seat and drawing a hand across an imaginary ticker tape in front of him. 'Minister wastes twenty billion pounds of public money in the middle of a recession. That's what they'll print. You know that as well as I do.'

Pryor went quiet suddenly, as if he expected me to offer him some kind of reassurance. I didn't. I stayed silent. We were both smart enough to know he was telling the truth, and I wasn't going to sit there and fire off empty reassurances at the man. His career was quite possibly in ruins. The MP who lost the country twenty billion through his own stupidity would never, ever be Prime Minister. What use was there in me pulling the wool over his eyes?

Then he smiled, a small sly, grin. 'I'm sure you can see there are political advantages to publicly opposing the deal.'

'No,' I said. 'Like what?'

Pryor rolled his eyes.

'Use your imagination, Jack. Young politician opposes takeover of government office by fabulously wealthy businessman. Young politician *saves* the taxpayer twenty billion. I could build my whole career on that. Blair did something similar in the early Nineties. All that stuff he said about being tough on crime and tough on the causes of crime. All turned out to be bollocks in the end, of course, but that didn't matter. The voters saw that crime was his thing and he was launched. This could be mine. Pollsters can argue till they're blue in the face about the effect of this or that policy, but all it comes down to is being memorable in the minds of the voters. People remembered that slogan of Blair's above everything else. The important thing was it swayed them when they went to the ballot box, not what he ultimately did about crime. If I blocked the GIC takeover, it could make my name in the same way.'

I smiled inwardly. Pryor had already reached that point where politicians instinctively think more about the consequences of this or that decision for their career prospects, instead of whether it was purely the right or wrong thing to do. He was going to go far.

I said, 'Maybe Valentine is bluffing. He's invested all this time and effort in you.'

'No.' Pryor's voice was flat and definite. 'He isn't bluffing, Jack.'

'You sound pretty sure of yourself.'

'That's because I am.'

'But this man is trying to blackmail you. Nine times out of ten, you call their bluff and nothing happens. You don't know for sure that isn't the case with Valentine.'

'But I do,' said Pryor. He looked at me for a long moment. His eyes were like white studs buttoned into his face. The corners of his lips and eyes were creasing. He looked like he was choosing whether to break out into laughter or tears, and still hadn't decided which way to go. He held that look for a long time. Longer than I imagined was comfortable.

Then he simply said, 'I'm not the first person Edward has blackmailed. In fact, he's been doing it for years. Key figures in government, backbenchers. Cabinet ministers. And believe me, he's never bluffed once.'

Monika brought us over two more coffees. She tried a smile on me. Not the best she'd ever pulled off, but at least she was trying. I smiled back. I liked Monika. Then I dumped three sugars in the coffee and knocked back half the cup in a couple of swigs. I was hot and sick and tired. I felt like I was at the tail end of the world's longest hangover. I dropped the smile and swivelled my eyes to Pryor. I was listening to a potential future Prime Minister tell me that for several decades senior figures in government had been dancing to the tune of a multi-millionaire with a charming manner. Neither of us said anything for the longest while. Then I opened my mouth, as much to break off the uncomfortable silence as anything else.

'Do you have any proof?' I asked.

Pryor made a face at me. Like he was squinting at dark clouds gathered over his head.

'What do you mean, proof?'

He thought it was a dumb question. I thought it was a dumb answer.

I said. 'Like, taped phone calls, implicating emails, texts, letters. Something that would stand up in court.' I suddenly felt like we were acting out a scene in a TV police procedural.

'No,' Pryor shook his head decisively. 'Nothing like that.'

'Then how can you be so sure?'

'Because of the rumours.' He tapped his fingers on the table edge. Hadn't touched his second coffee. 'You hear a lot of things in Whitehall. A lot of it is just frivolous gossip. But every now and then there's a trace of truth in something. You hear enough of it, you get an ear for what's true and what's a lie. You just know. And I know. Believe me, I know. It's not just the whispers. It's the way people talk about him. You don't think it's funny, that everyone in government holds Edward in such high esteem? It's not because he's a benefactor to a few rather obscure societies, you know. Edward has serious influence. The kind lobbyists would peel their eyelids off for.'

I said, 'Who else has he blackmailed?'

Pryor said, 'You want names?' He laughed somewhere deep in his throat. 'No, I can't say that now. Let's just say that they are people right at the top of the food chain.'

A man like Pryor, if he doesn't want to say something, he won't say it, no matter how hard you press. I moved on.

'And the setup is the same each time? Blackmail in order to get a dodgy deal in his favour? Like the AMob scheme?'

Pryor shook his head again. 'Edward is too slick to pull off the same stunt twice and hope nobody notices. Let me ask you, what do you know about his business interests?'

I shrugged. The honest answer was I didn't know. I hadn't really asked questions about the how, the why or the when of Valentine's wealth. On that score I had failed the first test of every reporter. I felt somewhat ashamed of myself.

'I know he's rich,' I offered tamely.

'Edward is worth a hundred and twenty-seven million, according to the Sunday Times Rich List. I suppose that valuation is correct, if you're only counting his various holdings and shares. But the most valuable thing Edward has is his contacts book.'

'Okay ,' I said.

'Valentine's original business was roses. He owned farmland in Kenya. Inherited from his parents. When Valentine took control of the land, he started growing roses.'

A smile tickled the corners of Pryor's lips.

'Did you know,' he said, 'that one in three roses in the world is grown in Kenya?'

'No. But I do now.'

Pryor pretended to find me funny. I almost believed him. Like I said, he was good.

'But you don't get to be as rich and powerful as someone like Edward by sticking to the rose trade. He had to branch out. He moved to London. His Kenyan business brought him back into contact with all those white farmer types. The ones with expensive educations and serious connections over here. They introduced Edward into the inner circles of power.'

'And from there, he what, just decided off the cuff to start blackmailing people?'

Pryor rubbed his temples. Like he was trying to recall some fact he had learned a long time ago. 'All I know is, it was something to do with the roses. One of his main importers happened to be a former member of Cabinet, and he was in some kind of trouble. Edward offered to help.'

'In exchange for?'

Pryor shrugged at me.

'Money. Shares. A tax break. Who knows. It was twenty years ago.'

I spluttered on my coffee, spitting most of a mouthful right back into my cup. Caught a rogue bead of it trailing down my chin with my forefinger.

'Christ. That long? And no one's ever reported him?'

'Anyone who tried would be committing political and possibly actual suicide.' He stopped rubbing his temples and screwed his eyes shut and sighed heavily. 'And that's the situation I'm in, Jack. So now you know.'

I said nothing. I sat there in the middle of Portcullis House, the cradle of British democracy, and watched a man physically fall apart two feet from where I was sitting. I didn't know who I felt worse for. Zoe or Kat or Pryor. Or the suckers who went out and voted.

'This is huge,' I said finally.

Pryor stared at the ceiling. Sighed again.

'You could go public,' I said.

Pryor laughed.

'Do me a favour, Jack, and give me some real advice.'

I fell silent again. Let it play out between us. Pryor and I had covered a lot of ground in a short space of time. We needed to let everything settle around us. Both of us did. Give it time to settle, then you'll see the best path to take. At least, I was hoping that kind of hokum would help me out here.

Then Pryor said something unexpected.

'Thank you, Jack.'

I looked at him curiously.

'What for?'

'For listening. Christ, you don't know how long I've been carrying all that around inside. Years, Jack. Pippa doesn't know. No one does. Only you, Edward and me.'

My bowels squirmed at that last statement. Me. Valentine. Pryor. I was now in their squalid little gang.

My mobile kicked up again in my jacket pocket. I ignored the vibration and tried to formulate my next question.

'What is Edward using to blackmail you?' I said. 'The crash?'

'Nothing specific,' he said. 'But I don't know what else it could be.'

'Are you sure? What about Kat?'

Pryor's confused face appeared again.

'How would he do that?' he said.

'He could be holding her somewhere,' I said, 'And be waiting for the right moment to let her out to tell her story.'

As I said it, I realised how ridiculous the idea sounded.

Pryor frowned. 'Are you serious? How would he do that? Kat would never go along with that kind of plan. She wouldn't keep quiet until Edward told her she was allowed to talk. You met the girl, you saw what she's like. Would she tell the papers about sleeping with me but not mention being kidnapped by him? Not a chance. You really haven't thought that through.'

'No,' I said slowly. 'I can't have done.'

I asked myself a question: why else would Kat have been taken? The first answer that appeared in my mind made my chest go tight.

So many things didn't make sense. I wasn't sure if I believed that Valentine had Kat, or if I wanted to believe it. Because if he did, what was he going to do with her? As Pryor said, he wasn't going to be able to let her go and have her say whatever he wanted, whenever he wanted her to say it. If he really had taken Kat, the only possibility was that he would make sure she never talked and I still hadn't figured Valentine for a killer. And then I remembered Naz. Maybe Valentine had someone to do the killing for him.

I hoped Kat had gone somewhere secret for some quiet thinking time and Valentine was simply trying to scare Pryor into action using the crash as leverage. But Pryor wasn't listening to me try to tell him that. He was in full-on self-pity mode. He was making restless shapes with his hands, like he was working some misshapen lump on a pottery kiln. Like he was trying to smooth it back into shape.

In the background, Pryor went on, unaware of what I was thinking. 'Edward says, if I don't do as he says, he'll destroy me.'

'He's bluffing,' I said a little too quickly. Pryor wasn't the only one getting worked up. Valentine was getting under my skin too. 'He likes you, remember.'

'I've been so bloody stupid,' he said. 'All this time, I told myself that Edward had my best interests at heart. That he loved the party and the country. That he wanted to see a real outsider do well. Someone he identified with. Like me. And the way he treated me, he made me feel like I was family to him.' He let his hands fall uselessly between his thighs. 'And now this. It was for nothing. All of it. It was for worse than nothing. It was lies.'

I leaned in to Pryor. I had to get his head back in the game. He was no use to me if he was full of loathing and bad vibes. Experience has taught me that the only way out of a tricky situation is to take a deep breath and not panic. If you panic, you make bad decisions. So if you don't panic, you're more likely to make a good call.

I said, 'So what do you want to do?'

'I need your help to fix it, Jack.'

'How?'

Pryor looked at me and for the first time I saw something else in his face. Not political destiny or fear, but the look of a man whose fate was out of his own hands and was entrusting it to the hands of the guy on the other side of the table.

'How?' Pryor repeated. 'That's up to you, Jack.'

My phone buzzed into angry life again. I went to reach for it, then realized the buzzing was coming from the other side of the table. Pryor grimaced and raised his backside from the seat as he rooted around in his trouser pockets, then his jacket side pockets, coming up short each time. Then he dug a hand into his breast pocket and retrieved his phone. Swiped the call. Stood up and paced away from me. He spoke in a low voice with his mouth pressed tight to the phone. I couldn't hear a word. I sat there and finished my coffee and worried about how I would take down a blackmailing multi-millionaire. The idea I'd hatched that morning while laying in bed with Zoe suddenly didn't seem so bright. I'd need to work the angles better. And above all, I'd need to be careful. I was in new and dangerous professional territory.

Then Pryor hung up. The call had lasted thirty seconds but had aged Pryor ten years. He came back looking like someone had poured bleach in his coffee. He was pale and emaciated and his jaw was slack. He didn't sit down. Just stood there, limp and numb, staring at the screen of his mobile as it dimmed. Kept staring at its black expanse and not moving.

'Adam?' I said. 'Everything okay?'

'Yes,' he replied absently. Then a snap of his head and a frown. 'No. I mean, it's Imogen.'

I looked at Pryor blankly. Imogen. I racked my brains. Had he mentioned this woman before? I wasn't sure he had. Maybe that was his secretary? I asked myself. Aide? Friend? I thought about asking Pryor who she was, but he looked like he was in a foul mood. So I pretended to know who he was talking about and said, 'What happened?'

Pryor said. 'She's in hospital.' And then he kind of scowled at the ceiling, like he had some personal beef with the ceiling way above us, and said it again, like he expected the meaning to sink in, and it clearly hadn't.

'My sister is in hospital, Jack.'

Not for the first time that morning, or even that hour, I looked for something to say and came up short. I just gave him my best concerned face. It didn't do much good. Pryor surrendered his eyes to the floor and looked at me and said, 'She's taken another overdose.'

14

The BMW cut down through Millbank. I checked my watch. Ten to eleven in the morning. We had spent the thick end of two hours talking in the café. Two hours of listening to Pryor banging on about the finer aspects of Edward Valentine's business acumen. My head felt fuzzy and numb.

The pounding between my temples was my brain telling me I knew too much, that I was now up to my neck in it, and if Pryor was caught up in it, now I was too. I soothed my temples. I needed painkillers. I wondered if there was some kind of a pill to un-remember stuff too. They ever invent a pill that gives you amnesia, I'll be the first guy in the queue. I have years of crap I would gladly forget.

My mind drifted for a long moment. I wondered, briefly, why I hadn't had the balls to go back to newspapers, and a job with a salary. If I hadn't been so desperate for work then maybe I wouldn't have been so quick to pick up the phone when Valentine called, and maybe I wouldn't be sitting here in the back of a BMW the size of a two-ton truck with a bodyguard made of right angles, feeling the secrets piling on top of my chest like rocks and making it harder and harder to breathe.

Then I shook myself out of my stupor. I just did it. One shake, and I was back in the game. Let me tell you something. There is a whole other world of maybes out there. Maybe you didn't marry your true love. Maybe you took that job. Maybe that kid didn't step out in front of your car. The world of maybes is a bitter and lonely place, and as soon as you sense the door opening on it, you have to slam it shut. The here and now is all that matters. That's what I did. I slammed the door inside my head, said goodbye to the world of maybes, and focused on the reality in front of me.

I turned to Pryor and said, 'Was it pills?'

Pryor raised his right eyebrow. He was gazing out of the window. The tint had to be at least fifty percent. I wasn't even sure it was legal, let alone that you could see anything out of it. He was silent for a cold second. I looked out of my window. The world had been crushed into a sheet of dull metal. Faces were chrome blurs. Trees were the colour of midnight. We passed Westminster Abbey, standing like a jet-black monolith in a sea of grey.

'It was heroin, Jack. It always is,' he said in a familiar way, as if I already knew this. I didn't, and it bugged the hell out of me, made me question what else Pryor had neglected to tell me. But this wasn't the time to bring him to task. He needed sympathy. I threw him a nod.

'I warned her the last time,' Pryor went on. 'She told me she wanted help. I said I'd do whatever it took. I told her about all these programmes and ground-breaking treatments they have these days. It's not like it was ten years ago, when they just gave you a load of methadone and told you to be on your way and best of luck.'

I continued gazing out at a blanket of vague and distorted greys. London swept past in giddy brushstrokes. It almost looked better when viewed through a heavy tint. You couldn't see all the decay.

'The fucking bitch,' Pryor said. The sudden viciousness in his voice sent bolts of electricity jerking up my spine. 'I knew. Soon as the phone rang. This always happens. When I got elected as an MP, that night should have been the happiest moment of my life. But Imogen overdosed then too. That's it now. I've had enough. Once she's out of there she's on her own. She can't keep relying on adrenalin shots from paramedics to keep her alive.'

'I'm sorry,' I said, which is a very English way of saying that I didn't know what to say. The English have been saying sorry to each other for the past five hundred years, and it never did them any harm.

'And now look,' Pryor said. He flapped his arms in front of him, as if the disaster he was describing was sitting on his lap. 'Just when everything is coming together, she goes and screws up again.'

We glided down Millbank. I looked at Pryor. His head was locked grimly ahead. I looked past Pryor. The Thames was unfurling beyond the road like a great grey tongue. Then we were tearing through the junction at Vauxhall Bridge Road and onto Grosvenor Road. Stacks of apartments winked the sun at me from across the other side of the river. The blocks were new and futuristic. They looked like prototype rockets assembled on a launch pad, waiting to whizz into the sky and map out brave new worlds. I felt like joining them. It might be lonely up there, but at least there would be no Edward Valentine to worry about, no Pryor to keep me up at night.

I mimicked Pryor and stared at the road ahead and said, 'Where is she?'

'Chelsea and Westminster,' said Pryor. 'She's a familiar face around the place.'

'How long has this been going on?'

Pryor sighed heavily.

'Fifteen years,' he said. 'Maybe a couple more. She was always difficult, even when we were kids. I was always young and enthusiastic, but she was different. Quiet, angry even. She was restless, but she was also incredibly jealous.'

'Of you?'

'Of course me,' he said, his tone harsh and biting. 'The problem is, she was a really bright girl. But she could never be bothered. I don't think she was lazy, but she was always distracted. By men. By friends. By partying. I think she found it hard to sit down and squirrel away at something and where we grew up, that usually meant you got into trouble. I never had that problem. Thank God.'

We slugged through onto Chelsea Embankment. The buildings to my right were Georgian and the colour of cheesecake. I hated this part of town. Everything was old. The buildings. The people. The money.

'She fell in with the wrong crowd,' said Pryor. 'I suppose I didn't really notice at first. Or maybe I did, and I just tried to pretend not to see it. By the time I realized she had a problem, it was too late.'

I felt a vein thumping away above my left temple. I touched a hand to it. Felt it pulsing. I was angry at Pryor. Angry that he hadn't told me about his sister and her smack problem. Angry that he was behaving childishly about the situation. He was doing what all good celebrities do when a story comes out: they make the story all about themselves.

'How come I never heard about this?' I said.

'She's been clean for four years,' he said. 'It hasn't been a problem for a long time.'

'And you think it is now?'

'The situation has changed. You must see that, surely.'

I did, but in my experience it is always better to guide someone to the answer rather than press them until they bleed it out. Pryor was already teetering dangerously on the brink, and I needed to rein in his anxiety. Arguing with him about Imogen would do neither of us any good. I'd have plenty of time to be mad at Pryor later.

'The press didn't care before,' Pryor went on. 'Who's interested in grubby stories about a new MP's sister? We covered our tracks like mad that night and she's been on the straight and narrow. But I'm about to become a Cabinet minister, for Christ's sake. That makes Imogen fair game. All it takes is someone at the hospital to open their mouth, and tomorrow it'll be all over the papers.'

'What about your colleagues?' I said as the BMW hurled past the Albert Bridge towards the World's End Estate, and Battersea Park and the power station shrank in the rear view mirror. 'Do the other MPs know about Imogen?'

'What difference would that make?'

I shrugged. 'None, I guess.'

The World's End Estate loomed into view. The name suited the place. It was the colour of dried mud, sprawled over a landscape of sad grass and holocaust trees, angular and inappropriate.

'The ones who need to know, do.' Then Pryor swivelled his head away from me and eyeballed Battersea Bridge, and the conversation was over.

The driver hooked a right at the end of World's End. We nosed north on Edith Grove. I flipped out my mobile and tapped in my pass code. I had three missed calls. They were all from the same number. Not a number I had stored in my phone. But I recognised the first seven digits as belonging to the offices of the *Sunday Legend*. I felt my guts lurch as the driver swung right again onto Fulham Road. I was sure he was way over the speed limit.

Thirty seconds later we jerked to a halt outside Chelsea and Westminster Hospital.

Pryor and the bodyguard flung open their doors at the same time. I unglued myself from my seat and crawled out a few moments later. Joined them on the pavement. Stood there, wedged between Pryor and the weasel, and felt a bit awkward. People were sucking hard on cigarettes by the door. A guy was being wheeled out in a dressing gown. He weighed all of about seven stone and had a face like petrified wood and lips like a sucked orange. He looked at me meanly. Like he was thinking, *why me and not you, arsehole?* as he dragged on his cigarette. No one seemed to have noticed the no-smoking signs plastered everywhere. Or they were all past caring.

We entered the hospital. It smelled like a lot of money had been spent trying to cover up the smell all hospitals carry. Like someone had pissed on the lino a week ago, a cleaner had just come along and poured a bucket of bleach over it and then another person had pumped a load of air freshener in. You didn't get that everywhere in the NHS – only hospitals in rich areas, like this one, where locals who didn't need to work spent their time raising funds to benefit others. And to make them feel good about themselves.

I hate hospitals. I used to be okay about them, but a few days on life support changed all that. Now I was convinced that the next time I went into one I'd never come out. I took a step backwards.

'You guys go ahead,' I said.

Pryor blinked at me.

'Something the matter, Jack?'

I waved my phone apologetically.

'I need to make a few calls.'

Pryor and the weasel swapped faces.

'Fine,' Pryor turning on his heels away from me. 'We'll see you in there when you're ready. Find us in the High Dependency Unit.'

'Sure,' I said, like I was promising a girl who just broke my heart that we would always be friends.

The weasel gave me his back too, and the pair of them trooped towards the entrance. As the doors sucked open, they disappeared inside, letting a smell of antiseptic drift out of the reception, slashing through the fog of cigarette smoke. It hit me and made me want to puke. I watched the guy in the wheelchair sit there in his dressing gown and socks. The woman pushing the chair was half his age and four times his weight. Could've been his daughter. He smoked his cigarette in his twig-like hand. His eye met mine.

I turned away from the crowd and stepped out of the hospital. The first thing I saw was a black Range Rover parked to the left of the door, a few cars down. I felt like I was seeing them everywhere now. Like I was being watched. I turned right and walked a few paces away from the door and found a quiet spot around the corner, a slip of a road called Nightingale Place, flanked by a Starbucks and a seven-storey block of vanilla-coloured flats. They were supposed to be swish and desirable. They looked cold and utilitarian to me. A bunch of For Sale signs were stickered to the windows. Someone ever wants to get a snapshot of Britain in the twenty-first century, of what went wrong, they could do a hell of a lot worse than come pay a visit to Nightingale Place.

I walked away from the traffic of Fulham Road and looked over my shoulder. No Range Rover. I called the number back. Someone picked up second dial.

'At bloody last,' Rachel Kirk said. 'And there was Bull saying you're permanently glued to your phone. Seems to me like you're permanently missing things.'

'I was in a meeting.'

'Really. I was beginning to think you'd retired,' Rachel said. 'Probably about time.'

She sounded breathless. I could hear the din of office noise in the background. The clatter of keyboards and the bleat of office phones, underlined by the drone of a corporate aircon. working overtime.

'Now, why would I go and do a thing like that?'

'Look. I called to tell you something.' Rachel cutting to the chase. Her voice was serious and hushed.

'Jack? Are you there?'

I got the impression she was speaking discreetly into her phone. Like she was making a call that she didn't want anyone to overhear. Not easy in today's open-planned nightmares.

'I'm here,' I said. 'I'm listening.'

'There's a lot of rumours around here that the guys over at the *Daily* are going to run a story.'

Dailies and their sister Sunday papers have oddly dysfunctional relationships. They're usually owned by the same overall Group, and often occupy the same building, though not necessarily the same floors. But there's an inherent distrust between the two. Both sides have their own beef: the dailies employ more staff than the Sundays and the Sundays have more cash to spend on big stories. The Dailies think the Sundays are sleazy and have it easy, only producing one paper a week and with all that money to spend. The Sundays think they pay for the Dailies' existence so they should stop moaning and be grateful. And as for the two trusting each other, there was more chance of me sprouting wings and flying to Barbados.

At the *Legend* there were maybe thirty people on the Sunday edition. The weekday paper had double that on the payroll. The us-against-them mentality at play meant that information and sources were never shared between the papers. Same for stories that were about to break.

I said, 'What are they running?'

Rachel said, 'It's about Pryor.'

I froze.

Rachel said, 'It's a big, big story. And it's running tomorrow.'

I blazed up. Like someone had doused me in petrol and lit a match. And yet, these are the moments when I really come into my own. Some people panic, it's like they lose control. They surrender. Me, I somehow manage to crawl away from the fear. I find my calm place in the back of my head, away from the noise and the fear. I shut the door on the world. I stay in that calm place until I have figured out what to do. I crawled into my calm place now and said, 'What kind of story are we talking about?'

Rachel was quiet for a few seconds. I heard people chatting away in the background. Then the chatter faded and she came back on the line.

'I'm not sure exactly,' she said.

'How did you hear about this?' I asked, knowing that the *Daily Legend* would have fought hard to keep this story locked down.

'I didn't. Bull did,' she said, suddenly throwing everything into clear light. Rachel wasn't calling me because she was looking out for me. Bull had asked her to put in the call, being indisposed himself, and she was just seeing through the favour.

'What else did he tell you?'

I could almost hear Rachel shrug.

'That was it. He just said to pass on the message.'

'There must be something else,' I said. 'Think.'

Another pause. Loaded with anger. I waited for Rachel to give it to me with both barrels. I know when women are about to lose their rag at me. I've seen it more than enough times. First they fall really quiet. Rachel fell really quiet. Then they let you have it. And Rachel let me have it.

'I'm not your bloody secretary, Jack. Nick asked me to call you and give you the message. I did that. And you didn't even say thank you for calling you, when I've got a million good reasons not to want to speak to you ever again. Looks like you failed this time, Jack. Retirement might be your best option after all. Goodbye.'

Click.

I stood there, angry and numb. That feeling you get when you're so cold that it actually burns your skin. That's how I felt all over. I stood on Nightingale Place, listening to the dead air of the dial tone coming down the line, and wondering how much worse it was going to get for Adam Pryor, and for me. I needed a new plan.

I ducked out of Nightingale Place and paced east along Fulham Road. Headed away from the Chelsea and Westminster Hospital and the BMW brooding out front, slick and black, like a beached whale. I figured Pryor wouldn't miss me. He had a sister to interrogate. Questions to answer. I had another story that needed killing, and I needed something to clear my head. It was either a brisk walk or a large measure of Jack Daniel's, and I figured it was a little too early for Jack.

I schlepped down the street. Took out my mobile and dialled Bull. Hoped he would pick up, because my battery was at 4% and about to die. I made a mental note that I should get rich by inventing the world's longest-lasting battery. Probably easier than babysitting Pryor. Bull didn't answer. I got his gruff voicemail –

You know the drill. Either leave a message or don't. Impatient as ever. I didn't leave a message.

Grand old redbrick mansion blocks gazed down at me. Looked like old boarding schools stacked on top of one another. The shops in the street were entirely of the kind that rich people frequent. Boutique and discreet and unnecessary. If you wanted an ancient Japanese vase or an antique globe of the world, this was your market. I wondered where people around here bought things like toilet paper and milk. Maybe they didn't need things like toilet paper and milk, in the bubble of richness they inhabited. I didn't know.

I had a text.

'Where are you? Call me.'

Pryor. I hit delete on the text. He could wait awhile. I needed to speak to Bull first. I didn't want to get in any deeper until I had the inside story.

The streets were refreshingly clear by London standards. Meaning that I could walk in a straight line without being barged, elbowed or shanked. I am a London man, and as such am grateful for small mercies such as this in a way that your average town resident simply isn't. I revelled in the freedom of the pavement. I bounced down that road at a good speed, my mind in tune with my steps, gears grinding, doors opening, others closing.

I was drawing close to Sloane Square when Bull finally called me back.

'Not on the phone,' Bull said before I could get a word in edgeways. 'Where are you now?'

'Sloane Avenue,' I said. 'Corner of Fulham Road.'

'Meet me at by the Round Pond at Kensington Palace Gardens. Can you get there in twenty?'

'I can try,' I said.

I hung up, hooked a left on Sloane Avenue and increased my stride to a fast walk. I powered past rows of Georgian townhouses. The street seemed to exist on a loop. The same houses, the same cars. The same people jogging up and down the street. I hiked all the way up to South Kensington tube. There were gaggles of tourists craning their necks at the sun, wondering where it had gone, why it had abandoned them. Wondering, like most English people wonder, when the rain would come. I slipped past them. Swung north onto Exhibition Road and my meeting with Bull.

I checked my phone. Three missed calls and a voicemail, all from Pryor. A text from Zoe saying that she missed me. I wondered if she'd feel the same when she found out I had a daughter closer to her age than mine. But there was no point thinking about that now. It was out of my control.

As was my phone's battery, which hadn't magically recharged itself. Another half an hour and it'd be flat dead. I bought a ham-and-cheese sandwich and a packet of crisps from a shop – how very English, I thought – and got three-fifty in change from a tenner. As I emerged from the shop I had the strange sensation that someone was watching me. Strange, I say, because that neck of the Kensington woods is crammed with people and at that moment there probably were several people looking at me. It's the nature of crowds. I mean, when was the last time you took the train and didn't observe your fellow passengers? But I had never had this feeling before. I glanced around, looking for some type of suspicious character. Maybe a grizzled guy in a fedora and a black trench coat, or a shaven-headed tough with a bomber jacket and a PhD in torture. Saw nothing of the sort. Put it down to a lack of sleep and my over-active imagination, and carried on.

I crossed the road and made my way into Hyde Park on the

West Carriage Drive walkway. Headed north and west, away from the Serpentine, towards the aptly-named Round Pound at the edge of Kensington Palace Gardens. The crowds thinned out. The east side of the park is always busier than the west side. I could never figure out why. I looked around the pond for Bull. Couldn't see him. Didn't try to look harder. Bull is not a man you can very easily miss. So I found a bench overlooking the pond, sat down, and wolfed down great big mouthfuls of bread and meat. My stomach and I were friends again.

Then a voice at my back said, 'Leave some for the ducks, you fat bastard.'

Bull propped himself down on the bench next to me. I tossed my sandwich wrapper in the bin and left the crisps. He hitched up his trousers at the knees and squinted at me and said, 'You didn't return my calls last night.'

I said, 'You sound like my ex.'

Bull didn't laugh.

'This is serious, Jack.'

'I was tired,' I said. 'It's been a long couple of days. But I got your message from Rachel and called you right back. And here I am.' I turned face-on to Bull. 'So what's the deal with Pryor and the *Daily*?'

Bull dead-eyed me. He was the one person I knew at the *Sunday Legend* capable of squeezing information out of the *Daily*. And he knew I knew.

'They found a photo,' he said. 'At Scannell's place. The *Daily* guys. Well, not them. The maid found it. They gave her a small bundle of Queen's heads.'

'What's the photo?'

Bull leaned in to me.

'Scannell getting his rocks off.'

'So?'

'Scannell getting his rocks off with a teenager.'

I frowned at Bull.

'He topped himself because he slept with a teenage girl?'

'Teenage *boy*,' said Bull.

Christ, said my mind. I searched the pond for answers. I looked back at Bull.

'Do the police know?'

'Do they fuck. The *Daily* are going to lead with it tomorrow. Biggest story of the year. Ticks all the boxes. Secretly gay high profile MP, supposedly happily married with kids, commits suicide. Like something from a soap opera. I overheard a couple of them talking about it over their fags outside. Bastards looking so pleased with themselves.'

'You're just bitter they beat you to it,' I said, trying to be sharp and cynically funny, and failing to pull it off.

Bull waved a hand at me.

'That's not real journalism anyway. Slipping some poor foreigner a few quid.' Then he narrowed his eyes at me. 'I heard about it, called you straight away. You need to get out of this mess you're in otherwise it will swallow you right up.'

'Why? What's Scannell got to do with me?'

'There's a link,' Bull said. 'A connection to what happened with your boy Pryor in Oxford. Scannell and his chum were in the same hotel as the one where you met Rachel Kirk. She recognised the place. Apparently the decor is distinctive.'

'Ever heard of the word coincidence?' I said, weakly. My mouth was dry.

Bull didn't even crack half a smile.

'Not when Scannell had been at a debate too and not when the bill was booked and paid for by the office of Edward Valentine.

Quite a regular occurrence there, according to the concierge, him coughing up for rooms other people stay in.'

'Have you found the boy?' I said.

Bull nodded. 'But we won't get anything from him. He's dead.'

I tried to hide the chilling effect those words had on me. Kat was still missing and she and this boy had played the same role.

'That's a shame,' I said. 'Would have been a great interview. What happened to him?'

'Accidental death,' Bull said. 'The local cops described it as "another drunk student falls in the river at the end of a night out." Happens regularly, apparently. Stupid way to go. That's why I don't drink near rivers.'

Bull lent forward, serious again.

'Jack,' he said. 'If you listen to what I say one more time in your life, make it now. You need to get yourself out of this. Away from Valentine and Pryor. I cannot tell you how important it is. You're in danger, boy. Serious danger. I don't know exactly what's going on here but Valentine is bad, bad news. The worst kind.'

It was there, gleaming like a flashing light on top of an ambulance, the connection between Edward Valentine, Andrew Scannell, Adam Pryor and an African mobile phone fortune. Billions of reasons why I should walk way and two why I couldn't: Kat and Zoe. Zoe's theory about Valentine wanting Kat to disappear forever didn't sound so ridiculous now. That would be the only way he could control her and it was becoming horribly clear to me that human lives didn't matter to him the way they did to most of us. Scannell was dead, too, and I couldn't be sure that was really suicide. And Pryor was next in line after Scannell.

'It's not that easy,' I said, and snapped my head away from Bull. The sky was smeared with clouds. They were smudged and heavy, like bags of cement.

'Why not?' said Bull. 'Just tell them you're not interested in the gig anymore, and walk away. Leave Pryor and Valentine to screw each other over. Take up that job offer with the Princess. Spend the rest of your days getting humiliated by me. What's so difficult about that?'

I said nothing.

In the corner of my eye I saw a smirk crawl out along Bull's cavernous mouth.

'You dirty bastard,' he said. 'You dirty, stupid bastard.'

I still said nothing.

'Zoe?'

For a split second I blushed. Not because of any embarrassment over Zoe. But because I had been blindsided by Bull. I frantically asked myself how he knew about Zoe. Then I thought about Rachel. She would've filled in Bull. Picked his brains. She would've mentioned Zoe being Valentine's stepdaughter. He knew my track record. It didn't take a genius to piece that puzzle together.

'Tell me you're not serious, my boy. Tell me I'm wrong.'

I couldn't tell Bull about my fears for Kat so I kept my vow of silence and let him think whatever he wanted to.

'You're a fucking idiot.'

I jerked my head back and stared at Bull. Stared at the man who had told me I was a fucking idiot many hundreds of times, each time spoken viciously but warmly. Our own little code for addressing each other. This was the first time Bull had said those words and really meant them.

'She needs my help,' I said to Bull, surprising myself with the force and fury in my own voice.

'What I hear, she needs a month in the Priory.'

I shook my head. I wasn't sure why I was being so defensive of

Zoe. I figured she needed my protection. I figured Valentine was a cockroach that needed crushing. I figured that she was irresistible. It was a complicated situation, and not one I wanted to unpick with Bull.

'You're playing with fire, Jack.' He raised his open palms in front of him. 'That's all I'm going to say on the matter. You're a big boy. You know what you're getting in to. All I'm saying is, be careful.'

I nodded.

'What about the *Daily* story?'

'I don't have any sway with them downstairs. Not even the Princess does. And I can't go rooting around down there, they'll clam up faster than a priest on the witness stand. So I don't know how much Pryor will feature in the story. But I thought you at least deserved the heads-up.'

'I owe you,' I said to Bull.

'Add it to the two hundred whiskey sours already on your tab.'

I smiled. A genuine smile; the rarest sort. He was a good friend. The thought hit me in the chest that I was running out of friends fast.

Bull stroked his considerable chin. Stared thoughtfully at the pond. He looked like a man deciding where to bury a dead body. Here in the pond? Or over here by the copse of trees?

'Good luck, kid,' he said, and stood up.

We went our separate ways. I headed west out of the park towards High Street Kensington. Thought I'd wander the long walk back to Earl's Court. Armed cops were milling about, submachine guns slung dramatically across their shoulders. I counted eight of them.

I used the last dregs of juice in my phone to send a message to Karl Wake. I kept the message brief, like I always do. The message

I sent Wake contained a single phone number and a request for a search for all messages sent during a specific twenty-four-hour period. Pleased with myself, I tapped Send and continued towards my flat. My mobile had just enough time and battery to flash up the response from Wake.

'No problem,' the message read.

15

Zoe was up by the time I returned to the flat. She was sitting on my sofa with her phone in front of her. Her eyes were red and she looked like she'd been crying. I saw my suit jacket hanging over the back of one of the chairs. The jacket with the eleven grand stashed inside.

'I've called everyone,' she said. 'And no one has seen Kat. No one knows where she is. We have to do this, Jack, and it has to work.'

She stood up and put her arms around me.

'It'll be fine,' I said. 'I'll make sure of it.'

My voice sounded much more confident than I felt.

She whispered into my ear, 'Will you make me one promise?'

'Of course,' I said.

'No secrets, Jack.'

'No secrets.'

'Promise?'

'I promise,' I said. And meant it.

'OK then, who's the girl?'

'What girl?'

'In the photograph by your bed. Who is she? Your sister?'

'She's my daughter,' I said, without hesitation.

Zoe's eyes widened. 'Your daughter?'

I felt her attitude to me change. In an instant I'd become older, more complicated. A man with a grown-up or teenage daughter was not what a twenty-four year old girl was after and I could already feel distance appearing between us. I wanted to reverse that shift and the only chance I had to do that was tell her the truth.

'Her name is Emily,' I said, the words tumbling out fast. 'She was born seventeen years ago, when I was that age too. I was at school with her mother, Marina. The pregnancy wasn't planned and Marina's family lost it with her. They were madly religious and threatened to cut her off if she had an abortion. Then they tried to convince me to marry her, told me it was the right thing to do and so on, but I was terrified and said I wanted to go to university, have a career and all that. So I broke up with Marina. I didn't think I had a choice. I was a kid and I was scared and I didn't love Marina.

'And then she went off to university and met a guy there, when Emily was two months old. The two of them went the distance. Got married a year out of university and Emily has grown up with him. She has his surname, a stable home, parents together. I do what I can but I'm mostly in the background.'

'How old is she in the photo?'

'Seven. It's my favourite photo of her, that's why I keep it there.'

'She's beautiful.'

I felt the warm glow any parent feels when someone whose opinion they respect praises their child. And I thought maybe Zoe would accept Emily and me after all.

I knew it for sure when she spoke again. 'I wish I'd had a father like you,' she said quietly.

'That's not funny,' I said. 'I'm no kind of father at all.'

'You are,' she said. 'You're a good father. I can see how much you care about her. That makes you good.'

I leaned in and kissed her hard, and she kissed me hard back.

Half an hour later I was watching sunlight fizzle and crack behind the too-thin curtains on my bedroom window, and listening to Zoe sleep beside me. Her flat tummy softly pressed against my side, her parted lips sighing hot, sleepy sighs onto my shoulder. I listened to the slow rhythm of her breathing and wished I could stay here a while. I thought back to Bull. There was a voice picking away at the back of my head that I couldn't blot out. A voice that said maybe Bull was right and I was in too deep. Maybe I should have pushed Zoe away. Maybe being in the middle of Edward Valentine, Adam Pryor and Kat was more than enough already.

There were a lot of Maybes in my head. I tried not to think about them. I turned my thoughts to my plan. Checked my watch. One fifty-five. I carefully withdrew my arm from around Zoe's head and slid out of the bed. Zoe rolled dreamily away from me, and made a sound in the back of her throat. I groped around for my clothes. Slipped on my trousers, tucked in my shirt. I could hear Zoe stirring behind me.

'Coffee,' Zoe said groggily. 'Black, no sugar. Very strong.'

I turned around. Zoe was sitting upright. Her right hand was thrust down and planted on the mattress. Her left hand was ruffling her hair. Brushstroke blonde strands dangled across her face. She made a face at them, like she had a personal beef with her own hair. She blew them away, smiled widely at me.

'What's the matter? A girl can't ask for coffee?'

'Coffee isn't the problem,' I said.

She tucked the smile away in some secret place I didn't know. Zoe struck me as the type of girl who had a lot of secret places.

'My step-father,' she said.

'We have to do something.'

'What about Kat?'

'She's still missing. We have to assume he had something to do with that.'

Zoe nodded quickly, like she didn't want to dwell on the thought. Neither of us did. I did us both a favour and moved quickly on.

There was something else on my mind. I had to know if Zoe was involved in what Valentine did with Scannell.

I said, 'I think your step-father was blackmailing Scannell.'

Zoe drew a blank look.

'Pryor's boss. The one doing a good impression of a dead man.'

'I thought he killed himself.'

I hesitated to go on. Did I tell Zoe about Bull and the *Daily Legend* getting their hands on the snap? I had to keep reminding myself that she was Valentine's step-daughter. That crack of doubt was beginning to split open inside me.

'I think he knows why Scannell topped himself,' I said. Zoe was quiet. She stared out of the window at the foamy London sunshine. She knew nothing about Scannell. Her reaction had just told me that.

'What do you want to do?' she said.

I buttoned up my sleeves. One by one.

Then I said, 'I have an idea. I think it could work, and it could get us both some answers. But it's going to mean doing some serious damage to your step-father.'

Zoe shuddered, like someone had blasted cold air over her. She looked away from the window. But she didn't fully turn to me. She was looking at me side-on, over the smooth curve of her shoulder, and the light is never great in my room but I swore I could see a tear growing under the curve of her right eye. Tracing a slow route down her cheek.

She kept on half-looking at me and half-not and said, 'I'm in. I can't live like this anymore.'

I waited for a little over an hour. Zoe spent the time showering and getting dressed. I passed the minutes in the living room. Made a phone call. Made a reservation. Then I hung up and sat there and listened to the furious hiss of the shower, looking out of the window, watching daylight seeping away. The sun was a purple cuticle on the horizon. The sky was cloudless and the colour of black denim. The shower stopped hissing. I ran through the plan in my head for the hundredth time. It wasn't perfect. There were weak points, plenty of things that could go wrong. But it was the best I could come up with. If it failed, it wouldn't have been for a lack of trying.

At a little past three o'clock I booked a taxi. Gave the operator my address. Then I gave him an address in Central London. The guy repeated both addresses to me. I felt we were getting somewhere. Zoe sauntered out of the bedroom and sat on my lap. Her hair was wet at the ends. The nape of her neck was like satin. I kissed her skin. It tasted like lavender. She bounced to her feet and did a little twirl. She had changed clothes. The roll-necked jumper and tracksuit trousers were ancient history. She was wearing a black skirt that finished just above the knee. The upper half of the skirt was overlaid by a matching black shirt with a classic-style collar, short sleeves and low neck revealing a generous amount of flesh. The shirt dipped at the back, ran a slinky curve down from the small of her back to the finish line on the skirt. She had a pair of white leather ballet shoes on her feet. They were classy. Like the rest of her. I gave her a look that said I was impressed. Inside, I was more than impressed. I was blown away.

The downstairs buzzer squawked.

'That's our ride,' I said, peeling myself off the chair. Zoe suddenly looked sad. I caught her eye and said, 'If you don't want to go ahead with this, I understand. No one's forcing you to do anything.'

Zoe shook her head.

'No. I want to do this, Jack.'

Her eyes met mine.

'I want to make that bastard pay.'

The taxi weaved and nosed its way towards Hammersmith Road. It was a brief ride. North on Earl's Court Road, west on West Cromwell Road, north again on Warwick Road. West again onto Hammersmith Road. The driver was the world's quietest cabbie. He didn't say a word from start to finish.

We turned north along Holland Park Road. We flew past Shepherd's Bush tube station and the tatty, downtrodden thoroughfare that snaked past a shopping centre that looked more like a giant crashed UFO. The shopping centre seemed to stretch on forever. Crowds of people were shuffling in and out of the doors, lugging designer shopping bags. Any newspaper tries to convince you times are bad and the economy is taking its toll and the bankers should be crucified, take them down to Westfield. At the tip of West Cross Road the taxi driver hit the Westway roundabout and pelted us east along the concrete overpass.

As we rolled along I noticed Zoe shooting a perplexed look at me.

'What's in the bag?' she asked, looking at the black gym bag I'd brought out with me from my flat.

'A present for your step-father,' I said.

'He doesn't like presents, never has,' Zoe said coldly. 'Whenever we tried to give him anything he always said he already had everything he wanted in me and Mum. Those words had a different meaning when I was a kid.'

'Trust me,' I said, 'This is one present he'll want to keep.'

'I trust you. The gadgets are all part of the plan, right?'

I nodded.

We went quiet again as London flew past beneath us, like a rapidly-flowing river of grey and brown.

I gave the driver two twenties and told him to keep the change. Then I hopped out of the taxi and grabbed the gym bag. Zoe joined me. Entwined her fingers with mine. Inside I felt warmer than I had in years.

A smug porter ushered us through a set of revolving glass doors. Zoe was behind me. I glanced back at her. Flashed her a reassuring smile. But she didn't seem to need it. Her face was strict and severe. I felt sorry for her again, having to become so hard. Despite all the privileges life had given her, Zoe had a kind of inner steel to her that I had to respect. She could have accepted her lot and I suppose some people settle for that trade-off, which is why many of the rich faces that smile in front of the cameras are so miserable when the camera turns away. But not Zoe. She wanted a real life, free from her step-father. She wanted to bring Valentine down as badly as I did. Maybe even more.

Our usher guided us across the lobby towards the reception. Everything was made of marble. The floors. The reception desk. The accents. It was the kind of place that tried to recreate a nostalgic ideal of Britain. The staff were dressed like Victorian butlers. There was a boutique selling Mulberry and Prada handbags. The shop was empty. I asked myself who the hell would buy their accessories in a five-star hotel. From the restaurant I heard the clinking of silver spoons against porcelain teacups, and the polite chatter, peculiar to rich people of a certain type, who valued discretion above ostentation. To people like me they were flamboyant, but not when compared to an oligarch's tastes.

Calming classical music tinkled discreetly out of unseen speakers. Or maybe someone was playing it live. It was the kind of place that might well pay a small fortune to a musician to sit there and fill their patrons' ears with pleasant sounds for ten hours a day, just for the sheer hell of it. A moderately famous comedian cut across our path. The chap turned at me and made a face, as if he recognized me. He was more famous for being fat than funny. Any other day I would've stopped, introduced myself, told him to give me a call someday. I could have networked the bejesus out of this place. Today though, I blanked him. Marched straight on for the reception desk and drew a frosted smile like dried blood from the brunette receptionist. A brass name badge told me her name was Evelina. 'Good afternoon,' the woman said, voice like she was chewing glass.

Zoe whispered into my ear, 'I heard that Victoria Beckham stayed here for a month.'

'I have a reservation,' I sad. 'Name of Jack Winter.'

Evelina tapped away at various keys in front of her.

'Two rooms,' she said after a pause.

'That's right,' I said.

'312 and 313?

'That's right,' I said again.

'And how will you be paying, sir?'

Said it in a way that actually asked a whole other question. Asking me, *Can you really afford a place like this, sir?* I handed her a black credit card and gave her a look which said, *Yes, a lot more easily than you can.*

She took the card and put it in a machine behind the counter. I tapped my pin number into a separate bit of kit and she gave me my card back in silence. Then she hit a few more keys and handed me two credit-card style swipe cards, and followed up with a bored run-through of the smoking policy and the special on today's menu and the dress code for the restaurant. It was a speech she gave maybe fifty times a day. I nodded like I cared.

The porter had been loitering behind Zoe the whole time. Now he rode with us in the lift to the third floor and took us down a warren of exquisitely-decorated corridors until we arrived at 312 and 313. The doors were next to each other and some seven metres apart. The porter went through an entirely unnecessary demonstration of how to swipe open the door locks, then waited patiently for me to fish out a tip from my pockets. I had a ten in coinage. I dumped the change in his palm. He frowned. Probably expected a couple of fifties, given the cost of the room. But the room was a necessary expense. The porter wasn't. His bad luck. He turned on his heels in a huff. We stepped into room 312, Zoe first, and I closed the door behind me.

Zoe looked at the room approvingly. It was bigger than my flat. It was certainly worth more per square metre too. The furniture was dark wood and intricately carved and the pictures on the walls looked Victorian to my untrained eye. The bed was the biggest I'd ever seen and the white duvet gave off a delicate, silky shine. There were two bedside tables and a desk with a Sony VAIO laptop open on it with a WELCOME TO REDBOROUGH screensaver playing out. There was a forty-inch flat-screen TV framed in an antique walnut unit. A fruit flower bouquet sat proudly on the desk, pineapples cut to look like sunflowers and watermelons arranged like leaves. If you weren't impressed with this place, you were either a billionaire or dead.

Zoe checked out the bathroom. I dumped the gym bag on the end of the bed. Unzipped it. Smiled. Inside was an iPad, a USB receiver, some batteries and a video camera and microphone. Except the video camera and microphone didn't look like spying equipment. They looked like a normal TV remote control.

Packed into one small black box, with SONY stamped on the front, it was a brilliant tool. No one thought anything suspicious of a remote control. Even if you looked closer, it didn't look dodgy. It had the normal battery spaces, it's just in this device they were used to power the video camera and microphone and then transmit the information to the receiver plugged into my iPad. This kind of stunt was so much easier now than when I started as a journalist. These days, you bought the kit, downloaded the app onto your iPad and away you went. Ready to go in five minutes.

All Zoe needed to do was remember to point the front of the remote control at what she wanted to video. And I knew she was too clever to mess up something like that.

When I was done, I returned to 312 and told Zoe to call Valentine. At my request she had been ignoring calls from him for the past twenty-four-hours. I knew Valentine would be desperate to get in touch with Zoe. As far as he knew, his daughter was off the grid and a loose end. I was sure that someone like Valentine viewed Zoe as a family member second and an asset first. As soon as she got in touch, he'd want to pin her down and make sure she wasn't about to compromise his plan with Pryor. But I also needed a carrot to tempt Valentine out from behind cover.

I sat in with Zoe while she made the call. She was great. She forced up a few tears. Her voice was cracked and papery, and she struck a beautiful balance between worried and hysterical. I could hear Valentine sweating on the other end of the line. She told him they needed to meet. She told him she thought she knew where Kat was. That got Valentine hopping mad. Zoe told him she was staying at the Redborough. She told him to be there in an hour. She told him she was in Room 313.

It was now getting on for six o'clock. Soon as Zoe killed the call I winked at her and said, 'We're almost there. Big night ahead of us. Let's eat.'

I called up room service and ordered a classic quarter pounder with chunky chips and a Diet Coke. Zoe went for a crab and langoustine spaghetti with a sparkling mineral water. Half an hour later, I was feasting on my burger, the first solid food I'd had since the sandwich with Bull some seven hours earlier at the park. I could have done with a little more industrial grease, but it hit the spot. Zoe picked tentatively at her plate, only managing a couple of mouthfuls. She wasn't feeling hungry. I didn't blame her. She was about to help me drive a train through her step-father's world. It doesn't matter if your dad is a tyrant. Family is family, and I appreciated what a difficult thing this was for Zoe to do, especially with her sick mother in the background. I stroked her hand and smiled at her. She smiled hopefully back, like she was daring to think of a life free from her step-father's shadow, for the first time.

I said, 'Everything's going to be alright, you know.'

She held the smile. Took a lot out of her, holding it like that. I could see the strain in her eyes. She said, 'I really want to believe you.'

We both fell silent. Zoe went back to picking at her food.

'So how is this going to work?' she asked, stabbing a piece of langoustine with her fork. 'You're going to be in here, and I'm going to be in the next room?'

I nodded.

'I've rigged it up so I'll have live audio and video feed. Everything you say will be played back live to me on the iPad, and it'll be recording at the same time.'

'Video too?' Zoe looked anxiously at me. 'Is that necessary, Jack?'

'Video is always better than just audio,' I said, feeding her one of my well-rehearsed lines. 'If we heard about man landing on the Moon but didn't see the video, no one would have believed Neil Armstrong about his small step for man.'

'What if he suspects something?'

'He won't,' I said. 'The camera and microphone are tiny.'

'You don't know my step-father,' she said. 'He's wicked but very sharp. He sees things everyone else misses. He's already going to be suspicious, all this Kat business. I shouldn't have said anything.'

Her voice was rising word by word. She was getting hysterical. I had to calm her down.

'We had to dangle Kat in front of him, to get his attention. It's a win-win for us. If he has Kat, he'll want to know why you lied or what you know. If he doesn't know where she is, he'll be desperate to find her. We'll find out either way. And remember, I'm right next door, listening in. If he tries anything, I'll come and grab you. But he won't. Trust me.'

I tried to make eye contact with Zoe. But it was impossible. She wasn't looking anywhere. She was staring into a void no one else could see.

'There's nothing to worry about,' I went on. 'You're safe with me, Zoe.'

She snapped out of her stupor. Shuddered, as if trying to shake off a grim thought. She stood up. Paced a couple of steps and stopped. Frowned, like she was trying to remember where X marked the spot.

'So what am I supposed to do?' she said.

'Just keep him talking,' I said. 'Guilty people, they talk long enough, sooner or later they slip up. Get him on to the subject of Pryor. Why it didn't work out this time. And the six MPs you slept with before. We need to know every detail from Valentine. All we have so far is rumours. But if Pryor is right, and we get Valentine confessing on camera, we have him bang to rights.'

Zoe's phone buzzed.

She stopped wearing a line into the floor.

Both of us eyeballed the phone. It was lying upright on the corner of the queen bed, screen glowing iridescent, the handset vibrating urgently. Zoe seized the phone. Didn't look at me. Swiped to take the call. It lasted all of ten seconds. Then she hung up and let the phone tumble out of her limp hand and drop to the bed.

'He's here,' she said.

16

Zoe rushed out of the door. I turned to my iPad. Panic rushed through my system. In the rush to prepare the room next door and prep Zoe, I'd forgotten to do a check on the camera and mic. I didn't know if the sound and video feed were working. I frantically hit the iPad camera app. My left foot tapped out a tune of tension as I waited for the screen to burst into life. It took forever. It took longer than forever. It took so long I was halfway to convincing myself that the feed wasn't working. I could feel my one shot at nailing Valentine slipping through my fingers. Then the screen faded out of black, came alive with colour, and broadcast a shot of the face of Edward Valentine.

If this was a guy who was pleased to see his daughter, he wasn't showing it. He started to fake-smile at Zoe and quit halfway through. The thought struck me that I had never actually seen Valentine in the flesh. He had been a face on the TV. Then he had been a voice on the other end of a phone. Now I was seeing the guy for the first time. Not quite face-to-face, I'll admit, but this was as close as dammit to the real thing. And I was struck, too, by the difference between the way he came across when he knew the camera was rolling, and his body language when he thought the camera was switched off.

I said before my professional interest in Valentine began with an appearance on TV. He had looked cold and arrogant and acted as if the studio and the female presenter were nuisances, like vermin in his kitchen. Or my kitchen. I suspect Valentine's kitchen hasn't seen vermin for a long time. Back then I had thought he needed coaching, to bring out his warm side – the one I heard on the phone – and come across like he was really enjoying himself.

But now there seemed to be no possibility of there being a warm side to Valentine. His slightly round face was set like stone. His bright blue eyes and thick salt and pepper hair was swept back above a mouth strict with tension. His lips were so straight you could balance a spirit level on them. His skin had an odd plasticky texture to it. He was medium height and apart from a slight paunch above his belt physically very average. Like most people, he looked much bigger on television.

Valentine appeared awkward on television, but in person he looked like he would have been a prime target for bullying at school. Maybe he was bullied. And maybe those experiences made him the ruthless bastard he was now. He wouldn't have been the first to react that way to hard times.

The screen shuffled and skipped and there was a muffled sound, like someone screwing up paper into a ball, as Zoe sat down on the armchair in room 313. Valentine remained standing. He was wearing a sharkskin suit, slate grey, wool, single-breasted with a two-button jacket. His shirt was immaculate white and his tie was a silk thing with a pansy blossom pattern on it. His shoes were brown-leather dust-point lace-ups. All perfect and all expensive, like he dressed to make a point about himself.

'I'm okay,' Zoe said. Valentine hadn't asked but she told him anyway. There was a distance between them. More like a chasm. It seemed to be that kind of relationship. 'This whole business with Kat has got me worked up.'

Valentine's breathing was heavy. I could hear it booming down the mike, like a brewing storm. He was stressed. Either that, or he had taken the stairs.

'I don't have all day. Tell me what you know,' Valentine said.

Zoe lowered her head.

'I know. I'm sorry.'

'You said you know where Kat is.'

'I said I *thought* I *might* know where she is.'

Valentine huffed impatiently, like a kid being told to put back a toy in a toy store. 'Well, do you or don't you know?'

Zoe shrugged casually.

'I thought we might be able to work it out together,' she said.

Valentine shook his head. There was anger in his voice.

'You don't know anything, do you? Tell me you don't know anything.'

Valentine folded his hands in front of him, like a man paying his respects to the dead. He took a deep breath. His eyes bored holes into Zoe. I could see why she lived in fear of the man. I was in another room, watching on a screen and still felt the bad vibes coming from his eyes.

'This is all Kat's fault,' Valentine suddenly burst out. 'That little fucking slut.'

He practically snorted the words. Zoe jumped a little. If I'm honest, I did too. It was a flash of a vicious streak I hadn't seen before.

'I knew she would be trouble,' he went on. 'The ones who look so innocent always are. Some English rose she turned out to be. Jesus. Look at the mess she's got us in now. You see me doing this so I can put out fires for our friend in the Cabinet? Paying that damned Winter a small fortune to keep him out of the headlines?'

Valentine's voice kept on rising.

'This was never a problem before. You know why? Because you kept your head low. I told you, no friends. No boyfriends. No problems. Stick to the plan and nothing can go wrong. You don't need sluts like Kat or boyfriends when you've got me to take care of you. I've always been here for you, haven't I?'

Zoe was sniffing and crying into her hands.

'Haven't I?' Valentine asked again, his voice booming off the walls, roaring down the mic and out of the iPad.

'Yes,' Zoe replied into the clammy, moist warmth of her hands. She didn't raise her head. Like she was afraid to look her father in the eye. Then she said, 'I'm sorry, Daddy. It's all my fault.'

Valentine stopped short. His breathing went silent. He angled his head at his daughter.

'What do you mean, your fault?'

'I didn't work hard enough at Adam Pryor. I mean, I tried to make him want me. I did, Daddy. But when I saw him leaning towards Kat, I didn't do enough to stop him. I let it happen. I let Pryor go for Kat. I'm sorry.'

Valentine went to say something, but Zoe kept going on now, letting it all out. I felt beads of sweat secreting out of the palms of my hands.

'Please don't be mad at me. I just didn't want to go through it all again. You don't know what it's like, Daddy. It's horrible.'

It was like Zoe had flicked a switch inside Valentine's head, the one marked 'Daddy'. The anger drained from his head all the way down to his feet. He took a couple of soft steps towards Zoe and reached down for her right hand. Cupped it between his and soothed her.

'I know how hard it is for you,' said Valentine.

I couldn't believe what I was seeing. His voice was smooth and frail. I had assumed Zoe was putting on an act, to lure Valentine into spilling his guts. But now, watching him comfort her like a father would, I wasn't quite so sure. He pulled her to her feet and she turned to face him, with her back to the camera. And then hugged her. Actually hugged her. I could see his face over her left shoulder and he smiled with what looked like genuine tenderness.

'Remember the deal?' said Valentine.

'Of course,' Zoe said. She'd turned her face to her right side, away from Valentine's. I wondered if she did that because she didn't want to look at him or because she was clever and realised the camera and microphone would catch what she said much better that way.

'One million for every MP we get.' Valentine's voice dropped to a whisper. I was barely picking up his voice. 'You remember what else I said, sweetheart?'

Zoe said, 'Pryor was the last one.'

'That's right. After him, no more of this. I promise.'

'I don't want to do it anymore,' she said.

'I know,' he said. 'You've done so well for me. You know I want you to be happy. I want the best for you, Zoe. I always have. And I will look after you and your mother. You know I will. I just need you to hold out for a little longer. Can you do that?'

Zoe looked over her shoulder, eyes focused on the wall but as if she could see me through it. I found myself touching her face on the screen.

'Yes,' she said to the camera. To me. 'I can do that.'

'Good girl,' said Valentine.

Zoe said nothing.

'You know I love you.'

Zoe still said nothing.

Valentine started stroking Zoe's back with his right hand, up and down. His hand moved up to her hair and for a second it seemed that in a warped way he really did care about Zoe.

And then his right hand moved down from Zoe's hair, over her back to the waistline of her skirt. He turned his face into her neck and inhaled deeply. I looked closer at the image playing out on the iPad screen. Something wasn't right.

Valentine traced his right down past the top of her skirt and onto the curves under the material. He pressed his hand hard against her and moaned. Zoe's eyes were clamped shut, like she was desperately trying to imagine herself somewhere else.

'You'll always be my little sweetheart,' Valentine said.

He turned Zoe round, spun her with force, so she was facing me with him standing behind her, his hands on her shoulders. He looked at her in the mirror. Her head was dipped and I couldn't see her eyes.

Then he moved his right hand down the front of her chest and ran it inside the left side of her blouse. He moaned again and his hand moved under the fabric and all I could do was sit and watch.

'We had some good times, didn't we,' Valentine said, his voice slightly breathless. 'It's been too long.'

His left hand moved to her stomach and pushed her body back into his. Zoe seemed to barely be there. She wasn't resisting Valentine but she wasn't responding to him either. Her body, with her face virtually out of my sight, seemed like a shell.

I was about ready to heave up the quarter pounder. I knew I couldn't just sit and watch this. Whatever had happened in the past – and it was obvious this was not new – was exactly that, the past. If I let events unfold next door, any kind of future Zoe and I might have would be blown to pieces. I already had a confession to use against Valentine on the video. This next part wasn't needed.

I would crash straight into the room, I decided. I had the key. That would be enough to stop Valentine, simply the sight of me in there with them.

On the screen Valentine's hand was still in Zoe's blouse.

I stood up. It was time to do the right thing.

And then Zoe spoke, quietly but with power.

'No,' she said. 'Please, no. I don't want you to do this.'

'You don't mean that,' Valentine said. 'I know you want this as much as I do.'

'I don't,' she said. 'I don't want this. Please, stop it.'

Her voice was even and firm. Maybe I wouldn't need to go in there after all.

Valentine looked up from Zoe's neck, trying to see her face in the mirror. But she was still looking to the side, away from him. I had a clear view of his face and he looked truly surprised by what Zoe was saying. He took his hands off and moved away a step. The surprise on his face gave way to a snarl and his right hand shot out, grabbed Zoe's right shoulder and span her round to face him. His right hand dropped back to his side and instantly moved upwards again, whipping out towards her cheek. I had never seen a man hit a woman before and the noise of the slap made me shudder. One part of me wanted to hold Zoe, to comfort her and tell her I'd always protect her. Another part wanted to take a baseball bat to Valentine's face. The final part felt ashamed for putting her in that room with him.

Zoe didn't make a sound. She just dipped her head. I wondered if that wasn't the first time Valentine had hit her and felt a bitter, deep hatred for the man.

'Fine,' he said. 'Have it your way. I'll let you off this time because I know you're worried about Kat. But don't expect me to be so understanding next time. I do things for you and you do things for me. That's our deal. It wouldn't be good for your mother if our arrangement ended. You should remember that.'

Zoe stood where Valentine left her. Perfectly still, her back to me. He moved out of shot on my screen and the door clicked open and then shut again loudly.

I heard Valentine's footsteps padding past my door. Expensive leather on expensive carpet. Then he stopped in front of my door. His shadow cut out the light sludging through the quarter-inch gap between the bottom of the door and the carpet. I stayed perfectly still. He moved on. I looked back at the iPad. Zoe still hadn't moved. I counted to twenty, until I was certain that Valentine was not coming back, and then I quietly slipped out of my room and knocked on the door of 313.

In a way I was glad I hadn't burst in and tried to smash Valentine's face in. As much as I hated to see Zoe suffering, the video was proof of his actions. And I didn't want Valentine to know that I was working against him, because that would scupper the rest of my plan. Besides, I'm no good in fights or barging down doors and it wouldn't have helped either of us if Valentine's bodyguard had appeared and broken my nose.

Zoe didn't come to the door. I knocked again, as gentle as one can rap their knuckles on a solid walnut door. Waited. And waited some more. A minute later Zoe sprung open the door. She had washed her face. There were blotches of mascara running like dirty rainwater out of the corners of her eyes and down her face. She had a red mark on her left cheek and wouldn't look me in the eye. She stood in the doorway, not really blocking the entrance but not really wanting me to come in either. She looked helpless and numb. In the end I took control, took Zoe by the hand and guided her back to room 312. Sat her down on the edge of the bed. I figured the quicker she was away from the scene of the crime, the better.

'Now you know,' she said. 'Step-father and stepdaughter. It's such a cliché.'

'I'm sorry,' I said.

'Don't be,' Zoe said. 'It's nothing to do with you.'

'Does anyone know?'

Zoe shook her head. 'That's why it's been going on for so long. I can't tell anyone. If I do, he'll abandon her.'

'Your mother?'

'Yes,' Zoe said, a resigned, numb tone in her voice. 'Because of her he owns me. I have to do what he says. That's my life.'

'Not for much longer,' I said. 'Now we've got that video he'll go down so hard, he'll never come back up. Do you see? It's better this way. It's all there. He can't deny what went on, with you or the MPs. Not now. We'll get him. We'll make him pay. I promise.'

Zoe sniffed a reply. Her eyes flicked around the room, as if seeing it for the very first time.

'I need a drink,' she said.

'Sure,' I said. I reached for the complimentary bottle of San Pellegrino on the desk. Grabbed a couple of upside-down tumblers. I was feeling pretty parched myself. I quickly loaded up the tumblers. Went to hand one to Zoe. But she had uprooted from the bed. She was kneeling by the table. She had cracked open the door disguising the mini-bar. She was grabbing drinks out of the cooler, ripping the caps off and necking them clean, one after the other. I watched emptied miniatures stack up around her feet. Vodka, rum, gin, cognac, anything she found, she drank. I knew trying to stop her was pointless. They say alcohol only makes things worse. But how could this get any worse for Zoe?

She tipped a final bottle of whisky down her throat and collapsed in a heap against the bed. She'd smashed down ten mini bottles. All that was left inside were two soda-sized cans of lager, and I doubt very much Zoe had had so much as a drop of lager her whole life.

I didn't know what to do. I racked my brain for something to say and drew a blank. My whole adult life I'd been comforting women, sometimes when I needed something from them, like a name, or an eyewitness account, or even a mobile phone. I had reassured women who had been assaulted, women who had been dating murderers and married to terrorists, women who had survived stab wounds to the head and been kidnapped in Afghanistan. But those women weren't real to me. They were stories, sources of information. I was involved with Zoe and Valentine in very different way; this was personal and intense. What do you say to a person who's been through that and when their darkest secret has been revealed to you?

I let the silence play out between us. Heard nothing but the Zoe's heavy breathing as she let all the anger out, and kept all the tears locked in.

Then I said, 'How long has it been going on?'

'Long enough,' Zoe said. 'Put it this way, he's been with my mother since before I can remember and he started with me when I was old enough to understand what would happen if he dropped her.'

I tried to think of something else to say. I felt like a driver turning up to the funeral of the little girl he accidentally hit. There was nothing in me but guilt. Maybe because I had watched the whole thing, that made me a part of it. Maybe not, I thought. Maybe because I set up the damned meeting and sent Zoe into a closed room with the step-father who has been abusing her for God knows how long. Maybe that's why I felt bad and she didn't want to talk about it. I felt helpless and angry and lost.

But not for long. Because this time tomorrow Valentine would be the one swimming in a pool of despair. I would do it for Zoe and I would do it for Kat, and for Pryor and Scannell and everyone who had been burned by Valentine. I would fix it for all of them. No more living with nightmares.

I turned to look at Zoe and almost jumped when I saw she was staring at me, with clear, intense eyes. To be able to do that after sinking all that alcohol was something I thought only Bull could do. She was a remarkable girl.

But something in Zoe's stare made me uncomfortable. She didn't look vulnerable any more. She looked like she'd made up her mind about something and was about to tell me. I felt like a guy who'd realised in a flash of subconscious calculation that he was about to be dumped.

'I can't do it,' she said, coldly. 'I'm sorry, Jack, but I can't do it. We have to wipe that video and find another way.'

'Why?' I said, pathetically.

'My mother,' Zoe said. 'Whatever we threaten him with, he has something bigger and worse to do to me. I don't care about the MPs or even Kat, really. Not next to my mother. And if the video goes public it'll be even worse. The world will know what he is and that would destroy her. Whatever we do, I lose. I'm sorry but I can't do this. It would kill my mother.'

I couldn't argue with Zoe because she was right. We hadn't thought it through properly. I hadn't thought it through properly. Whatever we did with that video, threatened Valentine with it, gave it to the police or a newspaper, the consequences would be devastating for Zoe and her mother, whether it was his retaliation or the fallout from bringing him down. I should have realised that. Should have known everything had to boil down to Zoe's mother. I'd failed her and I'd failed Kat. I knew it and Zoe knew it. We had nothing on him.

I thought of the biggest regrets of my life: the time I didn't spend with my daughter, the little girl I could have saved but didn't and the life in newspapers which I threw away. Now I had a new one to put alongside them. I'd messed this up as well.

Zoe picked up another bottle of alcohol and emptied it.

'That won't help, you know,' I said, as images of Emily's mother passed out drunk rolled through my mind.

I knew immediately I should have kept quiet. I had no right to criticise her and the cold silence in the room told me she thought the same. Zoe stood up and squinted at me, like she was trying to blink the drink out of her eyes, wiped her mouth, and brushed past me and headed for the door. She opened it and looked at me.

'Jack, please leave. I need to be on my own now.'

I felt like she was saying goodbye to whatever we could have become if I hadn't just seen what I'd seen and got the plan so wrong. If it was what she wanted, I had to leave. I couldn't tell her how to feel.

I tried to catch her eye on the way out but she was looking back into the room. She didn't want me in there with her. Wanted to pretend I didn't exist so she could block out her hellish day. I could understand that.

I walked slowly down the corridor. Heard the door to Room 313 thud closed behind me. I closed my own door, slumped on the bed and closed my eyes. Thought about Zoe on the other side of the wall. Sleeping in the room where she'd thought her life could change for the better, where I'd built up her hopes and taken her trust and torn them to pieces.

I lay down on the bed with no idea what I was going to do tomorrow.

***

Steven Finch could hardly believe his luck as he sat at the desk in the corner of his workshop. Three grand for that old banger – what a touch. He put the cash in the pocket of his overalls and grinned. It would come in very handy.

When the woman appeared outside his garage first thing that morning he thought she was a copper. It was still dark and he hadn't seen her waiting by the gate so when she said, 'Excuse me', he assumed she was about to whip out a warrant and demand to know the histories of the cars he had in stock. Which would have caused him a lot of trouble very quickly.

But when he saw she was wearing sunglasses he realised she wasn't police after all. A crazy hooker, that's what he took her for next. A high class one, mind you, because she was a beauty. But still a pro. Probably high on coke too, judging by the way her head was twitching from side to side – paranoid, that's what she was.

But when she spoke again he realised she wasn't selling herself, or anything else.

'I want to buy a car,' she said. 'Now.'

Right there outside his little garage, for cash, she said.

'How about that one?' Steven said, pointing at the car which looked the least battered.

She offered two grand for it before he could get another word out. For a stolen fifteen-year-old Vauxhall Nova. Madness. She hadn't even heard the heap of junk start.

'Three and it's yours,' was Steven's instant response. He thought of himself as a man who never missed the chance to earn a few quid and it was good to prove it every now and then.

'Done,' the woman said, not even bothering to negotiate. 'But there's just one thing. You have to report the car stolen. This didn't happen.'

She said it like she thought he might have a problem with that.

Steven nearly laughed at her. But he managed to control himself and nodded.

'No worries,' he said. 'You were never here.'

And that was it. She got in and drove off.

Steven wondered briefly why she needed the car so urgently. And what her name was. But he didn't really care about either of those things. The three grand in his pocket mattered much more.

Part Five: Saturday

237

17

I woke early. Saturday morning, hazy with promise, seven-thirty and a smudge of purplish light was creeping through my window and projecting halos into the wall. I stretched and showered and let the boiling hot water work some feeling back into my bones. My clothes were wrinkled and fuzzy. They felt less expensive and fine than when I slipped them on at my flat yesterday.

I wanted to see Zoe, to talk to her, to work out where we were going from here. But I didn't beat down a path to her door. Instead, I dithered in my room. Turned on the TV and flicked over to Sky News, like I always did. Bad habits die hard, I guess. Put the volume on low and pointlessly arranged bits and pieces.

I checked my emails. I emptied my spam folder. I noticed an odd scuff mark on one of my shoes. I was doing everything I physically could to avoid knocking on the door to room 313. Part of me wanted to comfort Zoe, sure. But a bigger part of me was afraid of stepping into that room.

Eventually I manned up, and headed for the door.

Then I froze.

Part of me had suspected that Zoe would be gone already. And maybe in a selfish way I secretly wanted it to be like that too. It was less awkward like this, for both of us.

I opened the note, expecting it to say she'd gone away and take care, short and sweet and to the point, much like Zoe herself. Which is why I hadn't expected Zoe to leave a note at all. I kind of suspected she would just breeze out into the Big Smoke and head off to wherever people like Zoe head off when their head is being pulled in a million different directions. Probably somewhere with a lot of vodka. Shame, I thought, and added a fresh regret to my long list.

I sat calmly down on the old chair. Drummed my fingers on the old desk. People had probably been drumming their fingers at this old piece of junk for hundreds of years. I started to read. *Jack*, she wrote, no *Dear* or *Hi*, just my name. The word was neatly written. One word in and the message was already clinical, emotionally detached. I could guess what was coming next.

Actually, no. Turned out I couldn't. The next few lines sucked the breath out of my lungs. The note read:

Kat's dead. The police called. They found her in the river and I have to go back to Oxford to officially identify her body because her mother is too ill to do it. They found her phone in her pocket so they're already almost certain it's her.

It was my father. I know it was. He killed Kat. There's no other explanation. He can't be allowed to go on like this. I won't let him. He is a monster.

Jack, I'm sorry about everything. I'm sorry you got dragged into my fucked up world and I'm sorry for what I'm doing to you. You don't deserve it. But you can still walk away. You're not involved like I am. I beg you, please, get yourself away from all this, for me.

I'll never forget you. Please don't forget me.

All my love, always,

Zoe.

I must have read the note a dozen times before its contents sank in.

Kat was dead.

Valentine killed her, just like he killed the boy Scannell slept with.

And Zoe was gone.

My first thought wasn't for Kat's parents. It was for me. Even three years on, Daisy Gill's death was still a gaping, raw wound in the centre of my life, every minute of every day. And now there was another one next to it, just as deep and painful, and marked Kat. Was Kat's death my fault? On the grounds I was trying to find her and had failed, yes it was. But I was rational enough to know you could argue it either way because she wasn't killed by my own hand. Then again neither was Daisy. The only thing I knew for certain was that some time this evening Kat would be joining Daisy in my nightmares.

I closed my eyes and saw Kat's face. And then I felt something stirring inside me. It was the urge to do something, to not sit here wallowing. There was still plenty left to fight for. You can't help her now, I told myself, but you can get revenge. I closed my eyes and thought about my next move.

Zoe was somewhere. But where? I had no idea. There was still Pryor for me to worry about and as for Edward Valentine, I was going to take care of him, somehow.

And it wasn't like I didn't have options. I had ammunition in those video files and I knew how to use them. I'd promised Zoe I wouldn't do that but things had changed now. So, options? I had plenty of those. But the situation I was in, it was like a straw poll. Pick the wrong one, and I was finished. I would end up like Kat. Or worse. And then there was Zoe's mother. I couldn't do anything to harm her.

I slumped forwards in the chair.

Then the TV noise cut through my fog of thought, and

suddenly my next move didn't matter all that much. I felt my hand move across to the remote, hike the volume all the way up to deaf-and-dumb.

Do you ever have those moments where you think someone on TV is looking directly at you? As opposed to the camera. Two days ago, I would dismiss that kind of thing as kooky nonsense. But that morning, sitting on a dark red armchair worth more than most people earn in a week in room 312 of the Redborough Hotel, I felt that sensation myself. Felt it the moment I saw the face looking back at me from the TV screen. It was a face I had never seen before. But the name the newsreader gave to the face made my guts turn to broken glass.

I was looking at Harry Slew.

'Mr Slew disappeared from this country nine years ago,' the newsreader said in a clipped voice perfect for Tube trains. 'But today he's been found, alive and well and living in Yamba in New South Wales.'

Yamba. I'd never heard of the place. It sounded Australian and dry and desolate. The screen transitioned to a map of Australia with a tiny dot in the top left hand corner. They cut back to the newsreader, interspersed her with the same shot of Harry Slew as an Aussie recluse. He looked chubby and had bags under his eyes the size of hockey pucks. His hair was thin and short as a Velcro patch. Defeated eyes the colour of dense fog. There was a certain resemblance to Pryor. He looked like Pryor might have done, had things not worked out so well for him.

They say you receive less information from an entire half hour of TV news than you get from the front page of *The Times*. I've no idea who works these things out, or the formula, but it seems about right to me. You watch any item on any news channel, after about thirty seconds you've learnt all there is to know. The trick the channels use to keep people watching is to repeat it whilst making it sound new. But I kept on listening anyway. I wanted to see if they had managed to corner Slew themselves.

They hadn't. About ten seconds later it became evident that the entire news piece had been lifted from the *Daily Legend*. It became evident because the ticker tape flashed the words ACCORDING TO THE DAILY LEGEND across, real slow and dramatic. Still, I couldn't see why this was Breaking News. Even in the world we live in today, the sudden discovery of a long-vanished witness halfway around the world isn't a big story. It's not even a small story. It's barely even a story.

Then the newsreader went on, 'Mr Slew left the country after a trial in which he was acquitted of causing death by dangerous driving. Mr Slew says he has come out of hiding because he wants the world to know he was not behind the wheel at the time of the accident. Instead he accuses MP Adam Pryor of being the driver.'

There was just enough time for the words to sink into the back of my skull. Like an axe. Splitting my head in two, in one powerful clean blow. I was numb. Then my mobile hummed on the table, and I jolted. Craned my neck at the screen. Pryor was calling. I didn't want to take the call. Not without taking stock of everything. My mind raced with what I knew. Pryor was on TV, being implicated in the death of an innocent by the man whose legal defence was funded by Valentine.

Slew's legal defence was funded by Edward Valentine, the same Valentine who was threatening to blackmail Pryor. The same Valentine who had tried to use his own daughter to entrap Pryor. The same Valentine who'd killed the girl who ruined his plan.

Now Pryor was reaching out to me. I picked up the mobile. It felt way too heavy in my grasp.

'Jack Winter,' said Pryor. I didn't like the way he said my full name. Like our relationship had somehow become formal. He said my name like it was a bad taste in his mouth. 'What the hell happened to you at the hospital yesterday?'

'Got a fear of hospitals. Since the accident.'

'What accident?'

I was finding it hard to focus. My palms were clammy. I was short of breath and light-headed. Either my fitness was really going down the plughole, or I was experiencing a full-blown panic attack.

'Sorry, I thought you knew. I was stabbed a few years ago.'

'Youth of today, eh?'

'It wasn't like that, Adam.'

Pryor was silent. I could hear classical music in the background. Seemed kind of incongruous, harmonious music playing out behind his anxious voice.

'I trust you've seen the headlines.'

'I have.'

I kept tight-lipped. Either Slew was a liar, or Pryor was. My money was on Slew. The photograph had creeped me out, and I felt Pryor had been straight with me. I was still looking out for him. But I wasn't taking any chances.

Pryor said, 'It's nonsense, of course.'

I said, 'Okay.'

Pryor said, 'Harry contacted Imogen.'

I said again, 'Okay.'

'That's why she did it.'

'Did what?'

Pryor blasted a sigh down the line.

'Took the overdose, dammit,' he said between gritted teeth. 'She got the message from Slew and then she went and plunged a load of smack into her bloodstream.'

I frowned at an old painting on the wall.

'How did he find her?'

'Same way everyone finds everyone these days.'

He waited for me to get it. I didn't get it.

'On Facebook, Jack.'

'Oh,' I said. Then, 'What did he say?'

'That he'd been traced by some of your tribe.' I guessed he meant reporters. I didn't ask. I let him go on, pacing up and down the hotel room myself, my ear burning. 'I don't know how they got hold of him but they did.'

I stopped pacing and looked at my shoes. I wasn't wearing any. I was halfway to stepping outside barefoot. I thought about Slew.

'It's easy enough to find anybody these days,' I said.

'How?'

'Same way everyone finds everyone else. On the Facebook.'

Pryor let out a smug laugh.

'How did you find out about the message? I thought your sister was in a coma.'

'No, Jack, you don't go into a coma after a heroin overdose,' Pryor said, pained, like he was talking while someone extracted snake venom from his foot. 'You either die or an adrenalin shot wakes you up. Haven't you seen Pulp Fiction? Anyway, Imogen is in hospital, getting stronger. I logged onto her account. I wasn't snooping. I just wanted to know what she'd been up to.'

That sounded like snooping to me, but I didn't press the point. I let Pryor continue while I rooted around for my socks and shoes.

'Harry being Harry, he didn't just drop a line saying "Hi." Oh no. He told Imogen that the journalists had caught up with him and said the story was going to run this weekend. He said he was very sorry. He said he'd walked into a trap. The journalist had gotten him drunk, apparently. One too many lagers and his tongue was loose.'

I nodded to myself. I'd done the same trick myself dozens of times. Police cannot question a suspect who is blazing drunk, but for journalists the looser the tongue the better. As I listened I pieced it all together inside my head. I could imagine the journalist hearing about Adam Pryor's imminent appointment to the Cabinet and doing what any hack does when someone comes into the spotlight. A full background check. Publicly-available court and police records would have revealed the crash inquiry and the subsequent dead-end. They would've run a search for Harry Slew and drawn a blank. They would know that Slew must have gone somewhere. They might have found him on Facebook, picked up a few clues that way. And then they would've widened their search. Every waking moment would have been dedicated to finding Slew. They would've looked under stones the police wouldn't touch. Anyone who might ever have known him would have been contacted and, sooner or later, for a bit of cash or simply the fun of being involved in a news story, someone would have talked. The reporter would've known he was in Australia in no time. Not much later they would have an anonymous contact on the phone swearing that Slew had called him a year back from an Australian number. The area code would have told them he was in northern New South Wales. By the time the journalist called it a night, he would've whittled it down to Yamba and then it was easy. I wondered briefly who had cracked it. I envied whoever had done the groundwork on this one. It was the kind of hunt I always enjoyed.

'We need to talk,' Pryor snapping me out of my daydream. 'There's something else going on that I need your advice on.'

'Sure,' I said. 'Later?'

'Now.'

'I'm not at home.'

'I know. I just tried your flat. Where are you?'

'The Redborough.'

Pryor paused a beat. I bet he stayed at the Redborough all the time. I could almost picture his head nodding in approval.

'Very nice. I hope the company was worth it.'

I shrugged at the furniture.

'Not sure.'

'I'll be there in ten. Meet me in the lobby.'

I killed the call. Placed the phone back down on the desk and watched the screen blacken like oil filling a lake. That's when it hit me. The iPad. It was lying there beside the bed like a fallen black slate from a roof. That was my proof that Edward Valentine was a monster. No matter what Zoe said about not wanting to use what was on there, I couldn't just leave it behind. I couldn't delete the video.

This wasn't some low whispers in the House of Commons, this was cold, hard evidence. And the only evidence I had. I didn't know what I was going to do with it but as long as it existed, I had options. A newspaper like the *Sunday Legend* could really go to town with. Despite Kat being dead, despite Zoe disappearing, despite my problems with Pryor and the rest of it, I still had the video. And as long as I had the video, I had a little bit more than nothing.

I had one last thing to do. I needed to stash the iPad somewhere safe. I had planned on dumping it and the listening gear at my flat. But with Pryor on the way I didn't have time to head back to Earls Court. I needed a safe place for it and quick. I rummaged frantically around the room, looking for a discreet place the maid wouldn't care to investigate. My search was hopeless. The room was devoid of good hiding places. A hotel this old and expensive, I was kind of disappointed there wasn't a secret door.

Then I found it. Not a perfect hiding place. Matter of fact it was nowhere near perfect. But it would have to do. It took me ten minutes from start to finish. Then I made a call to the reception and booked both rooms for another night. With the iPad safely hidden and the rooms reserved, I grabbed my phone and my wallet and my keys.

Opened my room door, and found myself face to face with Naz, who was pointing a gun at my forehead.

He said, 'Don't shout. Don't scream. Try anything funny and I'll shoot you in the face.'

'Hello Naz,' I said. He didn't reply. There was nothing friendly in his face. He was dressed the same as when we first met, brown brogues, jeans, round-neck jumper and blue shirt, except this time he had on his green Barbour coat. I wondered if that gun had been in the Range Rover when he drove me back from Oxford, or in one of the other ones which I was now certain had been following me around for the past few days.

I had never had a gun pointed at me before. It was a weird feeling. I wasn't rigid with fear. Instead I felt curious and surreal. Like I was having an out-of-body experience, looking down on myself standing there looking at the hole at the end of the barrel. What I believe they call the muzzle. I blinked at it. It didn't blink back. It was round and black and lethal. It looked bottomless. I imagined a bullet spearing out of that muzzle and smashing into my face. I could almost see it unfolding in slow motion, like a sports replay. Bits of my skull and brain exploding out of the back of my head. Curiously, I felt bad about my future dead self ruining the hotel room carpet. The cleaning bill would be massive, I thought.

Then I did a funny thing. I calmly stepped out of the room and into the corridor. It had that morning smell familiar to hotels the world over, a mixture of eggs and ham and liniment. I moved ahead of Naz and his gun. I followed the corridor towards the lifts. I couldn't feel my legs. It was like my body had taken charge of the situation, and my mind was just tagging along for the ride.

'There's a good girl,' Naz said at my back. 'Keep it quiet and nobody has to get hurt.'

'I think my feelings already did.'

'Oh dear,' he said. 'That's too bad.'

I drew towards the lift.

'No,' Naz said. 'Take the stairs.'

I nodded and carried on. Gone eight o'clock in the morning and the corridors were empty. I prayed that I'd bump into someone. Maybe a member of staff or better yet a retired general. I could throw myself at them, scream at the top of my voice. He wouldn't shoot me in front of a witness. I was pretty sure of that. He didn't have a silencer. The gunshot would make a lot of noise. People would jolt. Those same people would see him flee. Naz's face would be all over the news before he reached Baker Street station. But I saw nobody. I reminded myself that it was a Saturday morning in a five-star hotel in central London. None of the guests were mad enough to be stirring yet. None except me.

I trudged on towards the stairs. Thought again about that gun. It looked like new. I didn't know much about guns but I knew enough to know that it wasn't a revolver, it was the other type, a semi-automatic. I didn't know if that was better or worse. Probably worse.

And I thought about Naz and how small were my chances of escaping from him. He would eat someone like me for breakfast.

At the landing I steered left and headed for the lobby. My footsteps sounded impossibly loud on the marble steps. A dense *thunk-thunk-thunk* echoing inside my head. Tension was burning a hot circle into the nape of my neck. Burning downwards. Setting fire to my spine. I had no control of the situation; that's what made me blaze up inside. Naz was calling all the shots. I was paralysed. I tried to count the number of steps to the lobby. Got to ten then gave up. My whole body was shaking.

Then we hit the lobby, and I saw people.

Naz said in a low whisper, 'Do exactly what I tell you to or Zoe dies.'

Suddenly I didn't want to call his bluff.

Naz said, 'Take a right at the reception. Takes you down a corridor. You'll see a door at the end, says Staff Only. Head for that door. Do it nice and slow. And casual too. You're sweating badly.'

I moved past the reception. Evelina wasn't there. Some guy who looked like the manager was frowning hard at the computer. No one seemed to take any notice of us. I figured that Naz had concealed his gun. Somewhere people couldn't see it, but he could get hold of it easily. Like those bodyguards you see around presidents who wear smart suits but never, ever button them up. I felt like Naz and I were in our own little bubble, invisible to the rest of the world.

I turned right at the reception, like he told me to. The corridor was cold. The floor had been freshly mopped and my shoes squeaked on it. I felt my mobile humming away in my jacket pocket. It trilled six times. Three messages. I kept on walking.

In ten numb steps I reached the door that said STAFF ONLY. Gave the handle a tug. It opened up into a big industrial kitchen. Kitchen staff scurried about, carrying bags of this and that. A couple of chefs worked away at a big cooker, pans hissing and crackling with fat and oil. The air was greasy. I felt nauseous. No one gave us a second glance as I was ushered down the kitchen and through the exit. I pushed the crash bar. Stepped outside.

Morning light hit me, raw and tainted. I looked for the sun. Found nothing but a suffocating bank of clouds reminding me that there is a simple reason why England is the birthplace of modern democracy – the weather is all the oppression an Englishman can bear. And right now I felt about as oppressed as I'd ever been.

The rear exit backed onto a staff parking bay shaped like a tennis court. There was a train of dumpsters to my left and an avalanche of crushed cigarette butts on the floor in front of me. The asphalt was pockmarked with pockets of rainwater.

There was a car parked four metres from where I was standing.

I clocked it immediately as a Jaguar XJ sedan. I'm no car nut but I'd seen the posters splashed all over Euston train station and thought I wanted one of those one day, maybe to go with the dog and the house in the country. I had its futuristic curves seared into my brain. It was the colour of midnight and the windows were a fifty-percent tint. The engine was purring. The lights were on. I turned around to face Naz. He was smiling at me, a gentle, patronising grin which said he knew I was no threat to him.

I have never swung a punch in my life, and one look at Naz told me I wouldn't be popping my punching cherry anytime soon. There was a sign beside the door that said CAUTION! DO NOT OBSTRUCT. Next to Naz, it looked kind of appropriate.

He swept past me. Flipped open the rear passenger door on the Jaguar XJ. Waved the gun at the dark space inside.

'Get in,' he said.

I stepped closer to the Jaguar. Looked to my right. The parking lot lead into a back street. I thought about my chances of out-running the Jaguar and Naz. I was still light on my toes, when the situation called for it, but I doubted I could give Naz the slip.

I was even less confident I could outrun a bullet. So I took one last look at freedom and ducked into the passenger seats.

The driver was already gunning the engine as my door slammed shut on the outside world. The Jaguar had that new-car smell. The seats were leather and the front seat head-rests were embossed. Glossed ebony veneer, eight-inch touch screen fixed into the dash, Bowes & Wilkins premium sound system. The car probably cost more than my flat. Naz got into the front passenger seat. We surged out of the parking lot, hung a right and arrowed towards Euston.

I was conscious of a man sitting next to me. He was cast in shadows, Naz blocking the light from the windscreen. His face was shadowed too. But his eyes were a pair of white studs. I felt like I was being shown a pair of expensive diamonds in a jewellery store. Then the eyes grew bigger and the face leaned across to me and lunged out of the shadows, and I found myself looking into the cold eyes of Edward Valentine.

18

He was dressed in the same grey sharkskin suit as yesterday. The white shirt had been swapped for an arctic blue number, and he was sporting a plain white tie, loose and limp, his top button popped. He wore an altogether different face from the one I'd seen on the video feed at the Redborough. Then he'd just looked stern and cold. Now his features were knotted and strained into an impatient kind of angry. His legs were crossed. The Jaguar was big enough for him to do that, even with the heavy in the front sliding his seat all the way back. Valentine frowned at his leather lace-ups. Black today instead of brown. They were so polished he could stare at his reflection on the toe caps.

Then he cocked his head at me and said, 'Where is it?'

My turn to frown. 'I don't know what you mean.'

Valentine laughed inside his mouth. Made a hissing noise that sounded like he was cracking open a can of soda. His eyes searched me. They were unnaturally white.

'The thing about liars, Jack, is that their lies only work on the innocent. You try lying to a liar, he'll sniff you out in a second. The perception of truth is my area of expertise so please, don't test my patience. Just tell me where the video is.'

The driver did a hard right, beat the traffic lights and now we were skittering down Harley Street. I felt my guts tie themselves up into a ball. Valentine knew I'd been filming him. The ace up my sleeve had just been exposed.

'Zoe told me,' Valentine answering the question before it had a chance to float out of my mouth. Up front the gunman had whipped out an old clam-type mobile and was barking orders into it in a foreign language.

'She called me in the middle of the night,' Valentine continued. 'She was drunk. She wanted to tell me how much she hates me. But then she opened up, started confessing things. We have quite a bond.'

I thought about Zoe draining the mini-bar. Downing the spirit miniatures one after the other like they were going out of fashion.

'She told me all about the video and your little setup. I have to say, I'm impressed, Jack. You caught me red-handed. And if my step-daughter hadn't said anything, who knows. You might have succeeded. But you made a fatal mistake. The same one as I did, in fact.'

'Sleeping with your stepdaughter isn't a mistake. It's evil.'

'That wasn't a mistake, Jack,' he said. 'Thinking she could keep a secret was where I went wrong. And who are you to criticise my parenting? You're hardly dad of the year, are you? Emily must be seventeen now, I suppose. And what have you done for her? Nothing. The best thing you ever did was get out of her life so she could be brought up properly. How does that make you feel, Jack? Knowing your daughter has another man's surname? That would eat away at any man's soul. I guess that's why you drink so much.'

I never saw Clive Birch again after Daisy Gill was killed so the murderous rage I felt for him was only ever theoretical. I didn't get the chance to look directly at him and feel the urge to kill pulse through my body. But after hearing those words from Valentine, that's what I felt. I would have gladly put a bullet in his head or a knife in his heart. I've long suspected that all men are capable of killing, given the right circumstances. Sitting in that car, face to face with Edward Valentine, I'd found my circumstances.

A man like Valentine doesn't mention your family to show he's your friend. This was a threat, a warning.

He threatened my daughter so I wanted to kill him.

But I knew I couldn't follow through with it. When a man with a gun is sitting in front of you it would be suicide to even try.

Which left me with nothing. No plan A, no plan B, no plan C. All I could do was play for time and try to think of something.

'You're a monster,' I said, knowing how pathetic I sounded.

'No, Jack. You need to grow up. Monsters are things that go bump in the night. I'm a man who gets things done. There's a big difference. Now, the video.'

'I don't have it.'

Valentine considered me for a moment. Looked me dead in the eye, like he was trying to decipher a puzzle. Then he shrugged and glanced out of the window.

'Doesn't matter if you tell me or not. Right now I have my best people scouring the hotel room. And your flat. We're talking about men with decades of intelligence know-how. They'll find the video sooner or later. It's a question of when, not if. But if you save me a few hours and tell me now, who knows? Perhaps I'll go easy on you. I can't say the same for Naz, though.' He gestured to the front seat. 'People who cross him tend to go home in pieces. I mean that literally, by the way. He'd make you eat your own balls if I asked him to.'

Valentine's threats felt a bit like having that gun stuck in my face, surreal and almost as if they were happening to someone else. That weirdness gave me enough time to process what was behind Valentine's words and I realised they confirmed two things to me. First, I should keep my mouth shut about Kat. If Valentine knew Zoe had told me he killed her, the odds of me ending up face down in an alley would rocket. Second, Valentine had no idea what I'd done with the video and he was terrified of it. For all he knew I might have left it with someone, accompanied by instructions about what to do with it if anything happened to me. And he must have known what I'd do with it if anything happened to Emily. For the time being Valentine was as stuck as I was. He wanted to unleash Naz on me but he couldn't. Not yet, anyway. But my time was limited.

We reached the end of Harley Street. Swung a left onto Wigmore, then a right onto Regent Street. Skittered down towards the throng and bustle of Oxford Circus. I looked out of the window for answers.

'If I'm honest, I quite like you,' Valentine said. 'You're a devious, backstabbing bastard with scant regard for morals. Reminds me a little of myself.'

I watched the shops slink past. Designer brands jostling for attention, hordes of shoppers shuffling along the pavement, heads shooting this way and that, like pigeons. I groped uselessly around my head for a plan.

'Why did you hire me?' I said, turning to Valentine. 'If you wanted to blackmail Pryor, why turn to someone who kills stories for a living?'

'Because Pryor went for the wrong girl. I couldn't control Kat. She seems quiet and sensible when you first meet her but deep down she's a wild one.' I shivered inwardly as he talked about her in the present tense. Something about the way he spoke told me he had tried to control Kat before. Maybe the same way he controlled Zoe.

'So you figured, kill this story to keep it out of the papers, but keep it dangling over Pryor's head as a permanent threat?'

'Exactly. All I needed you to do was to stop Kat from running to the press. But that simple task was beyond you. If I'd known how useless you were, the job would have been done differently, you might say.'

A hundred metres or so down Regents Street the car hooked a right onto Maddox Street. The discreetly rich shopping district, with its five-grand watches and ten-grand dresses. Maddox quickly became Grosvenor Street. We were heading into paid-in-full Mayfair.

Naz was closing the clam phone and turning in his seat. It was like an oil tanker doing a one-eighty. He glanced at me. Then looked at Valentine and shook his head.

'Are you sure?' Valentine said.

'Not there.'

'What about the flat?'

'Nothing.'

Valentine cursed under his breath. Then he looked across at me.

'What did you do with video?'

I said nothing.

'Where is it, Jack?'

I still said nothing.

'Fine.' Valentine straightened himself, stared grimly ahead. 'If you want to play this game, I'm more than happy to indulge you. Just remember, you wanted it this way.'

He said nothing else after that. It was a short ride down Grosvenor. The driver took a left and after sixty metres or so a second left, and we came to a halt. Valentine patted my knee and said, 'We're here.'

He got out. Naz circled the Jaguar and cracked open my door. I stepped out onto the pavement. We were outside a four-storey whitewashed building at the corner of the street. The door was an imposing black thing with a brass doorknob. The first-floor windows doubled up as doors opening up onto balconies festooned with all kinds of plants. The second- and third-floor sash windows were draped with net curtains. A black wrought-iron gate separated the ground floor from a series of steps leading to the basement. In the country, this was probably considered an out-house. Here, in Mayfair, it qualified as a mansion.

'This is your home?' I asked Valentine.

He laughed.

'This is my office.'

He stood there on the street and looked thoughtfully at the house.

'Maybe once this is over I'll give it to Adam,' he said. 'As a thank you. What do you think, Jack?'

I thought that Edward Valentine in the flesh was a lot crazier than on the end of a phone. Naz pushed open the wrought-iron gate and shoved me in before him. We trotted down the steps leading to the basement flat. I looked back over my shoulder. Valentine was smiling cruelly at me as he carted down at a leisurely pace. At the door Naz thumbed a button on an intercom located on the wall. He waited. I waited. Valentine joined us and waited too. A couple of seconds later the door buzzed and Naz flung it open.

'Ladies first,' he said and gave me a shove. I stepped inside, and did a double-take.

I imagined the upstairs aspect of the house was lavishly decorated, corporate, stacked high with swish furniture and exotic modern art. The basement flat was like a crack den. The entranceway was cramped and dingy. The doorway was narrow and the carpet had been stripped away. The walls were plaster-bare. I followed Naz into a room on the left. Entered what had once been a living room, in a past life. A living room after the bailiffs had finished with it. The same exposed plaster. The same stains dyed into the floorboards. Generations of dust on the fireplace mantelpiece and the window sills. A single seventies-style wooden chair in the middle of the room. I noticed something strange. There were bars over the windows. The rear of the living room ushered into a kitchen. The window panes were made of distorted glass, so I couldn't see much of anything beyond, but these frames were also barred over. I felt like I was in a prison.

Valentine snorted air, rubbed his nose and gestured to the wooden chair.

'Take a seat,' he said.

Naz disappeared out of the room. Valentine stood over me. Hands in his pockets. Anger burning in his eyes.

'Cards on the table,' he said. 'You and I both know that the video would finish me for good.'

I didn't reply. I was looking at the bars on the windows, and wondering what they meant.

'I've worked too hard and too long to get to where I am.'

I looked away from the windows and asked, 'Why did you do it to Zoe?'

Valentine raised his eyebrows.

'You mean, why do I fuck her? Just spell it out, man. No need for beating about the bush. I'm a straight talker, you ought to know that much.'

'Okay,' I said. Meeting Valentine's stare halfway. 'Why do you fuck Zoe?'

Valentine took a step back from me.

'You think I'm a sick man, right? You think I'm like those perverts who lock their step-daughters in the basement. I'm nothing like them. I fuck Zoe because it's the only way to buy her silence. It keeps her loyal, keeps her under control.'

I worked my face into a curious stare.

'The thing that separates the winners from the losers is this,' Valentine said. 'Winners know that people serve one purpose, and one purpose only. To advance their own ambitions. Zoe was beautiful and alluring and she was going nowhere in life fast. I knew she could be of use to me. Until she loses her looks, that is. Once they're gone she'll be just another tired old whore.'

I felt sick at the way Valentine described her.

He rubbed his face, like he was wiping off mud. In the filmy light of the living room I noticed that his features were red and haggard.

'You want that tape to find its way into the newspapers and TV stations,' Valentine straightening his tie, catching his breath. 'I know that. God, if I was in your shoes I might even try and do the same thing. No doubt you have some feelings for my daughter which are clouding your mind too, because if you were thinking clearly you would realise that tape would destroy her life too. The world would know what she is. But if your intention is to protect Pryor, then you're making an even bigger mistake.'

Valentine was wearing that cruel smile again. Sharp at the corners, like a carving knife. The smile suited him. He dipped a hand into his breast pocket. Removed an object that I instantly recognized as the reporter's most important tool in the field. It was a grey plastic device and the size of an old Nokia mobile. It had a digital display and a white casing and an Olympus logo branded onto the top of the device.

I shifted in the chair.

'Do you know what this is?' Valentine said.

'Sure,' I said back. 'It's a Dictaphone.'

'Very good, Jack.' The smile turned into a full-blown grin. 'Now listen carefully.'

Valentine hit the Play button.

I couldn't hear anything. He dialled the volume on the speaker all the way up. The room swelled with the noise of nothing, an electric hiss bristling out of the speaker like radio static. Then I heard a voice crackle into life. The first voice was Valentine. A second voice replied, hushed and furtive. The echo was distorting the sounds but I recognized the second voice instantly. I listened and looked at Valentine. I listened to Adam Pryor saying, almost whispering, 'I said, dammit, I want Harry Slew dead.'

19

The air in the room rocketed from Arctic to Sahara. I was hot and pale at the same time, and my mouth felt like I had been chewing on sawdust. I felt my neck muscles straining. Valentine just standing in front of me and grinning, watching my best-laid plan falling apart. Neither of us speaking. Both of us listening to a pair of disembodied voices crackling over the Dictaphone speaker.

The scene assembled in my mind as if I was listening to a radio play. I could picture Pryor looking straight at Valentine, almost insisting that Valentine help him. He'd seen a way out of the mess he was in, just like that first time he and I met. The cornered fox, again.

PRYOR: Well? Can you do it?

VALENTINE: Can I, or will I?

PRYOR: Don't play games with me, Edward. This is serious.

VALENTINE: I know exactly how serious this is.

PRYOR: And I need your help.

VALENTINE: I know you do.

PRYOR: You're the only person I'd trust with something like this.

VALENTINE: It's a difficult situation.

PRYOR: There's no alternative. I've thought about it over and over. Christ, if there was any other option, I'd go for it, you know that. But taking Harry out of the equation is the only way I can stay clean.

VALENTINE: But you want him taken out—
PRYOR: Permanently. Yes.

A two-beat pause. Somebody coughed.

VALENTINE: you realise if I do this, we cross a line.

'Stop the tape,' I said. Valentine clicked it off. 'This is useless for blackmail. If you use any of this you're implicating yourself along with him.'

Valentine smiled. 'Be patient, Jack,' he said. 'This isn't about blackmail. All I want to do is show you a side to Adam Pryor you haven't seen yet.'

He started the tape again.

PRYOR: I understand that. We have no choice.
VALENTINE: And there can be no loose ends. What about that sister of yours?
PRYOR: Imogen.
VALENTINE: Can we trust her?
PRYOR: She's my sister, Eddie.
VALENTINE: Yes, but can we trust her?
PRYOR: Yes. We can trust her.
VALENTINE: I'm asking because it needs to be asked. She strikes me as a loose cannon. You must bear in mind that she'll have to lie to the police, and she'll have to live with that lie. So will you.
PRYOR: I can live with that.
VALENTINE: And she can too?
PRYOR: Yes. I'll make sure of it.
VALENTINE: Good. Because when she sits down with the

detectives, they're going to ask her who was behind the wheel. And she's going to have to lie and say it wasn't you. And she's going to have to say it like she means it.

Valentine stopped the tape.

The hiss cut out.

He was still grinning, smug now in a way he wasn't before.

'Adam Pryor is not the man you think he is,' Valentine said. 'Now you know.'

'Pryor was driving that night,' I said.

Valentine nodded.

'He killed the woman?'

'Her name was Katarina Pilot,' said Valentine. 'She had come over from a small town in Poland to work as a nanny. She was twenty-six years old.' The grin broadened across his face. For a shy second I almost thought Valentine was feeling sorry for her. Then he went on, 'Pity I never got the chance to thank her. She was a delightful and unexpected gift.'

'Pryor said he wasn't driving.'

Valentine harrumphed.

'Adam has many qualities. Among them his ability to pull the wool over the eyes of those around him.'

'I guess that depends whether you think lying is a quality or not.'

'For a politician?' Valentine laughed. 'I'd say it's essential.'

I paused and thought hard about something.

'But Harry Slew isn't dead. I just saw him on TV.'

Valentine sighed, heavy and deep and long.

'Just because Adam clicks his fingers, doesn't mean I'll jump. I realized that Harry Slew would be worth more to me alive than dead. He was the only other person in the car that night who knew what really happened. Other than Adam, of course. So I got Harry a decent lawyer and got him off.'

'And Imogen?' I asked. The way Valentine talked unnerved me. He had a kind of casual weariness to his voice that made him sound like a tired desk jockey explaining the job to his replacement.

'Imogen,' Valentine repeated. 'She was a concern.'

I thought about something else. Said, 'She's in hospital. She overdosed on heroin.'

'I know,' said Valentine. 'Adam told me.'

'Pryor said something else. He told me she'd been an addict for ten years. Which means she started around the time of the accident.'

'She found out about Adam wanting me to kill Slew. It was hard on her. She believed her brother had tried to arrange for a man to die, as well as lying to the police and having a dead woman's blood on his hands. He was her idol. She started drinking heavily. Calling Adam in the middle of the night, telling him she was going to kill herself. All a bluff, of course. Then she started on the drugs.'

I heard Naz walking down the hallway. He strode into the living room and nodded at Valentine. Valentine smiled and seemed lost in thought for a moment. Then he went on.

'When Adam found out she was doing heroin, he was a very relieved man. I mean, who would take the word of a junkie over that of a future Prime Minister? And Harry Slew has developed something of a problem with drink over the years as well, which is rather helpful. A guilty conscience, I expect. So the thought of Adam up against a junkie and an alcoholic in a truth contest doesn't worry me a great deal. The British people trust Adam, don't forget that.'

I was lost for words. I believed my profession had exposed me to the worst that humanity had to offer. The rapists and the murderers and the sexual abusers and the people who would sooner trample over you than help you. But I had never heard a man speak, like Valentine did, of people overjoyed at their sibling's drug addiction, or relieved that a childhood friend was drowning in booze, or happy to have got away with causing the death of an innocent woman.

'Adam indulged Imogen,' Valentine said, as though Pryor had been doing her a favour. 'He made it easy for her to score the heroin. He always helped her out financially, so she never had to steal to fund her habit. I did warn him that it would end in tears with her. But the man couldn't see it. I should have done something a long time ago.'

'She's an innocent,' I said. 'You both drove her to this.'

Valentine scoffed.

'She's a drug addict, Jack. She would've been a drug addict without the car crash hanging over her. Don't go getting all moralistic on me.'

'You use people. You used your own daughter.'

'I gave her a purpose.'

'Adam trusted you, and you used him too. You taped your conversation so you had a backup option in case he ever went against your wishes.'

Valentine laughed and smoothed a crinkle out of his tie.

'Of course I did,' he said. 'I'm surprised at how naïve you sound, Jack. You of all people should understand. You and Zoe did exactly the same thing to me last night. Why? Because in this world you're either in control of other people or they're in control of you. I prefer the former.'

'People like Andrew Scannell,' I said. I wanted to hear him say it.

Valentine nodded and frowned. 'Scannell was a weak man in every way,' he said. 'I did what I needed to do.'

I scratched an itch at the back of my neck.

'So once Scannell was out of the way and you had Pryor by the balls on the crash, why bother trying to frame him with Zoe? You could have blackmailed him to push the GIC deal through without her.'

'Could I?' Valentine said. 'If I threatened to go public with what I know about the crash, I would have implicated myself too because I paid for the lawyer. I made an error of judgment there. So I needed something fresh to hold over Adam and I needed it quickly. That was where Zoe came in.'

Valentine gave me his back and stared out of the sash windows. The bars were chopping up weak sunlight into ice blocks. He was quiet for a while and lost deep in thought. Naz departed to take another call. I could hear his muffled voice in the hallway, machine-gunning down the line.

Valentine turned back to me.

'You could work with me,' he said. 'Help me stop Pryor. My enemy's enemy is my friend, after all. And believe me, you'd much rather have me as a friend.'

The image of Valentine's hands all over Zoe flashed in front of me. Zoe turning her face away from the camera because she didn't want me to see her. Biting her lip and trying very hard not to cry. I knew Valentine didn't want me to work for him, not really. He wanted the files, that was all. This was just another way to try to get them from me.

'I created a monster,' Valentine went on. 'Adam needs to be stopped. Unless something drastic happens that man will reach the top of British politics sooner rather than later and because he's so young he'll be there for a long time.'

'That's not my problem,' I said.

'If he's willing to kill an innocent man to escape punishment, and let his sister spiral into drug addiction, what else do you think that man is capable of? Imagine him in charge of a country. He's dangerous. I want to bring him down, and you could help me do it.'

'But only after he's rubber-stamped your GIC deal.'

'Of course,' Valentine said. 'That must go through. I've put too much into it. There's twenty billion pounds waiting for me at the end of it. Do you understand how much money that is?'

I didn't speak.

'Of course you don't,' Valentine said. 'Let me put it like this. There are maybe twenty people on the planet who are worth that kind of money. Those are the people who run the world, Jack. I'm going to be one of them. And don't forget Adam was in on the gig. He'd have been rich too. But then he decided it would be better for his career to oppose it. He chose his political career over our project.'

I said nothing.

'Adam Pryor will be Prime Minister one day,' he said, his eyes searching me, trying to get a reading on me. 'His career has already been meticulously mapped out. You and I are the only people who can stop him. Help me, Jack.'

'I don't care about GIC. I don't care about Pryor,' I said. 'I don't even really care about you. But I do care about Zoe and Imogen. And Kat.'

I watched for a reaction to her name. There was nothing. Either Valentine had a supreme poker face or he was so ice cold he really didn't care about the girl he'd killed. He took a couple of steps closer to me.

'You killed her. Didn't you. And the boy with Scannell.'

Valentine gave me his shark smile and looked into my eyes. At that moment, right there, I learned what fear really is. Forget having a knife stuck in your guts, looking into the eyes of a killer without a conscience is much, much worse.

'No,' he said. 'I didn't.'

Valentine sounded so confidently that for a second I thought I had everything wrong. But when he spoke again I knew I was right after all.

'That's what I pay my friend out there for,' Valentine said, and nodded towards the door. 'You're so naive, Jack. I did what had to be done. Kat didn't matter. Neither of them mattered.'

My mouth opened and closed and I felt my throat tighten as I began to panic. I started to cough and Valentine slapped me hard around the face. My head swayed listlessly from side to side, the momentum of the blow gradually fading.

'Get a grip, Jack,' he said, putting his hand on my shoulder and squeezing so hard it hurt. 'Be a man. This is what leads to true power, doing what has to be done. Letting nothing get in your way. Not Kat, not Zoe, no one. That's where I'm going. You can be part of it if you want to. And you can help Zoe and make Adam pay as well. We can do that. I can make that happen for you. But first, I need that video.'

I clocked Naz in the periphery of my vision. He had come back to the room and was by a small table in the corner, with his back to me. He was busy arranging things on the table, silently. He finished what he was doing and turned to face me. I saw what he'd been laying out: knives. Different sizes, all shiny and clean, like a high class chef's. I felt an impossible weight crushing me, like rocks being piled high on my chest.

'Tell me,' Valentine said urgently. 'Or my friend here will make life very difficult for you.'

I looked at Valentine. I looked at Naz. I looked at the knives.

Part of me wanted to defy Valentine. But the greater part of me is not a hero or a superman and had no wish to be tortured. I do not think I would've resisted for long, under the circumstances. My pain threshold is not especially high. And then there was Emily. What would Naz do to her?

I couldn't deny it any longer. I was trapped, and it was merely a question of when I would tell Valentine what he wanted. Not if. The only variable was the degree of punishment I was prepared to go through beforehand. And if the damage they did would be permanent.

I also figured there was a twisted logic to what Valentine was saying about stopping Pryor. But the fact is I did what I did next out of fear, not intelligence or bravery. There can be no glossing or spinning. I did what I did, and I must live with that, like I'm used to living with my mistakes.

'It's at the Redborough. That's where the video is.'

Valentine cocked an eyebrow at me.

'Try again, Jack. We already searched your room.'

'It's not in the room,' I said.

'Where, then?'

'I'll show you.'

Valentine snapped his head at Naz.

'We're going to the Redborough,' he said, and started to walk out of the room. I felt a jab in my back as Naz directed me to follow, like a farmer herding cattle with a prod.

'You're coming with us,' he said. 'I don't trust you.'

A few feet ahead of me Valentine stopped in the doorway. Smiled at me and said in his best fake voice, 'Thank you, Jack. This is a good thing you're doing. I'll try and think of some way of rewarding you.'

I didn't like the way Valentine said reward, especially when Naz's gun was jabbing me in the ribs. Valentine smoothed the grin out of his face and stepped out into the hallway and made for the front door, me a few feet behind and Naz behind me. I heard the crank and shudder of the front door and watched it open.

The car was in front of us, passenger side – the side I got in and out of – closest to us. As Valentine approached the car there was a solid click as it unlocked. He walked to the front, making for his usual seat behind the driver. As he stepped into the road he turned to me and smiled, a grin of victory which made me ashamed of how badly wrong my plans had gone.

Then I heard the high pitched grind of a car revving hard in first gear. From my left, behind Valentine, a scruffy red car shot into the road, its tyres squealing and back end fishtailing as the driver revved the engine far too hard. The car was writhing along the tarmac as its tyres tried to grip the road surface.

When the car started travelling in a straight line its revs went even higher, squealing as the driver pushed the needle well into the red. As it got closer Valentine clocked the noise it was making and looked over his right shoulder with an angry expression on his face, as if the civilised veneer of his posh neighbourhood should not be tarnished by such yobbish behaviour. He gave the car the kind of evil stare which he was using to break me only a few minutes ago.

But as the car got closer, his expression changed. His frowning eyebrows jumped an inch up his forehead. His eyes widened and his jaw relaxed and dropped open.

I've seen people hit by cars before. Every time the human is thrown into the air and lands a few metres away, truly like a bag of bones. It's the simple consequence of a heavy, hard, fast-moving object hitting something much lighter and softer, like a tennis racket hitting a ball. But if a tennis racket hits a ball and on the other side of the ball is another tennis racket, the ball won't fly up into the air. The ball won't go anywhere.

And that's what happened to Valentine.

The right side of the front of the red car hit the far flank of his Jaguar exactly where he was standing, with a deep, metallic crunch and then, because of the angle of the impact, it scraped along the wing of the bigger vehicle, with Valentine's legs caught in between them.

Valentine didn't make a sound when the car hit him. His mouth stayed wide open, his whole expression freeze-framed.

When the red car came to a halt and stopped, I watched him fall sideways, towards the back of his car and away from the front of the red one. After he disappeared from my view the red car moved again, backwards a couple of feet and then forwards again, until it was past Valentine's Jaguar and right up against the next car.

And then it stopped.

20

I was around the car in four quick strides. Naz hadn't moved from the side of the pavement. I saw what looked like a bundle of clothes lying on the road beside the Jaguar.

I felt my legs turn to concrete. The bundle resolved itself into Edward Valentine. He was lying spent and crushed on the road, his body bent and dented in unnatural ways. His skull was split in half down the middle, like an axe taken to a coconut. His chest was crushed almost flat. Naz stood there at the side of the road, trying to process the situation.

I saw the passenger-side door on the Vauxhall swing open.

I saw a person stagger out. A woman with short, dark hair and big sunglasses over her eyes.

A woman with Zoe's jaw line, Zoe's lips and Zoe's body.

She didn't look at her father lying spent on the ground. She just touched a hand lightly to her forehead, as if about to faint. Her shoulders heaved up and down as she took deep breaths. Composing herself.

Then she faced me. I knew she was staring at me from behind those dark lenses. She began walking towards me. She moved smoothly on her feet with a deserted street behind her, the scene like a slow-mo from a Hollywood movie. The wig was still perfectly in place. She had black leather gloves on and her hands were steady. She looked like a professional assassin.

She'd left the Astra's engine running. I looked at the tyres. She'd hit him, waited for him to land and then reversed and run over him.

Zoe took a final step towards me and stopped, barely twelve inches away from me. We stepped forward at exactly the same time and met in a tight hug. I might have fallen over if Zoe hadn't been there to lean on. She felt so much more stable than I did.

I looked past Zoe at Valentine. His left foot was twitching. I wasn't an expert on car crashes or death. But it seemed to me that Edward Valentine wasn't much long for this world. I doubted a guy with his head split in half had much of a chance of surviving. I stroked Zoe's cheek. Her skin was cold and hard, like chilled plastic. She started shaking as shock from the impact of the crash kicked in. All that metal crushing and pulping all that flesh and bone.

I felt her body settle and then, with her face pressed against my chest, she screamed like I have never heard a person scream before, an explosion of fear, anger, pain and relief that shook me physically and mentally. When she had no more breath the scream stopped and Zoe started taking shallow, fast breaths.

I said as calmly as I could, 'It's going to be alright,' even though deep down, I knew that was far from certain. Maybe things would work out okay. Probably, they wouldn't. All I knew was, we were both a long way from being in the ballpark of okay.

'I had to do it, Jack,' Zoe said, her voice shaking. 'I saw Kat's body this morning. He had to die. Please don't hate me. This was what I wanted. What I needed.'

I smoothed her hair.

'I understand,' I said. 'I really do.'

'Now I need to disappear,' she said.

'No,' I said. 'You don't need to go anywhere.'

Stupid comments from a stupid man. When you have as much money as Zoe, disappearing is easy. And you don't have to be a hardened criminal to know that making yourself scarce when you've just killed someone is a good idea. But I didn't want her to go anywhere. I wanted her with me.

'I do,' she said. 'And I can. I did it properly, Jack. Bought the car in cash so it's untraceable, left no fingerprints on it. I could get away with it.'

'Maybe you could,' I said.

'I'm going away,' Zoe said. 'For a while. Might have to be forever.'

She was quiet for a double beat.

I looked around. Naz and the driver had vanished. I could hear the wail of an ambulance in the distance. Sirens screaming the screams that Valentine was no longer capable of. People were rubbernecking the scene. Someone had called the police. A couple of people were filming the scene live on their phones, every grotesque flicker of Valentine's leg recorded for posterity.

But none of them were filming us.

I peeled Zoe from her shoulder and looked her dead in the eye.

'It's not over yet,' I said.

I dropped my hand into my trouser pocket and took out the keys to my flat.

'Go to my place,' I said. 'Wait for me there. I can sort this out.'

Zoe stared at me from behind the glasses. She was completely still. Wasting time.

'How?' she said.

'You need to trust me,' I said. 'I will look after you. I promise.'

Zoe gave a small not. She trusted me.

'What about you?' she said.

'Pryor,' I said. 'I have to stop him. I thought your step-father was the one behind this whole thing. But I was wrong. He was a bad man. But Pryor wasn't far behind him. If I don't stop him now, he'll be too powerful and it will be too late.'

Zoe nodded, but didn't move.

'Now,' I said urgently, pushing the keys into her hand. 'Go to my place. As quick as you can.'

And squeezed her arm hard enough to snap her mind back into focus. She nodded, turned and jogged away.

A voice deep in my head piped up and said, maybe things were going to be okay after all.

The ambulance sirens were growing incessant and reckless.

I watched Zoe disappear round a corner and approached the dead body of Edward Valentine.

I am not overly familiar with death. The concept, yes. The limp, bleeding reality, less so. As I drew close to Valentine, glass crunching underfoot, I thought back to myself three years ago, and the woman who attacked me. Ever since I had tried to block that day out of my consciousness, but now it was looming at the gates, beating them down. I remembered feeling the blood drenching from my wound, the warmth of it, an almost surreal and peaceful feeling, the sensation of the strict tension in my muscles unwinding, my whole being letting go. I remembered, too, having something like an out-of-body experience. I am not a believer in such things, but at the point where I neared death, I opened my eyes, and instead of seeing sky above me, I saw myself below. Looked on passively, curiously almost, like someone studying their reflection in the mirror for the very first time. I wondered if Valentine was looking down on himself at this very moment. I wondered how he would feel about his life ending like this.

He was striking an odd pose. His arms and legs were bent at the elbows and knees. He looked like he was trying to spell out a letter visible to the skies above. His head was twisted to the side and his eyes were dim. The pool of blood glooping out of his skull was neat and thick and dark and reminded me of an oil spill. I was shaking. I didn't want to do this. But I had to do it. I needed the Dictaphone. I stooped down beside him. He had landed on his chest and the inside breast pocket on his jacket was draped over his left breast.

For the sake of the camera phone wielding rubberneckers I tried to make my actions look like I was checking him for signs of life, while also doing the best I could to keep my face hidden. I leaned carefully across his torso and dipped my thumb and forefinger into the pocket. I could almost feel the heavy dead weight of his body. There was a soft flopping sound coming from inside his chest. I gripped the Dictaphone and slid it out of the pocket. It had survived the crash intact. I stood up straight, and beat a path back from Valentine to the side of the road, where Zoe was sat, gazing hopelessly into the middle distance, her elbows resting on her knees.

I tucked the Dictaphone into my trouser pocket, and dug out my mobile. Called up Bull's mobile number from my contacts list. I had three text messages. They would have to wait. My battery was hovering above the ten percent mark and I felt my heart thumping against my breastplate as the call put through to Bull.

Three rings.

Come on, Bull, I thought. Pick up.

I caught the flicker of ambulance sirens down the street, cracking and popping.

Four rings.

The ambulance grinding to a halt behind the Astra. Doors urgently flying open. Couple of paramedics bouncing out of the back and scuttling with emergency equipment over to Valentine. More sirens booming away in the background. Another minute or so and the police would arrive.

The call was picked up on the sixth ring.

'Nick Bull's phone,' a female voice said. She sounded flustered. Breathless. Like she'd just jogged up twenty flights of stairs.

'Rachel,' I said. 'Please don't hang up.'

The breath shook itself out of her voice.

'Jack. What a pleasant surprise.'

'Where's Bull?' I said.

'In with the lawyers,' she said. 'Can't be disturbed.'

I thought quickly. I needed help from someone at the *Legend* and if Bull wasn't available, Rachel Kirk would have to do. I knew Bull rated her highly and she'd already impressed me. The only question was whether or not she'd want to do me any favours.

'I know you and I haven't gotten off to the best of starts,' I said. 'But I'm in a deep hole and I really need your help to get me out of it.'

I plugged my right ear and pressed the phone tight to my left. Started pacing away from the crash. I had a brief window to finish off Pryor. I wasn't going to let it slip through my fingers.

'And why should I help the man who's almost destroyed my career twice now?' Her voice was rising with anger.

'Listen to me—'

'No, Jack. You listen to me. I'm not going to help. Frankly you're the last person on earth I'd help out right now. So go ask someone else, because whatever sob story you're going to give me, I'm not going to bite.'

I said, 'This is the story of a lifetime.'

A pause. A glimmer of doubt. She was a reporter, and both a good and a desperate one. She'd be doing the maths – I was calling Bull on a Saturday afternoon and sounding desperate. She would have known something big was on and she couldn't resist that.

'I'm listening,' she said coldly.

'There's no time to explain on the phone. Where are you?'

'Right now? At my desk.'

'I need you to get across to Marylebone, right now. Go to the Redborough Hotel and into the shop in reception. There's a green handbag in the window. In the bag is an iPad. My iPad. Get it and meet me outside the hotel in thirty minutes. Got it?'

'Yes, but Jack, what's going—'

'Just do it,' I said, and hung up.

Ten percent battery.

I increased my pace down the street. Turned north onto Audley Street. I didn't have enough juice on my mobile to run Google Maps, but I knew the layout of Central London like the back of my hand. Marylebone was about a kilometre north of my location. Audley would carry me all the way past Oxford Street and onto Marylebone Road. If I hurried, I'd make it to the Redborough quicker than any taxi ride or Tube journey. I flicked through the text messages as I steered up Audley Street. There were three of them. They were all from the same number. They were forwarded messages, long streams of an exchange between two other numbers. The exchange pretty much confirmed what I already knew. It hardened my resolve to get the job done.

I was halfway up Audley Street, passing the statues of Eisenhower and Reagan and the endless train of blast-protection walls lining the front of the American Embassy. My mobile rattled into furious life. Incoming call. I eyed the display. It wasn't Rachel.

It was Pryor.

'Hey, man, where are you?' His voice was friendly and forced. 'You weren't at the hotel. I was getting worried about you.'

Pryor had previously blown a fuse whenever I'd been even a fraction of a second late. And yet here he was, acting nonchalant about being stood up in the hotel. I froze. The thought hit me in the guts like a fist.

Pryor knows.

He set me up.

He told Valentine where to find me.

'Where are you?' Pryor said again.

My mind accelerated ahead of me.

'Jack? You still there? Look. Tell me where you are, I'll come pick you up. We have a lot of catching up to do and I'm afraid it can't wait.'

'It's over, Adam.'

Pryor said nothing. I wondered if the line had cut out. But no. Four bars. Pryor was there, down the line, brooding and scheming.

I said, 'Valentine told me everything.'

'And you believed him? How sad.'

'He told me about the crash. Slew was telling the truth all along. You were the driver. You killed the woman, and you were happy to let your best friend take the fall for you. You're going to pay for this, just like Valentine paid. Oh yes. I forgot. He's dead,' I said. 'A car flattened him.'

Silence.

'It's true,' I continued. 'I just saw it happen. Seriously, Adam. You should see Valentine now. His head looks like someone went at him with a pickaxe. I went after Valentine and now I'm coming after you.'

Pryor sneered down the line.

'I know about Edward. Naz called me,' said Pryor. I could almost hear the smirk crawling across his smug face. 'You honestly thought it was going to be that easy? Take Valentine out of the equation, problem solved? Christ, Jack. You really are a joke.'

Then Pryor hung up.

I continued up Audley. The American Embassy shrinking behind me I was now beyond Oxford Street and approaching Portman Square. Not far to Marylebone Road. I sent a text to Rachel with the last squeeze of juice on my phone. Told her to fetch the iPad from the boutique shop inside the Redborough. This was personal for me now. The truth is, I didn't really care about GIC or investment scams or African mobile companies. I didn't care about Pryor and his merciless political ambitions. But I did care about Zoe and Kat and, more than any of them, Emily. Kat was dead. Zoe's future was in jeopardy. Valentine knew about Emily so it was a fair bet Pryor did too. And then there was the other innocent: Imogen, lying in a hospital bed.

The two of them had done enough damage. I wouldn't let them ruin another life.

Exactly twelve minutes later I arrived flustered and sweating at the front of the Redborough Hotel. The porter didn't recognize me as I made for the doors. Then he took a second look and stepped away apologetically. I looked ragged. My suit was crumpled, and not in the way Zoe had suggested a couple of nights back at my flat. I noticed spots of blood on the cuffs of my shirt. I spied Rachel hanging inside the lobby. Today she was dressed in a navy blazer, matching pencil skirt and a white blouse. Professional. Serious, even. She had a white leather shoulder bag hanging from her wrist, and she looked angry, furious even. She saw me. Didn't smile. I quickly seized her by the left arm and pulled her towards the entrance.

'Hey!' she said, standing her ground and trying to shrug off my grip. 'Get off me!'

'Not now,' I said. 'Have you got the iPad?'

'Of course,' she said. 'It's in here.' She patted the bag.

'Good. Now we have to get out of here.'

I glanced furtively around. Checked the faces in the crowd. They looked the same as yesterday. Old money and new money moving in circles, classical music wafting through the lobby. Evelina manning the reception. I didn't see anything suspicious. But that didn't relax me at all.

'What the hell's going on?' Rachel said. 'You're acting funny.'

I gave her a look.

'I mean, funnier than normal.'

I leaned in close, relaxing my grip and gently circling her. Like we were flirting. I said, 'I think someone might be watching us.'

Rachel hooked her eyebrows.

'Who?'

'Pryor.'

'Really?'

'Or people working for him and Valentine.'

'Jesus.'

'Only they're not working for Valentine anymore. He's dead.'

Rachel gasped. I gently led her towards the entrance. Kept looking across my shoulders. I was trying to keep my voice neutral. I didn't want to alarm Rachel. I needed her to think clearly and on the level, because in a few hours she would be breaking the biggest political story of the twenty-first century.

'What the hell happened?' Rachel asked.

'He had an accident.'

Rachel squeezed my bicep a little too hard.

'Really, Jack?'

'Well, maybe not an accident. But that's not important right now. What is important is that we get to your office before Pryor stops us.'

'What the hell have you got me into?' she said. 'I can't believe you.'

'Not now,' I said. 'We have to go.'

We broke outside and launched down the steps. The sun was high somewhere behind the clouds. A whitish splodge, like a dimming light bulb, marked its general spot. I looked around for a black cab. None presented themselves. Incredible. Lunchtime and not a single taxi in sight. I swung a left and headed for Baker Street tube station. It was a short hop away. A couple of hundred metres. The traffic down Marylebone Road was gridlocked. Even if we did hail a cab down here, it'd take decades to arrive at the *Sunday Legend* offices. Motorcycle couriers weaved crazy lines between the columns of traffic, going at the kind of speed that could break a swan's neck. The streets were filled with tourists. We hurried beyond a procession of Arabic phone shops and electrical stores. The Globe pub across the junction at our right. Tube station directly ahead. We cut through the crowds and threaded our way towards the steps.

Rachel said, 'Why would Pryor want to stop us?'

'That story your guys at the *Daily* ran today?'

'The one about Harry Slew?' She frowned at the lips. 'I didn't know anything about Slew, Jack. Neither did Nick. We told you everything we knew.'

'Slew was telling the truth,' I said. 'I can prove it.'

'How?' Rachel asked.

I didn't answer. I froze. Rachel looked at me quizzically.

'What is it?'

I pointed with my eyes to the Tube entrance. To a figure standing beside the newsagents, his hands stuffed in the pockets of his green Barbour coat. There was another man with him, taller, wider, with dark hair and wearing a black overcoat.

I said, 'That's Naz.'

'What are you talking about?' Rachel said, like I was losing my mind.

'He's one of Valentine's guys.'

Rachel said, 'I thought you said Valentine is dead.'

'He is. Naz must have changed sides. There's no point working for a dead boss, so he's with Pryor now.'

We were maybe twenty metres from Naz and his mate. He had been scanning the continuous wave of heads flooding up past the Tube entrance, many of them carting along to that most inexplicable of tourist attractions, Madame Tussauds. Then his eyes latched onto mine. I felt my breath trap in my throat. In the next instant he began pushing his way through the crowd towards us, the bigger man just behind him. I did a one-eighty and steered Rachel away from the tube.

'Great,' said Rachel. 'What are we going to do now?'

'I have an idea,' I said. 'But we need to lose this guy first.'

I turned to my mobile. The battery was crashing towards five percent. I had time to make one call. I had to make it count. I hung a right and led us up Park Road, past the tatty thoroughfare that converged on Regent's Park. Brought up Halliday's number and tapped Dial. Rachel kept looking back down the road.

'Jack,' she said. 'He's following us.'

I tried not to think about that. I focused all my energy on the phone plugged to my left ear. I needed Halliday to pick up. I had no other way of getting across to the *Legend*'s offices in Kensington. I didn't know if there were more eyes on us than Naz and the driver, but I knew one thing: I didn't want to test that theory out. I got Halliday on the fourth ring.

'Um, Jack. How are you, how are things?'

He sounded awkward, like he had answered my call by mistake

and was now regretting it. He'd probably figured I was calling in a rage to chase up my ten grand. Judging by the sob story he had laid at my door a few days ago, he probably fielded quite a few calls like that every day. Any other day, I would've been grilling him hard. Today, I had more important things to worry about.

'Where are you right now? Like, this very minute?' I said.

'At home,' Halliday said back. 'The hospital didn't take too kindly to me, uh, using your services. I'm suspended on full pay. That means I can't operate on anyone at all, no private clients either.'

'Sorry to hear that.'

'Don't be. My lawyer says that if they go ahead and sack me, we'll have a watertight case for unfair dismissal and compensation. Not to mention defamation and damages for that. I could be looking at millions, Jack. That'd wipe out my debts. Funny how these things work out, isn't it?'

'I need a favour,' I said, cutting to it.

'Sure, sure,' Halliday said quickly, eager to please. Or maybe just figuring that here was another ten grand he could shave off his debt pile. 'Anything, Jack.'

21

We trekked up to the junction at the end of Park Road. I led Rachel north on Wellington Road. Risked a glance over my shoulder. Naz was fifty metres back, alone. He was holding a bunched-up fist to his mouth and speaking into some kind of microphone. Telling his friends where to find us, I assumed. We were keeping a brisk pace but Naz looked like he was out for a gentle stroll. He wouldn't shoot us in public. At least, I hoped not.

Up ahead St John's Wood sprouted into life. It was a jumble of Sixties and Seventies brown-brick apartment blocks looking dangerously close to slums, straddling leafy streets and gated mansions. Lord's cricket ground towered gracefully to the north-west. The driver in the black coat popped out of St John's Wood tube, hung a left and started in our direction. I felt Rachel squeezing my hand tightly. He looked straight at us, his intentions obvious. He was forty metres ahead of us. I noticed a gaggle of Indian tourists across the street, taking turns to have their picture taken in front of Lord's. I looked back at Naz. Looked ahead at his mate. Had visions of them bundling Rachel and myself into the back of a blacked-out BMW. I suppose if this was an action movie I would have battered them to a pulp. But this wasn't Hollywood, and I had never hit a man in my life. So I did what came naturally to me.

I crossed the road.

I hustled over to the Indians. One of the guys was holding his mobile horizontally, like it was a camera, and trying to cram all his friends into a single shot. I tapped him on the shoulder, and made a sign that I would take the photo so they could all be in it. The man beamed a swarthy smile at me. He would never know the Englishman's politeness was due entirely to the threat of violence hanging over his head. I spent far too long lining up the picture. I deliberately took a bad snap, so I would have to take a second one. The two heavies stood on the other side of the road like a pair of severed testicles. I kept one eye on the traffic lights at the bottom of the road. They flashed green and a wave of buses and cars and vans came belting up the road. In a blur of motion that surprised even myself I chucked the mobile at the Indian, shook an entirely unnecessary wave and yanked Rachel down into the next left turning up from Lord's. I gathered my bearings and followed the directions Halliday had given me on the phone. I broke into a full-on run at this point. My lungs blazed, like I'd downed a pint of petrol and followed it up with a lit-match chaser. Muscles I had forgotten existed burst into reluctant, fiery life. I could hear nothing above the sound of my own breathing, and the sound of blood rushing inside my ears. I could hear Rachel faintly breathing at my back. A more steady, rhythmic pattern to it. She had a body that suggested she worked out. We took a left, then a right, then another left. Neither of us so much as looked back. We just needed to put as much distance between ourselves and the heavies as possible. We ventured into the placid heart of St John's Wood. The burr of motors left us behind and became a surreal underwater drone.

It didn't take us long to find Halliday's place. He lived on the corner of a road that looked like a slab of idyllic rural England. Redbrick façade, sash windows, pebbled front garden. Modest garage to the side of the place with a blue door. He was even richer than I thought. To put a place like this at risk, those gambling debts must have been astronomical.

Halliday was at the porch. He was hopping on his feet with nervous energy. He clocked me and waved us towards the garage. I looked back down the road. No sign of the heavies. We were okay for a few moments. I manoeuvred around the porch with its gnomes and frangipani and mini palm trees and joined Halliday as he hoisted up the garage door and flicked a switch on. An overhead light bulb sputtered into life. Threw blades of weak halogen light down over a mass of black tarpaulin cast like a tent over the back of the garage. Halliday grabbed a corner of the tarp and yanked it towards him, like a magician whipping a table cloth off a cluttered table.

'Well,' he said, turning to me. 'What do you think?'

'Honestly? If I don't die on this thing, it'll be a miracle.'

I was looking at a Kawasaki motorbike. It had a lethal shape to it, curved yet sharp, like a cat screwing its eyes tight and narrow. It was lime-green and had an engine that probably weighed more than my Vespa. There was a pillion seat cover at the back. The fender and tail panels were crusted with mud.

'This is the Ninja,' Halliday stroking an arm over the handlebars. 'A ZX-10R, to be precise. Not as smooth or as fluid as the Ducati,' Halliday nodding at another bike in the garage. 'But perfect for your needs. It'll get you from A to B in a jiffy. This thing goes faster than Concorde.'

I looked at the lime-green Ninja. Tried to imagine mild-mannered, middle-aged, clipped-accented Halliday tearing it along a country road, shrink-wrapped inside his leathers and visor. There was clearly a whole other side to this guy that I didn't know about.

'Nine-nine-eight cc engine, sixteen valve, liquid-cooled,' Halliday purring each word. 'There's a traction control system that'll stop you from going haywire or losing control at a turn. You'll be in good hands, Jack.'

'As long as it works,' I said.

Halliday stroked his chin at me.

'You've never ridden one of these before, have you?'

'Like I told you, I have a Vespa.'

'This is a whole other piece of machinery,' said Halliday. 'It'll feel completely different to riding your little scooter. Like sitting on a jet engine instead of a hairdryer with wheels. How long have you got to learn the basics?'

'I already know the basics,' I said.

When I bought my Vespa I did every motorbike training course and got every qualification under the sun. Not because I love bikes and speed but because I was terrified of taking to the road on two wheels. My Vespa topped out at 28mph. The Ninja was in a different league but I didn't have time for a refresher course. I knew about the throttle, the brake lever and the foot-operated gears. That would have to be enough.

Halliday continued stroking his chin, nodding, like he was trying to work out how to condense twenty hours of teaching into half a minute. He put a hand on my back and brought me closer to the Ninja.

'Jack, if you go down on this beast it's going to hurt like hell, and the paramedics will need a shovel to scrape you both off the road.'

Rachel shot me a bewildered look.

'Just remember, a little twist on the throttle goes a long way, so you don't want to be yanking your wrist down too hard, or you'll end up doing wheelies. I wasn't joking when I said this thing is like a jet engine on two wheels. Push it too hard and you will just about take off.'

'Got it,' I said.

I had the sudden, sinking feeling that riding the motorbike to the *Legend* offices was a bad idea.

'Good luck,' Halliday said much-too-cheerfully, his hands on his sides, gazing at the Ninja wistfully. Then he handed us a helmet each, shook his head and wheeled the Ninja out of the garage and into the street.

The heavies were on the horizon. They looked like insects from this distance. Like cockroaches. I climbed onto the bike in a hurry. Rachel climbed awkwardly onto the pillion seat. She wrapped her arms tight around my chest, like she was clinging on for dear life. Halliday chucked me the keys. I flipped down the red rocker switch with my right thumb, turning the kill switch to the 'on' position. Then I slotted the key into the ignition and gave it a clockwise twist. The Ninja growled into angry life. A bunch of lights flared up on the screen, like lights on a Christmas tree. A green-lit 'N' told me that I was in neutral. There was a button below the kill switch marked with a circular arrow surrounding a lightning bolt. I had the same button on the Vespa. This was the start button. I thumbed it and disengaged the clutch, and the engine roared as it turned over. We started moving forward. I gave a slight twist of the throttle and we picked up speed. I lifted my right foot off the ground and kicked up the kickstand with my left foot, allowing it to tuck underneath the body of the bike. We were moving forward. The engine was warming up. The speedometer and tachometer needles were springing into life.

I tried to remember everything I learned, but the panic of riding a powerful bike and Naz and his mate were fogging my mind. I almost lost control, felt the bike tipping over to the left side, Rachel tightening her arms across me, like a seatbelt locking, and then I overcompensated and twisted the throttle too hard, and the Ninja began to wobble. I feared we wouldn't make it to the end of the street. I looked back over my shoulder. Naz and the driver were no longer the size of insects. They were big and large and filling my field of vision. They were madly chasing us, pounding pavement, bombing down the road. They couldn't have been more than twenty metres back. I had to get us away. And then suddenly I found a moment of clarity in my mind. I relaxed, let the bike become part of me and I pulled the clutch lever with my left hand, and used my left foot to shift into first gear. Then I slowly released the clutch, and the Ninja moved forward at an increasingly smooth and steady rate, gaining momentum now. I felt us pulling away from the heavies. I wasn't afraid of the Ninja now. I was trusting it to do what I needed it to do. My hands were steadier. I started remembering the days of training I did. The bike's movements became smoother and more graceful. I accelerated down the road, steering us away from St John's Wood and towards the *Sunday Legend*.

We pelted central London at fifty miles per hour. Less than twenty minutes since we had sped away from the heavies and we were closing in on the *Legend* office fast. I felt like we were winning again.

Then we hit traffic, the kind of traffic that drives motorists to despair. It was three lanes deep and stretched on into the horizon like a lizard's tail. The cars ahead didn't move. They just sat there, groaning and sneezing fumes out of their exhausts. After a minute of going nowhere I hopped off the Ninja. Rachel unhooked her arms from my waist and shuffled down from the pillion. We took off down the road. We had passed Knightsbridge and were now just a few hundred metres east of the office along Kensington Gore. I figured we'd do the rest of the journey on foot. I left the

Ninja lying at the side of the road. Car horns protested my inconsiderate behaviour. But I was in a frantic hurry, and I couldn't exactly take the Ninja with me. Besides, something about the way Halliday had shaken my hand back at his home suggested he didn't expect to see his bike again anytime soon.

The *Legend* office shot into view up ahead.

It had been three years since I'd so much as set eyes on the place. A part of me didn't want to go inside. Actually, all of me didn't want to go inside. Too many bad memories. But I had no choice. Breaking the story about Pryor was my only hope of sorting out this mess the right way.

I suppose a less paranoid man might have marched to the nearest police station and laid out the evidence in front of the nearest copper. But there were malevolent forces at work. Pryor had long arms. Who knew how far or deep into the system they reached? The only people I was willing to trust were Bull and Rachel. The only audience I was interested in reaching were the eight million people who bought or read the *Sunday Legend* once a week.

The office was gleaming and corporate and bland, a towering ribcage of steel and glass. It was an anomaly set against the banks of industrial brown brick blocks and tattered newsagent facades. It was an anomaly of their own making, because just after I left, the private board of trustees who owned the *Legend* and its sister paper decided they'd had enough of nicotine-stained walls and keyboards, threadbare carpets and the directors with their permanently-closed doors and blinds pulled shut, and decided that open-plan and ergonomic was the way of the future. But they misjudged newspaper culture. The brooding rivalries between reporters that drove them on to get the better scoop, the tastier inside track. The moments of peace locked away in a cramped, dim office with nothing but a pack of Marlboro Reds for company, reaching into the air for inspiration, all of that disappeared overnight. In one fell swoop the suits ripped the soul out of the place. I was convinced neither paper had been quite the same since. Now, as I headed for the sheened glass entrance, I felt like I was returning to an old home, only to discover it had been demolished and replaced with a shopping mall.

'Where's your office?' I asked.

'Fourth floor,' Rachel said. 'All the Sunday hacks are on four. And I don't have an office. I have a pod.'

'No good. We need somewhere private.'

Rachel thought for a few brisk paces. Then she said, 'There's a conference room on the eighth floor.'

'Won't it be booked?'

'The ones on two and three, they're always full. But the eighth is usually empty, especially on a Saturday.' She smiled at the corners of her eyes. 'There's no lift between seven and eight. You have to take the stairs. You imagine someone like Bull taking the stairs?'

I had to admit it, I had a hard time picturing that one.

'So we'll go up to eight.'

'And then you'll give me my story of a lifetime?'

I nodded at Rachel. 'And your name will be on the front page.'

Along with Kat's murder, I thought, but decided to save that one for a bit later, when Bull was around to help share the burden of the bad news.

Rachel brushed hair away from her face and behind her ear and smiled. Said, 'Maybe you're not such a prick after all.'

Then Rachel looked past me and gasped, and I chased her line of sight, and the smile was wiped so far off my face it was on the floor.

By the entrance, two men in dark suits were standing next to a black Range Rover. They were staking out the street, the two of them. Naz must have clocked Kirk and known we would be heading here. One man was scanning the road, facing the opposite direction from myself and Rachel. The other was on his mobile and staring at his boots. The Phone looked impossibly small and fragile in his shovel-like hand. Rachel and I stood there for a cold moment, dumbstruck. The driver ended his call and had a brief word with the other man. Any second now, he'd direct his gaze our way.

'What do we do now?' Rachel asked.

'I don't know,' I said.

'Maybe we try and breeze past them. They won't do anything to us here, will they? We're in broad daylight, Jack.'

'Pryor's a desperate man. You don't know what he's capable of. They'll force us into the car. Speed us away. We'll never make it into the office.'

Rachel said, 'We can use the car park.'

I nodded. The *Legend* had an underground car park built into the basement of the building and accessed via a narrow side street. We could sneak in through the car park exit and a service elevator operated between the car park and the first floor. Reach the elevator, and we'd be home and dry.

We broke right and darted into Maple Street just as one of the men swung his eyes towards us. I didn't know if he'd clocked us or not. I didn't have time to worry about that. We shuttled past the dumpsters lining the side street and the gutter of crushed coffee cups and cigarette butts, and reached the mouth of the car park. A smooth tongue of asphalt led down from the side street and declined gently into the car park proper. A yellow automated arm barrier protected the entrance, an identical one blocking the parallel exit. We ducked under the barrier and descended into the filmy darkness of the car park. The place was packed out and I counted half a dozen neat rows of motors. Ford Focuses and Nissan Primeras packed tightly next to Benzes and Beemers. I could guess which motors belonged to the reporters, and which ones belonged to the directors. The air was musty and dry and overhead lights burned rectangles of sulphuric white light onto the gritty asphalt. I heard water dripping somewhere in the distance, and pipes clanging. The ground was marked with potholes and puddles. This was the one part of the building that had missed out on the renovation job upstairs. There was nobody about. The car park was ninety metres wide and a hundred and fifty long from entrance to the far wall, at the point where the service elevator was located.

We raced towards the elevator.

Then I heard a noise, a rumble, echoing through the car park. Sounded as if it was coming from behind us. I spun around, and Rachel did too.

Just in time to clock a black Lexus tearing through the barrier and heading straight at us.

22

The Lexus bombed down the asphalt. Its oversized grille gleaming and vicious beneath the fluorescent lights, like bared teeth. I had a second to react. Something kick-started inside my body, a survival instinct I had not been aware of. It flared up in my bowels. Sent bursts of electricity pulsing through my body. Suddenly the Lexus was fifteen short metres from us. Without thinking I found that my hands were locked around Rachel. I was hurling her into a gap between a BMW and a Range Rover. It was an involuntary movement, like a complicated flinch, like my mind had shut down and my body was running on automatic. The Lexus was still surging towards me. I knew if I paused I would be dead. I sprang to my right, powering forward on the balls of my feet and launching into a dive, throwing myself into the gap after Rachel. I landed with a heavy thud that reverberated through my skull, the same precise moment as the Lexus thundered past, engine roaring, passing close enough to the gap that I could feel its slipstream whipping my jacket and hair into a frenzy.

The tyres screeched. I poked my head out of the gap and saw the Lexus tail lights flaring as it lurched to a halt thirty metres ahead of us. It rested there for several seconds.

'What's he doing?' Rachel stammered at me.

'He's blocked us off from the lift. No way we can reach it from here.'

'What are we going to do, Jack?'

I was thinking about the Lexus, and about something I'd read a few months earlier, a random bit of trivia.

The Lexus engine revved.

'Jack?' Rachel asked again.

I pulled back from the gap. 'Look. I've got an idea. I'll distract the car. Soon as you get the chance, leg it for the lift.'

Rachel looked uneasy.

'What about you?' Her face stiffened. 'I'm not leaving you here.'

I rested a hand on Rachel's shoulder.

'I've got a bright idea, but you have to trust me. We don't have much time. Listen. You have a car down here, right?'

'A Focus. Light blue.' She jerked her head past my shoulder. 'Third row, at the back.'

'I see it,' I said. 'Give me the keys.'

'What for?'

'Like I said, you have to trust me, Rachel.'

The Lexus engine revved again. That spurred Rachel into action. She dipped a hand into her shoulder bag and rooted around inside. Came up with a bundle of keys on a keychain. She singled out the Focus key and passed it to me. I examined the fob. There were three buttons on the fob. A padlock symbol on one button was to lock the car. A second button was to unlock. I figured the third was to activate the alarm.

'And the iPad,' I said.

'Why?' Rachel said, suspicion in her voice. The prize was so close and she didn't want to let it out of her sight.

'He'll go after whoever has it,' I said. 'Keep it if you want.'

The iPad was out and handed over in an instant.

'So I'll meet you upstairs in the meeting room, right?' Rachel said.

'Eighth floor,' I said. 'Got it.'

'Down the corridor and on your left. Don't be late.'

Then I turned away from Rachel and burst out of the gap and stopped in full view of the Lexus, making sure the iPad was visible and hoping that those were not the last words I ever heard her speak.

Through the window I saw the driver's face. It was Naz. His face wore no expression at all. He looked focused and lethal. Then he did exactly what I hoped he would do. He backed up and sped towards me, tyres whining and groaning as he pushed the Lexus as hard as it would go. I ducked into the next row of cars. The Focus was in the next row on, six or seven metres away. I scurried on in a sort of crouching run, and threaded my way between several motors until I reached the Ford. The Lexus stopped again. I moved around to the back of the Focus until I was at the boot. I heard the Lexus backing up. Gears clunking and shunting. The Lexus headlamps drew arcs across the car park. The heavy was turning the Lexus around and gunning in my direction. If Rachel was sticking to the plan she'd be hurrying towards the lift at any second. I prayed she would make it. Then I backed off further and further from the Focus, putting ten metres between myself and the car, and then twenty metres. I stopped at the head of the row of cars. I had put six vehicles between myself and Rachel's Focus. I dropped to one knee by the rear wheel of a dull-grey Mercedes people carrier. I breathed solely through my nose, and waited. The Lexus slithered past the next row of cars. The heavy was moving slowly, casting his eyes over the crevices between each motor. I shuffled back slightly. Took the key fob, and raised it up into the air, like a periscope. A random bit of knowledge jangling around inside my head like a bag of loose nails.

By touching a key fob to your head, you can unlock a car from way further than the five-metre standard. I'd read. Google quickly told me this was rubbish. What mattered was line of sight. If the fob could get a direct line to the car, you were in. Manufacturers gave the five-metre figure so their customers would be pleasantly surprised when theirs worked from further away. I didn't own a car so this was new to me.

I had no idea how far away you had to be for the fob to work. If ten metres was too far, then my plan was going to fail.

The fob was up in the air. I depressed the unlock button. In the same instant I caught movement in the periphery of my right eye. Rachel making a run for the lift. The Lexus braked. There was a blind second when I thought the trick had failed and I had just signed Rachel's death sentence. Then the Focus squawked and flashed, and I heard the distinctive, industrial *thunk* of a car unlocking. Rachel carried on for the lift, scrambling as fast as she could, bag swinging from her shoulder. But Naz had been distracted by the Focus. He had a choice to make. Go after Rachel, or go after me.

He chose me.

Naz clambered out of the Lexus. Slammed the door. His sharp eyes flicked left and right. He slow burned at the Focus. He was clutching the gun in his right hand. He beat a path towards the Focus. I believe he had every intention of using that gun on me. He had seen the Focus unlock and figured I must be extremely close by, hidden from cover behind one of the nearby motors. He had no way of knowing that I was a lot further away than he thought. But as he neared the Focus, his shoes clicking against the ground, I realized my plan had a fatal flaw.

I'd banked on being able to distract Naz and then leg it towards the lift. But the service lift was currently shuttling Rachel up to the first floor. And even if the lift was ready and waiting, Naz had a clear line of sight towards it. If I tried making a run, he'd shoot me before I had a chance to press the call button.

I looked around for a way out.

Then I saw it.

A red box with a warning sign stickered to the front, fixed to the wall behind me. On one level a pointless facet of regulatory Britain. But now I saw it in an altogether different light. The box was set low, at waist height. It was directly behind me and out of sight of Naz, I was sure of that much. A rusted latch told me there had been a locking system on the box at one point, maybe a padlock, but for whatever reason the padlock was no longer in place. I put the iPad down and tried the door on the box. The hinges were rusted too, and it didn't give easily, but I was able to hook it open. Inside, just like the red box promised, was the fire extinguisher. It was a pitifully small thing. It looked to me like it would struggle to put out a match. But that wasn't my problem. I pulled the can out of the box. It felt surprisingly heavy in my hands. I peeked back at the Focus.

Naz was bent over and searching under the cars. He would be confused for only a few moments longer. Then he'd get suspicious. I had to act now.

I picked up the iPad and held it with my left hand close to my body. I had a good grip on the extinguisher in my right hand. I moved out from behind the people carrier. I was fully exposed. If I made so much as a scratch or a cough, Naz would have the drop on me. I had one shot at this. If I failed I was dead.

I buried my breath somewhere deep inside me. Felt like I was holding my breath underwater, my body swelling and my eyes bulging and my whole body feeling like it was going to explode. I kept my footsteps light but fast. I was making good progress. I was seven steps from him and he was still scrambling around on the floor, striking a pose like a big kid looking for the bogeyman under his bed.

I was three steps from Naz when my foot came crashing down into a puddle, and the sound was like a tsunami in my ears. Naz tensed, shot up like a rocket and shaped to spin around, and at two steps I thought I was dead, and there was nothing I could do but keep on going, no point in stopping now, except he was turning slowly, one of his feet had slipped, the leather sole on his shoe becoming slippery and letting him down at the moment he needed it the most, and then I was one step from him, and I was conscious of the fact that I had the fire extinguisher raised in my right hand, and I was bringing it down at his face.

The base of the extinguisher made a metallic thunk as it slammed into his temple.

The blow didn't feel all that powerful to me. But it knocked him clean off his feet. He stopped turning and started dropping. It took him a long time to drop. He deflated like a hot air balloon, muscle sinking into muscle. He rolled over on the ground and his eyes went into the back of his sockets. I stood there for I don't know how long. Maybe a second or two. Maybe a minute. Kind of amazed, and a little scared, of the damage I had done to this man. There was a dent in the side of his head deep enough to accommodate an orange. The gun had clattered to the ground on Naz's return to earth. It glittered under the lighting. I didn't pick it up. I let the extinguisher drop from my hand. I took one last look at Naz and decided he wasn't going to be on his feet any time soon. I didn't know if he was knocked unconscious, or what. All I knew was, I didn't intend to stick around long enough to find out.

The lift had swooped down to the car park by the time I had scarpered over to it. Made a nonchalant ping as the doors slid back and I stepped in. A minute later I was steaming onto the eighth floor. Kirk was by the conference room door. I said nothing to her. Just nodded, pulled out the Dictaphone, and arrowed into the room.

Bull was seated at one end of the table, Kirk went and sat down next to him.

'Foreplay's over, Jack,' he said. 'It's time for the serious stuff.'

I looked at Rachel. She was busying herself for the report, fiddling with her laptop and pens and notebooks. I looked at Bull. He was looking at me sombrely. He was sitting forward in his chair, his elbows propped on the edge of the table, his hands folded in front of him. His hair was actually combed and his tie straightened. He looked like a stockbroker about to tell me that the value of my investments had gone down, not up.

'Kat's dead,' I said, and the temperature in the room dropped by ten degrees.

Kirk's face was white. Bull, the hardest hack I ever knew, screwed up his mouth. I knew what he was thinking because I was thinking it too.

We failed her.

'The police pulled her out of a river in Oxford yesterday morning. They said she drowned. No suspicious circumstances. Accidental death. Just like the boy Scannell was with.'

Bull knew exactly what I meant. He said, 'I'm sorry, mate.'

'Me too,' I said.

I swung my eyes back at Rachel. She seemed to have snapped back into work mode and was plugging the iPad into the mains charger.

Bull tucked the bottom of his shirt deeper into the generous waistline of his trousers.

'Why don't you take a seat?' he said. 'You look knackered. Get you some water? Tea? Coffee?'

I surveyed the room. It oozed corporate social responsibility. The conference table was large and rectangular and white. There were four phones grouped in the middle of the table, and a whiteboard at one end covered in red and blue smears. Twelve chairs around the table, turquoise and painful-looking. The walls were lined with framed *Legend* front pages from down the years. Each one carried a lurid revelation. This Tory MP is gay. This celebrity is bulimic. This footballer is accused of rape. The headlines seemed to get more tawdry and desperate with each year. And yet, nothing on the walls compared to the bombshell we'd be dropping tomorrow about Adam Pryor and Edward Valentine.

The silence drifted and stretched, floating around us like thickening smoke.

Kirk broke it.

'You have the story of a lifetime for us, don't you, Jack?'

Her emotions had been parked, quickly. I couldn't say she would be one hell of a reporter one day any more. She already was one.

I nodded to the iPad.

'On there you'll find a video recording of a private meeting between Edward Valentine and Zoe Valentine at room 313 at the Redborough Hotel, yesterday evening.' Rachel furiously scribbled on her notepad. I continued, 'The plan was to film Valentine in order to get him to admit to the blackmailing of more than half a dozen MPs, including Pryor.'

I paused. Searched the eyes of everyone in that room.

'What I discovered was that Valentine was molesting Zoe. His step-daughter.'

Bull went wide-eyed. Rachel stopped scribbling. Just looked at me.

'Valentine was abusing Zoe. He was also using her to seduce sitting ministers, and then blackmailing in exchange for favours. I don't have all the details about past MPs. But I do know that Valentine planned to blackmail Pryor into rubber-stamping the sale of a government-owned investment company called GIC, to Valentine, for a ridiculously low price. The price is low because GIC has a secret asset, an African mobile phone company, which is worth far more than anyone except Valentine realised. Valentine planned to cash in on his shares soon after he'd taken control of GIC. The real value of the company would see him become a multi-billionaire overnight. He needed something to blackmail Pryor with in a hurry because of what happened to Scannell. Valentine tried to twist Scannell's arm with those hotel photos and we all know what happened to him.'

Bull folded his arms in deep thought. I'd just joined the dots for him.

'What about this Harry Slew business?' he said after a pause. 'Can't be a coincidence, he pops out of the woodwork at the same time.'

'Depends what you mean by coincidence. That wasn't planned by Valentine. Slew would have appeared whenever Pryor made it into the cabinet. That just happened to be this week.'

'Carry on,' Bull said.

'The setup went wrong. Pryor was supposed to sleep with Zoe. Instead he found himself attracted to Kat. Without Zoe, Valentine had no way of blackmailing Pryor over GIC. That's why he hired me. To stop Kat from going to the press. That would have scuppered Pryor's career, and that in turn would ruin Valentine's fraudulent takeover of GIC.'

Bull rolled his tongue around his mouth.

'So Valentine's fall-back plan was Harry Slew?'

I nodded.

'Valentine had the recording. That was a permanent sword hanging over Pryor's head, proof that he lied in court.'

'So Valentine hid Slew after the crash?' Rachel asked.

'Yes,' I said. 'He paid for the lawyers to get him off and then sent him out of the country with an envelope stuffed with cash and a one way ticket to Melbourne. But there was a problem for Valentine. He couldn't really use Slew to blackmail Pryor, because if he did, he'd be implicating himself too. Slew would only be useful to Valentine if Pryor thought Valentine was protected. Then Pryor got the promotion to the Cabinet, the reporters downstairs on the Daily made a few checks into his background, and hunted Slew down to Yamba.'

Bull frowned at the ceiling. Rested his ample hands behind his head, like a makeshift headrest.

He said, 'And that would cause Valentine a problem, because—'

'If he took Pryor down with the Slew story, chances are Valentine would have gone with him because he organised the lawyers. So he needed Slew under control,' I said. 'Just like he had Zoe under control. Just like he needed Kat under control. Valentine was a man who built his whole life around controlling other people.'

Rachel screwed up her lips.

'Kat dying is a coincidence too, then?'

'Maybe,' I said. 'Maybe not. She's not around to tell us and we're not going to get answers from Valentine in a hurry. He's dead too.'

Bull and Kirk's heads jerked upwards at exactly the same moment.

'How?' Bull said.

'Run over by a car. Another tragic accident. Another coincidence.'

I was still putting the pieces of the jigsaw together in my mind. I'd tell them the rest when I'd finished working it all out for myself.

'Fuck me,' Bull said. 'I've never seen a mess like this.'

'What's on the Dictaphone?' Kirk asked.

I could see that flash in her eyes, her mind working overtime, looking at the setup from a hundred different angles, picking apart the threads. She was fearless and analytical.

I was about to press Play on the Dictaphone when the door swung open and a woman stormed into the room. She was in her forties and dressed in a crisp dark suit. But the suit was no more than a nod to the corporate Gods. She had peace bands strapped around her wrists, a Mayan gemstone dangling around her neck, and her hair was blonde and flowing. She looked like a flower-power girl dressed up for a job interview. She had a steely look in her eyes as she marched over to me and said, 'There's someone in my office who wants to talk to you.'

I smiled and said, 'Hello, Princess.'

23

Jennifer Shaw screwed her face at me. Not unkindly, just in surprise. The only person at the *Legend* who called her that to her face was Bull. But I didn't work there anymore, and I was free to address her as I saw fit. She blushed a little, as if she was secretly pleased that her title was intact, that her reputation had not dimmed. Then she regained her composure.

'Nice to see you too, Jack.' She pointed to the door. 'You want to tell me why I have Adam Pryor barging into my office in the middle of a call, demanding your head on a plate?'

I did a double-take. Pryor was in the building. I saw Rachel shift uncomfortably in her seat, the pen falling from her hand.

'Pryor is in your office?'

Jennifer blinked at me, like I was thick.

'What did I just say? He's there right now, and he's spitting mad.'

'So he should be,' Rachel piped up.

'What do you mean?'

Jennifer didn't turn around, barely acknowledged the sound of her voice. She could be charming and fiendishly intelligent, but she came across as intimidating and standoffish to the younger reporters, the ones who hadn't proved themselves in her eyes and who hadn't gotten to know her, to understand where she came from, the balls she had to crush to get to where she was now.

'Jack has evidence that Pryor tried to have Harry Slew killed,' said Rachel. 'And that they both lied to the police about the car crash they were involved in.'

Jennifer blinked at me again. I felt like a foreigner asking for directions in my native tongue, and getting nowhere.

'Can you prove all this?' she asked. 'Or is this just more scurrilous gossip?'

'It's all here,' I said, tapping the Dictaphone. 'I'm telling you, Pryor is as ruthless as Valentine was.'

'You have a recording.' She raised her eyebrows sceptically. 'Is that it?'

'I have text messages on my phone, too,' I said, recalling the messages Wake had sent to me that morning from a pay as you go phone. They would be untraceable so I could do what I wanted with them, as long as I didn't tell anyone where I got them from, which I never would.

I said, 'They were sent to me by a man who works for a mobile network, in the same way the police get texts to use as evidence. The messages are an exchange between a mobile belonging to Pryor and Valentine's private mobile. They explicitly mention Scannell by name. This is two days before he was found dead. The messages also show Valentine was planning to do something with some incriminating photographs and Pryor knew about it. Someone put them through his door and when the maid found him she took a couple of pictures and sold them to you. They showed Scannell sleeping with a teenage boy. Valentine ordered the plant because he knew it would either make Scannell do exactly what he wanted, forever, or drive an old-value family man like him to suicide. Either way, Valentine would win. If Scannell stayed in the cabinet, he controlled him. If Pryor took his place, he controlled him too.'

'This all sounds a bit fanciful, don't you think?' She said.

I shrugged.

'A week ago, I wouldn't have believed a movie with a plot like that. Now, I'm wondering just what other skeletons are in Pryor's cupboard.'

Jennifer smiled wryly at me.

'Ask him yourself. He's in my office as we speak. Second door on your left,' she said.

The way she said it, it sounded like an order, not an invitation. And even though the Princess wasn't my boss, I found myself obeying her. She had that kind of voice, that kind of hypnotic certainty in her eyes which meant you knew she was right before she even said anything. I was being charmed by Jennifer all over again. I picked up the iPad and Dictaphone – after what I'd been through I wasn't going to let them out of my sight – and trooped out of the room and followed the corridor down to her office. The door was plain glass with a panel of frosting at eye level, to stop people from peering inside. All you could see from the outside was the frames on the walls and the bottom of the desk and sofa. I could see Adam Pryor's lace-ups through the bottom panel. Tap-tapping away manically. I cracked open the door. It slid smoothly back on the vanilla-coloured carpet. Entered a surprisingly modest office. Desk in front of me, shelves to my right, sofa to my left. Window behind the desk overlooking a balcony and the cluttered, satellite-dished rooftops of London.

Pryor was sitting at the chair opposite the desk. He spun around as I entered and bolted upright. He smiled an unreadable smile, and for a second I thought he was going to shake my hand and ask my how the devil I was doing. Much to my relief he did no such thing. Instead he propped himself on the corner of the desk, crossed his legs and sighed.

'I've always thought,' he said, 'that when I become Prime Minister, I should curb the worst excesses of the press. You chaps are all a bit reckless, aren't you?'

I closed the door behind me. Stood by the door, not wanting to get any closer to Pryor. Feeling sweat trickle down my back.

'I mean, look at what you did to Naz in the car park. He'll probably spend the rest of his days taking his food through a straw.'

Pryor sighed again, and unglued himself from the desk. Paraded around Jennifer's desk and stared out of the window at the rooftops.

'I thought the view would be nicer from up here,' he said. 'But it's not, is it? Just rooftops and rubbish. You can never really escape it. Not in this town.'

He turned around.

I said, 'What have you come here for?'

Pryor said, 'I'd like to cut a deal.'

'I'm not interested.'

'At least hear me out.'

'It's too late. The story is running. This time tomorrow, you'll be out of a job and on your way to jail. And I'll be sleeping easy.'

Pryor chuckled to himself. Like he was remembering an old joke. He traced a hand over the pictures on Jennifer's desk. He picked up one of Jennifer and a former Prime Minister. Pulled a face at it, then showed the picture to me.

'This is why I love politics,' he said. 'It's not about the money. It's not even really about the power. It's about the legacy. I mean, look at this man. He was perhaps the worst post-war Prime Minister of them all. His record in office was terrible, he made enemies left, right and centre, and when he walked out of Downing Street he left the country in an economic quicksand that will take us literally decades to get out of. And yet, he radiates something, you see? He must do. Otherwise, why would your boss have this picture on her desk?'

I shrugged.

'Maybe she has a thing for Scottish guys,' I said.

Pryor laughed. Reset the picture.

'I'm going to ask you for the Dictaphone,' he said, nodding at what I held in my hands. 'And your iPad too. So we can start putting this nonsense behind us.'

I looked at Pryor like he was mad. Quite possibly he was.

'You're kidding. You honestly think I'd hand over everything I've got to you?'

Pryor was giving me a curious look.

'Forget it,' I said, and made to leave the office.

'Imogen's dead,' Pryor said as I reached for the handle. 'She took another overdose an hour after she got out of hospital. Only this time she made sure no one would find her in time to get the adrenalin into her.'

I stopped. My hand resting on the handle. I didn't move. The way Pryor said it made my skin crawl. I heard his feet shuffling across the carpet. Drawing close to me.

'I can survive this,' he said. 'There's a way out for me. Jack, I didn't know Kat was going to be killed. I didn't want it to happen and I am so sorry for what Edward did. I really am. But we need to move past it. He's gone. You can't punish him now, so surely it's better to leave all that in the past. Pippa will get over my fling and the Prime Minister can't afford to lose me from the Cabinet after I've only been in the job for a few days. But I need you to do your bit, Jack. I need you to help me. Without you and what you've got on me, no one can touch me.'

I'd heard Pryor talk often enough now to know when he was lying and when he wasn't. And when he said he didn't know Valentine was going to kill Kat, he was telling the truth. Valentine was responsible for her death, not Pryor. I trusted my instincts on that.

I turned round slowly. Pryor was closer to me than I realised, barely two feet away. I looked him square in the eyes, as if we were boxers facing off before a bout. He was a couple of inches taller than me and a whole lot fitter and stronger but right now I knew I could tear him apart.

'You're right,' I said, still staring. 'But that still leaves one major problem for you. Why the hell should I let you off the hook?'

Pryor looked away, down and to the left.

'Jack,' he said, like he was about to cry. 'What did I do that was so wrong?'

'Well,' I said. 'Shall we start with trying to get Harry Slew killed? Then there's getting your sister hooked on drugs, trying to fleece the country for twenty billion and pushing Andrew Scannell to his death. Have I forgotten anything? Oh yes, killing an innocent woman. That's a decent charge sheet.'

That murderous rage I felt for Valentine flashed through me again. For an instant I wanted to physically hurt Pryor.

'I know,' he said, his head dropping. 'I was young and stupid. How many young men drive drunk and get away with it? Have you never done it? And the thing with getting Harry out of the way, I don't know what to say about that. I'm ashamed of it, truly I am. I was young and confused. And stupid. I am so, so sorry.'

Pryor's apology caught me by surprise, so I didn't answer.

'And yes, I had my head turned by Valentine and his money. But I underestimated him. I didn't know he was going to blackmail me when I got into the cabinet. I didn't realise how ruthless he was. I didn't know Scannell was going to die. I've learned my lesson, Jack, believe me. Please, you have to believe me. You don't need to destroy me. There's no point. No one would gain from it. Please just give me the files so we can move on.'

I carried on staring at Pryor. He was still hiding.

'And the woman?' I said. 'The dead woman. What about her?'

My tone was as harsh as I could make it without shouting. I was aware of where we were and I didn't want to be overheard.

'I didn't mean to kill her,' Pryor said. 'You won't understand this but that's a hard thing to carry around with you every day, the knowledge that you killed someone, even accidentally. I don't think my life is as perfect as you think, Jack.'

No matter what he said, I knew Pryor didn't care about the woman he killed in his car. So there was no comparison between how he felt about her and how I felt about Daisy Gill. None at all.

His whining was making me angry. He had no morals, no scruples at all. Here was the cornered fox again, desperate and devious.

'You're garbage,' I said. 'And you know it.'

'There's something about me you don't know,' Pryor said.

'I'm pretty sure I don't care either,' I said.

'Actually, you might,' Pryor said, and I saw something in his eyes I had only seen once before. Sadness, mixed with regret.

'We can't have children, Pippa and I. She has miscarried six times. I know what I did to that woman. Believe me, I know pain.'

'You told me she didn't want children,' I said. 'You said she wouldn't start a family until you were higher up the ladder.'

'I tell everyone that,' he said. 'It's easier that way. The truth is we both want children, doesn't everyone? But Mother Nature isn't doing us many favours.'

In an instant my mind built a fantasy of me and Zoe pushing a pram through a park on a sunny day, with Emily walking next to me, smiling. Happy to be with me. Happy I was her father.

Maybe I was going soft in my old age but Pryor was getting to me. I couldn't help it.

I snapped back into the present.

'Why are you telling me this?' I said.

Pryor's expression changed, his face hardened. 'Do you want children, Jack? Sorry, let me ask that again. Do you want more children, Jack?'

The question filled the room like poisonous gas. Pryor knew my weakness and went straight for it.

'It's about time we talked about your daughter,' he said. 'What's her name? Emily, that's right. Your daughter Emily.'

He paused, letting the meaning of his words sink in.

'I'm going to make this simple for you,' he said. 'If you don't give me all the recordings you have, well, teenage girls go missing all the time. You're a news man so you know what happens. Sometimes they never even find a body. The parents never find out what happened to their child. So do the right thing, Jack. Give me the files. For Emily's sake.'

My body felt cold and hollow. Valentine must have told Pryor about Emily. I suppose I shouldn't have been surprised. But was Pryor capable of following through on that threat? After what I'd found over the past couple of days, I knew it would be a huge risk to think he wasn't.

The adrenalin of the chase through London was fading and I didn't have the energy to get angry. The urge to shout and scream and strangle Pryor flickered and vanished. I was thinking clearly again. This wasn't just about me staying alive for the next ten minutes. It was about Emily, my daughter. She was more important to me than anything else. I hadn't done enough for her since the day she was born, since I cut her umbilical cord, held her in my two hands, that tiny, fragile little body I would have done anything to protect, even though I was still almost a child myself.

I had missed so much over the past seventeen years and I knew the damage my behaviour had done to our relationship was irreparable because I could never get those years back. I'd never have a second chance. But that didn't mean I could play games with her safety. I couldn't put her at risk for the sake of bringing Pryor down, and that meant I would kill the story in exchange for my daughter's safety. My job was buying and selling truth and lies, after all.

A question formed in my mind: what would I or anyone else gain from me giving those recordings to the *Legend*? The answer was simple: justice and a great set of headlines for the paper.

There were still more thoughts swirling. I've never supported one political party over another. I don't believe in ideologies. I'm a pragmatist – you deal with the circumstances in front of you in the best way you can. And so every time there's a general election I back whichever party I think will do a better job immediately afterwards. I work out what the benefits are of voting for each one and then choose the one which looks best overall. I don't care what colour their rosettes are.

So the important question was this: what would I or anyone else gain from me not giving those recordings to the *Legend*?

Three words circled in my mind. Emily, Zoe and Kat. They were all I cared about now. This whole tragic, sordid, disgusting mess had distilled down to those three words.

Emily – my daughter.

Zoe – my future, I hoped.

Kat – who needed justice.

'I won't give you the files,' I said.

24

When my words registered in his mind Pryor seemed to lose six inches of his height, his well-formed muscles lost their strength. Without his threat to hurt Emily he had nothing, no leverage, no hope. Here in a newspaper editor's office, I was safe. Right in front of him, but out of reach. His shoulders sagged, his head tipped forward and his eyes closed. I knew what was going through his head. Dreadful visions of how the next few weeks, months and years would turn out for him. How quickly would he be sacked from the Cabinet? How quickly would he be kicked out of Parliament? How long would he spend in jail? What kind of life would he have when he got out?

I enjoyed watching him suffer. I don't mind admitting that. Pryor deserved it. When his eyes opened again there was something in them which truly scared me. I knew then beyond doubt that he would not hesitate to hurt Emily, that he would do it for revenge even if he had no political career left to save. I spoke before he had the chance to.

'But I won't give them to the paper either,' I said.

'What do you mean?' Pryor said, confusion all over him, in his eyes, his face, his words, his unsteady posture.

'I'm going to keep them, for myself. Somewhere safe.'

'Why?' Pryor said.

'For Emily. For her sake I'm giving you a second chance. Just remember that if you step out of line, if you do anything I don't like the look of, it's very easy to leak things onto the internet these days. There are copies of this in lots of different places, with people who know that if anything ever happens to Emily or me, they're to be released. Which means tonight and every night from today onwards Emily gets home safely. Is that clear?'

Pryor nodded, a look of satisfaction on his face. He thought he'd won and I hated him for that. In a way I hated myself too, for letting him off the hook.

'I don't know what to say,' he said.

'From now on it's not what you say that matters,' I said. 'It's what you do. You won't have Edward Valentine to blame any more. Everything is on you.'

'I understand,' he said. 'But there is one more thing we need to clear up. Harry. He's back and talking. How can we keep him quiet?'

My reply came out with me barely having to think about it, my professional instincts still somehow working.

'Someone needs to point out to Harry that if he carries on telling the world you were driving that car then sooner or later the police are going to come for him as well as you. He lied in court and to the police. You'll both go down. Tell him that and he'll keep quiet forever.'

'Thank you, Jack,' he said. 'Thank you. I can't tell you how grateful I am.'

Pryor was back to his normal height, dreams reawakened, his future glowing again. He stuck out his right hand for me to shake, as if we were businessmen sealing a deal. I hesitated for a couple of seconds and then took his hand.

As I did so I took a small step forward with my left foot. When my weight was fully on it I brought my right knee up into Pryor's groin as hard as I could.

His hand went limp and he bent over, groaning pathetically, as

if someone had sucked all the air out of his lungs. With one hand
I pushed him in his left shoulder and he fell over slowly onto his
right side. When he was lying on the ground he curled up into a
ball, his eyes shut, his breathing shallow and irregular.

I knelt down next to him, pushed him onto his back and
grabbed his throat.

'One more thing,' I said, squeezing so hard his face turned red.
'If anything ever happens to Emily, I will kill you. I won't pay
someone else to do it for me, like you or Valentine would. I'll do
it myself. I'll get a gun and shoot you in the face.'

'Don't be stupid,' Pryor coughed as he put his hands around
my wrist. 'You'd never get away with it.'

Even when he was in pain and struggling to breath, Pryor's
cornered fox mind was still working angles for escape. Maybe that
was the difference between us.

'I wouldn't care about getting away with it,' I said. 'If anything
happens to Emily, I have nothing else to lose. Twenty years in
prison would be a small price to pay.'

Pryor made a choking noise and I let him go. As I stood up I
caught the look in his eyes. It told me he knew I meant every
word.

I turned away, my iPad and Dictaphone safely in my hands,
opened the door of the Princess's office and saw Bull blocking my
way, a deep frown on his face.

We looked at each for a second, then two, then three, until the
silence became uncomfortable. One of us had to break it. Bull did.

'These office doors are cheap and thin,' he said. 'Not good for
keeping private conversations private.'

'How much did you hear?' I said.

'Enough.'

'So?'

'You have a daughter,' Bull said. 'You never told me.'

'It's not something I advertise,' I said. 'She's seventeen. She has another man's surname. I'm a terrible father. That's about as far as it goes.'

Bull's face was blank as he processed the information. His view of me, formed over years of stories and drinks, was being quickly recalibrated. The seconds ticked past slowly. He frowned.

'So you want to take those with you,' he said, gesturing at what I was carrying in my left hand. 'And forget any of this happened. You know that would leave me hanging in the wind, no splash for Sunday and an angry editor on my back.'

'Sorry,' I said, because there was nothing else for me to say.

Bull was the most driven reporter I'd ever known. One who would rather lose a leg than a story. He had a decision to make.

'Do you remember the advice I gave you after our first story together?' Bull said. 'You nearly drove yourself crazy reeling that one in.'

'Of course I remember,' I said. 'You told me to always, always remember I was a man first and a reporter second.'

'But you forgot that, somewhere along the line.'

'Maybe,' I said.

'Lucky for you I didn't forget,' Bull said, and I felt some energy reappear in my body. 'So get out of here and take all that with you. Go and look after your daughter. The Princess will take some work but she owes me a favour or ten. Rachel won't be happy either but her job is safe now so she'll be fine.'

'Thank you,' I said.

'Don't forget my advice,' Bull said. 'You're always a man first.'

'Thank you,' I said again.

'I'm going to tell them you did a runner,' Bull said. I nodded gratefully. I paused, unsure of what to say next.

'That means you actually have to do one, Jack,' he said. 'And right now would be a good time.'

I could feel the past few days catching up with me, exhaustion hitting my body and mind. But I still had enough energy to get out of the building quickly, with my iPad and Dictaphone safely in my hands.

Outside I stopped at the spot where Sharon Gill stabbed me. I looked up at the night sky and said sorry for the thousandth time, even though I knew it would never be enough, for Daisy, for her mother, or for me.

I looked across the road. The Range Rover was still there, the outline of a big man in the driver's seat. The darkness meant I couldn't see his face.

I jogged up to the main road, hailed a taxi and gave him my address.

'I'm going home,' I said. 'There's someone waiting for me.'

www.ingramcontent.com/pod-product-compliance
Lightning Source LLC
Chambersburg PA
CBHW051636180726
48284CB00006B/1754